The Pyre

Also by David Hair

The Moontide Quartet

Mage's Blood
Scarlet Tides
Unholy War

DAVID HAIR

The Pyre

THE RETURN OF RAVANA
Book I

A version of this novel was first published as Pyre of Queens in India in 2011 by Penguin India
First published in Great Britain in 2015 by

Jo Fletcher Books
an imprint of
Quercus Publishing Ltd
Carmelite House
50 Victoria Embankment
London EC4Y 0DZ

An Hachette UK company

A CIP catalogue record for this book is available
from the British Library

PB ISBN 978 0 85705 360 2
EBOOK ISBN 978 1 78429 165 5

10 9 8 7 6 5 4 3

Typeset by Jouve (UK), Milton Keynes
Printed and bound in Great Britain by Clays Ltd, St Ives plc

This book is (once more) dedicated to Kerry, my wonderful wife,
and to Brendan and Melissa, my children.

Table of Contents

PROLOGUE

The Lost Journal

Mandore, Rajasthan, June 2010

The journal was right where he remembered putting it thirty years ago, buried two feet beneath the distinctive stone slab. It was wrapped in waterproof greased leather, in a painted wooden box that crumbled, rotten with age and damp, when he dug it out. To his considerable relief, it looked like the journal hadn't been further damaged by its burial. The pages were cotton cloth at the front, then varying grades of paper that became more refined as he flicked through. The book smelled musty and the binding was frail. Some of the oldest pages, the cotton ones at the front, were more than a thousand years old, and it was to the first page, the earliest, that he went. The script was ancient, but he found he knew it, and silently translated the words as he traced them with a trembling finger, not quite daring to touch the page.

If you are reading this journal, then I hope you are me – you know what I mean.

I have come to believe that certain stories develop a life of their own. They are powerful because they are so widely known, so much a part of our culture – indeed, of our daily lives – that they become more than mere words.

Imagine, if you will, a tale that defines a people. It has heroes and villains, good and evil deeds; its very words are sacred to us. It is like a chess set, its pieces inhabited by the same souls, game after game. Or perhaps this tale is a living thing, a script that constantly seeks actors, and when it finds them, it inhabits those actors and possesses them utterly, finding new ways to express and re-express itself, time and time again.

What must it be like to be one of those souls, doomed to live the same life time and again, over and over, always acting out the tale, sometimes glorifying it, sometimes enhancing it, and always at great cost to themselves, for their whole existence is a prison sentence. Their fate is to live constantly as a plaything of an idea.

But you know what that's like, don't you?

Such a story is like a tyrannical god, inflicting itself upon unwilling worshippers.

I know this is real, because I am living such a tale, and I am doomed to live it over and over, for ever more – and by 'I', I mean 'you'.

Over and over and yet again.

As he focused on the brief verse that followed, a thrill of unease – the same shivery feeling he always got when he saw those words – made the hairs on his arms stand up.

Time is water from the well of life
And I must draw that water with only my hands to bear it
My thin and fragile fingers cupped to receive it, every drop precious
But ere I have raised it to my lips, it has drained away
One day I will learn not to spill it and I will drink my fill

And finally be free
Aram Dhoop, Poet of Mandore

He blinked rapidly, remembering the last time he'd written those words, two years ago. He'd had to do a poem for English and though he'd had no idea then why, it had been one of the easiest assignments ever. The words had just flown from his pen, almost as if he were just copying out someone else's work. And when his teacher had asked him what he was trying to say, he'd started, 'It's about reincarnation—' and then stopped; he knew the poem *did* mean something important, but that was about as close as he could come to explaining it to someone else.

But that hadn't mattered, apparently, because the teacher had entered his work in the inter-schools' Poetry Cup competition that year – he'd been a little surprised how thrilled he'd felt when he'd got up in front of the whole school to accept the trophy from the headmaster.

And yet here were those very same words, set down in a strange – and yet not unfamiliar – hand on a page that pre-dated paper in a journal his forebears (if that was the right word) had been keeping for more than a thousand years.

He put the journal down. He would read it properly that night – though he knew already that the words would be as familiar as if he had written them yesterday.

There was one other thing hidden with the journal: a small leather pouch. It was empty. *Strange; I almost expected the necklace to be inside this time.* His hand still remembered the shape of the pendant: a pale crystal veined with burgundy streaks set into a tarnished decorative metal surround. He'd never forgotten the way it used to pulse queasily at his touch. Where the necklace was now, he had no idea.

The journal was unique, a scholar's dream, but he had no

intention of showing it to anyone. He had begun writing it many lifetimes and more than a thousand years ago, a record of his life that was centuries old; though the last time he had buried it was just thirty years ago.

And he himself was only seventeen years old.

Conspirator

Mandore, Rajasthan, AD *769*

As the winter draws to an end and the heat rises again, the winds begin to blow across the Thar Desert: great clouds of dirty orange dust billowing out of the west. The men, if they must venture outside, go muffled in scarves, while the women throw the loose end of their dupattas over their heads, so that they look like colourful insects, swaying in the mirages. The arid land leaches away what little other colour there is; the pallid shrubs become coated in sand, the tiny mud houses and canvas tents are the same muted hues as the desert itself. The vibrant clothes of the people provide the only brightness, the colours feeding hearts and lifting spirits.

It has not rained for months, nor will it for many more – the only real rain comes once a year here, at the end of the summer, when for six to eight weeks the land is revitalised by sudden, brief torrential downpours so fierce that anyone caught outside finds themselves staggering under the onslaught even as they dance in relief that the monsoon has come at all. But this winter has been drier than usual and the old folk are whispering of worse to come. When the skies are orange with dust, it is always a bad year, they say.

This, the third year of the reign of Devaraja Pratihara, son of

Nagabhata, certainly hasn't been a good one for the town of Mandore. He moved his court, the heart of the Gujara-Pratihara Empire, to Avanti, leaving the old capital of Mandore in the hands of Ravindra-Raj, his third wife's son. The desert folk whisper that the gods, displeased at this turn of events, have cursed Mandore; certainly the court and all its hangers-on have followed Devaraja to Avanti, leaving Mandore denuded and lost in dreams of its glorious royal past. Traders are few now, and houses that once thrived are abandoned, or taken over by squatters seeking shelter, or dismantled by stone-thieves looking for easy pickings. Some believe that Mandore's curse is embodied in Ravindra-Raj himself – not that they would ever voice their fears out loud to strangers – for his cruelty and oppression are amongst the reasons so many have left. Those who lay the city's current ills at Ravindra's door claim once-proud Mandore is being strangled by the raja and his many offences against the gods.

Madan Shastri, the senapati, or commander, of the raja's soldiers, watched Ravindra uneasily out of the corner of his eyes as he committed yet more such offences. Ravindra was not a man you ever looked at directly, not if you wanted to keep your eyes, as he was currently demonstrating.

'Speak, Gautam! *Speak!*' Ravindra roared as he pressed a white-hot iron to the naked prisoner's chest. Once again the dungeon cell filled with the smell of seared flesh, causing even the most hardened of the watching courtiers to wince. Gautam screamed silently: his mouth moved, but no sounds emanated from him, for by now he was beyond speech. His whole body was so covered in welts and burns and cuts to make him unrecognisable to even his closest friends. Even if Ravindra were to show him mercy now, Gautam would never be the same. True mercy would be to slay him swiftly.

Shastri longed to end this, but one did not come between Ravindra and his pleasures. He looked away, only to be met by a sight almost as unpleasant – the smiling jowls of the raja's favoured son, Prince Chetan.

'Why Senapati Shastri, I do believe you look a little unwell,' the prince drawled as he sipped a lemon sherbet. His expression kept changing as he was alternately bored and amused by the proceedings. 'I'd have thought our noble captain would have the stomach for such unpleasant sights when it is in defence of my father and his realm.' He lowered his voice and in a sly whisper he added, 'Or is it fear of what Gautam might say that makes you look so very ill at ease?'

Shastri stiffened slightly. 'Of course I have nothing to fear,' he replied. 'The conspiracy must be rooted out. All traitors must die.'

'But you and Gautam were quite friendly, I thought?' Prince Chetan's eyes were sparkling with unfriendly mischief. The prince was a big man, larger even than his father, with heavy, slab-like muscles, and though he wasn't a clever man, he was cunning, and in Ravindra's court of whispers and cruelty that mattered more.

'He was my superior. One must always cultivate amiable relations with those above us,' Shastri replied uncomfortably.

Chetan grinned maliciously. 'So your apparent amiable nature towards my father and me is just pretence, Senapati?'

Shastri frantically groped for the right words to lead him out of this dangerous little maze Chetan had woven, but he was saved from having to reply immediately when the door to the dungeon was flung open and Ravindra's chief wife sashayed in. Rani Halika was wearing a vivid jewel-encrusted red sari and enough gold to ransom her husband.

She looked at Gautam's shattered frame and tittered elegantly. 'My lord, I trust he has not expired just yet? I wish to teach my sister-wives a lesson in loyalty.' She looked about the dungeon, taking in the bloodstained floor, the nauseous courtiers and the grinning torturers lounging against the walls watching, and Chetan, her favourite son. She gave Shastri a voluptuous smile. 'Senapati, how nice of you to join us. Are you well entertained?'

The raja turned to her. He was clad in armour inlaid with gold and silver and embossed with intricate tracing of hunting nobles and fleeing beasts. A speared tiger died eternally in the middle of his blood-speckled breastplate. His oiled moustaches and beard gleamed and his flushed cheeks were ruddy in the flickering torchlight. Though he had been here all night, destroying the body and mind of the latest man alleged to have conspired against him, he showed no trace of exhaustion. 'Senapati Shastri has been our witness, my dear. Everyone trusts the good captain, so my brother's confession will have greater credence if spoken in his presence.'

Shastri wondered if that truly was the only reason for his presence, for this was not normally something the raja insisted on when he tortured a man.

'And do we have any interesting new names?' the rani asked curiously.

Ravindra shrugged. 'No one of note – a dozen of Gautam's guards, a few scribes, a merchant or two – a disappointing conspiracy, doomed from the start to fail. How sad, that my own brother had so few real allies,' he reflected with mock sorrow. He stroked his brother's flayed chest. 'Bring in the other wives, then, if you think it needful.'

'My lord, no—!' protested Shastri, but Ravindra cut him off with a chopping gesture.

Halika clapped her hands and a demure procession of six young women walked in, all except for one clad in bright saris of yellow and green and orange. The last girl wore a shapeless black robe that enveloped her entire form, leaving only a narrow slit for her eyes. Shastri watched her, feeling a distress that he couldn't quite bring himself to understand. Darya was the raja's latest bride, and the only foreign one. She'd been given to Ravindra by a Mohameddan from the western side of the desert. Something about her intense eyes and upright bearing always drew his attention.

He tore his gaze away and flashed a reassuring look at Padma, his little sister, the second youngest of Ravindra's wives. It was supposed to be an honour, to be chosen by the raja, but he knew Padma dwelt in misery. Her girlish prettiness had already faded and she didn't look healthy. She looked back at him dazedly and then dropped her gaze, almost as if she were frightened to meet his eye.

His nerves tightened.

All the girls recoiled when they saw the bloody form hanging from the chains in the centre of the room, but Rani Halika clapped her hands and crowed, 'See what we have here, girls!' She gestured at the broken man. 'A failed plotter! Do you even know who it is?' She peered at the vacant-faced girl nearest her. 'Do you know who it is, Meena?'

Meena shook her head, her face frightened. Two of the ranis involuntarily backed away, pretty Rakhi going pale and rake-thin Jyoti vomiting against the wall. Even hollow-eyed Aruna looked frightened, despite the clear signs of opium intoxication in her glazed eyes.

'Why, Meena, do you not recognise your own dear brother-in-law? Surely you know Prince Gautam? It appears that Gautam thought he could turn the guards against our lord and master. But of course our guards are totally loyal, aren't they, my beloved husband?' Halika stroked Ravindra's mailed arm.

The young queens all shuddered, unable to tear their eyes

from the bloodied mess that was all that remained of proud Prince Gautam. Shastri watched them all as they stood trembling – except Rani Darya. Through the narrow eye-slit he momentarily met a composed gaze, then as she became aware of his regard, she too started shaking, and for a moment it crossed his mind that she was just mimicking the others.

Surely not. Of course she must be as upset as the rest of them . . .

He wondered what she looked like under that thick black robe – a burkha – was she beautiful? His sister Padma spoke well enough of her, but said that she seldom interacted with the other wives. Was she intelligent and gentle? Were there hidden reserves? Her eyes were the most enchanting green he had ever seen, the few glimpses he'd had of her face revealed features that were angular and pleasing, and her hands were long and elegant. But only Ravindra had the privilege of seeing what lay beneath that heavy robe.

He caught the girl returning his stare and flicked his eyes away – straight into Ravindra's predatory gaze. He flattened his expression, dreading what the raja might have read in his face, but his ruler merely smiled knowingly before returning his gaze to his brother.

'I think Gautam's told us all he knows,' he said sadly. 'Bring in that poet fellow and let him say a few words. Then we'll release my poor brother from his torment.'

Shastri looked carefully at the floor and prayed that Gautam could hold out until he was 'released'.

Aram Dhoop, the Court Poet, was dozing, huddled uncomfortably against the wall outside the dungeon, where he had been for the last ten hours. At first the cries of the tortured prince had made sleep impossible, but it was amazing what one could endure if one tried. His reverie was shattered by a rough hand on his shoulder shaking him awake: one of the dungeon guards, a hard-faced man with a world-weary manner. Aram quite liked Pranav, except when the gaoler was hurting people for his lord, when he became a different person entirely. 'I do what I must, or I face the consequences,' Pranav had explained quietly once, after Aram had wondered aloud how he slept at night.

'But then, who am I to judge?' he acknowledged quietly to himself. 'I've slept most of the night in earshot of the one good man in this kingdom being eviscerated.' He straightened as the guard gestured, indicating that he was wanted inside; Pranav's expression gave nothing away. Aram hurried inside, hoping that all they wanted was his poetic abilities.

It appeared that was indeed the case, so the Court Poet murmured a few words of consolation over the tortured form of the only decent man in the fortress before blessing him in the name of the gods. Aram wasn't a priest, but the last of the holy men had fled months ago when it became apparent just what sort of a man Ravindra-Raj was. Many of the soldiers had deserted as well, but Ravindra had bribed, charmed or terrified enough men to maintain control. There was something unsettling about him, something of the cobra in his hooded eyes. Just being close to him was enough to paralyse thought.

As he finished his blessing, Aram glanced along the line of wives. While he counted every man here a beast, he felt sorry for these delicate creatures – except for Halika, of course, who was every bit as bad as Ravindra. *At least I need only recite poetry to the raja*, he reflected as he ran his eye down the line. *These poor creatures must bear his children*. Only the long-term wives, Halika, Meena and Rakhi, had given Ravindra male heirs thus far; Jyoti and Aruna had produced daughters. And only Chetan had so far survived to adulthood, but there were more in the nurseries. Imagining how *intimate* these women had to be with their lord and husband was nauseating.

Empathy was a curse, here in dying Mandore.

His eyes flickered nervously past Padma, Senapati Shastri's little sister. He feared she was beginning to take a dangerous liking to him. She asked for him to sing too often, watched him too avidly. The raja had executed men for less. But even as he reminded himself of this, he could not help his own gaze drifting to the black-clad girl at the end of the line and feeling a now-familiar twinge of longing.

Apart from the eunuchs and the raja himself, he was the only man allowed to see her face uncovered, when called to the zenana to play for the entertainment of the women. Darya's face had melted his heart the moment he had seen her reclining beside a pond in the women's quarters. Loneliness, loss, the courage to endure, all had been captured in her expression. She was like a hawk, tethered but not tamed; a poem far beyond his skills to write. In his most secret dreams he worshipped her.

Rani Halika clapped her hands a third time. 'Now, girls, the lesson for the day is this: there is but one god and his name is Ravindra-Raj. He rules every part of this world that you will ever know. He owns your body, and he owns your soul, and you owe him *everything* – in life and in death. May you be as thankful as you ought, for you see what befalls those who conspire against him.' She knelt, prostrating herself before the raja, and Ravindra smiled coldly as the other women followed suit, a line of genuflecting gaudy birds with wide-eyed, terrified faces . . . except for one. Darya lifted her head haughtily, turned her back and stomped away.

Halika looked outraged, but before she could say a word, Ravindra smiled and commanded, 'Send her to me tonight.'

The chief wife looked displeased. 'My lord—'

But her protest died on her lips when Ravindra looked at her sternly. She bowed her head and stayed silent.

Ravindra turned back to his younger brother and stroked his swollen purple cheek. 'Now, dear brother, I think your lesson is learned. Shall I release you?'

The prisoner quivered, and Aram realised to his horror that Gautam was still aware.

With a soft, almost sensuous sigh, Ravindra rammed the poker through Gautam's chest and into his heart. There was a great crack and a tearing sound and the prince's blood came spurting, sizzling, from the wound and coated the raja. A stench of roasting meat overwhelmed the chamber. Then in a grotesque parody of remorse, Ravindra closed his eyes and hugged his dying brother.

Aram Dhoop closed his eyes and sang. His voice floated through the walled garden to the carved red sandstone latticework that hid the faces of the queens. Somewhere up there, Darya would be sitting alone, he was sure, shunned by the other wives as a Mohameddan; lonely, lost, yearning for a gentle touch: *his* touch. He knew this with complete certainty. He sang of love and hope. He sang for her.

What is she thinking as she sits up there, staring through the grille at me? Does she know these songs are for her?

Aram Dhoop had been born here in Mandore. It was always clear he was going to be too small to be a warrior, but his father had ensured he was educated. Not only could he read and write, but he had become a fine musician. He'd hoped to be taken to Avanti when Devaraja Pratihara shifted his court, but the raja had an enormous entourage and many poets and musicians, and he'd been overlooked. It hadn't been for any lack of talent, but his high-birthed fellow poets – as vicious a flock of songbirds as ever pecked down a rival – had never accepted him as one of their clique, ostracising him and ensuring he never had the chance to catch the ear of the maharaja. Now, left behind in the obscurity of Mandore, he lived on his nerves in the cruel, deadly court of Ravindra-Raj, where a slip of the tongue could be as fatal as a sip of poison.

Would that I could ride free like one of those lumbering warriors! How unfair is a world that allows talentless brutes to prosper while the artistic must live hand-to-mouth . . .

His dream extended, as it was wont to do, to include a beautiful Persian girl at his side, laughing at his wit, weeping at the beauty of his voice and gazing at him in adoration as the priests made them one.

Does she feel as I do? Does she yearn for me as I yearn for her? Does her heart swell as my voice swells? Does it beat in time to the rhythm of my song?

But no matter how passionately he sang, or how prettily he played, the red sandstone latticework walls of the zenana gave him no sign that he was heard at all.

Senapati Madan Shastri stood stolidly as Rani Halika wafted towards him across the rosewater-perfumed room. He felt awkward standing there on the threshold of the women's quarters, but Halika herself had commanded his presence.

'Ah, Senapati, thank you for coming. Have you brought the eunuch?'

He nodded wordlessly and gestured to the pasty-faced man. He found the practice of castrating servants revolting, but the court had many such creatures now that Ravindra reigned. Still, at least the eunuch's presence meant that he wasn't alone with Rani Halika. That carried far too many dangers, for all that her worldly sensuality repulsed him. He turned away, anxious to be gone.

But the head wife had not yet finished playing with him. 'Stay, Shastri, please. The other girls are skittish tonight; they may need to be restrained while we sedate them. Don't worry, your sister is no problem. Padma is such a *compliant* girl.' She made this observation sound both complimentary and sneering.

Before Shastri could respond, the eunuch, Uday, simpered, 'I have brought an extra-strong dose for her, mistress.'

The fluting sound of Uday's voice was enough to make Shastri wince, but Halika was pleased. 'Good, good. Come with me.'

Shastri could scarcely hide his disgust at this task, but Uday's expression was well schooled. *He's better than me at this*, Shastri thought, as he followed the queen and the eunuch to the first of the bedrooms – scarcely larger than a prison cell – where the queens slept.

Halika was the eldest queen, a courtesan Ravindra had chosen as his bride when he was just another strutting nobleman of the Pratihara court, albeit more vicious and skilled than most. Their union had been the start of his ascent. Halika was in her early forties now, and still a striking woman, despite bearing three children to her lord.

Halika might be a bride chosen as a kindred soul, but Ravindra's later wives were all chosen for social advantage. Meena, a plump and stupid woman now in her thirties, had brought with her a huge dowry. Rakhi was a prize of tribal warfare; first choice of the spoils following Ravindra's victory on the battlefield. Jyoti, the only daughter of a high priest, brought great kudos, while Aruna, as the daughter of a man infamous for his ability to source opium from the north, brought great power. And Padma had secured the alliance with Shastri's family at a time when that had meant something. Shastri's father had approved the union in his dotage, something the senapati had never forgiven, even at his father's grave-side.

Only Darya, the Persian girl, did not fit this pattern. No one knew what had driven Ravindra to pursue her, but there was endless speculation.

The first five wives all took their 'medicine' calmly – and in Aruna's case, eagerly, which filled Shastri with pity as he watched them succumb to the poppy-milk. Clearly the debilitating dream-life of the addict was preferable to the reality of life in the claws of Ravindra and Halika. Padma was already snoring as he left her and he sighed, remembering with sadness the lively intelligence that had once shone in her eyes.

It was the newest rani who was resisting, which was no surprise. Darya spat at them when her cell was opened, snarling and shrieking like a wildcat. When Halika commanded Shastri to restrain her, she bundled herself in her burkha, hiding her face.

'Must she take that damned stuff?' he asked plaintively.

A slow, speculative smile crawled across Halika's face as she measured his words and what they revealed. 'Of course she must,' she chuckled. 'It's to help her sleep.' She tugged the corner of Darya's burkha. 'Pull it off her, Shastri. Then hold her down.'

What he saw in Halika's mocking face told him that to refuse was to risk ending up like Gautam. Any sign of disobedience in this court would always be interpreted in the worst possible way. It made him rage inside to have to lay hands on the young woman and wrench her cover-all away. His throat caught when he set eyes on what he found beneath: a young and nubile body, unblemished by age or child-bearing, clad in a short, thin shift that barely covered her thighs. Barely sixteen, he guessed, half his own age, and beautiful – so very beautiful, as lovely and wild as a doe antelope. Her face was contorted in rage, but that didn't conceal the handsomeness of her high cheekbones, aquiline nose and dazzling emerald eyes.

Tearing the burkha away felt horribly like the prelude to rape, though, and that quenched any other emotion he might have felt, leaving him trembling in disgust. *Perhaps that's what Halika intended*. Sick to the stomach, he grasped the girl's arms. *Forgive me*, he whispered as he pinned her down, but there was only hatred in her face for all of them. Halika held her nose to make her open her mouth, then tipped the drug down her throat, even as Darya tried to spit it out and breathe at the same time. Uday just shook his head sadly, but Halika seemed to relish the struggle; Shastri could see her quivering with excitement as she stood over the girl and held her down until her eyes rolled backwards in her skull.

She let Darya go and laid a hand on Shastri's arm. 'Thank you,' she murmured, panting and flushed. She waved the eunuch away and Uday backed out, leaving them alone. 'How strong you are,' she murmured, flashing her eyes and tilting her head closer, her lips opening.

For a second, her perfume caught in his throat and almost . . . *almost* . . .

He flinched, and fled.

'All praise a loyal servant,' Uday murmured as he passed him outside.

Shastri shot the eunuch a venomous look, and hurried away.

'Senapati Shastri, are you loyal to your lord?'

Shastri schooled the expression on his face carefully as he knelt before the throne of the raja and his son. 'Of course, Prince Chetan.' He kept his gaze fixed upon the feet of Ravindra-Raj, who was seated upon a seat shaped like a peacock with a fanned tail. A hookah of gold and enamel sat at Ravindra's feet. The opium fumes filling the room were making Shastri's head spin dangerously, and the profusion of flowers and plants depicted on the walls surrounding them, a mass of bright clashing colours all tangled together, wasn't helping.

'You have no wife, Senapati,' observed Ravindra. Apart from the punkah-walla, whose tongue had been cut out long before, they were alone. 'Why is that?'

'No time, my lord.'

And no desire to bind myself to someone whose safety could be used against me. No desire to bring children into this foul city that had been a good place to live until you were given its rule.

'Your last remaining parent died last year,' added Ravindra, watching him carefully. 'You have few ties to bind you to Mandore.'

What is he inferring? 'I have my sister, lord.'

'Mmm. Pretty Padma,' the raja purred. 'Quite my favourite wife. So . . . *amenable*.'

'And I have my love for Mandore,' Shastri replied, staring at the wall. His sister's marriage to his lord was a source of constant pain.

Ravindra smiled. 'How touching. Your love for a decaying town in the middle of a barren desert? A petty kingdom sidelined by the emperor's lack-witted decision to take his court elsewhere? Very romantic, I am sure. How old are you, Shastri?'

'Thirty-two, lord.'

'It really is high time you were married then. I shall arrange it. Have any women taken your eye?'

He shook his head numbly.

'What, none of the fair desert flowers of Mandore have caught your fancy? You are one of the most powerful men of the kingdom; you know you could have any woman you wanted . . .'

No, thought Shastri, *I have no power here. I am just a tool, one who lives in terror of being discarded. And the only woman I want is . . .*

He kept his silence, shaking his head slowly.

Ravindra looked at Chetan. 'My son and I will discuss this. It is not right that you are unmarried. We will arrange a suitable union.' He tapped his fingers on the throne, studying Shastri closely, then he changed the subject completely. 'But this was not my reason for summoning you. I must tell you that my health is poor. I am not expected to live long, according to my physicians.'

Shastri stared at him. The raja looked the picture of good health, and he sounded remarkably relaxed for a man announcing his impending death.

'My lord—' He stopped and started again, trying to sound as sincere as he was shocked. 'My lord, that is truly terrible news . . .' He stuttered to a halt.

Ravindra-Raj dying? *Could my prayers really be answered so easily?*

Ravindra raised a negligent hand. 'Yes, yes, Shastri. I have come to terms with it. But I wished you to know so that you can prepare yourself. When I die, it is likely there will be some unrest. You must be prepared to secure the kingdom for my son.'

Shastri bowed, his heart racing, but he didn't miss Chetan eyeing him suspiciously. The prince had his own favourites among the guards, killers like One-Eyed Jeet; Shastri wondered how long he would be allowed to keep his position once Chetan was crowned and the succession assured. 'I will give Prince Chetan all my support, of course. My commiserations on this dreadful news, Lord.'

Ravindra waved a hand dismissively. 'Yes, yes. You may go, Senapati.'

Shastri started bowing his way out, managing to contain his relief, but just as he thought he'd escaped, Ravindra spoke again. 'By the way, Shastri, Prince Gautam . . .'

Shastri stiffened, did not turn.

'My foolish brother did not name his main co-conspirator. I know there is one.'

Shastri swallowed carefully. 'That is unfortunate, my lord.'

'Find the men he did name and bring them to the dungeons. We will root out the key name – it is a matter of some urgency.'

Shastri forced himself to breathe. 'Yes, my lord.'

Only years of military discipline enabled him to walk steadily from the throne-room.

When Three Meet (Again)

Jodhpur, Rajasthan, March 2010

The white-clad fielders closed in as Warne tossed the ball from hand to hand. The MCG crowd roared, chanting not for the Aussie spinner, but calling the visiting batsman's name. He had won them over with his dazzling innings. 'Amanjit Singh! Amanjit Singh! Amanjit Singh!' He blocked out the wall of sound with an effort. *Concentrate*. Six to win, last ball . . . Gilchrist murmured something derisive to the batsman as he hunched behind the stumps. Lee smirked and Ponting scowled.

'You've got no chance, mate. Warney's gonna skittle ya.'

The blond spinner shuffled up to the stumps, his arm rolled over . . .

. . . Amanjit blinked . . . and he was back in reality, with Sanjay about to bowl the last ball before the end of lunch-break on a red-brown strip of rubbish-strewn dirt at the back of their tiny schoolyard in Jodhpur. The ball was a tennis ball stripped of its fur and carefully deflated so it bounced low like a cricket ball, and the bat was a plank of timber that had been chipped into shape and wrapped in tape. *But I'm still going to hit a six . . .*

Sanjay bowled, short, leg-side, as usual . . .

Thwack!

The boys all groaned except for Amanjit who skipped triumphantly down the pitch and roared, 'In your face, Warne!' at Sanjay. Sanjay's eyebrows shot up, then they all followed the flight of the ball as it sailed onto the roof of the main school building, three flights up.

'Amanjit, you kotte! You've lost the bloody ball AGAIN,' a chorus of young male voices cursed. 'You have to get it back!'

The bell rang, and everyone else groaned and fled, leaving Amanjit and Sanjay behind.

Amanjit looked at Sanjay. 'It's your ball.'

'You hit it – you know we banned sixers. You're always showing off.'

'If you weren't such a rubbish bowler I wouldn't have been able to hit it.'

'You get it back! That's our only decent ball!' Sanjay turned and ran after the rest of the boys pelting towards the classrooms.

Five minutes later Amanjit was crawling across the roof, praying to every god he could think of that none of the teachers on the upper floors were looking out of their windows. Fortunately he knew the roof well, even though it was officially out of bounds for students. It was a great place to hide whilst skipping class, and from up here you could see over the rooftops for miles on all sides. He'd always liked looking at the tangle of buildings, many of which were painted the ubiquitous sky-blue colour from which Jodhpur took its nickname, 'The Blue City'. Some people said the blue was considered auspicious, even holy, whilst others swore that it drove mosquitoes away. *Whatever!* he thought, rolling his eyes and looking about him.

Bal Vidya High School was on the south side of the city, beneath the shadow of the Mehrangarh, the huge fortress that surmounted the entire hill overlooking Jodhpur. It was the seat of the

Maharaja of Jodhpur, and had never been taken in battle. Amanjit was overcome with awe whenever he saw it.

Right now, though, he would rather have been looking at that bald old tennis ball . . .

The sun beat down, radiating heat. It was early spring, and the air was gritty from the sandstorms that always blew in from the desert at this time of year. He hated spring! It was worse than high summer. He had grit in his eyes, grit in the folds of his turban, grit in his ears, and he was going to have welts on his arse if any of the schoolmasters caught him up here again during class-time. A bead of sweat rolled from beneath his already damp turban and ran down his face. Feeling half-heroic, half-ridiculous, he crawled under windows, hearing fragments of the lessons being taught inside. He tiptoed over creaking beams and hopped over holes in the roof and around piles of rotting leaves and debris.

Where's that damned ball?

There! On an adjacent roof, he thought he'd spotted the dull black-brown sphere, nestled in a pile of . . . *something* . . . probably best not to think what. He winched himself up and crept quietly across the surface, trying not to make a sound, lest whoever was in the room below heard him. He balanced, perched precariously on his knee and elbow, and reached out . . .

. . . just as a furry brown arm reached in and grabbed.

No!

'Hey, give me that!' he hissed.

The monkey looked at the ball, sniffed it and bared its teeth at him.

'Let it go, you little rat!'

The monkey snickered at him, screeched and bounded away.

Damn!

Amanjit leapt after it, landing like a cat on the level below. The monkey watched him come, hissed and bounded away.

He should have shrugged and let it go, but he couldn't, not when it was their last ball and it was his fault. He gave chase.

He sprinted over the roofs, leaping between buildings, balancing along narrow ledges and climbing chest-high rises, and all the while the monkey capered in front of him, almost toying with him, more amused than scared. Then at last he had it trapped – well, sort of . . .

He rounded a corner and suddenly there were no more buildings in front of them; there was nowhere else for the monkey to run. It could have gone down the side of the building, maybe. For a second, Amanjit was afraid it would come at him – monkeys were no joke, with their powerful jaws and strong, grasping fingers, and they carried any number of noxious diseases. Then it darted to the edge of the roof and sized up the drop. They were right beside the open window of the music room – which was, by coincidence, exactly where he was supposed to be.

The monkey turned towards the window. 'No!' he hissed. 'Stand still! *Don't!*' The monkey grinned at him as if daring him to try stopping it. 'No! I'll do anything! I'll offer anything you like at the next Hanuman temple I see! Just don't – *oh no!*'

As the monkey leapt and sailed through the window and into the classroom, he lunged to intercept it, but he was too slow—

—and then chaos exploded.

Girls shrieked, boys hollered and the teacher roared as desks were overturned and something crashed to the floor . . .

'. . . and that's how the monkey ended up in class, sir,' Amanjit finished. 'I didn't deliberately chase it in, whatever those girls said,' he added defensively.

The professor looked at him, shaking his head. 'It sounds just about ridiculous enough to be true. But how did you end up falling to the lower roof?'

Amanjit's mouth dried up and he paused. Professor Choudhary waited. He was new here – a music scholar from Delhi, the headmistress had said in her introduction at Assembly, doing a research project on Rajasthani musical traditions and teaching part-time to help fund it.

'Well?' the professor asked.

Amanjit wasn't sure what to say, so he said nothing, until the silence had dragged out so long he had to break it. He muttered something about slipping.

'You're lucky you weren't hurt seriously, Amanjit.'

He nodded mutely. His back still hurt from landing heavily. But how could he tell the professor that he hadn't slipped at all.

I was pushed.

The blazing eyes of the ghostly woman were haunting him even now. As he'd turned to flee the scene, she'd been *right there*, somehow. Her icy hand had shoved him backwards and he'd stumbled and gone over the edge onto the roof below. If he hadn't known how to roll on landing, he might have died. As it was, he could still feel those cold fingers on his chest, even through his sweaty school shirt. And when he'd lifted his shirt to check, her handprint was actually there, like some kind of cold burn: proof that he hadn't imagined her.

It wasn't something he could explain to a teacher, though, not when she'd vanished without a trace, so he said nothing and hoped for leniency.

As the professor considered his fate, there was a knock at the door.

'Vikram!' commanded Mrs Poonam, and her English class fell silent, all eyes turning to the young man she'd singled out.

Vikram Khandavani stood up unsteadily. *This is why I hate English here, even though it's my favourite subject.*

'Come on, Vikram!' She put her hands on her hips. 'You've not long joined us from England: I presume they still speak English there?'

That's rich, coming from someone who doesn't even know what a predicate is, he didn't say: Mrs Poonam might not know the grammatical terms, but she was no one to mess with.

As he clambered to his feet, he felt the sea of eyes turn towards him. His mouth gummed up, which was absurd: he was perfectly good at English – in fact, he'd been top at his London grammar school, where he'd been happily ensconced until nine months ago. His parents had emigrated to England from Mumbai when he was seven, ten years ago, and he'd never expected to come back to India except maybe on holiday. Ten years of getting teased for having an Indian accent and now here he was, stuck at the back end of nowhere in provincial India getting teased for having an English accent. Life was *utterly* unfair.

It was while they were still in Britain that his parents' marriage had ended in wreckage. His dad's business had failed and his mother flounced back to Mumbai high society, shunning all contact with them. With half his assets disputed, his father had to swallow his pride and declare bankruptcy in the end, at the same time Vikram's grandparents – his father's parents – were dying in Rajasthan. His dad was obliged to return to India to sort out a horribly messy will – Indian families! – and what was supposed to be a short-term visit had rapidly turned into full repatriation to India. His family's affairs were so tangled – everything was in dispute and the Indian courts took *forever* to decide *anything* – and his father had been forced to set up a new business here just so they could both survive. The last two years had been the worst of his life by a long shot.

None of that really explained why he was standing tongue-tied in front of Mrs Poonam's English class, of course. The reason for that sat three desks away: a shimmering, radiant piece of loveliness whose mere presence reduced his brain to mush. The new girl was Professor Choudhary's daughter from Delhi. Deepika Choudhary.

Deepika, Deepika, Deepika, how I adore you!

Mrs Poonam was still waiting, and she was getting cross now. 'Vikram, don't be shy. You know you're the best poet in class; you've no reason to be self-conscious.'

Oh yes, I so have.

He rubbed his glasses and took a deep breath. He realised he was shaking. He clutched the piece of paper in his hand. The poem scrawled over it had so much crossing-out it was barely legible . . . and it was probably the worst, most lovesick doggerel he'd ever scrawled in his life. It had nothing to do with the topic they were supposed to be making verses about. Deserts – what did he know about deserts anyway? No, it was entirely concerned with—

'For goodness sake! Badri, you read Vikram's poem!' snapped Mrs Poonam impatiently and Vikram's neighbour smirked and held out a hand.

'No! No! I'll do it!' cried Vikram, but it was too late. Grinning like a fiend, Badri snatched the sheet of paper out of his hand, looked at it and sniggered.

'It's called "Deepika", ma'am,' he announced to the class. The object of the poem cringed and hid her face. Vikram looked around for a hole to crawl into and die . . .

'. . . and that's why I've been sent to you for detention, sir,' Vikram explained to Professor Choudhary. *Deepika's father.* And also the acting head of Prithviraj House. Punishments of a 'non-serious' nature were referred to the housemasters rather than the deputy principal, which was sometimes a good thing – but not now, not this time: not when you've been sent there for writing love poetry about the *housemaster*'s daughter. At least it had been tasteful. Rubbish, maybe, but not smutty. The poem in question was lying crumpled in front of the teacher on his desk.

What was worse, Amanjit Singh, who was probably the most popular boy in school, was listening from the corner with a grin that spread from ear to ear. All *he'd* done was chase a monkey into the music room – that was the stuff heroes were made of. Being caught writing love poems was social death.

Not that I wasn't socially dead anyway . . . Nine months wasn't long enough for an ex-pat to settle back into a country he'd barely known before he left. The heat and squalor of Rajasthan was too much after the damp orderliness of London, and he'd not yet learned when to shut his mouth and stop complaining. That he did it in a British grammar school accent didn't help to endear him either. Getting ragged at break time had become such a part of life since he'd come here that he'd taken to hiding in the library and writing poems.

After all, what harm could poetry do?

Professor Choudhary raised his grey bushy eyebrows and tapped his pen thoughtfully. 'This poem, "Deepika" . . . this is about *my daughter* Deepika?'

Vikram nodded mutely.

The professor drummed the desk with the fingers of one hand, all the while staring at Vikram with an unreadable expression on his face. In the corner, Amanjit appeared to be having to physically restrain himself from collapsing on the floor in hysterics.

The Professor's going to kill me, Vikram reflected sadly. *Tomorrow's headline in the Rajasthan Patrika:"Student strangled by Teacher in Love-Poem Scandal".*

Just when Vikram thought things could get no worse, the door opened and the object of his adoration walked in. She paused when she realised her father wasn't alone. 'Oh, sorry Papa – I'll come back—'

Then Deepika looked around, her eyes sweeping over Vikram and Amanjit. When she saw Vikram her expression went flat, the sort of look she probably reserved for crawling insects and unwanted food. Then she looked at Amanjit and flushed. He looked back at her and his eyes went wide. Vikram was a little surprised, then he realised that Amanjit was in the other senior class so he'd probably never seen her properly before. And after all, she *was* stunning—

Then they both looked at Vikram, and suddenly time froze.

Amanjit and Deepika were overlaid with myriad other faces and bodies, old and young, tall and short, dressed in a hundred different ways, from armour to uniforms, saris to burkhas, and everything between. There were dozens of them, each distinctly different, and yet each also the same.

Vikram reeled in shock. The scariest part was that he was pretty sure – though he had *no* idea how – that if he really, *really* tried, he could have put a name to many of those faces, though of course that was completely impossible.

And then he saw Amanjit and Deepika looking at him in the same way and felt a dizzy rush. He closed his eyes to block it all out, to make it stop, and when he opened them a few seconds later, everything was normal – or at least he could no longer see phantom faces. But the other two were looking at him open-mouthed and he guessed that they had had a similar experience. He wondered how many faces they had seen on him, and if they recognised any of them too.

As one, the three of them remembered they weren't alone, and turned towards Professor Choudhary, who was sitting back in his chair, still drumming his fingers. Unbelievably, he didn't appear to have noticed anything untoward at all.

'Vikram,' he said, oblivious to the astonished faces before him, 'I do not wish to hear of any similar incidents, you understand? You will keep your thoughts on your fellow students to yourself in future, yes?' When Vikram nodded sheepishly, he added, 'As penance, I want a handwritten biography of a Rajasthani poet of your choice on my desk tomorrow morning. Understood?'

Vikram nodded mutely, not quite believing that he had got off so lightly. *Some teachers would have walloped me into next week for that* . . . He could dash off a simple bio in double-quick time. And he would never have been able to speak to Deepika again in his life anyway.

Professor Choudhary turned to the young Sikh. 'Amanjit, I don't believe in corporal punishment. You will pick up all the litter on the sports field tomorrow morning before school. You may both go.'

The two boys fled before he changed his mind, but both cast back glances at the girl as they left, and they saw she was staring after them with troubled eyes.

Amanjit and Vikram hurried out together into the schoolyard, but they had missed the bus, and Amanjit resigned himself to the half-hour walk home through the busy streets of Jodhpur. No doubt Vikram's father would be at the gates with his car as usual; he'd seen him a number of times, waiting impatiently for his son. But after what had happened in Professor Choudhary's office, Amanjit didn't think he could just walk away without a word.

'You saw that too, didn't you?' he asked, feeling unusually hesitant. He realised this was probably the first time he'd spoken to Vikram without teasing him, or telling him what he thought of his whining; he was all, *London this, England that* . . . Right from the start he'd thought Vikram needed to get over it and deal with living in India, and he hadn't been slow to say so.

Vikram nodded. 'I did.'

'I think that girl, Deepika, she saw something too,' Amanjit went on. 'I saw her face. She looked like . . . like a dozen women at least, all at once . . . and you—'

'Yes? What did you see in me?' Vikram asked. He sounded both eager and fearful at the same time.

'I saw . . . well, *you*, but all *kinds* of you.' He couldn't explain it better than that: there had been all these different versions of Vikram, each almost clamouring for attention before being swept aside by the others. He spread his hands. 'It's hard to explain,' he finished apologetically.

'I saw many of you as well,' Vikram admitted.

They stared out across the yard. The wind was picking up again, but it felt like the dust storms were over at last; the breeze was lifting the dirt from the nooks and crannies and blowing it away, and for some reason Amanjit found himself wondering what it would uncover.

Then he remembered what had happened before they'd all had that strange vision and couldn't help laughing. 'By the way, nice poem!' he chuckled. 'I think she was impressed.'

Vikram groaned. 'More like she wants to slap me!'

Amanjit grinned at him. 'No, she was moved, man. You should write more of them.'

'Liar!' And suddenly Vikram was grinning too, in spite of himself, and they laughed together in genuine warmth and amusement. Suddenly Vikram didn't seem like too bad a guy after all. He knew he was being teased, but not maliciously, and he took it in good spirit. If you wanted friends, you needed to be able to handle some banter without getting riled up. So maybe they were from the same planet after all.

You're okay, Vikram Khandavani, Amanjit thought. *We may never be best buddies, but you're okay.*

Then Amanjit suddenly remembered the woman with the frigid hands, and almost felt her handprint steal the heat from his body again. The moment of levity passed and a faintly chilly wind blew across the courtyard, as if it had just wafted over a decayed corpse. They both shuddered at the same time.

'Hey,' said Vikram, 'my dad will be waiting for me. D'you want a lift home?'

Normally Amanjit wouldn't have been seen dead with a dweeb like Vikram, but for some reason he found himself accepting the offer with sincere gratitude. It might have been the shared vision, or maybe that moment of levity – *no, actually, it was the memory of that woman on the rooftops . . .*

Overheard

Mandore, Rajasthan, AD *769*

Darya ak'Alitan had been sold in marriage after a protracted negotiation by her Persian father to secure a trading agreement on the Silk Road, near Kabul. She had been born under inauspicious stars, with Mars in ascendance and the moon dark, things men took seriously. More importantly her father was not rich, so she wasn't a good catch twice over. No one of status had wanted her – not until, quite out of the blue, the Raja of Mandore had come and sued for her hand. At first she had been grateful, but now she looked back upon that moment as the beginning of the end of her life.

There was no one here in Mandore she could talk to. Her family was hundreds of miles away, and anyway, they did not care: once the agreed wedding goods had been received she had effectively become dead to them, even though her royal husband Ravindra was a monster three times her age, and his son Prince Chetan the lesser of evils only by degrees. Whenever she was summoned to Ravindra's chambers she was savaged and left bruised and battered. Thankfully she had not yet conceived, but it was inevitable that she would soon bear her husband – the Beast King, as she thought of him – a child.

It might have been bearable if she'd had someone to turn to in her misery, someone to share the pain. But the other wives were all drugged, and anyway, most of them were stupid or, in the case of Halika, malicious and overbearing. She liked Padma, but they were both so often groggy with the opium. She hated the feeling of numb helplessness, but there was no choice: the raja liked his ranis complacent. None of the guards would lift a finger to help, either out of fear or because they were obviously deep in his counsel, like the handsome senapati, Shastri. Everyone went in terror of their master, so they were eager to abet Ravindra's urges, no matter how obscene, if it meant they'd be left alone. Only the poet seemed at all sympathetic, but he was a pathetic creature, too weak and scared to be of any real use.

Though the opium at least gave her somewhere to hide inside from what was happening around her, she knew all too well what the poppy could do. She had seen too many die from excessive use in her own homeland. So now she always refused it – by making them force it down her, at least she knew that she still owned her own mind. It was a fruitless rebellion; they insisted on the poppy-milk nightly now, no matter whether she pleaded and begged, or raged and fought, they always won, drugging her to make her sluggish and pliant, to stop her screaming or crying. She prayed to Allah for release, but none came. She was in a nightmare from which she could never wake.

That night Darya was so lost in her miserable thoughts that she didn't hear Halika slither into her tiny chamber until she pulled the sheets away, revealing Darya's naked beaten body. She closed her eyes, not wanting to see the bruises and welts that marred her own skin, nor the hideous expression on Halika's face, those gloating, leering eyes . . .

She grabbed at the sheet to cover herself. 'Go away,' she tried to snap, but it came out more like begging.

'Not until I have told you something. Something important.' Halika sat down beside Darya's pallet. 'I need to tell you about one of our ancient and revered customs. It is called sati. Do you know of it?'

Darya shook her head.

Halika was almost purring with relish as she explained, 'Sati is named for the first wife of Lord Shiva, who burned herself to death on a ceremonial fire when her father insulted Shiva-ji. She was reborn as Parvati, and after her penance she remarried Lord Shiva. Because of this noble sacrifice, it has become the custom amongst highborn Hindus that when a man dies, the widow casts herself upon the pyre.' She smiled malevolently. 'Or is cast upon it, in some cases, should she for some inexplicable reason not be willing.'

Darya stared at her in disbelief. 'But that's *horrible*,' she exclaimed, shocked. 'It's *barbaric*!'

'Nevertheless, that is the custom.' Halika smiled. 'But of course, our beloved lord is young still, and virile. Long may he live.'

'Long may he live,' agreed Darya, suddenly yearning for the numbing taste of poppy-milk on her tongue.

Aram Dhoop was often forgotten. The raja had little appreciation of poetry and his son even less. Only Gautam had appreciated him, and Gautam was . . .

Aram tried not to think about that.

He had been overlooked again: Ravindra-Raj had asked him to sit behind one of the grilled windows while he interviewed a merchant from Gujarat – he sometimes did this, ostensibly to ensure nothing important was missed during the conversation.

Aram would be called upon to report back in due course. The acoustics were so cleverly ordered in the meeting chamber that a person huddled behind one of the ceiling lattices could hear the whispered remarks of guests to each other as clearly as if they had been murmuring into their ear.

Today it appeared that the raja had forgotten Aram for he had not been dismissed from his station and after a few hours he'd fallen asleep. He'd awakened with a start when he heard Senapati Shastri below him, hauling in a guardsman. The man was bound and gagged, his ankles chained together.

'This is the last one, my lord,' Shastri said. He sounded tired.

'Ahhh,' Ravindra said in a smoky, self-satisfied voice. 'Gautam's bodyguard, wasn't he? Wait, let me remember . . . Devi, isn't it?'

The prisoner whimpered.

'And what has been done to him?'

Shastri's voice was carefully neutral, but Aram could hear the strain. 'He has been whipped, beaten and castrated, my lord, but I fear he has given us nothing we did not already have. In fact, I'm not convinced he was involved at all.'

Ravindra sighed. 'Ah well, that is the way of it sometimes. Loyalty is such a double-edged virtue, isn't it?'

'Yes, my lord,' Shastri replied stiffly.

He suspects you, Aram thought. *He thinks you were in it too, Shastri, but he's not sure, so he's giving you the benefit of the doubt. Maybe. For now.*

Ravindra tapped his fingers on the arm of his throne thoughtfully, then made a decision. 'Kill him, Shastri.'

The commander of the raja's soldiers bowed. 'Yes sir.' He turned to go, one hand on the prisoner's shoulder.

'No, Senapati. Kill him yourself, here, and now.'

'But my lord . . . the floor. Your carpets—'

'That is of no moment. Kill him.'

Aram stared through the grille as Shastri pulled out his dagger. He willed the soldier to throw it into the breast of the raja instead, but there were other guards present, and hidden watchers like himself, only better armed. Any such move would be suicidal, and Shastri would know that.

He hoped he was the only man to see the captain's hand tremble a little before he drew his weapon across the throat of the prisoner, holding him upright as he slumped. A great gout of scarlet covered Shastri and marred the rich carpets.

'Shall I have the servants clean the carpet, Father?' Chetan's voice floated up from beside Ravindra.

'No, leave it.' Ravindra clapped his hands. 'Leave us, all of you.' He didn't move his head, but he did raise his voice as he added, 'Including you, Aram Dhoop.'

So I wasn't forgotten at all . . . he wanted me to see that . . .

Aram left his place silently, nodding to a eunuch he passed outside the chamber. No one stayed to guard the passage leading back to the tiny listening chamber and it was a simple matter to turn and creep silently back – simple, and the most nerve-wracking thing he had done in his life. *Why am I doing this?* he asked himself. But he didn't stop, though every footfall could bring disaster – his clothes could snag on the wall, or catch and tear, and even the slightest sound would carry back down . . . and yet he didn't stop. He moved noiselessly past his previous post to the grilled window that looked down upon the raja himself. He knew better than to go too close – if Ravindra glanced up, he could see inside that chamber – so he needed to stay out of the raja's direct line of sight. It wouldn't matter that the sound would not be as clear here, for Aram's excellent hearing had been finely tuned by his musical training.

'When, Father?' Chetan's voice was unnervingly loud.

'Soon, my son. Within the week.'

'And the kingdom will really be mine?' Chetan sounded doubtful.

Ravindra laughed softly. 'Of course. Why would I want so paltry a thing as a mere kingdom when death will bring me so much more?'

'I don't understand,' Chetan complained. 'Why do you need this ruse? Why should you give up the throne in this way? It makes no sense.'

'I don't need you to understand, Chetan. I just need you to do exactly as I have instructed. You will place my body on the pyre, together with all seven of my wives.'

'Sati,' intoned Chetan, his voice filled with dread, and something baser. 'What a waste – especially of the Muslim girl.'

'They must *all* go on the pyre, Chetan: and remember, I will be watching. *I will know*. Burn all seven – and each must be wearing the gemstone I have given them.' His voice took on a threatening tone. 'Remember this above all: I will be watching you, even when the world thinks me dead, and if you fail me, *I will know*. And I will *not* be pleased.'

Aram heard Chetan choke out, 'I will not fail you, Father. I swear it!'

Ravindra chuckled. 'Good, good. And when I am gone, all of this will be yours, to do with as you will – to let live, or to let die.'

Chetan laughed. 'I can scarcely wait. And the first death will be Senapati Shastri: that man stinks of secrets – and he's far too popular.' Then he recollected himself and added quickly, 'Of course, it will grieve me that you will not be here, Father – but I will know that you are alive in another realm!' He laughed uncertainly.

Ravindra laughed with him: a rolling, throaty laughter that

curdled the blood in Aram's veins. He'd heard enough. He crept away, shaking, full of terror – but even stronger than his own fear was the horror that his rani, the queen of his life, was to be thrown upon the pyre to burn alive.

'Rani Darya, I won't let them do this!' Aram promised under his breath. 'I swear I'll save you!'

Private Life

Jodhpur, Rajasthan, March 2010

Dinesh Khandavani was waiting beside their little Swift, combing his already immaculate hair carefully in the side-mirror. It was jet-black, thanks to some expensive dye from a mall in Mumbai, as was his carefully waxed moustache. His face glistened in the late heat. He wasn't a big man, but he had a confident dignity in his bearing. As soon as he saw that his son had company, he stood up straight and thrust a firm hand at the boy.

'Vikram, who is your friend?' he enquired, gripping Amanjit's hand, his handshake as steady and respectful as if he were the chairman of some powerful board or company.

Amanjit looked at Vikram. 'Friend' wasn't a word they'd ever associated with each other before now. Vikram broke the silence before it stretched too long. 'Uh, this is Amanjit Singh, Baba. He and I – we just, er, did some extra work for one of the teachers. Can we drop him home?'

He bowed slightly and beamed. 'Of course, of course. Any friend of my son is a friend of mine,' he said warmly, opening the back door of the car, which was stacked with bails of fabric and books of swatches. 'Vikram, move those over and you'll be able to squeeze in. Your friend can have the front seat.'

Amanjit winked at Vikram and settled into the comparative luxury of the front seat while Vikram, wondering why he'd offered the Sikh lummox a lift in the first place, struggled into the back. The first hairpin turn, which on Jodhpur's streets wouldn't be long in coming, would bury him in two tons of spiral-bound fashion statements.

Vikram's life had undergone a painful collapse in the past few years, but he knew it had been infinitely worse for his father. Dinesh Khandavani had gone to England a married man with a family and full of hope for the future. He'd returned almost penniless, his British assets lost and his Indian assets frozen while the divorce from his second wife dragged on. Vikram had come upon him in tears more than once, and decided that was something no son should ever see.

But his father was a resourceful man, and once they'd arrived in India he'd soon put himself back on his feet. He'd started in a new business, as a cloth purchaser, affiliated to a number of upmarket fashion houses in Mumbai. It was a two-way process: the fashion houses wanted to dictate to their cloth producers, but they were always looking for inspiration, so their procurers needed to be more than order-takers; they also had to be talent-spotters, and his father had always had an eye for such things. Vikram wanted to stay in Mumbai – at least that was a real city! – but his father needed to be based in his new territory, so off they'd gone to Rajasthan. But business quickly picked up, and Vikram got on well with his dad – after all, they'd been through a lot together. His real mother had died when he was four, and though his memories were more about smell and warmth and shelter than specific words and deeds, she remained in his mind an ideal of gentle care and patience. She was *Mother*, a special kind of goddess who had departed but was always present. His stepmother . . . well, she was a different matter entirely, and in all honesty, he didn't miss her at all. She'd entered his life when he was still young and she'd always treated him as secondary to her own son, his half-brother. Once let loose in London she'd spent money on herself wantonly, leaving his father deep in debt, then abandoning him. He doubted that she'd ever seen anything in his father beyond an easy mark, but his father had taken a long time to recover emotionally.

While his father prattled on about nothing in particular to Amanjit in the front, Vikram desperately tried to stop the shifting piles of samples from collapsing onto him as they wound their way through the narrow streets past handcarts and autos and cows and motorbikes, honking every few seconds, sending pedestrians scattering and facing down oncoming vehicles until they veered aside. Driving in India after the orderly streets of England was like a continuous game of Chicken. As they made their way into the old city, following Amanjit's instructions, the dusty air clogged their nostrils. The Swift's aircon didn't work all that well and it wasn't long before they were all bathed in sweat despite the gathering gloom of evening.

'Our house is down there,' Amanjit said finally, indicating an alley. He looked across at Dinesh, clearly weighing up his social obligations for accepting a lift. 'Uh, can I offer you water, sir?'

Vikram knew his father well; and he watched curiosity overcome the need to get home on his father's face. In all likelihood, the hesitation Amanjit had shown in inviting them in had only made him more inquisitive. He groaned silently as his dad courteously accepted. This was exactly the sort of thing that landed his father into trouble all too often.

They parked the car at the head of the lane, where an old chaiwallah promised to keep an eye on it, then followed Amanjit between the blue-painted walls, trying to avoid the piles of litter and lumps of cowshit everywhere. The whole alley stank worse than a public urinal. There was some furious honking and a motor-bike ridden by a youth with his head wrapped in a scarf ploughed past them. Amanjit guided them to an ancient carved door that hung off one hinge; beyond was a dusty courtyard where an old crone, bent almost double, was rearranging the sand with a bracken sweep. She eyed Vikram and his father suspiciously.

Amanjit led them to another doorway, painted and in better repair generally, and up narrow stone stairs worn smooth with age. As the smell of cooking wafted down to meet them, erasing the stink of outside, Vikram contemplated another quirk of India: that public spaces were often neglected, but private dwellings were invariably tended with inordinate care and pride. He still didn't really get it.

Somewhere deeper in the house a woman was singing absently, tuneless meanderings that floated on the cooking smells. The house might be small and plain, but it was clean, and very tidy. His father nodded approvingly.

'Mum! I'm home!' Amanjit called as he topped the stairs to a landing with several doors leading off it. Another set of stairs continued up to the next level, and Vikram could hear a radio playing somewhere up there.

The singing stopped. 'About time! You were supposed to be here hours ago!' A door opened onto a pokey kitchen and a harried but elegant woman with a narrow face and a cascade of greying hair caught in a loose ponytail peered out. 'Did you remember to—? Oh!' She stared at the visitors.

Amanjit fidgeted awkwardly. 'Mum, this is Mr . . . um . . .' He visibly cursed his faulty memory, but Vikram's father smoothly stepped into the breach.

'Dinesh Khandavani,' he said, bowing. 'My son Vikram is a school fellow of Amanjit's.'

Amanjit's mother wiped her hands on her apron, then tentatively offered a hand, western-style. 'Kiran Kaur Bajaj.' She looked questioningly at Amanjit.

'Uh, Mr Khandavani gave me a ride home after I, er, had to stay late at school. I offered him water before they go home.'

Kiran looked relieved. 'Oh! Oh, of course – I am most grateful, sir.'

'Please, call me Dinesh, Mrs Bajaj.' He had an infectious smile, and Vikram had never seen him not coax a return smile from another person if he tried – except his stepmother, of course.

Kiran blinked. She had a long, horsey face and a classic narrow beak-like north Indian nose that dominated her face. She looked melancholic and anxious, but she smiled slowly, as if suddenly remembering how to, and it transformed her instantly, softening her features dramatically. 'Please, please come in. Amanjit, go and get Ras.' She backed into the kitchen. 'Come in, please, there are seats through here.'

She led them through the little kitchen, which was heavy with the scents of turmeric, curry-leaf, pepper, roasting capsicum and fresh coriander, into a small dining-cum-living room where worn furniture, clearly once expensive, filled the space. A small television, the sound muted, perched on a chest of drawers. The scent of roses seeped from a bowl of pot-pourri, blending with the kitchen smells in a bittersweet mix. A big photograph of a severe-looking Sikh man in military uniform dominated the largest wall. It was garlanded with drooping marigolds and prayer-beads.

'Please, sit,' Kiran said a little breathlessly, and vanished into the kitchen.

The sound of a shrill girl's voice echoed from the stairwell:

'And apparently they read the poem out to the whole class!' She started laughing hysterically, before shrieking, 'I wish I could have seen it!'

Vikram buried his head in his hands as Amanjit led an almost painfully skinny girl into the room. He vaguely recognised her. She was a younger version of her mother, but her face was full of lively mischief. She stifled her laughter when she saw him, then her eyes bulged in recognition and she went red, trembling with the effort of suppressing her mirth.

Amanjit nudged her to try and shut her up, then announced, 'Mr Khandavani, sir, this is my sister, Ras. She's at our school too.'

Ras acknowledged Dinesh's little bow, then flicked a glance at Vikram, her nose twitching. 'I'll go help Mum,' she volunteered quickly, and fled. Vikram groaned as he heard another burst of laughter from the kitchen.

'Clearly she has had a happy day,' his father observed, looking at the boys, who both looked at their feet.

Amanjit's mother brought iced water and while they sipped slowly, Vikram's father briefly told her about his profession and his family, the awkward exchange of newly met strangers. He was well-practised at meeting people, though, and could talk effortlessly about local fabrics and trends, and soon the two adults were deep in conversation about clothing.

The three teenagers looked at each other uncomfortably until Amanjit's mother suggested, 'Why don't you take Vikram up to the roof? You may have a soft drink, if you wish.'

Amanjit looked at Vikram enquiringly and he nodded. Ras remained beside her mother; though she clearly wished to go too, Vikram was glad she didn't – he could do without yet more teasing over the whole love-poem débâcle.

Amanjit picked up a lidded bucket from the kitchen, then led the way up the steep stairs, past two more doors and out onto the flat, open rooftop where a canvas awning – suspended between the top of a water tank and a TV aerial – shaded a couple of mattresses. A real Spaghetti Junction of wires ran from the main power-line.

He picked up a rock from the top step of the stairs and peered about warily before sending it crashing against the far wall, a foot from the head of a small brown rhesus monkey which hissed and darted away. Then he took the lid from the bucket, pulled out two bottles of cola rebottled into old Mountain Dew bottles and uncapped them with the rusted bottle opener tied to the handle of the bucket. He passed one to Vikram, then sank to the ground. 'Sorry, no seats,' he said, leaning back against the outer wall. Vikram shrugged and sat a few feet from him, and they looked at each other, neither really sure what to say.

Vikram looked around. This was another thing that was strange to him: that here the roof was used like another room of the house. Of course, that was only possible in a place where the year's entire rainfall happened over six weeks in mid-summer. The monsoon was still months away, due in June, and Amanjit's family's rooftop was cluttered with personal possessions. Vikram spied the pair of mattresses under the awning, and asked, 'Um . . . is this where, um—'

Amanjit cocked his head. 'Yeah, this is where I sleep with my brother when he's not sleeping in his taxi. Except during the monsoon. Then I have to go inside and sleep on the landing. Mum has the main room and Ras gets the other one.' He frowned a little. 'My sister gets the best room because she has a serious illness. The doctors say she has a hole in the heart, and bad lungs too. She won't live long . . .'

Vikram had no idea what to say to that. 'What about your father?' he asked tentatively.

'The photo downstairs? That's him. He's not with us any more.' Amanjit gnawed his bottom lip. 'He was a tank commander in the army. His tank got blown up in Kashmir a couple of years ago. He was killed, his crew too.'

'Sorry,' Vikram said, not knowing what else to say. He peered about surreptitiously. Amanjit's family would have been well-off while his dad was alive, he supposed – a tank commander would be well paid – but it looked like money was tight now. The house looked pretty run down – not neglected, but it was obvious old things were being used past their usefulness. He had no idea what to say, and Amanjit obviously didn't wish to talk any more, so they sat in uncomfortable silence as the minutes dragged by.

Just as he was thinking, *Surely Dad must be ready to go by now?* Ras appeared at the top of the stairs. She came over and reached into the bucket for a cola. She looked at Amanjit and now all traces of her earlier laughter had gone, making her look grim and determined, and much more like her mother. 'You-know-who just got here,' she said, putting a book beside her as she sat. Vikram peered; it was a battered copy of the *Ramayana*. She looked at Vikram. 'You're the Love Poet,' she said finally, her face cracking into a grin. 'You're already a legend!'

Vikram ducked his head. 'Maybe I'd better go down,' he said.

'I wouldn't. My uncle just got here, and he's being all "Mr Big Man". You'll be called down soon enough, don't worry.' She didn't sound like she liked her uncle at all. 'So, your dad is a widower, huh?' Her eyes sparkled. 'Uncle Charanpreet was giving him the third degree when I left. Uncle Charan thinks he owns Mum.'

'He does,' muttered Amanjit darkly.

Vikram nodded uncomfortably. He didn't really want to know this family's problems. 'My mother died when I was young.'

Ras looked at Amanjit, ignoring Vikram's comment. 'Uncle

Charan *really* didn't like seeing another man in the house, but he couldn't just chuck him out, so now he's trying to lord it over him. I bet he'll give you a thrashing for inviting them in.' She sounded semi-sympathetic.

Vikram looked at the brother and sister uncomfortably. 'Sorry if we've caused trouble.'

'It's not your fault,' Amanjit said softly. 'I invited you in, after all.'

'Does your uncle live here?' Vikram asked tentatively.

Amanjit pulled a face, clearly weighing his words. 'Uncle Charan is Dad's brother. He was always jealous of him. He comes round here all the time. There's a lot of gossip – the people round here think we don't hear them but they reckon if he could get rid of his wife, he would, and then he'd marry Mum.' He bunched his fists unconsciously. 'I wish he'd just mind his own bloody business.'

'But he's Dad's executor, so he's got control of Mum's money,' Ras went on chattily. 'I've heard Mum argue with him late at night – the walls are so thin you could hear a mouse poop, let alone Uncle Charanpreet when he's mad. Once I heard Mum accuse him of pocketing most of Father's pension – of course he denies it, but he refuses to let us see the accounts. I *hate* him! So does Mum!' Then she started and threw a glance back at the stairwell, as if afraid she might be overheard. 'Anyway, what's your family like?' she asked Vikram.

'There's just Dad and me. Well, sort of.'

'Sort of?' the girl asked, leaning forward. 'What does that mean?'

Vikram sighed and leaned back against the wall. He didn't normally talk about these things, but Ras was nice, and he'd not got any real friends here, not since leaving England. He decided he could risk sharing this.

'It's a little complicated. There's me and Dad. My mum died. And well . . .' He ducked his head, suddenly embarrassed. 'My dad remarried this other woman, this absolute dragon from Mumbai.' He scowled, then spread his hands helplessly. 'Actually, she hid her true colours in the early days – or maybe she changed. I mean, she and I, we never really clicked, you know, but she and Dad seemed happy. We all moved to London – I was seven then. They had a boy, my half-brother . . . things were okay, but soon they were arguing all the time and it went on and on and I hated my life. She was really, really pretty and she liked to go out all the time, and soon it was Dad looking after me and her son and lots of arguing in the bedroom when they thought we were asleep, and then finally they divorced, and that was a *huge* relief . . .'

The word 'divorced' hung in the air. He'd already discovered divorce wasn't common here in India; it carried a deep stigma – and Amanjit and Ras were looking at one another furtively. When Vikram caught the glance he said defensively, 'That was years ago.' Then he admitted, 'But it does put off most people. My half-brother lives with the Dragon – I haven't seen them for five years or so. So Dad and I were left in London, having to do everything ourselves. In England nobody has servants except the super-rich, because labour's way too expensive over there. Then Dad's business went down and we lost everything, so all we had left was just the joint property here in India, but even that's been a nightmare because the divorce was contested, so either Dad's assets went to the Dragon or they got frozen until the court process finished. In England it'd be over in a few months, but this is India.'

He ignored Amanjit's raised eyebrows and went on before he could say anything, 'It's been nearly *forever* and it's all still dragging on! That's why we had to come back to India, to fight for it—' He clenched his fists, angry just thinking about it.

Amanjit and Ras *tsked* sympathetically and Ras asked curiously, 'But why didn't you stay in Mumbai? Why'd you come to Jodhpur?'

'We were originally Rajasthani, at least on my dad's side, and my grandparents lived in Jodhpur – but they died, and we'd just come back anyway, so Baba brought us here so he could deal with the funerals and will and stuff. My dad used to work with my grandfather before, so it made sense for him to take over his business, buying and selling cloth. And here we are.'

'But you don't like it,' Amanjit said coolly.

'Well . . . I kind of got used to England, where things *work*, at least mostly. There's plenty of clean water, no dust, no power-cuts, traffic that obeys the rules, rubbish gets collected regularly, proper footpaths, trains that run to time. If we'd stayed in Mumbai it probably wouldn't matter so much, but here . . .' His voice trailed off as he realised that he'd lapsed into complaining again. *No wonder I've made no friends when all I ever do is bitch about this country. Not that there isn't good reason* . . . The only thing he and his dad argued about was this stupid insistence on living in Rajasthan, and making him live there too. But if he was going to make friends he'd better learn to shut his mouth a bit more, or better yet, just get over it.

He sighed and admitted, 'It's not that England was perfect. Plenty of people treated me like shit just for being Indian, and I was always getting bullied at school, and the winters were *dreadful*: weeks – no, *months* – on end of rain and sleet and fog and sometimes even snow, and it was *so* cold, this horrible dank cold that gets right down to the bone, and even worse was never seeing the sun from November to March . . . but I'd got used to it, you know. I thought I'd be going to Oxford University! Instead I'm going to Mumbai next year when I finish school,' he ended, with a little, grudging, satisfaction.

'My marks aren't good enough for university,' Amanjit said, sounding resigned. 'Uncle Charan's going to have me driving taxis by July.' He picked up a ball and tossed it against the wall, watched it bounce back and neatly caught it. 'But I don't want to work for that arsehole.'

They lapsed into silence again while Ras stared intently at Vikram. Suddenly she patted the book beside her. 'Hey, if your dad and our mum got together, it would be like the *Ramayana*. We're studying it in class,' she added. 'The king had three wives and four sons.' She looked at Vikram. 'Remember? King Dasaratha had three wives, and they each ate the sacred kheer sent by the gods, but one got two servings, so she had twins.'

'That's stupid,' Amanjit said crossly. 'Mother will never remarry, not while Uncle Charanpreet controls everything.' He glared at Vikram as if it were his fault.

'Don't look at me – I don't even like kheer,' Vikram said, throwing up his hands. 'Rice pudding? Yuck!'

Ras snorted in amusement, Amanjit rolled his eyes and they started laughing companionably until they were interrupted by a booming male voice shouting aggressively, 'Amanjit! Amanjit! Get down here and bring your friend!'

Ras looked at her brother. 'You're going to get it, bhaiya,' she warned.

Amanjit looked positively ill as he glanced at Vikram. 'Come on. You and your dad have to go now,' he said, straightened his shoulders and set off down the stairs.

The uncle was a burly man, running to fat, dressed in the uniform of an officer of the Indian Army, with a pale blue turban. His face was pockmarked with chickenpox scars and his thick lips were twisted into what Vikram suspected was a permanent sneer. He looked down with ill-disguised contempt, put out his hand and almost crushed Vikram's when he shook it. He towered over everybody in the room.

'Thank you for your hospitality,' Vikram's father said, bowing to Amanjit's mother and smiling serenely as if all were well. He said goodbye to Amanjit and Ras, and then led Vikram down the stairs, to all appearances completely at ease. Once the door was closed behind them, he looked at Vikram and gave a sad shake of the head. 'A lovely lady,' he breathed, 'with a perfectly horrendous brother-in-law.'

From above, the sound of a man's voice shouting rang down the stairs and rattled the door.

The Pyre

Mandore, Rajasthan, AD 769

The news of the sudden death of Ravindra-Raj swept through both the city and the surrounding countryside faster than a grass-fire in drought season. Chetan had immediately grasped the reins of power, moving swiftly to secure his succession, proclaiming his accession to the throne by sending messengers to the neighbouring rajas – and of course to the Maharaja – reminding them of truces made, rights bequeathed – and of course, of hostages exchanged and currently housed as honoured guests, living in luxurious comfort within the royal palace.

He decreed a week of public mourning, so that proper respects could be paid, then Ravindra-Raj's body would be consigned to the flames.

Royalty was always revered, but the king had also been dreaded by many and was loathed by many more, so there was no clear way to react to his unexpected death. Did one rejoice or mourn when the hated son had so seamlessly replaced his detested father? It felt fitting to be cautious. The people were muted in both their mourning and their celebrations.

Senapati Shastri rode widely about the kingdom, apparently

completely loyal to his new master. His visibility served to calm the populace: the captain was a popular man, and his honest, battered face reassured people a little. Not that anyone believed all was well – how could they, when a misspoken word could condemn one to public lashing, or a visit to the raja's infamous dungeons? But Shastri had always been known as a fair man, not one to abuse his position, and many people believed that his influence had tempered Ravindra's renowned cruelty a little.

They were desperately hoping that Senapati Shastri would retain his place in the new regime, and many took the risk of expressing this wish to him. He was invited to take refreshments in any number of homes across the city while his soldiers milled outside, and if people did suggest such things, they went to great lengths to ensure they were only expressed in passing, in quiet, *private* conversations.

Shastri knew his own future was far from secure, but for the time being at least, he was still in charge of the army, and there were duties to perform, chief among them the dead king's cremation. He would immerse himself in such things and demonstrate his usefulness, in the hope it would be enough. And he sent more than a few prayers winging to the ears of Vishnu, the Protector God favoured by soldiers.

In that fraught situation, rivalries intensified. He and One-Eyed Jeet had been friends once, but not any more: it was no secret that Jeet wanted Shastri's job, he had Chetan's ear and it felt like he was increasingly pushing ahead of Shastri, now everyone knew they were competing for favour. Only one could prosper, and Shastri had been pondering on who could help him, but it was looking increasingly like anyone who might once have had some influence in the court had evaporated like steam before the heat of Chetan's gaze. A summons to the raja's inner court had become a trial: each time he entered, he felt like the air had become thinner, more rarefied, and harder for the likes of him to breathe.

The atmosphere of impending doom in the palace was underpinned by the wails of lamentation rising from the women's chambers, permeating the ancient stones. The voices were ragged, hoarse; to an ear not tuned to such matters it might have sounded like deep, genuine grief, but he had heard enough of the real thing to know the difference: no voice within wailed with real sorrow. His sister Padma and her fellow wives – except Halika, of course – wept through a haze of drugs. The little Mohameddan, Darya, screamed from time to time, until Jeet and the eunuchs drugged her again, but that was pure fury. Shastri was thankful Jeet had taken over the drugging duty; he had hated his own hands for having held that girl down, though he raged also at the thought of what Jeet might do to her.

Meanwhile, Halika's mourning was a virtuoso performance, her ululations pitched musically for best effect, accompanied by much theatrical pulling of her hair. No one could accuse her of containing her grief.

But what haunted him more than anything else was the serene face of the raja two weeks ago, when Ravindra had first spoken of his impending death. He had not appeared to care at all . . . as if it were not real.

As if none of this were real . . .

It took two days to gain Chetan's permission, but it finally came, via one of the eunuchs: yes, Senapati Shastri could visit his sister Padma. He walked the gardens with her clinging to his arm. She was clad all in white, the colour of death, of old bones and ash, and in just a few days' time that was what she would be. They did not speak of it; instead they talked quietly of people they knew, the fashions this year in jewellery and clothing, and the poem Aram Dhoop had recited the previous night at Chetan's crowning feast: trivial things, as if she were not condemned to die and he not walking a knife-edge.

'I am sorry, behan,' he whispered. 'I am sorry for marrying you to him, and sorry for everything you've already gone through.'

Padma hung her head. 'You had no choice, bhaiya. And it has not been as bad for me as the others.' She leaned closer. 'He never came to my chamber, brother – not once. Not even on the wedding night.'

He stared at her in puzzlement. *The marriage was not consummated? Why not? What did that mean?* He'd heard of unconsummated marriages where the union had been for state reasons and children weren't desired – perhaps because a certain heir was already in place – but never when the bride had been deliberately pursued: Ravindra had actively vied with others for Padma's hand. And Padma was far from ugly – she was a healthy, pretty girl, one any man might want.

Is there some way I can use this to stop her being burned on his pyre?

Padma put a hand on his arm and stopped his thoughts dead, as if she'd heard every thought. 'It wouldn't work, bhaiya. Halika knows, and the question has already been raised and refused,' she told him. 'There is no escape that way. In any case, it is Chetan who would judge the matter, and he wants us all to burn.' Her voice was full of fear. She hugged him tightly and whispered in his ear, 'You should run, brother, before it's too late.'

He stiffened awkwardly. 'I cannot,' he said finally. Why, he couldn't easily say, for surely running was the logical thing? To stay was to openly court death. *Who do I think I'm fooling, acting the loyal sworn man, when all can see the way things are going? I am juggling two fates: to be hunted to the death as an outlaw, or executed as a traitor.*

So where was the middle path to safety? Could he ride to a neighbouring kingdom, Oshiyan, maybe, and beg admittance? His competence as a soldier was well attested. Perhaps he could take Padma with him, and just ride and ride? But she would never survive such a flight, not as she was now. And anyway, where would they go?

A movement caught his eye: a man, half-hidden in the far alcove, watching them. There were eyes everywhere.

He turned suddenly and threw his arms around his sister, clasping her to him. Her heart fluttered like a trapped bird against his chest and her shoulders shook. A hundred plans were considered and discarded in the minutes that crawled past, and then the waiting eunuch coughed discreetly. It was time to go.

'Take the poppy-milk, behan,' he whispered.

Tears rolled slowly down her cheeks. 'I don't want to die, brother,' she whispered. She fumbled at a chain at her neck, her hands shaking, until she had managed to unclasp it. It was silver, and from it hung a crystal shot through with dark maroon veins, set in a silver surround. 'The raja himself gave me this,' she whispered. 'He called it my "heart-stone". He gave a "heart-stone" to each of us on the night he died.' She shuddered. 'Not that I believe he is dead. Evil things never die.'

'Don't say that.' He took the pendant from her.

'Ravindra-Raj said that it is my heart now. So you should give it to Aram.'

Aram Dhoop? Shastri stared at her, shocked. *What's the poet to her?*

Her voice dropped to a whisper, filled with horrified awe. 'Before Ravindra gave us these, he chanted spells over them. He told us that we must wear them always, because they bind our souls.'

'Then won't it be missed?' Shastri looked worried.

'I have other gems that look similar,' she murmured. 'Please, brother, give it to Aram for me, for I cannot.'

'Aram Dhoop? Why him?' Despite his best efforts he knew he sounded incredulous.

'Because he has my heart. Because I love him.' Her big eyes filled with tears again.

'Aram Dhoop?' he repeated, stuffing the necklace into his pouch.

'Yes, brother: *Aram Dhoop*. Are you blind? I love him – I always have! But I know I will never see him again, unless it is when I stare out from the pyre . . .' She swayed, and then her eyes fluttered closed and he caught her as she fainted dead away.

With the eunuch Uday leading the way, he carried her to the zenana and deposited her gently on her pallet in her narrow chamber. He kissed her forehead, but Padma didn't stir.

'Goodbye, dearest sister,' he whispered finally, when Uday signalled that he must leave. 'May the gods bear you safely to paradise – and may you finally find the happiness denied you in this life.'

As Shastri left his sister's dark cell, Halika emerged, clad in a diaphanous white sari that left little to the imagination. 'Oh Senapati Shastri, how sad we all are,' she said, swaying seductively towards him. 'How we all lament and tremble – and what little comfort we have in these, our final hours.' She reached for him, beseeching him, 'Hold me, please—!'

He stared at her and his resolve almost weakened – but then she blinked, and for an instant something corrupt shone from her eyes. It gave him the strength – or the fear – to tear his gaze from her voluptuous form. Ignoring her theatrics, he pushed past her to the courtyard outside and stood panting slightly, breathing in the dusty air as if it were the most refreshing mountain breeze.

He pulled Padma's heart-pendant from his belt-pouch and examined it, but as the great veined stone lay on his palm he shuddered: for a moment it almost felt like it was pulsing in his hand. He thrust it back into his pouch, his hand shaking.

The Pit

Jodhpur, Rajasthan, March 2010

The monkey with six arms taunted him. He knew he shouldn't follow it, but he couldn't help himself. He flew from roof to roof, always just behind it. It juggled a tennis ball with two of its hands and threw stones at him with two more, using the other two to climb. It was too nimble for him, but he was gaining; he was sure he was catching up. The strangest thing was that every so often, it wasn't a monkey at all, it was the nerd Vikram from school. And he nearly had him!

Then he rounded a corner and SHE was there.

Her jet-black hair was loose, a curtain of midnight, flowing over her bared shoulders. Her face was pale as a ghost, her lips a bloody slash. Her perfume reached out for him; it clogged his mouth, a sickly-sweet cinnamon, overlaid with something that reeked of burning meat. Her sari was red and orange and yellow, composed of fire and smoke, and beneath it her body was half-visible, lush and seductive as she swayed towards him.

'Shastri,' the woman before him purred. He was afraid suddenly that he knew her – that if he wanted, he could speak her name. Her hand came up and reached out. Her nails were three inches long. Her teeth flashed between those ruby lips. 'Madan Shastri, it's been so long.'

Her hand snaked out and reached inside his chest.

He stared down at it, realising as he did that he was clad in armour and holding a sword which now fell from his grasp. He watched in horror as the hand buried itself to the wrist in his chest and gripped his heart. Then he was falling, falling off the school roof, with nothing beneath to catch him; and as the ground opened, flames rose to swallow him . . .

Amanjit woke up with a muffled shout, his heart pounding. On the mattress beside his, Bishin – his elder brother – stirred. The canvas overhead hung limply. In the alley below dogs were barking at something, and then he heard them whimper and slink away. A wisp of cloud passed across the moon. The air was stale, laden with sweat, but somehow, impossibly, cold air radiated from the deepest shadows. He dared not move. If he used his imagination, he would be able to make out the shape of a human form in the far corner of the rooftop, draped in material that rippled in unfelt breezes. He stared at it, willing it to vanish, scarcely able to breathe.

He still hadn't moved, nor had he slept again, when the sun finally rose, and he had never prayed so vehemently in all his life. But as the sky lightened, the shape turned out to be some washing Mum had left out and at last he fell asleep as dawn kissed the Mehrangarh, the fort on the hills, with golden lips. They had humble beds, his brother and he, but the best view in the world.

Amanjit's grandfather had come here from Jaisalmer when he retired from the army and bought a taxi business. Father had inherited it when Grandpa had died of lung cancer, but by then he was in the army himself, so he had hired drivers until his sons came of age. His plan didn't quite work out, though, for he himself had died before that and Uncle Charanpreet managed things now. When Bishin was eighteen, old enough for his license, he had been ordered to leave school and take up driving, and Amanjit was expecting the same command when he finished high school.

It wasn't his dream life – but who got to live out their fantasies anyway? Bishin was keen for Amanjit to join the company too, so they could lay off another driver and keep more money in the family. And of course so Uncle Charan could pay Amanjit less than the driver he replaced and pocket the additional profit. In his dreams, Amanjit drove a tank like his father, or even a jet fighter. Mother was supportive, but Uncle Charanpreet kept telling him he was too stupid for the Air Force. Uncle Charan was an infantry officer, and he believed families should be run on instant obedience, just like his regiment. Amanjit avoided him as much as he could; the only times they exchanged more than a polite greeting they generally ended up having a blazing row.

Bishin was already up by the time Amanjit came to. He washed on the roof, using the bucket of cold water his brother had left him, before blearily making his way downstairs. Bishin waved mutely as Amanjit grabbed a handful of chapatti and a bowl of daal, kissed his mother on the cheek and went outside to eat his breakfast on the back step. There was room inside, but he preferred this. Ras, the other family rebel, joined him on the steps.

'So, how'd it go with You-know-who?' she asked sympathetically. She looked pale and sickly. Mornings were always hard for her, but Amanjit tried not to let her see how worried he was – she looked almost corpse-like today.

'He yelled a lot. I shut up and let him get on with it.' He patted his bruised cheek and shrugged. 'He only hit me once.' He'd had worse.

'Why were you late back from school last night anyway?'

'I got caught on the school roof and got hauled up before the housemaster,' he said, not bothering with the tedious details – telling her the whole thing would take too long, and anyway, her friends at school would soon fill her in.

'Again.'

'Uh-huh. Oh shit – I've got to clean the playground this morning,' he suddenly remembered. 'The new housemaster doesn't do corporal punishment; what a wimp!'

'Then you better get going, bhaiya.'

'Yeah.' He scowled. 'Having to pick up rubbish is demeaning. I'm not going to do detentions if this is what we get. I'd rather get the cane. Bloody Vikram just had to write about some poet,' he grumbled.

'Lucky you didn't have to,' Ras told him. 'You can't even spell.'

'Can too, cheeky witch.' But he decided that he probably was better off with the punishment he'd been given – he wouldn't even know how to begin finding out about some lame old poet.

Professor Choudhary looked curiously at the sheets of paper before him, and then across the desk at Vikram. "I must admit, I was expecting Surajmal Misrana, or perhaps Chand Bardai,' he observed. He glanced at the library book Vikram had given him, the source of his report. 'I've never heard of this Aram Dhoop.'

Vikram wasn't sure if he should take that as a good thing or not. He'd found the little book at the public library on the way home – weirdly, it was like the book had chosen him, rather than the other way round, falling into his hand when he had been reaching for another one entirely. But fate was fate; he'd thought, 'Why not?' and that was that.

'He lived more than a thousand years ago, sir. He was a local poet, but he isn't very well known any more – the librarian said he's virtually forgotten these days.'

Professor Choudhary looked through Vikram's biography. 'A local poet? It says here that he's from Mandore – where is that?'

'Just a few miles north of here, sir. He fled the city, though, and never returned.' The book hadn't had many details, but reading between the lines there had been lots of hints of a pretty interesting life.

The professor looked slightly intrigued despite himself. 'Hmmm. A brief report on a barely noteworthy subject? It's not really what I had in mind for this detention, Mr Khandavani.'

Vikram groaned internally. He had plenty of homework to do without having to repeat his detention.

Professor Choudhary looked at him and relented. 'But it will do. You may consider your detention served – but no more poems about any of the girls, understand? And especially not that one, eh?'

Vikram let out his breath with visible relief. 'Yes, sir!'

'You're seventeen years old, Vikram – in fact, almost eighteen, I see. You are a bright student, intelligent, and you have lived abroad. I expect more maturity from you going forward, yes? You need to put aside teenage crushes and concentrate on your future. Understood?'

Vikram felt the weight of the professor's stare and the gravity in his voice and nodded mutely. The strangeness of the last few days served only to reinforce his words: *something* was happening, something for which he had to be ready, though he had not the faintest idea what that might be.

He's right. Childhood's over.

It was a ruin, like the ones her father liked to clamber through, muttering obscure phrases like 'Pre-Mughal architecture' and 'Greco-Roman influences'. It was beautiful – with wonderfully intricate, graceful carvings, and artistically laid out to enhance the feeling of space and openness. But it was empty and in ruins now, and the shadows were moving. Bats clung to the ceiling, large ones that gibbered at her as she passed beneath, their saliva dripping towards her.

She had to find something in here: something dreadfully important. She just wasn't sure what it was.

A pale shape wisped past one of the arches and she followed it. She must have been running because she was panting now – was she hunting something, or being hunted? She wasn't sure about that either.

This is a dream, *she thought – but even thinking that didn't wake her up. She stopped, her heart leaping, as a tiger passed by, so close she could touch it, but it didn't see her. It yawned, and she glimpsed massive incisors, smelled the rankness of its breath.*

A voice broke the silence, a young man's voice, reciting poetry. It was a love poem to her, from that idiot boy in her class who kept staring at her; she recognised his voice. His name eluded her, though it was on the tip of her tongue.

Then he fell silent and a new voice started.

'Darya,' it whispered. 'Darya . . .'

It wasn't a friendly voice. It was feminine, but somehow reptilian. The bats squeaked and scrabbled above her, looking down, leering at her, reaching with hook-handed wings. Drool slavered from their bared fangs.

'She's here,' another female voice exclaimed. 'She's in here!'

Footsteps clicked on paving stones, coming closer.

Deepika broke cover and became the hunted. Corridor followed chamber followed courtyard, all blurring past, each as shadowy and menacing as the last. Pale shapes were closing in on her.

'Where is she? Where? *Can you see her, sisters?' There were at least three voices, and they all sounded dry, silky, cold . . . and very, very hungry.*

She took to her heels again, running through the maze of rooms peopled only with images of carven stone, of gods and demons entwined. The deathly women's voices called from all sides, driving her on, until all at once she burst into another empty chamber, a great circular room with a pit in the middle . . . and no other exit.

The tiger was on the other side of the pit. It saw her, and opened its mouth.

'Darya,' it purred, in a man's deep voice. 'We've all been waiting so long.'

She turned, but an armoured man now blocked her exit. His face flashed: for an instant he was a grim, scar-faced man with a full beard, and then it was the young man from school, the Sikh she'd seen in her father's office. Again, her memory refused to yield a name.

She turned back to the tiger as five white shapes glided into the chamber through the walls, their dead eyes flashing. The remains of their saris clung to decayed flesh, exposing ivory bones. They raised imploring hands towards her.

'You've been so hard to find,' the tiger said. 'But now you're here.'

The pit burst into fire, the flames roaring and jumping, and the tiger leapt into it. Its fur caught fire as it stalked across the burning pit towards her, but it was oblivious.

The stone gripped her feet; she couldn't run. As the ghosts of the women closed in, the tiger reared up on its hind legs and walked like a man towards her, his jaws opening impossibly wide.

She screamed . . .

. . . and woke.

Deepika hugged herself and realised she was shaking like a leaf. Her bedclothes were sodden with sweat; her brow was dripping, though the air-conditioning had her room as cool as usual. Trembling uncontrollably, she grabbed the top sheet and pulled it around her. She didn't dare close her eyes again for fear of revisiting that frightful scene. She reached out abruptly, grasped the glass of water of the nightstand and tipped it over her face.

That had been the worst one yet.

Ever since they had moved from Delhi two weeks ago she had been having bad dreams: always the tiger and the dead women; always chasing her. Papa said it was just nerves, because she was unsettled at having to come to a new place, and Ma said the same thing when she talked to her on the phone. 'You'll be fine when I get there, darling,' she would say, as if Deepika was still a baby. All the same, she wished Ma were here – but Ma had a job in the hotel industry that involved a lot of travel. It would be July before the family could be reunited.

She wished she could go next door and wake Papa, but what would she say? That she'd had a bad dream again? She'd sound like a little girl, not the nearly grown-up woman she was. She wished he would just cancel this project and go back home – she still didn't understand why she hadn't been allowed to stay in Delhi; she could have gone to boarding school, after all. Why did they all have to pack up every time Papa got a bee in his bonnet over something or other? It wasn't fair! And Jodhpur was such a dump . . . That horrible fortress gave her the creeps, towering oppressively over the city, and the old town was even more chaotic than Chandni Chowk in Old Delhi; a crowded, stinky maze! She missed their apartment in Safdarjung Enclave, and her own room. She missed the giant malls in Gurgaon – her 'natural habitat', as she liked to call them. She *really* missed her friends. She kept using up her credits on her mobile, but long phone calls and drawn-out text conversations with her girlfriends back home just weren't the same. Papa had been buying her airtime, but he was beginning to get grumpy about it – and then what would happen?

She toyed with her mobile, but it was no good; she couldn't call anyone. The clock said 3:23 a.m. and they'd all be asleep. *Ugh!* Hours till dawn . . .

She didn't think she'd be able to fall asleep again, but even if she could, she daren't try.

Papa pulled into the staff car park and Deepika kissed his cheek before heading for the library. She was always one of the first in, along with the other children of staff members. They were like a little club, clustered among the books, but none of the others ever spoke to her. They were all dark-skinned, bony Rajasthanis and she was a pale Delhi-miss, an outsider. She'd tried, but they wouldn't unbend. The girls all ignored her and the boys all stared at her – or made up poetry like that twerp Vikram! She trembled slightly with embarrassed fury at the memory.

A big, burly figure in an ill-tied turban was slouching about the sports field, picking up litter, and after a moment she recognised him: the other boy from yesterday, the Sikh – what was his name? That had been so weird: all of a sudden her eyes had gone funny and it was like she'd been seeing him in a dozen different ways at once. And not just him but that bloody Vikram as well! It had to have been the bad dreams . . . but he'd looked at her oddly too. So perhaps something had happened . . .

On a sudden impulse, she turned away from the library and walked towards him. 'Hey!' she called, realising she didn't know his name.

He looked up and she suddenly didn't know what to say. He wasn't fat, like she'd thought at first, but big and muscular, and he badly needed to shave away that rubbishy bum-fluff that might one day become a manly beard but was nowhere near that yet. He was pretty slovenly dressed, too. He looked as if he had been lost in thought, unable to find his way out.

'Hi,' he said, and blinked twice before focusing on her properly. 'Oh, hello.' He grinned suddenly. 'So, did you see it all too?'

Her first reaction was defensive – she certainly wasn't going to share too much with this unkempt young man. 'See what?'

'You know! Yesterday, in the office – that—' He stopped suddenly, as if he couldn't find the words he was searching for. 'You know,' he finished lamely.

She did – and oddly, she discovered she *did* want to talk about it. There was an openness to the Sikh that she liked. He looked like he couldn't keep a secret if his life depended on it – so if she could read him that easily, then she reckoned she could trust him. But it wasn't just that, there was something else . . .

So she admitted, 'I do know. And yes, I saw strange things too.'

He thrust a hand towards her. 'Amanjit Singh Bajaj.'

She took his hand cautiously, but nothing strange happened when they touched, just normal things, like noticing that for all his sloppy airs and lack of attention to personal appearance, he was rather handsome, and he had a lovely smile . . .

Vikram saw them sitting together on the playground bench and he felt a strange twist in his stomach. *His* Deepika and that oaf Amanjit were leaning towards each other, talking quickly, oblivious to everything around them. He didn't admit to the emotion that numbed his throat, but he almost ran towards them, desperate to intervene before it was too late.

'Hi! Amanjit! Deepika!'

They both went still, then glanced up like surprised cats, not sure whether to freeze or flee.

He looked at Deepika and then at Amanjit and something stirred: he felt it again, that unique shock of recognition, of déjà vu. Then that feeling faded, as if he had nothing further to say, having got their attention. But at least they had stopped talking in that *confidential* way and were now self-consciously leaning away from each other.

'Hi guys,' he said, plucking up his courage. 'I think we need to talk.'

They looked at each other and then at him and nodded.

Vikram sat down in the middle, forcing both to shuffle aside to make space for him. 'I had a weird dream last night,' he started, and felt as much as saw Deepika and Amanjit both flinch. *Ahhh, so they did too!* 'I dreamed I was in a palace – not a large one, but somehow I knew its name: *Mandore*. I was hiding, and listening to these two men talking. They were plotting something evil. I couldn't hear what it was, but I knew it meant danger . . .'

'Danger? Who to?' Deepika breathed.

He caught himself staring at her lovely face and blushed. 'To you.' He looked at Amanjit suddenly. 'You were there too. You were one of the soldiers. One of the bad guys.'

Amanjit looked at him and then burst out laughing. 'Yeah, sure, Vikram. Of course I'd be the bad guy, right? Just because I bullied you a few months ago? Look, I'm sorry about that. I've grown out of it. And in *my* dream I wasn't the bad guy at all . . .' He stopped and stared out into space for a moment, and then finished, 'In my dream I was *murdered* – by a ghostly woman!'

Vikram and Amanjit both turned to Deepika, who visibly swallowed before saying, 'In *my* dream I was being chased by ghost-women – and a tiger. And there was a fire. And bats. It was scary, really, *really* scary – but last night wasn't the first time. I've been having this dream every night since I came here.'

They digested this in silence for a few minutes, then Vikram said, 'You know what I think? I think we should go to Mandore and look around. It's not far, just ten miles north or so, and the ruins of the old palace are still there – I looked it up. We should visit it.'

Amanjit folded his arms. 'We? Who's "we", Vikram? You and Deepika, or the three of us? Or am I too much of a "bad guy"?'

Vikram chewed his bottom lip. Of course he'd love to be alone with Deepika; that would be wonderful. But he didn't think she'd go with just him, not after the whole love-poem fiasco, and anyway, Amanjit was involved too, that was clear. He sighed and said grudgingly, 'I meant the three of us.'

'Okay then,' Amanjit said thoughtfully. 'I can get us a car. How about Saturday afternoon, after morning school and football?'

A bell rang and Amanjit stood slowly. 'I've got to see your father and get my detention signed off,' he said to Deepika, then he smiled at her. 'Hey, what about we do a movie Saturday night, just you and me?'

'What, like a date?' She arched an eyebrow. 'Do people date, out here in this *pata nahim kaham* village?' she asked, then with a slight sneer added, 'I thought you could only take out your wives and sisters and cousins?'

Amanjit snorted. 'Well, hang it, then: we'll get married and *then* do a movie!'

Deepika laughed. 'Dream on, Turban-boy. Go and see my father before he makes you clean up the whole school.'

'Sure, and I'll ask him for your hand while I'm getting my detention clearance. I do like a good movie!' He sauntered off, laughing loudly.

Vikram frowned after him. 'Good people don't date, here in Jodhpur,' he observed. 'They're very traditional, you know.'

'Really?' drawled Deepika. 'You shock me.' Then the smile fled her face. 'You know, I didn't want to say anything to him, but in my dream he was a bad guy too. Just like in yours.' She met his gaze fearfully.

His heart pounded just to be so close to her, but at least this time he had the sense not to do anything stupid to ruin the moment. He went to pat her arm reassuringly, lost his nerve and settled for saying, 'Don't worry. We'll sort it out somehow.'

'Hey, it's the Love Guru! Write me a poem!' someone hollered as Vikram darted into class. He'd been desperately hoping that the teacher would already be there, but no such luck. Deepika had claimed she needed to go to her locker first, which he suspected was to avoid arriving with him; not that he blamed her for that. The whole class had swung about to stare at him as he entered and the noise became deafening as the derisive chorus continued.

Then Priti – the alpha-female of the group who already bent the boys around her little finger at will – demanded, 'I want a poem all about *me*!' Her coterie of friends, the popular, noisy girls, laughed cruelly as she swayed towards Vikram while everyone else in the room melted away from him.

His classmates were all on the verge of adulthood and individually, they could be very mature, but collectively they just reverted straight back to kindergarten-levels of behaviour, Vikram thought with a sigh. This wasn't going to go away for a *very* long time.

He fled to his desk, his face red with embarrassment, put his books down and went to sit, but Badri yanked his chair away and he landed painfully on his tail-bone. Suddenly the world was a painful place, cluttered with the legs of chairs, desks and other students.

Priti towered over him. 'Come on, Love Guru, get up and compose for me! I need to know how beautiful I am!'

Vikram was writhing in pain and could barely think, let alone wax poetic – and anyway, he thought Priti was a complete bitch. He flailed about him, trying for purchase so he could haul himself up, then Priti snatched his glasses from his face and the world became just a smear of light. There was more laughter, and nastier now.

'Come on, Casanova, give me a verse,' a Priti-shaped blur jeered, waving something sparkling – his glasses, he presumed.

He finally managed to stumble to his feet. 'I need my glasses,' he said, putting out his hand. 'If I can't see you, how can I be inspired?'

'Just think of a cow chewing grass,' Deepika's voice snapped out of nowhere. The Delhi-miss stepped from behind Priti, snatched Vikram's glasses and thrust them into his out-stretched hand. By the time he had them on, Deepika and Priti were squaring off to each other while the rest of the class looked on avidly or backed off, depending on how much they liked Priti.

Vikram was not the only person to notice that it took just about three seconds of staring into each other's eyes for Priti to decide that she didn't fancy this confrontation after all. There was something steely and implacable in Deepika's gaze and stance: she wasn't at all defensive. He might even have described her as *aggressive*, as if she was relishing the chance to take out her frustrations on the other girl; her whole demeanour made it clear that if this went further, someone would get hurt, and it wouldn't be her. He would never have suspected it, but there was something wild inside Deepika, and it both chilled and stirred him.

She is more Durga the warrior-woman than Parvati the gentle wife . . .

Priti muttered something mildly sneering to save face and backed away in the face of Deepika's stare – then Mrs Poonam hurried in and the whole class set about pretending nothing had happened. Vikram sat carefully, glaring at Badri, who just shrugged.

Deepika was going to fight Priti on my behalf, Vikram realised, unsure whether to be horribly embarrassed and ashamed, or immeasurably proud.

Then Kumar, one of the studious boys he half-liked, tapped him on the shoulder and, after looking round to make sure no one was listening, whispered shyly, 'Hey, Love Guru . . . could you please write me a poem for Drishti?'

Pursuit

Mandore, Rajasthan, AD 769

There was a square below the fortress, in the middle of the tangle of mean houses beneath the walls where the raja traditionally convened his public court. Once a week their lord would sit before his people and the common folk, no matter how poor or lowly, could come and present their complaints so he could arbitrate their petty conflicts. Under previous rulers these courts had been popular; the people would leave satisfied that justice had been done. But Ravindra-Raj had turned the courts into darker affairs, with unpredictable and corrupt judgements and hideous, unexpected sentences. Complainants grew fewer and sycophants more plentiful.

Today, though, the square had a quite different aspect. This was the day the dead raja would burn, along with his still-living wives. As Aram Dhoop watched the growing crowd, nausea threatened to overpower him once more. As no priest would come to this godforsaken place, he had been charged with reciting the blessings over the dead raja and his living queens before they all burned to ashes. He wished he were drunk; a strong swig of madhu might have given him the courage he needed to stand before the new raja and his bloodthirsty minions and speak the words of farewell for the most frightening man he had ever known. But he couldn't afford to be intoxicated, not with so much at stake. Instead, he would have to find the courage inside himself.

The crowds grew bigger by the minute – no one dared to stay away for fear that their absence would be noticed – and the square was overflowing into the narrow alleys that led off in all directions. The stench of so many unwashed bodies was overpowering. Aram held a perfumed cloth to his nose, inhaling through it, and gazed down on the fire-pit before him. Underneath the wooden platform there was a great pile of bone-dry tinder. Soon the body of the raja would be brought out, followed by his wives. Aram's mouth was dry with terror.

There were women in the crowd, and that stunned him. *What woman could possibly want to watch another burn?* he wondered. But many looked as eager as the worst of the men for the show to start. Then the crowd was tossed into a fresh ferment by the blare of trumpets, and the funerary procession descended from the fortress, bearing the body of Ravindra-Raj.

Aram wanted to leap up, to scream, 'It's not him, it's not him, he's not really dead!' – anything to stop this travesty. He accounted himself as devoted a Hindu as any man, but the recent revival of sati, an ancient practice that had all but died out, horrified him, as he believed it should any civilised man. *The gods cannot want this!* he screamed inside. But the gods – or even civilised men – appeared to be in short supply today.

Where is Ravindra really? After all, the raja had been very clear when he told Chetan that he would be watching. Aram scanned the crowd and peered at the windows overlooking the square; he checked out the gaps in the stonework, looking anywhere a spy might be hidden, but could find no trace of that fearful visage.

Where are *you, Ravindra?*

The crowd was certainly sure their lord was no longer alive, at least where he was. They pulled at the orange sheets wrapped about the raja's body and peered at the waxen face. Some even reached out and touched the cold skin, as if ensuring their oppressor was dead, though no one dared to celebrate yet, not when the tyrant's son still sat above them. Aram stole a glance: Chetan was sitting on his father's peacock throne fanning himself. The new raja was sweating profusely. *As well you might, you bloated toad!*

The drums boomed and the conches blew and Chetan stood up and recited a long speech about the glories of his father. Then it was Aram's turn to speak the blessings. He made his way to the head of the platform, bowed to Chetan, then gazed down on the corpse of the raja. As he prepared himself, he saw the wives being brought out. The courtyard fell silent, and all he could hear was the slow rumble of the drums, throbbing at heartbeat-pace, reverberating off the stone walls that bordered the courtyard. Then a slow moan, somewhere between pleasure and sorrow, rose from the crowd, and emotions running from horror and pity to bloodlust were almost palpable in the smoky air.

Ravindra's ranis had been covered in loose white shrouds, but clearly visible beneath were colourful saris embroidered with precious metal threads; they were all dripping with gold and gemstones, their accoutrements worth more than the annual incomes of most of those watching – and about to burn away to nothing. The sense of material waste accentuated the rage Aram felt; it pricked his courage as he scanned down the line of women.

Halika led the wives out, of course, her head held high, her face proud. Her eyes were heavily kohled, her lips painted vibrant red, and she was festooned with so much gold jewellery Aram was surprised she could move under all that weight. She was a vivid contrast to the rest, who were shuffling along clumsily, swaying from side to side, their eyes glazed; surely even the dullest peasant here could see that they were drugged? Yet to his eyes, none of them had ever looked so lovely; dull Meena looked young again, her anxious face smoothed by the drugs to serenity. Rakhi looked like a ghost already, and Jyoti like a skeleton, but their eyes were luminous, as if sucking in the light of their last sights. Aruna the addict was calm and smiling, as if this were a picnic outing. Aram doubted that she had any idea what was happening – and that was probably for the better. Padma, the senapati's sister, cast Aram a look full of open longing that scared him, lest Chetan notice. It was almost as if she was trying to tell him something – but whatever it was, he didn't want to know.

His eyes went instead to the girl at the end of the line. They had removed her burkha and unlike the other queens, she had been dressed not in an expensive sari but in what looked like a threadbare cotton salwar kameez, not one of silk, embroidered with jewels and threads of gold and silver, but a mean one, meant for a servant. A final humiliation from the chief wife to her most despised fellow queen. But Darya's face shone with an unearthly beauty the others would never own, not even Halika, and everyone watching could see that.

Then Aram sucked in his breath in fresh horror as he realised that Darya's face was alert and defiant: they had not even given her the mercy of opium! He shuddered at the realisation that they intended her to feel all the agony of being burned alive!

He wanted to race to her side, but he restrained himself. The courtyard fell silent again, and Chetan gestured impatiently at him to get on with it. As they placed Ravindra's funerary palanquin on the unlit pyre, Aram began to pray. He heard himself speak of kings and their bond with the land and their people, all the while inwardly marvelling that the gods could ever permit this terrible thing. His voice became increasingly hoarse and ragged as he spoke, but no one appeared to notice, or even to be listening. It was an unutterable relief to be able to pause for breath as the initial invocations ended.

Beside him, a stony-faced Senapati Shastri signalled, and the soldiers standing at intervals around the great fire-pit marched forward and touched their torches to the wood.

There were more prayers required, and Aram swallowed to moisten his throat, then began to speak again, this time words of duty and virtue, as Halika stepped onto the pyre. He saw her exultant face as the flames licked her skin and he shuddered. Then Padma was prodded until she moved up beside Halika and Aram risked a glance about him, looking for Shastri. There he was: standing bolt upright, his demeanour that of the trusted soldier, and all the while his face had crumpled and tears were streaming down his face.

He never thought he would see such a thing; he had always thought of the senapati as forged in steel . . . but after all, Padma was the captain's sister, his only living relative, burning alive before his eyes. He looked back at the pyre. The queens already on it were enveloped in flames and more were being added, like fresh kindling: Meena, then Aruna. The heat rose and Aram stuttered, but when the first girl started screaming his throat dried up completely and he stopped speaking.

No one noticed that he'd stopped praying, that he had turned away from Chetan, that he had left the platform and was moving through the crowd. They had eyes for only one thing: the funeral pyre. The heavily embroidered saris must have been soaked in something in preparation for this moment, for they caught fire within moments as each queen was pushed into the flames. He reached the fringe just as Jyoti, the last but one of the queens, was cast screaming and struggling into the fire. So much for the traditional concept that the wives went willingly. Now only Darya remained. She stood silently, her expression empty, her arms held tight by a stony-faced soldier.

Aram glanced up at Halika, who stood there with her arms extended, her hair afire, staring out at the silent crowds with an exultant expression upon her face. The pain must have been excruciating, but Ravindra's chief wife never even flinched. Rani Halika's expression was one of triumph, as if she had won some great and terrible victory. Beside her, the other burning queens had collapsed, screaming. Their contorting, spasming bodies were already blackening in the intense conflagration. They must have been in torment; no amount of poppy-milk could ever have sufficed to wipe out the torture of the blazing inferno. The heat was intense, the smell dreadful, and all he could beg the gods for now was that the smoke would overcome the queens swiftly. He whispered his final prayer to Ganesha, for luck, and committed the first act of violence of his life.

He drove a dagger up under the jaw of the guard holding Darya and into his brain.

Then he grabbed her hand, and he ran.

Mandore

Jodhpur, Rajasthan, March 2010

The blue shirts of the Chelsea players massed at the edge of their penalty box, jostling and pushing, and he pushed back. Terry shoved him and Lampard barked something obscene. The crowd was in uproar. One minute to go, and his team were a goal down. 'Amanjit, Amanjit, Amanjit!' the crowd chanted, punching the air: sixty thousand hopes and prayers, all focused on one man, one moment.

The free kick floated up to the edge of the box and Amanjit was away, anticipating the flick-on. Up went the red shirts, up went the blue, the ball spun off a head and fell into his path. Terry lunged, but he was already away. For an instant he steadied himself, then he rolled his shot past the onrushing goalkeeper and into the corner of the net.

'In your face, Chelsea!' Amanjit screamed, to the bemusement of the parents of the visiting team from Bikaner High School, sixty miles north of Jodhpur. He punched the air, as did his teammates and some three-quarters of the two dozen spectators around the undersized pitch behind the school.

The whistle blew and the black-clad referee raised a hand to signal . . .

'Offside,' he shouted. 'No goal.'

'What?'

Amanjit strode towards the referee, his fists clenched.

The referee stared down at him contemptuously. 'You were offside. No goal.'

'NO WAY!'

His teammates crowded around and Dalmeet shouted, 'No way, Ref! It's where you are when the ball is kicked! He was onside! Don't you know the rules?'

The referee stroked his impressive moustaches and signalled a free kick for the defending team.

Amanjit felt something fairly flimsy snap inside him: his self-control. 'You're a goddamned idiot! You're not fit to referee a kindergarten kabaddi game!'

The referee's eyes bulged and his nostrils flared. He reached for his top pocket.

Oops. I probably shouldn't have said that.

They drove in silence for a while, Amanjit negotiating the traffic with casual grace, sliding unscathed through the morass of cars, trucks, auto-rickshaws, motorcycles, hand-carts and everything else with wheels or feet or hooves clogging the streets.

Amanjit normally liked driving – though he didn't want to spend his life driving taxis – but right now he was still fuming about the football game.

'So what exactly does a red card mean?' asked Deepika, sitting beside him in the passenger seat.

'It means you've been sent off,' answered Vikram from the back seat. 'It means you're a bloody idiot,' he added unnecessarily.

'But there was only a minute to go anyway, so I guess it doesn't really matter,' Deepika said with all the offhand logic of one who has no idea what she's talking about.

'It'll matter when he's banned for the next two games,' Vikram muttered.

'It was the last game of the season anyway,' snapped Amanjit. 'It doesn't matter a damn. And the ref was an egotistical numb-skull. Can we talk about something else?'

Silence ensued instead. It was mid-afternoon and out here the traffic was only moderately busy. The roads up this way weren't too bad; they weren't far from the Pakistan border and the army shifted a lot of troops around here, so the ministry kept even the side roads in pretty good order. They arrived at what might have been just another dusty little roadside town, but was in fact all that was left of the pre-mediaeval kingdom of Mandore. But just as they were congratulating themselves on getting there more quickly than anyone had expected, they hit the back of a traffic jam – all manner of vehicles were crowding down from three lanes into one, and as no one was giving way to anyone else, they lurched to a virtual standstill. In seconds the heat inside had risen two or three degrees and they all slumped into their seats, fanning themselves futilely while Amanjit fought for every tiny gap, inching into the town bit by bit.

Deepika was the first to break the silence. 'So, you used to live in England?' she asked Vikram, and that rankled Amanjit – he'd really rather she didn't have any curiosity about anyone else at all, let alone Vikram. But he found himself listening with interest anyway as Vikram talked about his old life in London, even though he'd heard most of it the other night.

'I wanted to go to England when I was young,' Deepika admitted when Vikram fell silent. 'Or America – some of my friends have gone there. But you know what: it's not always better. I had a friend who went to Florida with her family. Fatima and I kept in touch, and though they tried to put a brave face on it, they were miserable for the longest time. They hadn't expected to miss the extended family, you see, or not so much. Think about it: we grow up *surrounded* here – we can hardly escape them, even when we want to. Everyone's got hundreds of aunties and uncles and cousins, whether they like it or not. But when you emigrate – well, Fatima and her parents called it "this great void". Americans haven't any idea what "family" really means . . .'

'That's exactly right,' Vikram agreed. 'We didn't know anyone over in England. You know, Indians who emigrate go two ways: some become ultra-traditional and cling to the past, even though their children go to local schools and make friends with local kids and grow up completely westernised – a lot of my Indian friends in England were like that, and they fought with their parents pretty much all the time. And other families go in completely the opposite direction: they become ultra-western and go tearing off in all different directions – and then marriages break down because husbands and wives are suddenly feeling free and they want to explore, and then the children are left with no heritage. I tell you, emigration is hard.'

'Even the money isn't what people make out,' Deepika added. 'Fatima's parents suddenly couldn't afford servants, and her mother had to work twice as hard at home – and she had to get a job as well! All right, it was only part-time, but she wouldn't have had to do that in Delhi!'

Typical Delhi-miss, with her servants and maids, Amanjit thought enviously. But he couldn't resent her, not when she was so pretty.

For himself, he'd always dreamed of travel, of amassing riches in far-away lands, but he'd never really thought it would be possible. *Not with damned Uncle Charan determined to ruin my life*. It was weirdly consoling to find out that escaping to England or America wasn't all it was cracked up to be. He knew from taxi-talk that emigration agents made millions of rupees selling the foreign dream to people who could barely afford it, even helping them falsify documents if they didn't qualify according to the rules. *No matter how much I want out, I'll steer well clear of that scam*, he told himself.

They fell silent again for a while, until Vikram started, 'I did some research—'

'No kidding, girly-swot,' said Amanjit grumpily. He was still smarting from the football débâcle. 'What did you find out? The average rainfall of the Amazon basin? The batting average of the Mumbai cricket team?'

'Give him a break, Amanjit,' Deepika told him, which shut him up. 'So go on then: what did you find out?'

Despite himself, Amanjit was actually keen to hear what Vikram had to say. He didn't intend to say any more about it, but those bloody nightmares were definitely getting worse. Every time he closed his eyes that ghostly woman was there. *She calls me 'Shastri'*. . . But before he could start remembering other details, Vikram started talking, and though he would never in a million years have admitted it, he was pleased to have that particular train of thought derailed.

'So it turns out Mandore was actually a pretty important place before Jodhpur existed.' Vikram's voice had taken on the tone of a teacher delivering a lecture about a subject they were passionate about, but Amanjit didn't mind: this concerned all of them. 'It ended up part of the Marwar Kingdom, but it was originally an older and smaller fief and it changed hands several times, being passed around the larger kingdoms. Back then, around 770, Mandore was part of the Gujara-Pratihara Empire, which pre-dates Marwar. I'm pretty sure that's the time our dreams are set in.'

'And why is that, O Learned One?' Amanjit asked drily.

Vikram threw him a look, to see if he was being teased or not. 'Well, partly because of a coincidence. For my detention I had to write a biography of a poet, and I found this book of poems by a Mandore poet called Aram Dhoop – it just kind of fell into my hand, and it was short, so . . . well, anyway, he was from that period. So in the book, it said the kingdom was at its height then, but it started falling apart just a hundred years later.'

These ancient names meant absolutely nothing to Amanjit; anything before he was born was ancient history and therefore irrelevant to him. He nodded in what he hoped was an intelligent manner though, because Deepika did appear to be interested, judging by the way she was tapping her fingers on the dashboard and looking thoughtful.

'Was there a palace then?' she asked.

'There was,' Vikram said enthusiastically. 'The Raja of Mandore ruled back then – Jodhpur didn't exist then, and this was long before the Mehrangarh was built. Mandore was originally the capital of the whole empire, but the maharaja decided it was too small for him and he and his court upped sticks and moved to Avanti. It was several hundred years later, around 1450, and a whole other dynasty, the Rahores, who built the Mehrangarh on the Bhaurcheeria – that's the name of the hill; it means "mountain of birds".'

Vikram paused when he caught Amanjit rolling his eyes in the rear-view mirror, but ignored him and went on, 'Anyway, Mandore was a real backwater by then – the local people had pulled down the old palace and used the stone for other buildings. Then it was rebuilt, then abandoned again, until the ruler, Rao Jodha – who, by the way, was the *twenty-fourth* son of Rao Ranmal! – decided Mandore wasn't safe enough and had the Mehrangarh built. Apparently very little remains of what used to be in Mandore – not even the experts are really sure where the boundaries of the old palace are—'

'Huh! So much for the experts!' Amanjit exclaimed, then had to break off again as a bit of a gap appeared in the traffic, and he concentrated on forcing his way deeper into the swarm of vehicles. It sounded like everyone in the town was honking their horns and shouting at the same time. He couldn't see any reason for all the racket, so he just pressed on, heading into the older part of Mandore. 'So, what's left then?' he asked as he weaved between cars, the occasional wandering cow, donkey- and hand-carts, auto-rickshaws, mopeds and pedestrians, all jamming the narrow, twisting streets of hard-packed red clay.

'I'll bet there's still something to see on the north side,' Vikram said. 'I read that there are the remains of the gardens and palace, and an old altar where they say Ravana married his first queen, Mandodari.'

'Who's Ravana?' Amanjit asked.

'Don't you remember your *Ramayana*, Amanjit?' asked Deepika teasingly.

'I'm a Sikh,' Amanjit reminded her. 'We don't believe in your Hindu fairy-stories.' He regretted his words immediately, for Deepika turned and scowled at him. 'I mean, maybe they were true once, like old history or something,' he added hastily. 'Who knows, really?'

The girl from Delhi didn't look much placated by his apology. 'In the *Ramayana*, Ravana was the big demonic baddie,' she explained. 'Ten heads, monstrous ego – you know the type.'

Amanjit grimaced; he did indeed know one very good example of the type, who answered to the name 'Uncle Charanpreet'.

'Actually, there is a small temple to Ravana in Jodhpur,' Vikram put in. 'Ravana was a Shiva devotee, supposedly very wise and knowledgeable. I was reading all these wild theories online, suggesting that the *Ramayana* might have been based upon memories of the Indus Valley cultures around 3000 BC, or the later Vedic kingdoms. It's kind of controversial, apparently.' He tailed off, as if realising that he was babbling.

'Another link to the *Ramayana*,' Amanjit said, remembering what Ras had said the other day. Not that he wanted his mother to marry Vikram's father, mind!

Vikram frowned. 'That's not funny.'

'Am I missing something?' Deepika asked.

Amanjit looked at Vikram slyly. 'Only that his father phoned my mother last night to ask her out to dinner.'

Deepika raised her eyebrows. 'So? What's that got to do with the *Ramayana*?'

'Oh, it's just that my sister Ras noticed that if our families combined, we'd have the same family make-up as the *Ramayana*: four sons from three separate wives.' He chuckled. 'It's all rubbish, of course. Uncle Charan is going to beat the crap out of your dad just for asking. He's got plenty of cop friends and ex-army mates and they're all huge. Your dad will be lucky if they don't break both his legs.'

Vikram squirmed uncomfortably. 'Well, she said no,' he replied defensively. 'And it's not illegal to ask, is it? They're both single—'

'Uncle Charan was in the room when he phoned. Bet your dad didn't know that,' Amanjit replied. 'Anyway, enough of that,' he added, noticing that Deepika wore a pained, faraway expression, and that her fists clenched and her knuckles were white. 'Did you dream again last night?' he asked her gently. Forgetting his resolution not to talk about the dreams.

She hesitated, then murmured, 'Yeah . . .'

'Do your dreams take place in an old palace too?' he asked.

'Yeah . . .'

'Do you want to talk about it?'

'No,' she said emphatically, as they finally crept through a gap and into a square crammed with parked cars. A rough-clad man with broken teeth came over and demanded a few rupees in return for a parking space and his personal guarantee to watch their car for them. As they clambered out of the vehicle, Vikram was the first to spot the gate in the wall with signs above it pointing through to the palace gardens. After locking up and handing over a fistful of coins, they joined the short queue for tickets to enter the monument, and once inside, the clangour and filth of the dirty old town outside faded away, swiftly forgotten in the peaceful gardens with their lush lawns and profligate flowerbeds set before the cenotaphs of old rulers.

Vikram launched into a lecture about the architecture of the curved conical domes and how they fitted into Hindu traditional architecture. *He might find it all fascinating*, Amanjit thought, *but honestly, I couldn't give a toss*. There was a low hill behind the gardens, and the remains of what would have once been a pretty extensive fortress containing a temple. That was much more like it as far as he was concerned. *I am a Sikh: we are warriors. We belong in places like this*.

They made their way about the fortress, sweltering amongst the sun-baked stones as they looked around curiously. None of them had a clear idea what they were looking for, but as they wandered the ancient stone halls, Deepika was the first to voice her thoughts. 'This is it,' she whispered. 'It's the palace in my dreams, the one where the women and the tiger chase me.' She sounded scared, and Amanjit badly wanted to put an arm around her.

Despite this revelation, nothing untoward occurred and they drifted back down into the gardens. The Hall of Heroes contained depictions of Rajput warriors and their deeds; Amanjit looked carefully for a 'Shastri' and was a little disappointed not to find one. He'd been certain that the name was significant in some way. The temple of 33 crore gods didn't appear to have anything to do with their dreams either, colourful though it was. 'Three hundred and thirty million gods!' Amanjit said, awed, looking around. 'How does anyone remember to pray to them all?'

'The scholars say that it is a number meant to suggest infinity,' Vikram replied studiously. 'Some say it's just a mistranslation of the ancient texts, and of course, Hinduism itself has gone through many phases of—'

'Vikram, I think it was a rhetorical question,' Deepika interrupted, while Amanjit looked skywards and chuckled at Vikram's endless enthusiasm for strange facts.

Eventually they emerged into a sort of courtyard with an overgrown lawn bounded by an ancient wall. A few old men were playing cards on the rough patch of grass, and they all looked up and gave the trio the once-over before shuffling the deck and dealing a new round. The walls were all falling down, and there was all manner of rubbish piled alongside them. In the centre was some kind of well or pit. It'd been partially filled in, and the earth within it was black as ash.

Deepika sucked in her breath. 'It's just like in my dreams,' she murmured, so softly Amanjit barely caught the words, and he was certain she'd not meant him to hear her. He was feeling less and less comfortable with every passing moment, and beginning to wish now that they'd not come here at all. The other two looked just as affected, and all three of them stood staring at the pit as if in a trance until a voice broke through their reveries.

'Namaste,' said an old man in dirty orange robes. 'Welcome to Mandore.' He detached himself from the wall he'd been leaning against and hobbled over to them. There was something odd about the way he walked, almost as if he were a puppet being moved by invisible strings. His voice was rough-edged and awkward, the words slurred. He looked like a sadhu, an itinerant holy man, but there was something else about him, Amanjit thought, something . . . *wrong*.

He grunted a non-committal response, wishing the old man would go away.

'A great palace, this once was. A great raja dwelt here.' The old man's eyes burned feverishly.

Deepika took a step away from the old sadhu, as if she found the old man threatening, even though that took her closer to the blackened pit. Amanjit stepped in front of the old man, instinctively protecting her.

'A great raja,' the old man repeated, 'the greatest who ever lived.' His voice was slurred, and for a weird moment, Amanjit thought that the sadhu was nothing but shadow and air.

Impossible. He shook his head to clear it. 'Here in Mandore?' he sneered, wanting to break the uncanny mood the sadhu had brought. 'In this old dump?'

Deepika took another step towards the pit. He could hear her breath, coming too quickly, and when he glanced over at Vikram, he saw he too looked a bit frightened, even though there was no visible threat to any of them. *What's going on?*

'Oh, this was once an important place: capital of the whole empire. But the greatness of a man lies not in his kingdom but in his conquests,' the old sadhu wheezed.

'Then he was doubly a loser,' Amanjit said dismissively. 'What did Mandore ever conquer?'

'Death. The Raja of Mandore conquered death.' The old holy man looked up at him with soulless eyes and Amanjit found himself taking a step back.

He bumped into Deepika, who stumbled into the shallow pit,

and when he turned, he saw her stiffen, then she sucked in a frightened breath and suddenly it looked to Amanjit like she was surrounded by flames, and there were hundreds of ghostly people all around them, all shouting things and chanting what sounded like slogans – or maybe they were prayers?

He went to grab her, but the sadhu gripped his arm. 'He conquered death, did the Raja of Mandore,' the sadhu hissed, 'and he will conquer again!'

There was something truly repulsive about the holy man, though Amanjit couldn't say quite what it was. He went to push him aside but the old man stepped nimbly back and suddenly started snarling like a beast.

Amanjit twisted away from him in disgust and anger, grabbed Deepika and pulled her from the pit. As she clung to him, shaking, he realised the air about her had become strangely hot.

The sadhu leered at them, and suddenly Amanjit felt afraid of this vile old man, as *unholy* a being as he had ever seen, though he couldn't think of any reason why he should – he was horrible, but that was all . . . but Amanjit was shaking, all the same, and couldn't move. Then to his surprise – because Vikram too had looked paralysed with fright – Vikram stepped between him and the sadhu. Amanjit didn't try to stop him but grabbed Deepika and pulled her away. She was clearly upset, and a strange stench of burned meat clung to her.

The old card-players in the corner of the garden were all staring at Amanjit, but none of them made any move to help. In a way he was glad; he trusted nothing here. He decided enough was enough; time to get Deepika out of here. Vikram was still talking to the old man – who knew what about? – but he looked back at Amanjit and nodded once, and Amanjit took that to be approval for getting Deepika away, so he led her towards the entrance to the small garden, intending to take her all the way back to the car. She calmed as soon as she was away from the fire-pit though, and self-consciously pulled herself from his grasp.

'What happened?' he asked. 'What did you see?'

She wiped her eyes and looked up at him. 'Fire!' she said, almost incoherently, then she shook her head as if to clear her thoughts. 'There was this huge fire, and people everywhere, and I saw—'

Her eyes flew past his face and he turned and took in the four leather-clad men lounging by the gate. The security guards were gone. They were all brandishing knives and cudgels, and the leader, a man with one eye hidden behind a leather eye-patch, held a long ornate dagger. Somewhere deep inside, Amanjit thought he recognised him – but he couldn't quite grasp the memory, and anyway, there was no time . . .

'Going somewhere?' asked the one-eyed man.

Vikram had no clear plan in mind when he stepped between the old sadhu and his companions; he was just buying time for Amanjit to get Deepika out, because she was clearly badly affected by something. The stink of fire and roasting meat clung to this place, churning his belly. He waved at Amanjit to urge him to hurry, then faced the sadhu again. There was definitely something strange about the old man – then he glanced downwards, and his skin prickled.

The old man cast no shadow.

'Aram Dhoop,' breathed the sadhu. 'So we meet again.'

The breath that washed over Vikram was the foul air of the grave, or a cold pyre.

'How appropriate that it is here.' The strange man waved his arm about. 'This was the old town, built into the lee of the fortress; it did not become a garden until centuries after *our* time – but perhaps you already remember this?'

'*Ravindra?*' The name had leapt into his mind from somewhere, though he'd never heard or read it before in his life.

Or had he?

The sadhu smiled. 'Ah, so you remember my name! But do you remember the rest yet? Do you remember how it ends?' The black eyes glittered with malice.

Vikram stared at him, then slowly shook his head.

'You will,' the old man rasped. 'You will remember it all, as you always do: every single failure, every death, every pointless wasted life you have ever lived. And finally you will remember that in each life I have danced upon your grave, as I will in this one.'

Vikram's throat closed up and his lungs laboured and he tried to breathe steadily, but still he managed defiance: 'You're not even really here.'

The sadhu spat, a gobbet of phlegm that vanished as it left his mouth. 'You've caught me between hosts, that's all: a circumstance that won't last for long, boy. You've got days at most and you've not even remembered who you really are.'

Vikram didn't know what to say; he could barely think straight through his growing terror.

The sadhu's eyes narrowed as he examined Vikram. 'The dance begins anew, Aram Dhoop – do you not feel it? We are gathered once more, but this time, we are all here: all of us! You, me, the queens, Shastri, even One-Eyed Jeet . . . and yes, even the ghost of my delicious Padma has been seen! The four who thwarted me that fateful day is gathered again, right here in Mandore where it all began. And this time, Aram Dhoop – this time we are playing for keeps. We are duelling for eternity – and look at you! You are nothing but a foolish boy, and one scarce grown at that! What hope have you this time?'

Vikram backed away, filling his lungs to shout for help, but the shadows arose as if from nowhere, the old man stepped back into the darkness and faded from view like a waking dream. He saw the card-players staring at him, apparently amused at this display, and he suddenly wondered whether they had even seen the old man – or had he only been present to him and Amanjit and Deepika; he *knew* they had seen him.

Then he realised that Deepika and Amanjit were gone and he felt a lurch of fear for them. For the first time he noticed the coldness of the air and gulped. He wrapped his arms around himself to try and still his shaking, then looked fearfully about him.

He couldn't see either of the others – until he heard his name being shouted and saw Amanjit and Deepika, sprinting hand-in-hand back through the archway into the fire-pit garden where he stood. He felt a spasm of jealousy that instantly dissolved as four men emerged behind them, shouting and waving weapons.

The Stolen Queen

Mandore, Rajasthan, AD 769

It was some kind of dream, a vivid opium vision, or a nightmare coming true. Aram tried to drag the young queen away, but she was dazed and unsteady on her feet, tottering for a few seconds as she tried to take in her rescue. The sea of faces turned towards him and he realised it wasn't only women who were screaming; that his name was on everyone's lips as they gaped at him in amazement.

They'll tear me apart.

They didn't attack, though: they backed away as if his very presence might be malignly infectious. Confusion spilled from one man to the next as everyone looked to someone else to act. The guards were yards away, caught up in the press of people, and the men of the court could barely see through the smoke from their vantage point above. The commoners, faced by a bloody-handed figure with a look of glazed determination stamped on his face, gave way like goats before a wild dog.

He had never felt so powerful in his life as in those few moments. He thrust his blade out in front of him and followed it through a parting sea of frightened faces. '*Where is the arch?*' he yelled to himself, then, '*There!*' He pulled the girl after him, then took a moment to glance back at her and found to his shock that she was now completely alert; her eyes were focused and fierce and her limbs were moving of her own volition.

'Run!' he shouted at her, and she pounded after him through the crowd, shoving aside anyone who got in their way. Still no one tried to impede them, though the alarm had finally gone up; he could hear shouting, lots of it – then suddenly arrows started flying, shot indiscriminately from the royal platform. A woman some way from him screamed and went down, clutching the shaft that jutted from her shoulder. Then an old man fell sprawling and all they could do was leap over him and into the shadow of the southern arch. Maybe the archers were just bad shots, or perhaps the next arrow would take him in the back. He wasn't going to hang around to find out which was right.

The young beggar was right where he'd promised to be, holding the reins of the horse Aram had bought the previous night. He was leaning against the dressed stone of the southern gate, as he had been paid to do, but he was looking scared, as if he was beginning to realise what madness he was assisting. As Aram emerged from the press with blood on his clothing and one of the queens in his grasp the boy shouted, 'Sorry—!' as he dropped the reins and took to his heels.

'Can you ride?' Aram shouted at Darya.

'Of course! Can you?'

Well, no. That was one weakness of the plan. 'Sort of – come on, get up – we have to flee!'

She scrambled up with practised ease, and to his embarrassment sat herself firmly at the front, so that he had no choice but to climb up behind her. He'd not sat on a horse since an uncle let him as a child, and he wasted too many precious moments in heaving himself onto the beast's back now, and clinging to her waist.

'I was supposed to be in front!' he shouted. 'Give me the reins and—'

She ignored him, shouting, 'Hang on!' and kicking her heels into the horse's flanks; the beast tossed its head and leapt into motion, careering down the road away from the southern gate.

He glanced back, shouting in alarm as two bowmen burst through the arch and loosed their shafts, and this time there was no doubt they were aiming straight for him, but the horse was moving fast and the roadway was choked with vendors and shoppers, all of whom dived for cover as the arrows started flying. Then the natural curve of the street took them out of sight.

'That bitch Halika refused me the poppy-milk!' Darya shouted. 'Thanks be to Allah!' She swore as a cart pulled in front of them. 'Hold on!' The horse's back legs bunched up as it galloped, and then it sailed over the cart. When it landed the crunch to his groin knocked the breath out of him and almost sent him flying. Somehow he managed to cling on; he didn't think she would return for him should he fall.

'Which way?' Darya shouted, and she glanced backwards, revealing vivid wild eyes, full of fury and fire: a blaze to match that hideous pyre burning behind them.

He had no idea. Perhaps that was another weakness in the plan. 'Um . . . south!' he decided, trying to sound assured.

'South?' She threw an uncertain look back over her shoulder, though the horse never slowed, not for an instant, as they headed for the open spaces. Here at the edge of Mandore all was quiet – almost everyone had decided to attend the spectacle at the palace – and the thunder of their beast's hooves on the packed red earth was the loudest sound around. But it wouldn't be so for long; already he could imagine the menacing clamour rising behind, the shouted orders and the jingle of harness and the dying screams of the other queens.

'Where are we going?' she shouted. 'Where are your men? How many are there? Who are you taking me to?'

'Er . . . it's just me.'

'Just you?' She swore in her native tongue; *was it Persian?* he wondered. He clung to her waist – that narrow, lissom waist he'd dreamed of holding for so many months – and prayed to every god he could name as they thundered out of Mandore, scattering a few stragglers, a camel and some curious donkeys, and clattered away down the southern road.

Below Madan Shastri's position on the wall all was utter confusion. The soldiers had flooded into the square as Chetan started waving his hands in every direction and shrieking orders from his throne. People were fleeing, panicked by the sudden charge of the soldiers, and those men, thinking there was a riot breaking out, reacted by bludgeoning them to the ground with spear-butts and shield-rims.

Shastri saw the insanity unfold through a veil of tears, but his mind was caught up in that blazing pyre. Which of those dark shapes huddled in the burning timber was his sister? It was impossible to say. He had pledged to his dying father that he would always protect her, but instead had seen her handed over to that monster Ravindra without even trying to stop the marriage. Now he had stood aside and watched her being led to the pyre. He hadn't even found the courage to intervene when the flames caught in her golden sari and engulfed her.

With his gaze and his mind wrapped up in Padma's last moments, he hadn't really seen what happened. The smoke, the press of people, his tears: they had reduced everything to a wet smear. Then suddenly the whole crowd had convulsed, women had started screaming and then soldiers were piling in from all sides, no one knowing what was going on, everyone lashing out in their fear. He should have been in there, helping them sort this mess out, but still the after-image of Padma's face in those last instants held him. All he could truly hear was his sister's cry as she entered the flames, and the whoosh as her clothes caught fire. She was heavily drugged – Chetan had sworn that; he had promised she would not feel a thing – but Shastri didn't truly believe that, and even so, it was still death, either way. He could feel that cursed heart-stone pulsing in his belt-pouch – he could have sworn he felt it go hot as she burned, and for a moment he had had to fight an almost overwhelming urge to throw it into the pyre. But he had made a promise, the last promise he could ever keep for his beloved sister . . .

May the gods bear you up, sweet sister . . .

Only Halika and Darya had not been drugged before they stepped onto the pyre; Darya had been denied out of sheer malice, he guessed, because Halika wanted her to feel every single second of the pain . . . and Halika, because she was insane enough to desire the agony, to crave such a death.

Still his reverie held him as he saw Ravindra's body atop the pyre be swallowed up by the hungry fire. No one could tell him what Ravindra had died of. No one seemed to know, not even Chetan, his favoured son. Illness, suicide, murder . . . everything had been whispered, but there had been no signs of anything amiss with him; to look at him, he had looked in the peak of health. It made no sense . . .

It finally dawned on Shastri that something untoward was happening below. He saw his soldiers hammer into the throng, finally heard someone yelling his name. He shook his head and came out of his stupor.

'Senapati, Senapati!' shouted Tilak, his most reliable sergeant. 'The poet has stolen Queen Darya!' He was standing at the edge of the press below, waving his arms in the air, gesturing wildly.

'What? The poet?' He would swear that the pulsing heart-pendant in his belt-pouch quivered – or was that his own heart? He threw a glance back over his shoulder and caught a glimpse of One-Eyed Jeet lounging against the door, watching him. One hand was resting on the ornate hilt of his dagger.

He bristled at the implied threat, but before he could move, Chetan was roaring down at him from his throne.

'Senapati! Shastri – *Shastri!* Bring that girl back! Bring her back – your life depends on it!'

My life . . . what *life? Lord Shiva protect me!* But right now he had no choice but to react, in public like this as he was, and surrounded by Chetan's men. He shouted for his horse and ordered Tilak to round up two squads.

It took far too long to muster the thirty men and get them mounted up, time in which their quarry was adding to his significant head-start, but there was no help for it. The town was in uproar, simmering on the edge of a full-scale riot, and chaos reigned. The pyre had collapsed under the weight and the heat of the raging flames and Ravindra's body had fallen to the edge of the fire-pit. It was a horrifying sight: though the corpse was hideously burned, the raja was still recognisable. The heat had driven even the most curious back, but a sudden breeze blew sparks through the throng. They danced in the air, a cloud of viciously glowing fireflies, which landed on clothing, and hair, and in the trees. A dupatta caught alight, an old man's beard, then the fire took hold of a branch, and another, and a great cry went up as someone's washing, hung on a roof to dry in the hot sun, suddenly blazed up, sending even more of the lethal sparks scattering across the area. Shastri's men hadn't been able to clear the square and all the streets leading from it were blocked with panicking people running from the pyre and wildfires now springing up all over the place. Even the horses couldn't push their way through, and they were getting increasingly skittish as they caught the scent of the fires and tried to flee the flames.

Shastri could see a group of men lifting Ravindra's charred body back onto the collapsed pyre. '*Burn, you bastard!*' he muttered to himself as he tried to peer through the smoke; apart from the still-erect figure that must be Halika, no one else was recognisable in the depths of the flames. Ravindra's chief wife no longer looked remotely human; she was just a collection of charring bones now, though somehow she was still standing upright. He shuddered involuntarily; he imagined he could hear her whispering in his ear and he shook his head hard as if that might dislodge the sound. He scolded himself for letting his mind wander when his life was at stake.

At last his soldiers had assembled and were ready to force their way out. Shastri swung himself up into his own saddle, cursing in frustration, and started laying about him with a whip, desperate to clear the onlookers out of the way. He was mindful of how brutal the act would look to anyone paying attention, but he could see no other choice. There would be many more lying dead in the alleys of Mandore before this day was over if they couldn't clear the square and set some men to fighting the fires.

'Come on!' he snarled as they finally reached the southern arch and there was room for the horses to go faster than walking pace. He kicked his own mount into a trot and led the way. *If that poet knows anything about riding, they could be anywhere*, he thought, then realised he'd never seen the man anywhere near a horse before, let alone actually riding one. It wasn't much to pin his hopes on.

He glanced behind at his column of soldiers, counting heads – and stiffened: One-Eyed Jeet was four horses back, his dark eye gleaming as it focused on him.

'Jeet, you stay here and get those fires out! I'll lead the—'

Jeet shook his head insolently. 'I'm with the pursuit,' he

growled. 'The raja's orders. Jagat can see to the fires.' His face dared Shastri to contradict him.

So that's the way of it, is it? Jagat's loyal to me, and we both know it. Instead I'll have you with me like a shadow. And what are your orders, Jeet? To ensure that I don't return, I'm willing to bet . . .

But right now there was nothing to be gained by countermanding Chetan's orders. He reined in, turned back to his men and shouted, 'Right . . . Kalyan, Vilas, Ratnam: you go to the poet's house – see if he has any family. Tilak, you take four men and scout the road ahead. Keep me informed – the poet and the rani can't have got far. Let's move it!'

Tilak nodded grimly. He didn't look like he relished the job he'd been given. *Well, neither do I.*

One of Tilak's scouts was waiting for them at the first major crossroads. 'He's still heading south, sir,' he reported, 'and he's not got all that much of a head-start, by all accounts. Some children collecting dung saw them pass.'

Shastri looked at the sun: mid-afternoon already, but enough time for the fugitives to reach any of three nearby settlements, though all were within Chetan's control, at least nominally. It was more likely they would take refuge in the wild.

'If we don't find them before the sun goes down, this could get complicated,' he muttered to no one in particular. He turned his horse and as he started to address the column he realised that three-quarters of them were Jeet's cronies. *Worse and worse.* But that couldn't be remedied, not now. He'd just have to watch his back, that was all.

'Men, that idiot poet has stolen Queen Darya from the sati pyre. He has broken the law of the gods. He must die, and she . . .' He swallowed, fighting for the words. 'And the rani must burn, as the raja intended.'

Gods above, hear my words and not my heart! He faced the ring of hard-faced men and found it inside him to match their callous expressions. 'They've gone south. He's no rider and no warrior. He'll be easy meat. Let's get him!'

The column sprang into a canter and thundered down the road behind him, kicking up a cloud of dust that towered into the sky behind them.

The land rose and fell in front of the fugitives, but the choice of directions was limited: only the hard-pack of the cart roads could easily support a horse's hooves at the gallop. But there'd be patrols on all the roads, of course there would be, so they couldn't stick to the main routes. About them dirty brown farms became dirty brown dunes of sand, speckled with sickly trees standing up like thinning fur on a mangy dog. For most of the time the only colours were the blue of the sky and the brown of the earth and the grey of the drought-stricken trees. Occasionally they saw bright spindly shapes in the distance: women bearing water on their heads from the wells. Normally placid cattle, wild camels and red deer, spooked by their headlong gallop, scattered across the landscape, but even with that sudden movement there could scarcely have been greater contrast between here and the chaos about the pyre.

'What's that?' Darya called back to Aram, pointing towards the great broken mass of a hill the locals called *Bhaurcheeria*: Hill of Birds. The massive outcropping dominated all the lands about them like a crouching tiger. Aram had written poems about it, his imagination caught by the way it brooded over the landscape, but he'd never gone all the way there himself, for all that it was less than half a day's ride away. The south road led around it.

'It's the Bhaurcheeria,' he replied. 'It's just a barren hill, though I've heard there is a hermit who lives up there, and a shrine.' He barely attended his own words because his mind was still pounding away at the impossibility of all this: *I'm holding on to Rani Darya, a queen, the woman I have dreamed of ever since she came here. I'm pressed against her back, my arms about her waist. And all the demons of the underworld are coming for us.*

The girl spat. 'Heathen idols! Does the road turn west?'

'Yes, there is a crossroads south of the Bhaurcheeria. We can go in any direction there.'

She looked up at the sun. 'We will stay clear of the hill. Let's circle it on the eastern side, then once we strike the crossroads we will go west, to my father's people, once the sun goes down. Did you pack us food and water, and blankets for the night?'

'Yes!' He had known at least enough for that.

'That bitch Halika didn't drug me,' Darya said again, and Aram was pressed so close to her he could feel her shudder. 'She wanted me to feel all of the pain. Ha! If she had, you'd never have got me out of there.'

There was no arguing with that.

'And I never said thank you,' said the queen, suddenly, making his heart glow within his chest. 'And another thing . . . I don't even know your name.'

Something inside him fluttered. *How can she not know my name, after all those songs? I thought . . .*

He put that to one side. 'Um, er, it's Aram. Aram Dhoop.'

'Then thank you, Aram Dhoop. Now hold on tight, we're going to gallop again!'

Old Ash

Jodhpur, Rajasthan, March 2010

Amanjit saw Vikram's eyes go wide behind his glasses as he stood there gaping at the four toughs who were sauntering into the small garden. Some people thrived in the midst of action. Others were like rabbits caught in the headlights. It looked like Vikram was one of the latter.

But Amanjit was not. 'Run, you fool!' he shouted, then turned to Deepika, whose eyes were round but moving: she had her wits about her too, thankfully. 'Run, both of you!' He shoved her in the direction of some steps leading to another exit from the garden, then lunged sideways and snatched up a bamboo cane from beside one of the card players. Then something blurred at the corner of his eyes and he moved entirely by instinct, diving into a forward roll, right through the fire-pit, as what he thought might be a cudgel whistled past his ear . . .

Vikram stared at the four men in dark leathers, saw the cudgels in their hands, and for a second he froze. Then Deepika snatched his hand and yanked him after her and that wrenched him from his daze. He turned and ran.

I can't fight worth a damn, but I know how to get away from bullies!

Two of the men thudded after them as they raced up some old steps and leapt through a gap in the wall and into a narrow open-roofed passage. For a second his vision lurched and he thought he was looking at some kind of ancient town, full of people in odd dress – lots of soldiers, and servants, maybe – he wasn't sure. Beside him he heard Deepika gasp beside him and knew she was seeing it too, then he blinked and as they tore across a small lawn towards an exit from the ruins, the vision was gone. They burst through a rusted turnstile and into the narrow streets of the oldest part of Mandore. Tall, rundown buildings were all around them, festooned with a bird's nest of electrical wire. They heard running footsteps right behind them and without a word increased their own speed, flashing around a corner to find themselves at a T-junction.

There was no time to discuss: Deepika went left as Vikram went right and even if they'd wanted to turn back there was no time because the two pursuers were between them in an instant. As they pelted in opposite directions, Vikram prayed the alley he'd chosen led somewhere other than a dead end.

Amanjit rolled out of the pit, sharply aware of an acrid burning smell and sudden heat. He emerged on the far side from the two remaining thugs. He looked towards the steps where Deepika and Vikram had vanished and for an instant it looked like they were still there, but dressed strangely, and Vikram was covered in blood and brandishing a knife, waving it all around him as if to keep people away. Then he blinked and the figures were gone and reality re-imposed itself: a reality in which two grown men looked fair set to beat the shit out of him.

The biggest of the thugs, a burly, moustachioed man with a

pockmarked face, now blocked the exit. Amanjit looked back across the pit at One-Eye, trying to measure the distances.

The card-players were on their feet now. There were five of them, all grey-heads. Would they intervene? Could they? They didn't look keen, backing against the wall like that; they were definitely looking towards the exit.

One-Eye was acting strangely nervous of the pit which separated them. 'Do I know you?' he asked Amanjit as he stepped sideways around it. There was a strange lilt to his voice. 'I feel I should, but I don't know why. . .'

Yeah, you too, but I don't know why either . . .

'You've got the wrong guy,' Amanjit tried. Pock-Face was circling the other way, trying to outflank him. He had about five seconds before Pock-Face was on him.

One-Eye shook his head. 'Oh no, you're the three I was sent to find, no mistake there. But there's something familiar about you.'

'Perhaps you've seen my latest movie,' Amanjit quipped.

'I've seen how it ends,' One-Eye drawled. He looked at his colleague. 'Get him.'

Speaking of movies, Amanjit thought, *what would Shah Rukh Khan do in this circumstance? Or Hrithik?*

Dance, probably. Good advice!

As the two men closed in, he leapt sideways to the left and holding the bamboo cane in both hands, swung at Pock-Face's ugly visage. The man was slow; he howled as the cane smashed across the bridge of his nose and went down in a heap.

Hah! Take that, Bollywood!

Then he swallowed as One-Eye pulled out a gun.

Deepika ran fast. She'd done athletics for years and had always trained hard. She was, however, dressed in jeans and a T-shirt, a nice pink Calvin Klein with sequins – and all she could think was if the bastard on her tail dirtied it, she would kill him! At least she was in flat shoes! She ran past shocked-looking women hanging up their linens and shouted apologies as she bowled over a chai-wallah. Behind her she could hear the grunting of the leather-clad thug, who staggered for a moment as he clattered through the spilled tea-stand, then speeded up. He was getting closer now . . . she had to try something! For a moment she contemplated throwing her handbag away, in case that might make her run faster, but instead she tucked it tight to her side and redoubled her efforts.

She darted left, ran up onto a cart then leapt on the tail so that the front reared up; she felt it jolt as the thug tried and failed to make the jump. He flailed and fell back while she leapt nimbly off it, landing easily on her feet. She glanced back as she took off again: ten yards gained. Surely there were policemen here somewhere! What sort of wasteland had they come to?

'*Help! Help!*' she called, but no one even looked at her.

'Shut up, girl!' her pursuer snarled. He was gaining on her again.

She went up some stairs and into a courtyard, but she'd made a huge mistake: this was a dead end! A man repairing a bicycle looked up at her and opened his mouth, but before he could say anything the thug burst in behind her. She ducked behind a pillar, but she knew she'd run out of options.

'Hey! What's going on?' the bicycle-man asked inanely.

'Help me!' she hollered at him.

The thug cursed, then snarled, 'Shut up, girly.'

'Yeah? I'll give you "girly". Help! He's attacking me!' she hollered at the top of her voice, and half a dozen windows opened onto the courtyard from above and faces appeared. The thug snarled and reached for something in his pocket. She shook, horribly afraid she knew what it was – then remembered something and fumbled in her handbag. The man with the bike leapt to his feet, his mouth dropping open to shout something, then blanched as he saw the thug pull out a gun and in slow motion angle it towards Deepika's face . . .

Vikram tore around a corner and felt fingers brush his denim jacket. He yelped and sprinted even faster, past rubbish piles and a heap of bricks, then he checked himself just in time before he fell into a square well. He jumped over it, finding himself at the foot of some stairs that ascended a rough slope near the perimeter of the palace ruins. He tore up them, hearing his pursuer panting a little further behind. He reached the top ten steps clear and pulled away, thanking the years of running away from bullies at school that had apparently left him well-trained for this particular chase.

He was seeking a direction for his flight, somewhere he could lose his pursuer, when suddenly it felt as if he were running through treacle: the air around him shifted and coalesced, like water turning to clotted blood, and that in turn changed into people: thousands of people all around him, and a tall, lordly man holding the hand of a beautiful, majestic woman clad like a bride in brilliant scarlet and gold cloth. They stood at the top of the stairs where a stone altar had been placed, overhung by a stone lintel bearing ten symbols etched deeply into it. Below the lintel was an image of Shiva, festooned with flowers and candles and offerings of worship.

This must be the place where Ravana married Mandodari . . . but how can I be seeing the Demon King of Lanka marrying the daughter of the King of the Asuras?

The lordly man turned and glared at Vikram, then said something that made the air ripple. Unseen forces bunched like a fist and punched him sideways off the stairs, leaving him sprawling on the rocky slope. Suddenly the crowds were gone and the lord's furious face was the last thing Vikram saw vanishing from view as he flew through the air and landed heavily, the air jolted from his lungs. He groaned as he sprawled on the jagged stones, trying not to slide down the slope and gasping for breath.

The thug loomed above him, grinning savagely.

Vikram lashed out desperately with his foot and caught the man on his knee, making him overbalance; he tripped on the edge of the step and rolled away, howling in fury, but Vikram had already jack-knifed to his feet and was staggering across the rugged slope towards the wall dividing the parkland from the town. He leapt from rock to rock, tearing off his jacket as he ran, until he reached the stone wall about fifteen paces ahead of his chaser. He wrapped the denim around his hands and leapt for the top of the wall, which was studded with broken glass. One vicious shard snapped and his jacket tore; the thug lunged at his legs but he was already swinging them up and over, barely missing shredding his groin on the glass, then he launched himself over the top and into an alley, somehow landing on his feet. On the other side of the wall he could hear his pursuer swearing furiously. Vikram had barely moved when the man launched himself over the top and landed heavily six feet away. The thug squealed like a child as his ankle twisted, but he still came after Vikram.

They zigzagged through the alleys, shoving through bewildered townsfolk, until he made a wrong turn and found himself in a dead end. The alley ended in an archway, and cursing, Vikram sprinted through and found himself in the courtyard of a temple. Without thinking, he reached up and chimed the bell above the gate as he passed through. There were maybe a dozen worshippers inside, clustered before a statue of Vishnu seated on a serpent bearing a lotus, and they all turned as he ran in. A few seconds behind him, the chasing man banged his head on the bell and swore angrily.

Vikram looked around, desperately searching for a way out, but there were no visible exits. He turned back to the archway and gasped in sudden fright: there were now no worshippers, and no sign of where they had gone – in fact, the whole temple was different. When he'd entered it had been freshly painted; now it was suddenly run down and filthy; it stank of old incense and rotting offerings – it felt somehow both newer and older.

A monkey chattered from above, but when his eyes found it, it seemed to have too many limbs. It was gone before he could look closer. Even the air tasted different: there was smoke still, but without the carbon monoxide tang of diesel.

The man chasing him slowed to a limping halt and looked about him, and then peered down at his clothes: his battered brown leathers had transformed into an old white kurta. But his knife was still the same. He looked spooked, though, as if this was as unexpected to him as to Vikram, and just as frightening – but he seemed to blame the change on Vikram, because he backed away, his mouth opening and closing in voiceless confusion. 'What—? How—?' he finally managed. He looked down at the knife in his hand again, then he turned and fled. In a second he was gone.

Vikram stared after him for a moment, panting, trying to catch his breath, then he looked down at himself. He was completely blue – all of his skin was painted the colour of divinity – except for a white loincloth about his waist. In his right hand was a bow, and he held a clutch of arrows in his left. He looked like one of those religious fanatics who dressed up on feast days as their patron god, then made a packet posing for tourists. Then Vikram realised that his glasses were gone, yet he could see clearer than ever before in his life.

An old man clad in white with an orange sash emerged from the back of the temple: the pandit, Vikram guessed, the priest of this temple, and he looked terrified. Vikram glanced at a shrine and saw inside an image of an unfamiliar god with ten heads, all of which were turned his way. As his mind leapt toward some terrifying conjectures, the pandit bowed and then backed away, obviously afraid of him.

Vikram stared again at his blue-painted hands, which he suddenly realised weren't painted at all, then he gasped and ran back into the alley, heedless of whether the man who'd been chasing him was waiting outside or not.

•

The hoodlum's gun rose slowly, but Deepika's can of mace didn't: she wrenched it from her handbag and gave him a jet in the face, then spun behind the pillar as his finger tightened involuntarily on the trigger as the gas seared his eyes. Two thunderous blasts numbed her ears and chips of stone and plaster ricocheted about the courtyard, then the man was staggering away, screaming, brandishing his gun blindly as his other hand clutched his face. The man who'd been repairing the bike dived through a doorway and the windows above crashed shut. The gunman fired blindly at the sounds, sending another two bullets into the square of clear sky above.

While the man howled out his pain Deepika darted from her pillar to the next, but he heard her running footsteps and turned in her direction.

'You fucking little bitch! I'm going to fucking *kill* you!' he screamed, opening his arms wide and groping for balance. She could see tears streaming down his face. 'You're *dead*!'

She picked up a pot plant and threw it to one side, opposite the entrance, and as it shattered noisily he spun and fired in the direction of the sound, then fired again, swearing wildly. But she had already gone the other way, out of the courtyard and into the narrow street again. She tore off towards where she hoped the car was. She prayed none of the residents would get hurt, but there wasn't anything she could do, not now.

It wasn't until she found the car that she began to shake uncontrollably.

What is happening to us?

Vikram was staring about him dazedly on the steps outside the temple when the pandit emerged, looking at him wide-eyed. The thug was gone, and everything appeared normal. Vikram saw that he was back to normal skin colour, dressed in his everyday clothes, and his glasses were perched on his nose as usual. He pulled them off and the world blurred. *Damn, I could have got used to that.* He'd not had clear eyesight since he was eight.

'How old is this place?' he asked the priest.

The pandit took several seconds to respond. 'Very old, sahib, very old.' His voice was tremulous with wonder and fear, as if he'd seen something he didn't quite believe and couldn't recapture. 'Two thousand years. Maybe three.'

'And who is it a temple to?'

'To Vishnu, our Protector.'

I bet it wasn't always dedicated to Vishnu, Vikram thought to himself. He looked around carefully, but his attacker was gone. He walked cautiously back the way he'd come, darting from corner to corner, peering around before proceeding. The alleys were completely empty; it looked like everyone had fled inside at the first sounds of trouble, with that instinct people had for survival. *It might have been nice if they also had an instinct for helping people*, he reflected ruefully. *But I suppose that might have got them shot . . .*

He found Deepika huddled, her arms wrapped about her shins, on some steps near the car, shaking violently. She wasn't crying, though; she looked utterly furious. Sirens blared in the distance. He cautiously put a hand on her shoulder, just to calm down. Her T-shirt was damp with perspiration and she was breathing heavily, and so was he. The air of the street felt suddenly cold as their bodies chilled.

'What're the police like here?' she asked abruptly, looking off into the distance. 'In Delhi you only call them if you're certain you aren't going to get hauled off yourself.'

Vikram had no idea: police were the good guys, weren't they? Protectors of the law? Keepers of peace who made the world safe . . . weren't they? But he wasn't in Britain and he didn't really know about such things here. All he knew was that the world didn't feel safe any more – and after what he'd just seen, he didn't think he could give an adequate explanation of what had happened to anyone.

Deepika looked at him and made up her own mind. 'If those guys are locals, the police will take their side. We should go. Where's Amanjit?'

He looked back at her, hoping his fear didn't show on his face. 'I don't know.'

After the Burning

Mandore, Rajasthan, AD *769*

The square was empty. Only Chetan remained: the new raja, alone at his father's pyre. 'Aram Dhoop, you will die slowly,' he promised aloud, then thought, *Damn them all! Especially the poet! I'll eviscerate him ...* Recently his father had traded with the Persians for a device that corkscrewed a spike into a man's belly and then slowly pulled out his entrails, twist by twist. *Aram Dhoop, your bleeding guts will spill out at my feet as you plead for mercy, but I will be deaf to your pleas.*

The pyre still burned, stinking of smoke and pitch and casting a dull orange light over the courtyard. The guards had slain sixteen people, including several women, in the riots that had followed the abduction of Rani Darya. He didn't need to imagine the whispers; this was an inauspicious beginning to his reign. The rumours would have already started, for the people took the luck of their ruler – or the lack of it – as a sign of divine favour.

Ill-starred, ill-fated ... the poet has poisoned the beginning of my reign and for that he will die the most dreadful death I can imagine.

He kicked a piece of wood to liven up the bonfire and watched the flames lick a skull that rolled to the edge. *Which of them was it,* he wondered. *Meena, maybe? Or Padma* . . . He grinned savagely as he recalled the tears on Shastri's face. The man was weak: a real man did not weep, no matter the cause. But he would not be returning; Jeet would see to that.

He peered deeper into the pyre at the still upright bones of Halika and shivered slightly. His mother had been the oldest of the ranis, and yet she remained the most beautiful, the most powerful, the most frightening of them all. She had been the only one fit for the title of queen: a match for his terrible father in every respect.

'Where are you, Mother? Burning in some demon-realm, or already installed as a handmaiden to Durga, Queen of Heaven?'

Something whispered in the air and he shivered slightly. He tried to dismiss it as fancy, that sound so like his mother's voice. *I am raja now*, he reminded himself. *I need fear no one*. But he knew that was a lie. To be raja was to fear *everyone*.

Someone moaned, a low sigh of pain from the far side of the pyre, and he jumped, startled. The soldiers were supposed to have dealt with all the bodies, disposed of all the stupid rioting imbeciles they had been forced to slaughter. How could they possibly have missed one?

He walked around the fire-pit and peered in – and nearly swallowed his tongue in terror as he gazed on a charred form crawling on its belly out of the pyre. It was impossible to tell if it was male or female, until it raised its head—

'Father!' His heart almost stopped.

Ravindra's muscular body had been stripped of skin and the flesh beneath had been roasted to char, with cracks of running fluids flowing between the blackened slabs. His hair and clothing were gone, his face pared back almost to the bone. His lips were burned away, leaving a row of teeth gleaming between the charcoal remnants of flesh.

'Help me!' the stricken raja hissed. '*Help me!*'

Chetan stood above him, frozen in dread. His mouth worked, but no sounds emerged.

Slowly, the awful figure stood. Behind it, six forms of smoke and ash formed and fluttered in the breeze. He recognised his mother – then one of them blew away, leaving only five, growing more and more substantial as he watched. He dragged his eyes back to Ravindra's hideously deformed face and the dreadful shape filled his sight.

Ravindra pushed his head forward until he was just inches away and croaked, 'You have failed me!'

His visage was too dreadful to take in and Chetan shut his eyes, though he knew he could never forget that awful sight. 'But . . . How—?' he started.

'Where is Darya? Where is my seventh queen?'

Chetan willed himself to back away, but his limbs would not obey. 'I don't understand . . .'

'They *all* had to die!' Ravindra snarled, as loudly as his ruined throat could manage. 'All of them! And then I would be returned, perfect and immortal, the living incarnation of Dark Ravana, Lord of All!' Those dreadful eyes blazed and now his voice roared up from the bowels of the underworld. 'WHERE IS DARYA?'

'Gone . . . gone,' Chetan managed at last. 'It wasn't my fault – I ordered them all to burn – the poet took her! Aram Dhoop – it was all his fault—'

'*ARAM DHOOP? THEN BRING HIM TO ME! AND BRING ME MY QUEEN! I WILL NOT BE THWARTED!*'

Chetan fell to his knees, sobbing, 'Father, please! Jeet is pursuing him – he will return soon, with both Dhoop and the queen. All will be well, I promise!'

A searing hot hand fell on his shoulder and burned straight through the silken robe to his flesh.

'Stand, my son.'

He tried to rise, but his knees wouldn't take his weight. 'Father, please . . .'

'Stand, Chetan.' Incredibly strong hands picked him up and held him upright. The heat was dreadfully painful, more than Chetan could bear. He closed his eyes again.

'Look at me,' Ravindra-Raj commanded him quietly.

Chetan began to cry.

'Look at me.' The low voice was implacable.

'Please . . .'

One hand lifted his chin and he opened his eyes.

The blackened face, oozing steaming fluids, was the most hideous, hypnotic thing he'd ever seen, but most terrifying of all was the agonised intellect behind the eyes, all that remained intact of his father.

Chetan quailed before him as Ravindra's jaws opened horribly wide – his teeth had lengthened; they were now three inches long and razor-sharp, and so hot they scorched his flesh as his father closed his jaws and his teeth pierced Chetan's right jugular vein. He had been bent over backwards and was staring up at the evening sky, helplessly pinned by his dead father's immensely powerful arms and weakening by the second. Smoke like cooking fires rose from his father's mouth as he bit down again – that was *his* blood he could hear, sizzling, and he could feel his father drinking as he became dizzy, and then the sky swung above him and his skull cracked on the marble slabs beneath him.

I am dying. I can feel my heart slowing. I am dying.

His father's voice rasped above him, harsh and uncaring. 'Feed, my queens. Replenish yourselves. We must be far from the light when the sun comes.'

The women hissed like snakes and Chetan felt them close in on him. He tried to wail, but all that came from his torn throat was a mewling sound. But he was still alive to hear his father's voice take on a note of consternation. 'Where is Padma? Did she not die with her heart-stone at her breast?'

The ghostly shapes shimmered uncertainly and Ravindra snarled, 'Damn you all! Can you do *nothing* right?' He glared down at Chetan, his ruined face savage with anger. 'I have no pity in my heart for you, for you have failed me twice. You are no longer my son.'

Dusky shapes of ash and air wrapped themselves about Chetan and semi-substantial nails ripped his clothing. He screamed one last time as five mouths tore into his flesh.

Death came, unimaginably slowly.

Ancient Echoes

Jodhpur, Rajasthan, March 2010

One-Eye levelled the gun at Amanjit's chest and smiled slowly. On the ground, Pock-Face groaned, clutching his bloodied face, but his eyes were on Amanjit as well, and filled with murder. The frightened card-players were all on their feet, their hands in the air, backs against the wall.

'Drop the stick, boy,' One-Eye drawled.

'Kill him, Jeetan,' snarled Pock-Face. 'Kill the bastard.' He slowly got to his feet and lurched to one side, still dazed.

Amanjit stared down the barrel of the gun. It looked huge, even from ten yards away across the ash-pit. Jeetan's eyes were filled with hatred and purpose: it was clear the man would shoot if he needed to . . . or perhaps just for the satisfaction.

He dropped the stick, sending it clattering across the marble slabs.

Run, Deepika! he willed them. *Run, Vikram!*

Jeetan smiled and walked towards him. 'On your knees, boy.'

In his moment of triumph he had forgotten his earlier reaction to the fire-pit, but as Amanjit watched, the man's shoes scrunched into the blackened circle and a sudden burning smell accompanied a whiff of smoke, blooming around Jeetan's feet. The stench was overpowering, and as Amanjit heard the gunman gasp he looked up to see the one-eyed man standing in the midst of the ash-pit, the gun in his hand and a look of utmost horror on his face. His legs bunched as he tried to leap clear, but instead he suddenly screamed and collapsed, his hands flailing as if to bat something away. The gun dropped to his feet.

He looks like he's slipped into a vat of acid, Amanjit thought. *Or a blazing fire,* he amended as a wall of heat suddenly flowed from the pit and he found himself driven backwards.

He needed two sets of senses: his hearing encompassed the present, in which the card-players and Pock-Face were staring at the screaming Jeetan, and at the same time he could also hear the cries and chants of a crowd of unseen people, and the roar of flames. He could even see other figures in the flames, all of them women, wreathed in fire. His eyes saw both the burning pyre surrounded by crowds of people in primitive clothing, and also a near-empty garden in which one man was apparently thrashing about in incredible agony. Even his nostrils were taking in two sets of odours: one of the stale rot of the modern garden and the other of that terrible pyre from the past.

He backed away while Pock-Face looked at him with saucer-like eyes, his bloodied face and broken nose forgotten as he tried to understand what had happened. 'Who *are* you?' he cried. Then he stepped into the pit, utterly unaffected by whatever had struck Jeetan down, and tried to pull his mate to his feet. Throwing a glance over his shoulder at Amanjit, he stooped to pick up the gun.

'You: don't move!' he ordered, but Amanjit ignored him, spun around and ran and was gone from the garden before Pock-Face could take aim, though he heard a bullet ricochet off the stone wall behind him as he fled. The man didn't follow.

Where are Deepika and Vikram? He was suddenly struck by a great wave of fear: what if Deepika was in their hands? Vikram was no use in a fight, and Deepika—

He almost froze with dread for her. What might they do to her? She was only a girl!

He ran through the gardens, shouting her name, and getting back to the car felt like it took for ever.

'What kept you?' Deepika was leaning against the car, casually tapping her fingers on her mobile phone. Vikram was beside her, looking slightly flushed but otherwise absolutely normal.

Amanjit stopped and gaped. 'Are you all right?'

So much for worrying about them . . .

'Of course – I'm a Delhi girl, remember? We don't take shit from anyone, especially not jerks like that.' She looked him up and down as he panted, suddenly exhausted by his frantic search for her. Her look said 'I can handle all manner of things', leaving him feeling slightly foolish.

'But we should probably get going,' Vikram put in anxiously. 'The cops are coming.'

'Ah, sure.' Amanjit flicked out his car keys, trying not to let the others see that his hands were still shaking. 'Let's get out of here!'

The traffic on the drive home was so slow that if the gunmen had still been chasing them, they'd have easily caught them – on foot. Once they hit the motorway they were able to weave a path through the traffic at a more respectable twenty miles an hour. They all compared notes, with first Amanjit then Deepika describing their experiences, while Vikram asked probing questions from the back. It was strange, trying to describe what they had seen when it sounded so crazy – completely far-fetched, something out of a fantasy novel or a computer game.

Amanjit felt embarrassed to be telling his mad tale of the one-eyed man, Jeetan, and how he just collapsed as if he'd been burning in invisible flames – if someone had told him a tale like that he'd have sworn they were playing a joke on him. But neither Deepika nor Vikram laughed at him: they had all experienced these interlinked dreams and none of them were in any doubt that however crazy, what they had just endured was very real, for all its impossibility.

Then it was Deepika's turn, and Amanjit found himself gripping the steering wheel and trembling with fury at the thought of her being menaced by a gunman. He laughed when she got to the bit with the mace, thinking admiringly, *But she handled it*. His Delhi-miss was no coward, that was for sure.

Vikram's tale was the hardest to follow. The sadhu's words had chilled them all, but he'd kept talking to Vikram after the other two had left, and now the young student told them the definitely-not-holy man had mentioned that name again – 'Shastri' – as well as others, "One-eyed Jeet' and 'Padma' – and a lot of what sounded to Amanjit like gibberish about queens and past lives.

Once Vikram had finished describing his strange encounter with the sadhu, what he'd seen at the place where Ravana had married and then his experience in the old temple, he paused for a moment, thinking, and then announced, 'I think I'm starting to pull it all together.'

'Good man, Sherlock!' said Amanjit sincerely, because nothing was yet making any sense whatsoever to him. 'I'm all ears.'

'Go on then: do the big reveal!' Deepika added.

Vikram pulled off his glasses and looked at them, then started polishing them on his shirt-sleeve. 'You know, for a moment I could see perfectly without my glasses,' he said yearningly. 'It was *wonderful*. I've never been able to do that before.'

'Yeah, well, the eyes might be good, but you try explaining

the blue skin to normal people,' Amanjit grunted. 'Come on; you can get your eyes lasered later. Tell us what you're thinking, Chameleon Man.'

'Well,' Vikram began, 'I think it all comes back to these dreams of ours. Don't laugh – but I think that the three of us were part of something that happened in a past life, back in Mandore a thousand years ago – something to do with that fire. The spooky sadhu called me "Aram Dhoop" – and that's the name of the poet whose book I found in the library the other day! And I've heard Amanjit's alter ego called "Shastri" in my dreams, and so has Deepika, and the sadhu mentioned him too, so I guess that's who you were, Amanjit.'

'The so-called bad guy.' Amanjit couldn't keep the sarcasm from his tones.

'Not the main bad guy.' Vikram shifted uncomfortably. 'I'm only saying it's beginning to be pretty clear that you were Shastri – and I was this poet, Aram Dhoop. Get over it.'

'If it's a past life, then it's a past life. It's what you do now that counts,' said Deepika diplomatically. 'And I don't think you are a bad man now, Amanjit.'

The young Sikh flashed her a grateful look, though he still wasn't ready to fully buy into this whole 'past lives' thing – surely there had to be other explanations?

But Vikram went on, 'The two places we all had weird experiences in Mandore were the two really ancient places – the old palace gardens and the temple. The temple is around two thousand years old, maybe even more, and it might once have been dedicated to Ravana, well before it was re-consecrated to Vishnu – they used to do that all the time as gods came in and out of favour. And Amanjit, you said that the one-eyed man – Jeetan? – you said he could see and feel the flames too, and I think that means he was around then too, in that same past life. So that gels with what that old sadhu said – he also mentioned "One-Eyed Jeet", didn't he? Oh, and I forgot the other thing he said – that was, that he is called "Ravindra" – and I'm pretty sure that was the name of the raja in my dream. If that's the case, he is *not* a nice person, I can tell you that for sure.'

'That sadhu didn't wish us well,' Amanjit agreed. 'You say he vanished?'

'Into thin air,' Vikram confirmed.

'Okay, so I guess that makes some sense – but what about the ghostly women?' Deepika asked.

'Well, Amanjit said he had this kind-of flashback vision, where he saw women in the fire-pit, and crowds watching – and someone who looked like me and someone like you running away.' Vikram leaned forward. 'So what if it was a vision of the past: *our* past?'

He looked a little surprised when neither Amanjit nor Deepika laughed at him, and when Amanjit glanced at Deepika, he could see she was taking the suggestion as calmly as if Vikram had suggested a chai-break.

'If it was the past, it was a bloody dangerous one,' Amanjit observed. He wondered if he really wanted to know more – but that was stupid: if this Jeetan knew about them, he might still be trying to find them. He might even track him down to his home, and that would put his mother and sister at risk too. The thought chilled him, so he said encouragingly to Vikram, 'Go on.'

'Well, what if this poet – this Aram Dhoop – rescued one of the women from the fire? What if it was you?' he added, looking at Deepika. 'It looked like sati, like the women were being cast on a funeral pyre.'

'*Sati*,' Deepika echoed, going pale. 'How ghastly.'

'I think we were all there, in a shared past life. I must have been this Aram, the poet. Deepika was a queen and Amanjit was a soldier named Shastri. I think Aram rescued the queen.'

'Nothing like recasting yourself as the hero of the story,' Amanjit commented drily, though he couldn't fault Vikram's reasoning, so far at least.

Vikram ignored him. 'Maybe it's because we've all met up, so we're remembering these past lives, and that must be somehow attracting others from the same time and place, like that one-eyed guy.'

'What else did that sadhu say?' asked Deepika.

'He said, "Now the four who thwarted me that fateful day are here", or something like that. Oh, and also, "The dance will begin again", or words to that effect.'

'That must mean that this has happened before.' Deepika swallowed. 'How horrible . . .'

Amanjit overtook a camel-cart and finally moved on to a stretch of empty highway. Ahead, the Mehrangarh towered above them and he found himself wondering what it must have been like to see it whilst riding across the desert, hunting. And out of the blue, unwanted memories arose and though he struggled to keep his eyes on the road, he couldn't quite cast them aside: *A flash of himself, riding alongside a one-eyed man . . .* He groaned and blinked the image away.

'The sadhu told me: "In each life I have danced on your grave",' Vikram said in a low voice, staring away into space. 'I believed him.'

'Why would he say that? Does that mean he thinks you're the main enemy?' Deepika asked Vikram. Then she exclaimed, 'Hey, does all this mean that reincarnation is real?'

Vikram pulled a thoughtful face. 'Maybe – maybe it does! I've never really believed in it, not really . . .'

'Some Hindu!' Amanjit snorted. 'It's only the central part of your religion!'

Vikram winced and shifted uncomfortably on the back seat. 'It's one thing to be dragged to temple every morning, quite another to have to read the scriptures for myself, or to work out if it might all be real,' he replied. Then he pulled a sly face. 'So where does that leave you, Mister Sikh?'

'We don't necessarily discount reincarnation,' Amanjit replied airily. 'So, anyway, what about that other person you told us that the sadhu talked about: something about "Padma's ghost"?'

'So there must be someone else involved,' Deepika said. 'You said "four", didn't you? Four people?'

'Maybe it's that one-eyed guy, Jeetan,' said Amanjit. 'He's certainly involved.'

'But the way the sadhu spoke . . . I'm not sure,' Vikram muttered. 'I think he meant us, and someone else. I really don't know.' He fell silent.

'So, what are we going to do next?' Deepika asked. 'Should I go back to Delhi? Perhaps that would make it stop?'

'No,' said Amanjit, emphatically.

'No,' echoed Vikram, then blushed.

Deepika rolled her eyes. 'Don't you guys both have an arranged marriage or something set up for you?' she enquired scathingly. 'Because I'm telling you right now, if being in the same place as you two is what set this off, I'm leaving town, right now. America, England, wherever it takes to make it stop!'

Amanjit dropped Vikram off at the main library. The studious youth looked engrossed in his own thoughts, and eager to hit the piles of dusty tomes.

'I'd help, but I have to get back to Papa and convince him to move back to Delhi,' Deepika said. 'And Amanjit probably can't read,' she added cheekily. 'Good luck, Vikram – and don't forget to let us both know how you get on.'

They all exchanged mobile numbers so they could keep in touch, then Vikram hurried off, a determined look on his face.

'He's got a huge crush on you,' observed Amanjit.

'Then he's got good taste,' replied Deepika crisply. 'Our house is on the east side, driver. Make it snappy.'

They drove in silence for a while as Amanjit negotiated the crowded streets, but finally he plucked up the nerve to ask her about herself, by way of her father. 'The headmaster said your father was educated in London?'

'Yeah: Papa went to England, and I was born there. Papa and Mum don't always see eye to eye about emigrating, though. She's a professional too, and she travels a lot in Asia, so we came back to Delhi to live when I was young. And when Papa decided to come out to Jodhpur for his research, it coincided with Mother having to travel to China on business, so I had to tag along with my father, otherwise I'd have been left alone in the house in Delhi, and no one wanted that. Except me of course. I would've had a great time!'

'It'd never happen out here: a girl being allowed to live on her own.'

'Yes, well, it didn't happen in my case either.' She looked slightly sulky. 'Instead I got landed in this dump, with no friends and nothing to do.' She grimaced, and added, 'And now I'm being chased from pillar to post by ghosts and gun-toting hoodlums, accompanied only by two young men labouring under the delusion that they're reincarnations from history.'

'I'll be your friend,' offered Amanjit.

'Yeah, sure, Turbanator. Like I'm ever going to date a small-town Sikh boy.'

'Jodhpur's a city – and it isn't a dump. We've got lots of good stuff – old palaces and the fort, and picture theatres and all.'

'Oooo, fancy. Whatever.'

'I'll show you round, if you like. We could go for a movie tonight.'

'Humph. Didn't you have to get my father's permission to marry me first?'

'Oh, he said yes,' Amanjit announced with a smile.

She burst out laughing. 'Yeah, right! What's on anyway?' She looked at him and added sharply, 'Not that I'm agreeing to anything.'

'There's that latest Shah Rukh Khan one – you know, singing, dancing, bahut mast plot-line. You know the stuff. I like Hollywood movies too, but we don't get so many here.'

'Delhi has dozens of good cinemas, ultra-modern, just like the West,' Deepika said.

'Did you grow up in England or Delhi?' Amanjit asked as he pulled up outside Deepika's apartment.

'All over. It's been Delhi since I was ten, so mostly there – I've even lost my English accent. Hey, thanks, for looking after me back there. It got pretty scary. Those flames . . .' She shuddered, and hugged her arms about her middle.

He rubbed his chin. 'Do you reckon Vikram is right about all this past-life stuff?'

After a moment she nodded slowly. 'I didn't want to believe, but it does kind of make sense . . . Do you?'

'I guess. Sort of. But I know this: there is no life, past or present, in which I would hurt you.'

She gave him a startled, blinking look. 'Thank you,' she said quietly. 'I would like to think I can believe that.'

He suddenly wished he could kiss her, but it was probably a little soon, he decided. He still didn't want to say goodbye, though. 'So, I still can't persuade you to come for that movie? I'll bring my sister along to chaperone.'

She began to refuse, and then stopped. 'Okay. Sure. Why not? Pick me up at seven.'

He grinned all the way home, the terrors of the day forgotten.

Vikram went into the library, which belonged to the Maharaja of Jodhpur – it was actually inside his palace, which was also now partly a hotel. He was torn between enthusiasm for the task and dread of what he would find – not to mention an unwillingness to leave Deepika behind with that charmer Amanjit. There was also the fact, not quite acknowledged even to himself, that he didn't want to be alone at all, after what he had gone through that day.

He glanced at his watch as he entered – 4:36 p.m., well before sunset. He felt a measure of safety in the number of people coming and going. He had membership through his father; it was always surprising just who Dad knew – it might only be a tailoring business but it appeared to take him everywhere. Vikram had been here often enough before that he was a well-known face to the ladies behind the front desk, but he still looked up in surprise as one of them called out, 'Hi, Vikram!' He was seldom greeted by name anywhere out of school.

It wasn't one of the usual matrons but a young woman – who on closer examination turned out to be Amanjit's younger sister, Ras. Now he thought about it, he'd often seen her here, but of course he'd not known who she was before. She smiled warmly at him and he grinned back. She'd been all right the other night, lively – and a bit cavalier; he'd liked that. She had some of the same spiky confidence her brother had, despite her skin-and-bones body and unhealthy pallor. She was obviously a fighter, but it was clear her biggest battle was with her own health. Not that she was what he thought of as 'his type of girl' – the ones he normally fancied were quiet and studious, and of course they were the ones who never dated anyone, let alone him. And that included Deepika, of course – although it now turned out she wasn't in the least bit meek and demure! He hadn't quite worked through that dilemma yet.

'Hi, Ras!' He waved and moved swiftly to his usual corner, where the old history tomes, the ones written in original Sanskrit, were kept. His father had surprised him with a pass for the restricted book section when he'd been working on a difficult project a while ago and now the guards and librarian for that section waved him through without even searching his bag. In just a few minutes he was wrestling with the ancient texts, immersing himself in tales of the early rulers of Rajasthan, the Pratihara kings.

His teachers might all say he had a gift for this type of research, but it was still hard work. It took him several hours, but at last he found what he was looking for. The dirty windows let only soft light in at the best of times, so he'd scarcely noticed the lengthening shadows. He stiffened when he saw the name, handwritten in Sanskrit on leathery old parchment. There was something odd about the handwriting, he thought as he hunched over, scrawling a rough translation on his pad. As he translated, he realised that he might have finally found what he needed. He whispered the name softly, like a magic spell.

'ravindra atrappatta, raja of mandore.'

There was much more and he transcribed it eagerly. This, at last, was real progress . . .

Ravindra ascended to the throne of Mandore when the capital moved to Avanti . . . Feared by his fellow rulers . . . Died in mysterious circumstances . . . His son Chetan, murdered the day of his father's cremation, ending the family line . . . Mandore declined until other dynasties revived local fortunes.

It was when he glanced from one document to the other, from the faded original, written hundreds of years ago in an entirely different alphabet and language, to his own neatly written script, that he realised what that odd thing about the handwriting was.

The old note was in *his* handwriting.

Vikram leaned back, his mind reeling, theories and possibilities colliding wildly.

What if I—? But surely—?

He glanced up, and nearly shrieked aloud.

There was a pale face pressed to the window.

Ras made room and pushed a book into its place, then peered through the glass doors into the restricted section, ostensibly taking a moment to catch her breath after the stacking. Even the smallest exertion was hard for her, but the family needed the extra money she brought in, and more than that, she liked working in the library. And tonight it was giving her the ideal opportunity to do a little spying: on Vikram Khandavani.

The object of her surreptitious attention was currently scribbling furiously into a notebook. He had been in there for hours.

It was ridiculous really: even though she had laughed at him the other day, she had to admit she quite liked Vikram. He was nothing like the guys she normally went for: the muscular, decisive, action-hero types. Her bedroom walls were covered in posters of Akshay Kumar, Salman Khan and the like – exactly the type she intended to marry. But still she couldn't stop herself sneaking looks at Vikram whenever she saw him, at school or in the library too, though they weren't in any of the same classes – she was no one's idea of a scholar, not like him. Even though he was a lot shorter than her brother, and wiry rather than muscular, not to mention kind of nerdy-looking with those glasses, he had this kind of fearlessness which made him stand out from the others. He would argue the point with anyone about anything and she respected that. Most of the guys were only interested in strutting about, trying to impress girls, rather than actually *talking* to them. And the more sensitive, intelligent ones were so *timid*. Vikram might be just as clever, but he had this inner steel, she could tell. Sometimes, when he looked up in a certain way, you could see the determination in his firm jaw and deep-set eyes.

He had the sort of body that would take to a good work-out, she was sure of it. *I could do a lot with you,* she thought. *Contact lenses for a start, and a hardcore weights programme . . .*

She caught herself and blushed deep red. Her brother would rag her endlessly if he ever got the slightest hint that she'd been thinking along these lines, even for an instant!

'Hey, Ras,' Bipasha called out. The grey-haired lady manned the desk outside the restricted section. She had a distinct sparkle in her eyes. 'Maybe you could return these books for me?' She winked mischievously.

Ras pulled a face as if in protest, but hurriedly scooped up the books and pushed open the door before Bipasha could change her mind. Vikram didn't see her enter; his attention was entirely consumed by something through the window. His whole demeanour had changed: his shoulders were stiff and his mouth hung wide open, and if she didn't know better, she'd have thought he was stuck trying to crawl backwards out of his chair. His eyes were huge behind his big round glasses, and when she walked over to him and peered into them, she could see they were filled with dread.

She glanced at the window, looking for whatever had so shocked Vikram – and stopped dead, her own mouth opening and closing like a goldfish.

A young woman was staring back at them. She was pretty, with rounded features. Traditional yellow-gold jewellery hung from her nose, ears and lips and about her neck. Her hair, beneath a veil of yellow silk, was tied back severely. But that was not what had made Ras stiffen and drop the books.

The woman's eyes blazed with orange light, and her lips were pulled back in a dreadful grin, revealing almost feral pointed yellow teeth.

And what was far worse: she was slowly walking through the wall into the room.

Ras' hands flew to her mouth and she gasped aloud. Vikram was frozen solid, and now so was she.

The woman's head turned, her eyes blazing, and talon-like hands with long, curved nails rose as her gaze moved from Vikram to Ras – and then her mouth split into a dreadful grimace.

'You!' the thing gasped at Ras as if in sudden fright. 'It's *you*!'

Flight

Mandore, Rajasthan, AD *769*

Their escape had taken on a truly nightmarish quality, Aram Dhoop thought. He was no horseman and the incessant hammering of his buttocks and thighs against the bulky hindquarters of the horse had been systematically destroying his body: his back felt as if a club was pummelling every inch of his spinal column.

He tried to hide his sigh of relief as the rani brought the beast to a halt and slipped lithely off its back; she'd already moved to its head and was comforting the creature before he'd managed to heave himself off, but he was certain she heard the deep groan he couldn't quite suppress.

'We need to give our poor horse a break,' she explained, her voice low, and she set off, whispering to it and stroking its neck as she led it forward, trying to keep it calm.

I wish someone would do that for me, Aram found himself wishing. *I need it more than that stupid animal does!* Then he blushed at the inappropriate thought and concentrated on keeping his footing on the uneven ground.

They had already left the main trail south when it became apparent that the dust cloud behind them was gaining rapidly;

Aram might be no tracker but even he realised that if they could see their pursuers' trail, then it was very likely their own was just as visible to the senapati's men.

He was concentrating on breathing deeply, trying to keep his rising panic under control, when Queen Darya stopped and pointed to one side. 'Look: see that dried-up streambed? We can use it – it looks like the footing might be hard enough to mask our hoof- and footprints.' She didn't wait for him to comment – it had been blindingly obvious from the start that he knew nothing much about anything but poetry . . . although he'd written some pretty good stuff about the countryside round here, he thought with a sigh. But she was right: best leave such things to her. *She's obviously got some experience of such matters*, Aram admitted to himself, and that set him to wondering about her childhood as he limped behind her up the channel, heading westwards.

He wrenched a branch off a shrubby plant of some kind and started to brush away their prints. When she turned and nodded approvingly, he felt unaccountably proud of himself for thinking of such a thing, even if he had only thought of it because he'd once read something like it in an epic by a Persian poet . . .

They continued on the path through the wilderness, below the rim of the wadi, winding and twisting but always heading westwards, but after an hour or so, it became clear their path was taking them places Darya hadn't wanted to go. She nudged his arm as he backed along the stream, sweeping at their footprints.

'Look,' she said, sounding worried, 'we're heading straight for that big hill after all.'

She was right; when he looked up he could see the Bhaurcheeria was now looming before them, blocking the way forward. Even worse, the road was now much closer again – it wasn't just that the streambed had veered back towards it, they had to actually traverse it beneath a stone bridge, or go back the way they'd come. After looking all around, listening hard, they decided to risk it.

It took just a few heartbeats for them to cross the road. With Darya still leading the horse, they scurried onto the streambed on the far side and Aram got sweeping again – then there came the sound of hooves, lots of them, thudding on the hard-packed road.

'Hurry!' Darya hissed, and they ran to the next bend of the dried-up stream, where a dip in the land got them out of sight of the road moments before the column of pursuers thundered into view. Judging from the dust-clouds thrown up by their galloping hooves, the chasing soldiers had split up into smaller groups to search for the stolen rani, and now blocked their desired route south.

'That's it,' he whispered to her, though there was no one else in earshot. 'The way to the crossroads is well and truly cut off.'

'So we're left with no choice but to walk on,' the queen said pragmatically, and started off again towards the uplands where the ground was more broken. 'Anyway, it might be a lot easier to stay out of sight up there,' she added, unconvincingly.

They avoided the occasional mean dwellings, the crude thatch huts and lean-tos housing those few farmers and herdsmen so desperate that they would try to eke out a living on this hard-scrabble land. Everyone knew the peasants had no love for the Raja of Mandore, who had taxed them into utter poverty, but the risk of betrayal was still too great to approach any of them for shelter. Surely even the smallest reward would tempt these people.

The horse was sweating badly, and panting. To Aram's refined nostrils it stank, but the queen didn't seem to mind. They found shelter from the sun in a cleft of the river bank and tied the beast to a khejri tree. They had climbed a little and when they crept to the rim of the bank and looked out, they could see the eastern plains spread beneath their eyes. It worried him, though: what he could see could potentially see him, and the cover was growing less the further up the slope they went. It certainly didn't look possible for a horse to travel unseen on the lower slopes of the Bhaurcheeria.

At last he voiced the words out loud. 'My queen, we cannot return to the roads. Our flight has come to a standstill, for I can see no way to escape the raja's net, not in the daylight—'

'We will hide here, then move again when the sun goes down,' Darya told him softly. Her calmness was soothing, enough that he felt just the faintest hope taking root inside him, that somehow they might just survive this ordeal.

'How is it you can ride so well, Rani-sahiba?' he asked her, forgetting himself and staring at her. *The detail of her beauty is like a painter's masterpiece*, he thought, *from the fine bone structure of her face to the deer-like litheness of her limbs, the soft swell of her breasts against her plain shift: each part of her contributes to a whole that is enough to make the mouth go dry and the heart drum*.

'My father could not afford a suitable dowry to marry me off, and I was too useful around the house as an unpaid servant,' she replied, her voice soft, her eyes lowered. 'So I remained unmarried and my father made use of me in his business. I learned numbers and writing, and one of my brothers taught me how to fight and how to ride. He always told me that if no man would marry me, then I should have the skills to protect myself. But his kind actions just made me more of a freak in the eyes of my people: I was the only woman in our village who learned such things.'

Aram couldn't imagine the stir a woman like her would cause in a small village. In Mandore, one's station was ordained by birth and gender. Aspiring to more was barely conceivable. 'It must have been difficult for you.'

'Yes and no,' the queen replied lightly. 'In fact, I loved learning such things – to ride especially was my greatest consolation.'

'I . . .' He dropped his own gaze. 'You are as a goddess to me, my rani.'

She grunted. 'You're very sweet, poet. I will speak well of you to my father when we return to him.'

'But he dwells far to the west! I had not thought to go so far . . .'

'Then you need not. But that is where I will go,' she said in a determined voice.

A thousand strange futures fluttered through his imagination. She was in all of them. 'I'll come with you,' he promised her. 'I will not abandon you, Rani-sahiba.'

She tilted her head coyly. 'Why would you do that, poet? You would have to cross the deserts and evade the nomad tribes with me. You would have to protect me, and I you. We would have to find food and clothing and refuge. And when we arrive, you will likely have to convert to the house of Islam.'

He shuddered at her words, but refused to be deterred. 'Even so,' he declared.

'Why would you do that? It is one thing to save a woman in need, but you should not throw away your whole life. You could go to other kingdoms and find safety, surely.'

'No,' he answered. 'I will go where you go.'

Because I love you.

He should have said it aloud, but somehow, despite all the heroically foolish things he had done that day, he could not find the courage to speak those words.

As twilight fell over the land they moved off, Darya leading the horse along the dried-up watercourse. They continued to keep away from any signs of habitation and dropped down into the deepest hollows whenever they heard horsemen nearby; the sounds of hoof-beats and shouting sent them into immediate concealment, and there they crouched, hearts thumping, until the land fell silent again.

Pallid stars slowly lit the skies above, and the sickle moon rose. Though it was spring, the nights could still be cold. They could not risk lighting their way, instead stumbling along as best they could, barely able to make out the rocks and bushes, or to see the slopes rising in front of them. Jackals whined and barked, not always far away, and occasionally other creatures padded past. Once, something coughed throatily: a deep rattling noise that made Aram quiver. Everyone knew there were terrible things that crept into the land of men once the sun was gone: rakshasas and asuras and bhoots, and a thousand others told of in all the old tales. Aram made the sign against evil, though it felt utterly inadequate against such beings.

But right now they were being hunted by men, who were a far greater threat, a much more tangible terror. They spotted them at times, bearing pitch torches to light their way as they combed the paths that crisscrossed the desert. Once they almost stumbled into a whole patrol as it passed by, the hunters oblivious to the darker shapes huddled into the broken hillside. Aram held his breath and prayed silently but fervently that the horse would remain quiet and not give them away. As the men moved off a great wave of nausea washed over him; he felt positively sick with relief.

Rani Darya moved like a ghost, gliding soundlessly over the ground: an avator of Durga, hunting different but equally deadly demons. The horse appeared to understand her completely: when it should go silent and stand still; when it could move freely and nicker softly to her, as if in conversation. As his admiration for the rani grew and grew, he saw himself more and more as a liability, a hindrance slowing her down.

But when he tried to put his fear into words, she shushed him.

'I will not leave you behind, Aram Dhoop,' she said plainly. 'You rescued me, and now I will rescue you.' Her words made his heart sing; they made this terrible flight endurable.

The horse went lame some time after midnight, pulling a muscle in the rapidly chilling air. If the setback made the rani despair, she did not show it; her face was calm and impassive. She swiftly unsaddled the beast, then stroked it, whispering into its pricked ear, before turning it loose. It pained Aram to see it go: horses were prized here and it had cost him almost every coin he had to secure one. They were usually reserved for the warriors, who prided themselves on their mastery of them, so it was no surprise he'd never learned to ride. But a lame animal was a liability, he could see that. So he helped Darya share out their gear into the saddle-bags and picked up the heavier one. He couldn't begin to imagine how they would walk all the way to Persia, alone, in dust-storm season, but Darya refused to weep – or if she did, it was done silently, her face hidden in the shadows as they slipped through the darkness towards the south-west. That kept him brave too.

It was only in the predawn light, when the bulk of the Bhaurcheeria loomed right above them, that they realised just where their winding, erratic path between their far-flung hunters had brought them. Queen Darya looked up at the great mass, blacker than black against the slowly brightening sky, and cursed.

'I had not meant to come near here,' she hissed in frustration.

'Why not?'

'Because it's such a large landmark – it's the only high place and so they will have sent men here to spy us out from above.'

'Then maybe it is best to be here after all?' he whispered back. 'Right where they won't think to look?'

She stared up at it, then she turned back to him, smiling a wolfish grin. 'You know, maybe you are right. It's a gamble, but we have no choice now. We must ascend before dawn.' She touched his shoulder lightly. 'Come.'

In the last hour before sunrise they made their way up to the top. The lower slopes were steep and covered in loose rocks and sand that made them treacherous, but the final ascent required climbing: it was hard work, and slow going. Once they discovered a campfire where three men lay wrapped in blankets; one was awake, but oblivious to them as they crept past them and made their way to the middle of the rugged mound towering above the plains. Dark things slithered between rocks, startled by their movement, but nothing hindered them and they did not stop until the light of the sun forced them to hide between two boulders leaning into each other, where they huddled together for warmth and prepared to sleep away the day.

Movie Show

Jodhpur, Rajasthan, March 2010

Ras stared, and then a wave of dizziness washed over her, blurring her sight.

For a second she was staring at herself through this ghastly spectre's eyes; she could feel dreadful sensations, of pain and hunger and heat. Her skin felt tight as a drum and hot as coals. Her throat was parched and she was thirsting horribly for something wet and metallic and oily, gushing from punctured skin into her mouth—

They touched, the woman's icy hand on hers, and something passed between them, almost like fluid being sucked up a straw, then the spectral shape shrieked and backed away. Ras felt her legs begin to go, and in a panicked second thought her weak heart would stop altogether.

A name dropped into her head. *Padma*. The ghost's name was Padma . . .

Vikram was sure he was dead. The bhoot – a burning dead woman – was stalking through the wall towards Ras, who had suddenly appeared at his side; the door was still banging on its hinges. His heart leapt into his mouth, but Ras' appearance had somehow broken the spell, for he could move again! But his momentary relief evaporated instantly as he realised that Ras herself was now the one in peril.

She could see the apparition too: he saw her drop the books she was carrying and stare into the face of the ghost – *who turned its attention to her!* As he stared in horror the ghost glided through the air towards Ras and started to reach out—

He didn't think; he just acted. Somehow he knew at once there was no time to get between them, but almost without him willing it to happen his hand had dipped into his pocket and grabbed a handful of coins – a mix of silver and coppers. He flung them as hard as he could at the spectral woman and the ghost looked shocked – and was suddenly gone, but not backwards through the walls or windows or doors; the dead woman gasped aloud as if in pain and *vanished*, just like that. The coins hit the wall and clattered to the floor while he ran to Ras and caught her in his arms as she swayed. Her face was white as snow, and she looked like she was going to—

'Padma,' she murmured, dazedly, and fainted.

She was so thin that even he could support her. He lowered her awkwardly to the floor and started calling for help.

Padma! That was the other name the sadhu mentioned: 'Even Padma's ghost has been seen.'

But what if that means . . .

He stared down at the young woman's face, swearing under his breath.

All the family taxis were out on jobs, even his brother's, so Amanjit took an auto-rickshaw to pick up Deepika. Ras wasn't back from her job at the library so there was only his mother to say farewell to.

'Where are you off to, son?' she asked, with lively interest. 'Look at you! You've washed your hair and put on your best turban – you've even tied it properly!' She sniffed the air around him and her eyes widened with wonder. 'You've put on perfume – it must be a girl!'

He ducked his head. 'It's *aftershave*, Mum! And . . . well, maybe . . .'

'Do I know her?'

He shook his head, flushing.

His mother's eyes narrowed, though she was still relaxed, as far as he could tell. 'Is she a good girl, Amanjit?' she asked. 'What do her parents do? Do I know them?'

'Mum, she's a teacher's daughter,' he replied, both nervous and exasperated. 'It's not really a date – we're just friends. Ras is supposed to be back to chaperone.'

'If it's not a date, why do you need a chaperone? In my day a girl went nowhere without her brothers at least. You young people today are too fast.'

'She doesn't have any brothers – and anyway, she's not here for long, just while her father is on an assignment. She's from Delhi.'

His mother frowned. 'Those Delhi girls, they are too loose there. Nearly as bad as those Bombay film-wannabes, but still . . . You be careful around her, Amanjit. You can't trust city misses. Don't let her break your heart.'

'Mum . . .' He sighed. His mother got all her ideas of romance from 1960s movies filled with preposterous storylines of true love and destiny.

A bit like what Vikram thinks we all went through hundreds of years ago, in fact . . .

She looked at him with pursed lips. 'Listen, if she doesn't produce a chaperone, you shouldn't go. It's up to her parents to protect her reputation: if there is no chaperone, you come right home!'

'Yes, Mum,' he intoned, kissing her on both cheeks, ''course I will. See you later, yeah?'

'This place smells,' Deepika said in a dubious tone.

Amanjit hated to admit it but she was right. Jodhpur didn't have any really modern cinemas and this one was pretty run down, even by normal standards, what with the stink of the previous sweaty occupants and their sticky fingerprints on the armrests, the spillages ingrained into the carpet, even the rotting remains of food shoved under the seats . . . She was clearly used to much better.

There was no chaperone. Deepika had paused for a few very long seconds when he knocked on the door without Ras. Then she had flashed a daring smile, slipped out and locked the door behind her. 'Papa is working late and I don't want to be alone in the house, not after what happened today. So, where's your sister?'

'Oh, she has this part-time job and she hadn't got back by the time I needed to leave,' he said airily, all the while holding his breath. *Please please please* . . . He couldn't be expected to keep track of what younger sisters did in their spare time, but perhaps this Delhi-miss wouldn't see it that way. 'She's probably going straight to the theatre, meeting her friends there.' He'd been trying Ras' mobile for ages, but she wasn't picking up – maybe she was doing overtime at the library.

Deepika had eyed him suspiciously, then winked. 'All right, but you behave, okay?'

So here they were in the local fleapit picture house, which had obviously seen better days – a *very* long time ago at that. The rest of the crowd were almost entirely male, and they were leering at

Deepika in a way that was making him very uncomfortable. Curvy Delhi girls in their tight jeans and blouses weren't a common sight here. He heard some comments from the back row that made him clench his fists, but so far he'd kept his temper. He felt eyes on their backs and he was dreading turning to see One-Eyed Jeetan and his cronies coming up behind them. Even when the lights went down it was no relief: there were too many people here, too many strangers in the darkness.

The movie began – not that anyone would've guessed from the levels of conversation or movement, which didn't change much at all. Movie-watching in Jodhpur was a social pastime, not a retreat into the world on the screen: here, you chatted with your friends, you sang along to the songs, you danced, you shouted out the next action – and if your mobile rang, you took the call. If you'd seen the movie already you told your neighbours what was going on and mimicked the dialogue – it was fun if you knew what to expect.

But he could see that Deepika was not really watching the film; her eyes were almost glazed over, except when she looked about nervously, which she did every few minutes. She kept shifting awkwardly in her seat and she wouldn't touch him, not even to let her shoulder brush his for a second, despite the cramped seats. Her unease was making him nervous too.

Then the movie changed.

He couldn't say exactly when it happened, or when he noticed, but at some point he realised that they were *alone*. It was as if the cinema had quietly emptied behind their backs, but before he could work out why, their own faces appeared on the screen in front of them, in grainy black and white.

Though it wasn't quite their faces at all . . .

. . . it was Shastri and Darya. He knew their names, just as he knew that they were also him and Deepika. The costumes weren't just old-fashioned but *ancient*: the sort of old-style armour he'd seen in the museum. The women's clothes were heavy with gold and silver embroidery and precious jewels, and the man was carrying an actual sword. But he knew they weren't costumes at all.

What he saw made him feel sick.

Shastri was holding Darya down while another woman – older, but still very beautiful, in a scary sort of way – forced Darya to drink a milky fluid; he knew it was some kind of drug. He couldn't take his eyes from the screen as that other woman bent over Shastri – HIM! – and pressed her body against him, while the young Queen Darya slumped back on her pallet, her eyes going slack. But he heard himself protesting – thank the gods! – and finally he tore his eyes from the screen to find that he and Deepika were both on their feet and that she was looking at him with such a look of shock and loathing that it tore his heart in two.

'No! I – Deepika—!'

'Sit down and shut up,' grumbled someone behind them and he spun around to see that they weren't alone any more but were back in the same Jodhpur cinema. He stared in confusion at the rows of irate faces glaring back at them, then looked at the screen again, where three brothers were bouncing through some comedy dialogue: it was the Hindi movie they'd come to see.

He looked back at Deepika, but she had shrunk away from him and was staring at him with round eyes. 'Please,' he whispered fervently, 'I wouldn't do that – never – you *know* that . . .'

She shook her head. 'I'm going home.'

'Sit down, chicky-babe,' complained someone behind them. 'I can't see.'

'Go bite yourself,' Deepika snapped back.

Someone chuckled evilly from the cinema's massive speakers, and Amanjit felt himself go cold.

'*Maybe I'll* bite *you*,' the voice replied.

As Deepika stared wildly about her the movie changed again, back to black and white, but this time with vivid flaring lights: a wild fire, out of control. Amanjit caught her arm. 'Don't go,' he hissed, even as his eyes were drawn irresistibly back to the screen. 'We don't know what's out there.'

Lights blinked, and again the cinema was empty except for the two of them.

'You're on *their* side,' Deepika snarled, shoving him backwards, so hard that he staggered against the seats, almost losing his footing. 'Don't *touch* me!'

He clenched his fists, fighting his temper. 'No!' he declared, 'No, Deepika: you have to believe me: I would *never* do that to you. *Never!*'

Five grey shapes floated out of the screen like drifting ash or spider-webs, growing more and more solid with each passing instant until five women dressed in translucent grey stood there, their eyes gleaming dully in the darkness. The one at the front sashayed towards them with gut-tightening grace.

Behind them something darker formed on the screen: a ruined face that called throatily, 'Get out of the way, Shastri. It's the girl we need – just the girl.'

On the Hill of Birds

Mandore, Rajasthan, AD *769*

A shaft of sunlight on Aram's face woke him and for an instant he blinked stupidly, his head full of holes and fog. Then he looked about him and tried to still his beating heart.

It was real – all of it! I didn't dream any of that madness!

He and Darya were lying wrapped in the horse blanket on the rocky earth in the lee of two huge boulders. They had clambered past a thorny little acacia, searching for any little cranny where they might conceal themselves. It had been black as pitch when they'd crawled into the nook, wrapped themselves in the stinking blanket and trembled until sleep overtook them; now the sun was high above.

Aram's throat was parched and his belly rumbled emptily. He wondered how much of the day had passed.

The young rani slept on and he calmed himself by watching her. Her angular face was softened in relaxation and she looked very lovely. Her lips were softly parted, her cheeks lightly dimpled, and faintly pink, as if they were lit by some lost piece of dawn sky. Her long eyelashes hid those gorgeously intense eyes, those flashing orbs that so entranced and unsettled him. Her long hair might be full of dust and sand and hopelessly tangled after yesterday's headlong flight, but it framed her glorious face perfectly. He longed to press himself against her, to feel her breath upon his face . . .

Her nose twitched, and she began to yawn. Then he heard voices.

He put a hand over her mouth and held her still, to stifle movement and sound. She came awake instantly, her eyes momentarily round with fright, then blinking as she too heard the sounds of men shouting to each other. She jerked her head slightly and he removed his hand, but other than that, neither dared move a muscle for fear of dislodging a rock and bringing their pursuers down upon them.

'How many?' she whispered after a moment.

He shook his head. 'I don't know.'

As slowly as if she were stalking some small creature, she turned over, and together they watched that tiny little triangle of light, peering through the branches of the acacia bush, seeking movement.

He almost cried out in fright when a man appeared right in front of them. This time it was Darya who put her hand against his mouth, an ironic smile on her lips.

'Anything?' someone shouted.

'No!' the man outside shouted back. 'Let's go back and take the other fork!' Then he turned and peered at the gap between the boulders, noticing the dark shadows. 'I'll just check down here.'

Aram choked back the urge to flee. *Where could we go, anyway?* They were completely trapped. Darya went so completely still that he thought she had stopped breathing. He was sure his own heart would go into seizure the moment the man saw them.

As his silhouette loomed closer, Aram knew discovery was inevitable.

Then the man gave a sudden squawk, and they saw him flinch violently as something rattled at his feet. He looked up and shouted furiously, 'Get lost, you little piece of dung!' He picked up a rock and flung it, crying, 'Get lost!'

'What's happening?' asked the distant voice.

'Damned monkey! It threw something at me!' the man outside their hideaway shouted back. 'I think there's a nest of the bloody things down here in the acacias!'

'Then back off – those little bastards can rip a man to pieces if there are enough of them. No one's going to be hiding there, are they?'

The man outside started backing away, his face pale, his eyes everywhere except on the little notch where Aram and Darya cowered, then he turned and fled.

Thank you Hanuman-ji, Aram breathed fervently.

They both let out a slow breath, then Darya turned his face to hers and pulled him down to her. He held back for an instant until he understood, then, almost disbelieving, he pressed his lips to hers. She tasted bitter-sweet, and so filled with tension and need. For one long frozen moment he felt as if the gods had touched him. Then she released him and pushed him away, looking both embarrassed and frightened.

It was just relief . . . it meant nothing . . . probably . . . But he knew already that he'd remember that kiss until he died. *Just . . . let that not be soon . . .*

'It's too dangerous to move now – we have to wait until dark,' she whispered. 'There are too many vantage points out there. They'd spot us at once.'

He nodded, his mouth dry. He reached out for her again, but she blocked his hand.

'Please, no. Don't . . .' She looked at him and added softly, 'I'm sorry – I shouldn't have. I was frightened.'

His heart twisted sourly inside him. 'No doubt there will be more frights to come,' he said, jesting to hold off heartbreak.

'It's not you,' she told him, 'I promise. But the raja— After him—' She broke off and shuddered violently.

He nodded slowly. He would never truly know exactly what she had been through at the hands of that evil beast.

They moved at dusk. They crawled out of their nook, relieved to leave that cramped and sweaty place behind and breathe cleaner air. Above them, all over the vast promontory, birds shrieked and wheeled in the sky; the Bhaurcheeria was indeed a Hill of Birds. Crows flapped heavily about the boulders, staring with hungry eyes at anything that moved, while kites and goshawks and vultures circled overhead. The dusk chorus was deafening. Lizards and snakes crawled cautiously from the shadows, awaiting the fall of darkness, and Aram felt like a gecko himself, squatting on the edge of daylight, scared to step from the protective gloom for fear of what predators might be lurking.

Darya crawled from the back of the little crevice and after sharing a grim look with him, crept slowly under the bush obscuring the crack where they'd hidden and peered around. After a few seconds she waved him forward and he slid out into the fading light, tugging the saddle-bags behind him.

Like the rani, he stood and stretched, straightening his aching body after a day in their cramped hiding place, and just unkinking his limbs felt better than the sweetest rose-water bath. He groaned in mixed pain and contentment, then looked down at himself. His clothes, like hers, were filthy. The red-brown dust that dulled her hair had marked his skin, and hers too, soaked into the sweat and was streaking their arms and faces. They looked like peasants, and he prayed that if they were spotted, they might be mistaken for such.

'Which way do we go?' he asked, looking around. As well as the larger path they'd followed up here there were a number of other paths, heading deeper into the rocks. The birds were still calling, and a pack of monkeys eyed them suspiciously from the rocks above them. Aram waved to them, deeply grateful for their actions, which had undoubtedly saved them both, but the monkeys gave no sign of understanding.

'What do you know about this Hill of Birds?' Darya asked him.

He consulted his memory, based on the reports of others, and said, 'The Bhaurcheeria is only about seventy parideshas long and no more than a few rajjus across,' he recalled. 'In broad daylight you could walk the length in half a morning, and clamber across the top in a quarter of that. But the landscape is rugged, and known to be dangerous to traverse, and we'll be moving at night. If we try to hurry, we risk falling, or we could stumble into our pursuers with nowhere to run. But if we go down to the flats, we will have nowhere to hide.'

As she pondered his words she crinkled her eyes and gnawed her lower lip. Finally she put her hands on her hips. 'I do not like this place. It is full of snakes and monkeys and it would not surprise me if there were more dangerous beasts also, like jackals or tigers. But if we think this, so too will our pursuers. Yesterday I thought I saw higher ground – west of here, yes?'

Aram thought about that. 'Yes, there are more heights to the west, broken land like this. If we can cross the Bhaurcheeria and the small valley on the other side, we can lose ourselves in those hills and make our way towards your homeland.'

'It's a decent plan,' she said approvingly. 'Shall we try it?'

He thought it through once again, then whispered softly, 'Lead on, Rani-sahiba.'

She touched his cheek. 'Good and faithful poet! I will never forget you.' She crept forward and began the climb, creeping from shadow to shadow.

Aram Dhoop had neither the choice nor the desire to do other than to follow her.

Madan Shastri had not slept since he arose from a poor night's rest before Ravindra's cremation and Padma's murder on the sati pyre. He felt like a restless ghost himself, with his mind full of sand and his heart of lead. All the colour had seeped from his vision, leaving only shades of grey, but at times that was overwhelmed with visions of his sister, burning amongst the flames.

Now he watched the sun set behind a promontory north of the Bhaurcheeria. He could feel Jeet's eye on his back, like the jab of a red-hot poker.

'Senapati,' Tilak mumbled, approaching him cautiously.

Shastri whirled. 'Anything?'

'Yes, sir. We've found the horse.'

Finally! A breakthrough! It had been a long, fruitless chase so far and he'd begun to fear that against all logic, the poet and the rani might actually have got away. They'd eluded his men for more than a day, which meant a much bigger search area, and now night was falling again, increasing his difficulties. 'Where?'

'Not far from here, northeast of the Hill of Birds. It is lame, Senapati, and the bags are gone. The scouts are retracing its trail to see if we can determine where it was abandoned.'

'The poet and Rani Darya?'

'No sign of them yet, sir.'

He pushed out a frustrated sigh. *Damn you, Aram Dhoop. You're going to be the death of me – literally.* He reached into his pocket and touched the strange gemstone Padma had given him. *My sister loved you . . . Did you even know?*

He looked back over his shoulder at the small lake where the horses were being watered; it was nearly dried out but there was just enough muddy water for their needs. Most of the men were spread far across the plains; there were ten or twelve with him, but Jeet and his cronies outnumbered those whose loyalty he could depend on.

'What news?' the one-eyed man asked, slouching towards them.

Tilak awaited Shastri's nod before replying, 'We've found their horse, sir. But the fugitives abandoned it a while ago.' He gestured away to the gloomy east, where dusk was settling. 'We found it out there.'

With his one eye fixed on Shastri, Jeet grunted, 'Then what are your plans, Senapati?'

He's happy enough to concede command when he knows where blame will fall, Shastri thought bitterly, but he answered all the same. 'They'll try and move at night. She is Persian, so she will try to flee to the west, to her people. Let all our torches be doused so that they cannot mark our disposition. We will hunt them by moonlight.'

'And what of the farmers out here?' Jeet asked.

'We will search their dwellings, but we will not despoil or damage their property, nor kill their beasts. Their lives are hard enough without such vandalism.'

Jeet shrugged noncommittally. 'I'll take my lot around the western perimeter of the Bhaurcheeria. I've a fancy they may be up there somewhere.' He clapped one of his cronies about the shoulder and roused the rest of them to their feet.

Shastri scratched his head. He'd been thinking to do the same thing. *I pity our runaways if Jeet finds them first.*

Tilak was watching Jeet's men mount, reeling off their names quietly: 'Dajji, Manoj, Jitan . . .'

He turned to Shastri. 'Killers, sir. They're all killers.'

'Killers, yes, but not real warriors, Til, just bullies and sneaks.' Shastri laid a hand on Tilak's shoulder and pulled him close. 'Keep your bow strung and your blade loose in its scabbard. There will be blood tonight.'

Tilak grunted and clapped a hand on Shastri's forearm. 'I know.' Then he strode among the remaining soldiers, shouting out orders. 'Right, on your feet, you rabble! Let's get ready to ride!'

The game of hide and seek amongst the boulders and crevices of the Bhaurcheeria played out with painstaking slowness beneath a waxing moon that wasn't too far from full. Its bright silver glow and the sea of stars gave Aram and Darya just enough light to see by. They wrapped their sandals in lengths of cloth torn from his kurta so that every footfall would be near-silent, even on the scree that covered these rocky slopes. The hilltop was a maze and even though it wasn't wide, a few thousand paces was a long way when you had to drop to your knees and crawl at the crack of stone on stone or the quavering call of a disturbed bird.

The soldiers were up here now, and they were definitely hunting them – maybe through guesswork, or perhaps the poor horse had given them way, but either way, it no longer mattered. Occasionally they glimpsed soldiers silhouetted against the night sky, but more often they heard them in the distance, calling to each other. They'd doused their torches, probably thinking they'd be able to creep up on the fugitives unawares, but it also meant they were hampered by not being able to see clearly in the darkness themselves. Sometimes Aram and Darya were forced to press themselves into crevices whilst patrols passed by, almost within touching distance. Distant sounds carried clearly on the night air, and once when they glimpsed the plains behind them, they saw a sudden fire flare up, far out in the desert. Perhaps the soldiers were burning a farmer's dwelling for having displeased them during the hunt for the missing queen. Perhaps it was nothing to do with them at all. There was no knowing.

The rani moved with uncanny skill, blending with the shadow and the rocks, moving in such silence a cat would have envied her. Aram felt clumsy and foolish by comparison, forever blundering through scree that crunched, or kicking stones that rattled away down the hillside, making them both freeze until they were certain they had not been discovered.

At last they found themselves overlooking a place where Darya thought they might be able to descend the western side of the hill, though it would be down a rock-strewn slope. Below was a gully filled with grey shadow; far to the south they could see what might be men on horses, slowly traversing distant paths with torches held high.

Darya breathed into Aram's ear, 'I cannot see anyone close. This is the most dangerous part, Aram: there is no cover on this slope. All we can do is go down, and pray there is no one to see us.'

He nodded. 'I am ready, Rani-sahiba.'

'Brave Aram.' She squeezed his forearm gently. 'I'll go first.'

'No, I should, my queen. It is you they want.'

'No, I am more used to this sort of landscape; I am surer of foot than you. I will be able to descend in silence and you can follow me. Watch where I tread. Wait here – and do not start down until I reach that big rock.' She pointed to a large black shape at the bottom of the slope.

He swallowed. *She is so much braver than I am*, he thought.

'Wish me luck,' she whispered, and then she stole out of their hiding place into the moonlight and began to creep down the exposed slope, keeping close to the edges where the loose rocks were fewest. Waiting behind her in the lee of a mound of earth,

Aram's lips expelled a silent torrent of prayer to every god and goddess he could think of.

Shastri's soldiers might be dispersed far and wide across the desert and out of sight of each other, but they were a slowly moving net of watchers. Those patrolling the main tracks had to use torches, to guard against the horses breaking their legs in unseen holes, but most of the men were on foot now. His group were strung out in a line, sweeping the foot of the Bhaurcheeria. They were supposed to be moving silently, but he could hear them muttering and calling to each other every few seconds. They were nervous, he could feel it, and seeking reassurance by checking that their comrades were well. There was a feeling of impending disaster, so thick in the air it was almost tangible.

My lads can sense that Jeet's thinking of trying something . . . They're wondering if they'll have to take sides . . .

He wished he knew for certain how many of them he could trust.

Jeet and his men were somewhere out to his right, further upslope and a little ahead, or so Til's last muttered report had him placed. Tilak had been spending more time scouting Jeet's men than looking for the rani and the poet, and Shastri was certain it had become very necessary. He felt exposed out here in the night with so many of Jeet's killers around them. Prudence told him he shouldn't be alone, but keeping track and covering such a wide area meant risk, and the biggest risk was to let their quarry slip through their fingers.

He glanced up to the left, where a high slope pitched up between two buttresses in the great hill, with a cleft at the top. It was a logical place for someone to descend, assuming that their quarry was even up there, but there were other places too, and too many gaps where they might slip through.

Curse this hunt for a grain in a sand dune! He sighed and settled behind a large boulder to watch the slope a while. He was careful to remain wrapped in his cloak so that no light could strike the metal of his mail, before propping himself against the boulder and laying his head onto his arms. His eyes stung from being awake so long: two days and almost two nights now.

It won't hurt, just to close them for a few moments . . .

. . . and Shastri woke with a jerk. He had no idea how much later it was. A tiny rockfall was running down the slope from the near edge, a stream of dust and gravel, but nothing else was moving. He stared up into the shadows and waited, panting slightly, not quite sure whether he was awake or asleep. He waited, scarcely breathing, but still nothing stirred.

It must have been a mouse, he told himself eventually. *Damn fool, asleep on watch – you're lucky you aren't choking on a slit throat, you imbecile!*

He started to move—

—and instantly froze again as a lithe little figure detached itself from the shadows where the rockfall had been triggered and stole down the slope, not very far above his hiding spot. Moonlight shimmered on a curtain of hair. The shape, little taller than a young boy, hunched over as it darted from one outcropping to the next, from a bush to a mound . . .

She moved well, the lovely Queen Darya, her limbs spread to distribute her weight and aid her balance . . . for it could only be her. He felt his mouth go dry and his hand shook as it found the carved hilt of his carefully sharpened dagger.

Aram couldn't stop himself moaning out loud when she stumbled and triggered a small rockslide that rattled off down the slope. He saw her freeze, and as she stood totally still and utterly silent she began to merge with the shadows until he could scarcely pick her out, even though he knew exactly where she was.

After a long pause he managed to calm himself, breathing deeply until his own heartbeat had returned to normal.

Eventually she moved again, staying low to the ground, creeping sideways with reptilian stealth and precision, blending into the shallow folds of the slope. She was a natural hunter, born to stalk. He tugged on his small beard anxiously. Not far to go now . . .

Please watch over her, all you gods and goddesses . . .

He began to gather his bags, ready for his turn.

May I not let her down . . .

He counted his breaths, up to fifteen, and she was fine . . . now thirty, and undiscovered . . . forty, and almost safe . . .

Then a black shape leapt from cover with a triumphant roar and bore her to the ground. It was followed swiftly by another, and far below, Aram could see a third man appearing from behind a boulder.

As his heart screamed, the rani's own voice pierced the night, her cry waking the darkness.

Without pausing for a moment to consider his options or to think about the consequences, Aram broke cover and pelted down the slope.

Madan Shastri sensed more than saw the girl pass his position. She looked to be heading for an outcropping at the far side of the slope. Soft moonlight lit her face briefly; her striking features were fixed in a mask of silent concentration. She was achingly beautiful. His hand released his dagger-hilt, opening and closing convulsively three or four times as his mind churned with indecision.

Then with a great bellow a man emerged from the shadow of the rocks she was making for and threw himself on top of her, and as she crumpled to the ground her heart-rending cry echoed across the hillside. Another man followed the first and he too was roaring in triumph. Far-off voices answered their cries.

The fog in his mind lifted, and he silently drew his sword.

The man on top of the girl laughed, grabbed her kameez at the neck and ripped it open. 'Come on, your Highness, let's see what you've got then,' he growled hungrily.

'Get off the bint and hold her legs, Biltan, you oaf!' the second man snapped, raising a hand, and Shastri could see a blade glinting in the moonlight. 'And you shut up too, Rani-ji, or I'll cut your pretty little ears off. The raja don't need you with ears, not for what he intends.'

Shastri recognised their voices: Dajji and Biltan, two of Jeet's intimates. He swallowed and circled his shoulders, loosening them in preparation, then glanced up the slope at the sound of loud footsteps crunching over the uneven ground, swiftly followed by the noise of someone slithering towards them, starting any number of mini-avalanches as he descended. If that was the poet, he was making no effort to conceal himself.

Shastri continued to lurk under the cover of the boulder; it wasn't yet the right time to reveal himself. He watched Jeet's men as they too heard the person coming down the hillside.

Dajji peered up the slope. 'There's the damned poet,' he said to Biltan. 'Go and get him.'

Biltan growled, 'You do it. I'm taking the girl.'

Aram was flailing helplessly as he slid down the slope, no longer in control of his descent, and Dajji sniggered as his movements grew ever more erratic. 'Look at the little eunuch! He can't even manage to stand on his own two feet!'

The poet tumbled to a halt a few paces away. His clothes were torn to shreds and Shastri guessed his face and arms must be bloodied and covered in scrapes and bruises. He groaned as he tried to stand, gazing helplessly at the rani, who was lying shaking in Biltan's grasp. Her kameez had been ripped open, and she was pinned in Biltan's big paws, sobbing as she fought for air.

Dajji had got up and was swaggering towards the fallen poet when Shastri stepped into view. 'Let her go, Biltan,' he told the soldier, his voice flat and hard.

Jeet's men spun their heads and Dajji drawled, 'Senapati Shastri! We found 'em, sir.' He drew his talwar.

'And now we're gonna have some fun with them,' added Biltan belligerently. He pawed the girl's chest. 'And you ain't stopping us. *Sir.*'

'The girl is still a queen,' Shastri snapped, 'and you will not harm her.'

Biltan stood up and placed a heavy foot on her chest, pinning her down. 'The girl is for the fire anyway, Captain, so it don't matter what we do to her, she's still burning.' He snickered evilly. 'We can always blame the poet.'

Shastri took another step forward and Dajji raised his sword. The two soldiers were using standard curved swords, the favoured weapon of a cavalry man, used to slash at enemies as they flashed by at a gallop. But Shastri favoured a longer, heavier straight sword, a footman's weapon.

Dajji eyed the weapon uneasily.

'Unhand her, Biltan, and step away. That is an order.'

The two glanced at each other, then Biltan drew his own talwar. The crescent of tempered steel gleamed in the night. 'No, Senapati, *you* step away,' he said insolently. 'You ain't going to live the night out anyway: Jeet's put a price on your head.'

Shastri felt a chill on the back of his neck. *So that's the way of it. At least I now know.*

Biltan was several paces away, still standing with his foot on the rani's chest, but Shastri didn't even glance at him; instead he went for Dajji, his straight sword slamming into the soldier's talwar with such force it shuddered in Dajji's grasp. The man staggered, then tried to leap away, but Shastri turned his second blow into a low thrust, pressing even closer; though the talwar swept down, he was already inside Dajji's guard. He caught the man's wrist with his left hand and rammed his sword into the man's belly, first once and then again. Dajji sagged, gasping, as hot blood steamed in the cold night air. It spurted everywhere, drenching Shastri's thighs and stomach.

The senapati shoved Dajji backwards and turned to deal with Biltan.

Jeet's man had dragged Queen Darya to her feet. Now he put his blade to her neck and cried, 'Stop – or the girl dies!' His voice filled the night, and Shastri heard others responding.

Jeet will be here any moment ...

He didn't stop walking forward. 'I don't damned well care if you kill her, Bil,' he snapped. *Ten paces.* 'What I care about is *you disobeying an order*!' *Six paces.* 'Drop her and run, or you're a dead man.' *Four paces.*

Biltan met Shastri's eyes and he read his death there. His own eyes went round with dread. He threw the girl to the ground and turned to run.

Step. Extend. Lunge.

The straight sword stabbed through Biltan's left armpit, scraped past a rib and skewered his heart. Biltan gurgled as blood darkened his lips; he toppled first to his knees, then to the ground as Shastri pulled out the blade. He watched as Biltan kept trying to draw a breath that wouldn't come. His head flopped sideways and his body convulsed, then went still.

Queen Darya gave a sobbing gasp. 'Be quiet, Rani-ji,' Shastri whispered, listening to the night air.

The poet crawled past the stricken man to get to the queen. Dajji was bent in half, attempting to hold his guts in; he too was labouring for air, but Aram barely even saw him. Shastri ignored the poet as well; he was concentrating on the noises further afield: the clatter of hooves and the shouting of men, Jeet's men, he thought, and all of them to the west, where the rani needed to go.

He turned and offered his arm. 'We must go, Rani-ji. Please.'

She looked up at him, trying to hold her ripped kameez closed. 'Senapati?' she said, that single word conveying *many* questions.

The poet, on his knees beside her, stared up at him, terrified, yet still determined to protect the rani.

What have they both been through?

'Rani, these men will kill us all, me included. We must go.'

'Where, Senapati?' she asked calmly, and Shastri found himself impressed with the young queen's instant grasp of both her own and his current situation – not to mention her understanding of where his loyalties perforce now lay.

He looked around him. Torches were gathering on all sides, and as Jeet's men had been closest, and in greatest numbers, he knew he could not wait for help here. They needed to reach somewhere defensible, a place where they could hold Jeet off until some kind of opportunity presented itself.

He looked up the slope. 'I am sorry, Highness, but we must climb back the way you came.'

Aram Dhoop clambered to his feet, staring at the senapati, his face a mixture of hope and fear. Did Madan Shastri really mean to aid them, or was this just some power struggle between the commanders? Were he and Darya to be taken back for execution, the only question now being which victor would claim the credit? He tried to meet Darya's eyes, but she was obviously still in shock, the way she was holding her clothing together and swaying unsteadily, as if she had been drugged. Aram knew how she felt. *Sweet Gods, she was a couple of breaths away from rape, and I was moments from a blade through my heart . . .*

But there was no time to dwell on their fortunes. The sounds of men and horses approaching through the darkness were getting louder as they closed in.

Darya turned her head away as Shastri went over to the dying man and cut his throat, but Aram watched, as if he might suddenly be able to inure himself to such sights. He had never before managed to view violent death with equanimity, even though it had been one of the many unpleasant facts of life in Ravindra-Raj's court.

Then the senapati strode into the shadows where the two men had concealed themselves and returned with an armload of gear. He held out a cloak to Darya, who took it wordlessly, fastened it about her neck then tied it around her waist with one of the dead soldier's sword-belts.

The act visibly steadied her; Aram took a deep breath and tried to follow her example.

'Can you shoot, poet?' Shastri asked him, his voice implacable, and though Aram shook his head, he was handed a sword-belt, a bow and a full quiver of arrows anyway. 'Do your best,' the senapati told him grimly, as he shouldered two small packs and added, 'Come, before we are taken.'

Aram draped the quiver over his shoulder as he had seen the warriors do, buckled the sword-belt over his own, and concentrated on keeping up as the captain set a fierce pace. Shastri helped them both to clamber back up the slope, despite lugging the packs he'd taken from the dead men as well as his own gear.

Whenever he looked back over his shoulder Aram could see

the flickering orange flames of the pitch torches converging below them. By the time he'd counted twenty he found he was able to go faster after all.

Darya, struggling along beside him, was slowly regaining her poise. Her face was beginning to lose that look of vacant shock that had so terrified him; she was focusing again. She turned and lifted her lips in a slight smile, as if to let him know that she was all right, then turned back and continued searching the route ahead.

They were two-thirds of the way up when suddenly bow-strings sang from far below and Aram stiffened in shock as an arrow skittered between them. Another buried itself in one of the packs Shastri carried, knocking the man to his knees. A third glanced off the captain's helmet.

'Stop, you fools! Cease fire!' bellowed a voice from below. 'No arrows! *No arrows*, damn you! We take them *alive*!'

The man shouting the orders arrived at a canter and as he reined in his mount at the foot of the slope Aram recognised him from the court: a nasty piece of work known to most as One-Eyed Jeet.

'Shastri!' the one-eyed man called, his voice echoing up the rocky slope.

'Don't stop, Rani-ji.' Shastri looked at Aram. 'Keep moving, poet!'

'Shastri!' Jeet roared. 'Shastri! Stop – or be declared traitor! You, and all you hold dear.'

As Aram and Darya staggered past him the senapati suddenly turned and stared down the slope, his face unreadable.

Suddenly the poet was afraid again. *What is Senapati Shastri's price?* he wondered, trying to stop his shaking hands. *What or whom does he hold dear?*

Research

Jodhpur, Rajasthan, March 2010

The lights on the ceiling blazed, illuminating the little cinema, and the small crowd jeered, drowning an echoing shriek as the five women dissolved in the light. Deepika and Amanjit stared wildly about them. They were standing up in the middle of the place and the entire audience was staring at them. Then most of the mouths beneath those angry eyes opened and a torrent of abuse poured out, immediately followed by a deluge of crisps and sweets.

They pulled their jackets over their heads and fled.

Amanjit caught up with Deepika as she ran out into the street and grabbed her arm. 'Hey! Deepika, stop! Listen! You have to talk to me. *It wasn't me!*'

She glared at him and spat out furiously, 'Why should I? *You know it was!*'

'Remember this morning?' he said, desperately searching for the right words. 'You yourself said it: "Past lives"! That's what you told Vikram and me – well, the same goes for you and me! *Past lives*, Deepika!' He was suddenly aware he was shouting, that people walking past them on the darkened street were looking at him like he'd lost his mind.

Maybe I have. Considering what he'd seen over the last couple of days, that might very well be the case. *At least it would explain everything . . .*

He put his hands on her shoulders, hoping she'd take it as a reassuring gesture, not a threat. She looked up at him and after a long, fraught moment, she managed a strained smile that didn't fool him one little bit. She was clearly terrified.

'Yeah, okay, Turbanator,' she said with forced levity. 'Past lives. You're right – well, *I'm right*, so I'm going to give you the benefit of the doubt – for now, anyway.' Then the attempt at a smile dropped away and she shuddered. 'But what's happening to us? It's like the whole world has gone mad.' She looked about them, past the staring passers-by, and admitted, 'I'm really scared now.'

'We were surrounded by people and yet they still got to us,' he muttered, trying not to admit just how menacing the night was feeling. 'What shall we do?'

In a small voice she murmured, 'I don't know. I'm sorry. I just want to go home.'

His heart sank. 'Okay,' he replied in a pained voice, 'of course I'll take you back.'

She shook her head. 'No, I want to go home to Delhi.'

He realised he was still holding her shoulders. Though he hated to let her go, he let his hands drop to his sides. 'Okay – but it's six hundred miles so I'll need to fill the car up with petrol.' He said it as a joke, but he meant it, too: if she wanted to be driven to somewhere she'd feel safe, of course he'd do it. He'd never before met anyone like her, but he already knew that – just like in any good Bollywood movie – he was smitten. Perhaps he should be practising his bhangra moves . . .

She smiled properly then; maybe she recognised that his offer was genuine. 'Idiot.' She patted her admirably flat stomach. 'Are you hungry?'

Amanjit led the way to a little dhaba near the clocktower; it smelled of burned rice, but he knew it was cleanish and the food was good. They got channa daal and hot chapattis, and icy-cold Coke to wash it down with. As Deepika scraped up the last of the chickpeas with a sliver of chapatti she said, 'We should call Vikram.'

Amanjit had been enjoying having Deepika to himself, despite their earlier fright – already it felt more like a bad dream, as if they'd both fallen asleep in the cinema. In fact . . . maybe that was what had happened—?

He didn't believe that, though; in his heart he knew whatever was going on was much worse than just a nightmare. 'Vikram will be busy following the clues,' he said after a moment, half believing his words. 'We shouldn't interrupt.'

She looked at him doubtfully, but didn't press it. They sat together in silence a while, looking out into the street through the grimy glass. The road was only a few feet wide here, just broad enough for an ox-cart going one way and a motorbike the other, provided they were both careful. People honked and vendors hollered; Krishna worshippers came past, clashing symbols and chanting, and then a sadhu – a *real* one, with matted dreadlocks and dirty orange robes – appeared, going door to door with a tin cup, begging chai and coin. Then came a crowd of young men, banging drums and leading a white horse with a brightly clad groom in the saddle, heading for his wedding with a stunned look on his face, as if he didn't honestly believe he was awake. Amanjit knew how he felt. Still, this was the Jodhpur he knew: never a quiet moment in this city, always something to see. It was difficult to believe in ghosts with hundreds of people out on the streets. Occasionally familiar faces went past: schoolmates, who noted the two of them together and stood outside the window smirking until Amanjit waved them away. By Monday everyone would know he'd dated the Delhi-miss – so kudos for him, cringe-time for her, no doubt.

Still, both were better than ghosts and gunmen. *Anything* was better than that.

'What on earth is going on?' he wondered aloud.

Deepika sighed. 'Well, so far: we've had those guys try to snatch me in Mandore.'

'And that Jeetan guy who had that weird fit when he stepped into the ash-pit,' Amanjit reminded her.

'And so did I, if you remember,' she said. 'Even though there was nothing there – and I *knew* that – but it was still like I was stepping into a fire. And on the movie screen Shastri was attacking the girl who used to be me—'

'Not attacking,' Amanjit objected, '*restraining*. And it looked to me like he was trying to avoid that other woman.'

'Maybe,' Deepika said noncommittally. 'But even so, I have absolutely no idea what it all means.' Her mobile rang and she jumped, then hesitantly peered at the display. 'It's Vikram,' she mouthed to Amanjit before answering, then, 'Hi, Vikram!'

Amanjit grunted. He really didn't want to be interrupted right now, and especially not by Vikram . . . but there was something wrong, because Deepika's voice had changed and now she sounded worried – *really* worried.

He stopped daydreaming and listened in as she said, '—*Amanjit's* sister? Really? Oh— No, no, of course we'll come over right now!' As she hung up she started, 'It's your sister – something happened at the Maharaja's Library – Vikram was there too. She fainted – he thinks we should get there as soon as we can.'

Ras!

Amanjit's mind was racing even as he leapt to his feet and grabbed his jacket.

If something has happened to my sister, there will be hell to pay . . .

Vikram looked up as Amanjit burst into the little private room at the back of the library, but he had eyes only for his sister. 'Ras!' he shouted, 'Ras?'

She was slumped in an armchair, but as he reached her he saw that she was sipping chai.

'Hi,' she said weakly.

'What happened?' Deepika demanded as she followed Amanjit into the room.

'I fainted,' Ras said.

Her voice sounded uncharacteristically dreamy – or drunk, even, Amanjit thought – but perhaps it was shock.

Vikram looked around to ensure they couldn't be overheard by anyone, staff or visitors, then he leaned forward and said conspiratorially, 'No, it's worse than that. Something made her faint: a ghost of a woman, a young woman, in a really ancient style of clothing, like a mediaeval princess.'

Deepika looked at Amanjit. 'Maybe we should tell Ras what we've seen—?'

Ras blinked blearily, but she was aware enough to look questioningly at Deepika. Amanjit, still looking worried, stroked her arm, trying as much to distract her as comfort her. *We shouldn't be speaking in front of her. This isn't anything to do with her . . . I hope . . .* But if she'd seen that ghostly woman, perhaps she was? In which case ignorance would be no protection. He decided it wasn't his decision alone and raised a hand. 'Wait – before we say any more, we have to decide: is Ras part of this, or not?'

His sister opened her mouth in protest. 'Hey! I'm the one

who saw that thing! I'm involved, whether I like it or not!' She stuck her chin out defiantly, much more the girl Amanjit was used to.

The shock must be wearing off, he thought. He didn't like the idea that she really was involved; far better she was kept well away from all this, in his view, but the dangers were too real to ignore. Amanjit looked to Deepika for support, but as she hesitated, Vikram jumped in.

'Look, I know you don't like it, but I think Ras *is* part of this,' he said quickly. 'I don't think she could have seen that ghost-woman if she wasn't. And you should have seen what happened . . . it was as if the ghost *recognised* her.'

Amanjit flinched.

Ras nodded emphatically, suddenly animated. 'He's right: it did! I saw the way it looked at me! And then – IT RAN AWAY FROM ME!' she exclaimed loudly, thumping the armrest. 'And I know her name: she's called *Padma*.' She looked triumphantly at Amanjit. 'See? I must be part of . . . whatever it is you're all doing!'

Amanjit sighed dejectedly. 'Okay, okay, you're in.' Ras lifted her chin and grinned at him and he said quickly, 'For now!' He rolled his eyes, then looked at Deepika. 'You see what I have to put up with?' he complained.

Ras listened, increasingly bewildered, as the three of them recounted their adventures, shaking her head as she looked from one to another. They'd been attacked at Mandore, in the old palace gardens; and her brother and Deepika – *who'd been on a date!* – had seen something strange at the cinema that they clearly weren't telling everything about.

Vikram clearly sensed there was more too, because he asked Amanjit, 'So what did you see on the screen again?'

'This "Shastri" was holding down one of the queens while another watched. But he wasn't trying to hurt her,' he said firmly, looking at Deepika.

Ras knew her brother – she knew that look. Her brother could be silly, reckless and careless, but he was truthful.

And he obviously really, really *likes this Delhi-miss . . .*

'Deepika?' Vikram asked, turning to her.

'I saw the same thing,' she replied, after sharing a wordless look with Amanjit.

Vikram didn't look satisfied, but with a heavy exhalation, he let it go. 'Well, then. We need to decide what to do next. I wouldn't be surprised if those men who chased us at Mandore know where we all live. This is coming to a head.'

The three of them looked at each other, then, reluctantly, at Ras. If the older teens weren't so earnest, she might have stormed away angrily; there was no room in her life for make-believe. Her illnesses were too real for that.

But it was her turn, and she reported what she'd experienced, saying finally, 'This is all too weird. If I hadn't seen that woman coming through the wall myself—' She shuddered and whispered, 'I thought my heart was going to seize up once and for all.' As she spoke, she couldn't stop looking fearfully at the window.

The library staff had helped Vikram revive her, and one of the older matrons, the one who'd brought her chai, was peering through the glass at them all now. All the ladies knew was that Ras had fainted, and though they knew she wasn't very strong at the best of times, it was quite clear they thought there was more to it than that, especially now the four of them were talking so animatedly.

The door was pushed open and the matron appeared with a tray with three more cups of chai. She peered at them curiously as they chorused their thanks, but no one said anything other than, 'Great tea!' – that was Amanjit, who'd taken a sip of the chai – very sweet, and heavily spiced with mint and cinnamon – and, 'Gosh, I needed that!' from Vikram, and, 'Thanks so much – you've been so kind to Ras.' That was Deepika.

Once the matron was gone, Vikram pulled out his notebook. 'Listen up,' he said confidently, 'I found some stuff I'm pretty sure relates to what's going on here – in fact, it's all starting to come together. As it turns out, I was right in my guesses.'

'Miraculous,' Amanjit remarked drolly. Deepika flashed him a warning look, and Ras punched him lightly. He pretended it hurt.

Vikram gave them all a martyred look, and went on, 'Listen up, okay? A thousand years ago or more, Jodhpur was barely a village – Mandore was the capital, and that palace we visited today was the heart of it. Actually, hardly anything is known about the period because the imperial court moved away to Avanti, but I did find this note here that talks about a Raja of Mandore called Ravindra Attrapatta – and this guy had six or seven queens and when he died, they were all cast into his funeral pyre. But his son Chetan died the same day, and there were no heirs of age so the dynasty ended. Apparently the maharaja took control of Mandore again, but then let it go into decay again and it never really recovered.'

Ras liked this new Vikram, full of passion and authority. It made him more like the person she imagined he could be; and she was pleased to see the respect her brother was showing him.

It looked like Vikram could barely contain his excitement as he picked up the shabby little tome and showed them a note, something he'd translated about this 'Ravindra Attrapatta'. 'Here's the thing, though: it's signed – look: "A.D." – it has to be Aram Dhoop, the same poet I did my detention essay about!'

'Why does it have to be this Dhoop guy? Those initials – they could just be a coincidence, couldn't they?' Deepika looked at Amanjit for support.

Vikram continued, 'Not when that sadhu in Mandore goes and calls me "Aram Dhoop", don't forget – *and* I'm dreaming dreams about his life.'

Ras stared at him. 'You're having weird dreams too?' she asked.

Everyone looked at her, and then at each other, and Amanjit groaned. 'Ras, are you also having nightmares?' he asked gently.

'Every night!' She bobbed her head. 'There's a fire. And this evil man and his wife . . . and a brother who just watches and never does anything to help.' She shot a look at Amanjit. 'Sound familiar?'

Amanjit hung his head and cursed. It was true; he didn't have a great track record when it came to helping out, both his sister and his mother. But if she was dreaming as well, then she really was involved, whether he liked it or not, and that was far worse.

He looked closer at his sister. 'Ras-didi, you don't look so good.'

They all turned. 'No, no, I'm fine,' she said dazedly. 'Really. I want to be—' But even as she spoke, a wave of dizziness and exhaustion struck her. Her vision blurred and swayed . . . and then—

Amanjit lunged in and caught his sister as she slumped forward. He eased her back into the armchair. 'Didi?' he said softly, 'Ras?'

Her eyes rolled up and her head swayed, then she half caught herself and stared at him dazedly. 'What?'

'Okay, that's it. I'm taking you home.' The library would be closing soon anyway, so they needed to get a move on themselves.

Ras protested halfheartedly, but Amanjit thought she looked relieved as they hailed a taxi. He got her into the back seat, with Deepika on the other side and Vikram in the front with the driver.

As they wound through the streets of Jodhpur, Deepika asked, 'Is she okay?'

He turned and glanced at her and shook his head. 'No. She's never been okay.' He looked down at the slight figure cradled in his arms, but Ras looked completely out of it, so he decided he could talk. 'The doctors are surprised she's made it this far.'

Deepika looked at him with horrified sympathy. 'Oh, Amanjit, that's awful.' She leaned forward and laid a hand on his shoulder and squeezed.

Was it wrong to luxuriate in such a moment with everything else that was going on? He didn't see why not – especially as Vikram looked sharply away.

She took her hand back and he turned and flashed her a grateful smile, then the taxi was out into the cut and thrust of the traffic. There were lots of people about, and lots of noise, but Ras remained asleep all the way home.

With Deepika and Vikram following, Amanjit carried her up the stairs. His mother was in the lounge, asleep on the couch, so they put Ras onto her bed and then crept up to the roof. The Mehrangarh loomed above the city, the lamps that lit its walls at night lending it majesty: an enthroned monarch brooding alone in the night.

Deepika exclaimed aloud at the view. 'It's even more beautiful than the Red Fort in Old Delhi,' she said, gazing at it in awe, which pleased Amanjit immensely.

They all stared at the old fortress, each wondering if what Vikram had said about their past lives really was true.

'So, what do we know?' Amanjit asked finally, as they settled against the walls of the roof and sipped Cokes.

Vikram produced a small, old-fashioned-looking book. The title page read, *The Latter Verse of Aram Dhoop, Poet of Mandore*. 'So look: there's this, a book by the poet Aram Dhoop, who may or may not have been me in a previous life. I found it in the school library during my detention. Aram Dhoop wrote lots of poetry – but most of his early work was lost, apparently, and anyway, he refers to it as "excrement" in the foreword to this book. There are three types of poems in this book: the main type is love-poetry, and lots of it. The object of his affections is always the same: a Persian girl for whom he has an overwhelming adoration, but she is oblivious to him. In the second type, he writes about the Hill of Birds – that's the Bhaurcheeria, the locals' name for the hill the Mehrangarh was built on. He obsesses about the place – not just the hill itself, but all the birds on it, the reptiles, the plants. And he especially writes about caves within the hill.'

'The Mehrangarh,' Amanjit repeated, looking up again, savouring the sound of the word. Like most Jodhpurians, he'd visited it many times. He'd loved climbing those walls, staring along the cannon-barrels on the battlements, imagining where the balls might strike if he fired them. He used to imagine armies besieging him there, and fighting them off with cannon and rifle. 'I didn't know there were caves . . .'

Vikram tapped the book. 'Well, Aram Dhoop clearly thought so. But listen, there was a third type of poem he wrote . . .' Vikram stopped and took a deep breath. He looked worried. 'So, the third lot are all about the *Ramayana*, especially this huge epic poem he wrote, about Rama and the overthrow of Ravana, the Demon King of Lanka, which is a retelling in verse of the epic.'

'Ha!' exclaimed Amanjit. 'The *Ramayana* again!'

'I think you're reading too much into this *Ramayana* thing,' Deepika said. 'I don't see how that can have anything to do with us . . .'

Vikram had moved from looking worried to unhappy. 'Yes, but . . . like we said the other day . . . if my father married Amanjit's mum, then the family structure would be exactly like the

Ramayana: three queens, four sons. Aram Dhoop was obsessed with the *Ramayana*. And Mandore was where Ravana the Demon King married Mandodari, the Queen of the Asuras. I know it's thin, but the link is definitely there . . .' His voice trailed off and they sat silently, gazing off into space.

Amanjit didn't know what to believe – he kept changing his mind – but Deepika was nodding as if she'd got it. Then again, Amanjit had nodded along with the other students in maths class for years just so he wouldn't appear stupid, and yet he still struggled with long division. Vikram was the only one of them who'd really got a handle on any of this. It felt odd, like a concession of leadership, to ask him for direction, but he found himself doing so anyway.

'So what do you think we should do?'

Vikram looked as if he'd been waiting for that very question. 'We need to go up there – to the Mehrangarh – and look for caves beneath. Those notes I showed you? They're just the main points – there are lots of hints in the full document, all about what happened to Ravindra and his son and the dead queens, and the Mehrangarh is mentioned more than once.' He looked about them. 'Tomorrow?'

Amanjit couldn't think why not, and after sharing a long look with Deepika, they both nodded in assent.

'Good.' Vikram let out his breath. 'But in the meantime, I don't think we should be together. It seems to me that it was all of us coming together that attracted these entities that are trailing us, and the more often we're together, the worse things get. And we shouldn't bring Ras along unless she is well,' he added in a low voice.

Amanjit agreed wholeheartedly with that bit at least. He suddenly remembered another thing. 'Hey, Vikram, you know something else? Ras . . . well, that's just her nickname, you know? Her full name . . . it's Rasita.'

Vikram looked at him and groaned. 'You're kidding me! Rasita . . . so, *Sita*?'

'As in Sita from the *Ramayana*, yes. And while we're at it, your name contains seventy-five per cent of the name "Rama",' he added with a humourless chuckle.

Vikram said emphatically, 'That's just coincidence, nothing more.'

All I Hold Dear

Mandore, Rajasthan, AD *769*

'All I hold dear?' Shastri said coldly, his voice carrying down the slope. '*All I hold dear?*' He spat. 'All I hold dear are *dead*, Jeet. Dead, or right here.'

Jeet grinned, his white teeth a distant gleam. 'At last! I have waited so long for this, Shastri. At last your true cowardly, treasonous nature is laid bare, O Renowned Senapati; at last we see you for the lecherous traitor you are.' He spread his hands, clearly speaking as much for his followers as to Shastri. 'How long have you been having the Persian girl? How long have you been despoiling the queen, bringing the curse of the gods on to us all? You adulterous traitor, prepare to die!'

A cloud of men gathered behind him, their weapons glittering in the moonlight. Their faces were angry; clearly they believed Jeet's words, even men he would have once believed loyal to him. His heart sank when he glimpsed Tilak, shouting along with the rest.

Jeet lifted a hand, pointing up the long slope towards the fugitives. 'Advance! Take them alive!'

Shastri turned and snapped at Aram, 'Run! *Run, damn you!*'

To his relief, the poet required no second command. His legs pumping, he went surging up the slope, gasping for air, as if terrified that in spite of Jeet's order, an arrow would hiss from the darkness and puncture his body. But to Shastri, such a clean death would be a kindness compared to what awaited if they were taken alive. He glanced at the rani and caught her eye, seeing that she knew what awaited them only too well.

If we fall into their hands, it mustn't be whilst we can still draw breath.

Shastri couldn't remember ever being so afraid in his life, and he'd seen battle, killed men, even cheated death a time or two. But he'd survived all that; he was damned if he wouldn't survive this. Rage at Jeet and his men fuelled his determination to live. Miracles *could* happen.

Beside him, Darya laboured purposefully, her face set and hard as she strained to control her own fear. He admired that; he admired her. If he had to die, better it be in her service than serving a monster like Chetan or Ravindra.

He muttered a prayer to Vishnu, asking his protection, then cast about him, surveying the lie of the land. They could not just flee blindly in the darkness: somewhere, somehow, they had to make a stand.

They reached the top of the slope where Aram and Darya had hidden only moments before – had it really been so short a space of time? As Aram turned and looked back, Darya ran past him, gasping. Then Shastri was beside him, throwing the packs down and snatching the bow from Aram's hand. With practised grace he pulled an arrow from the quiver on Aram's back, nocked it, drew and fired.

The leading soldier cried out and pitched backwards down the rocky slope, and the rest shouted in alarm and faltered. They were strung out, a ragged charge with the fittest and fastest pursuers at the front, the late arrivals just starting the climb.

'Keep moving!' Jeet's voice carried up from somewhere in the midst of the advancing pack. Aram could see that Shastri was trying to pick him out for his next arrow, but Jeet was too wily to make a target of himself.

Twang! Thock! A second soldier screamed and slumped forward, clutching an arrow in his thigh. Shastri grunted, groping for another arrow, but already the next two soldiers were nearly upon them.

'Senapati!' Darya called, 'let me!'

She took the bow, which he relinquished immediately, unable to hide his surprise – but there wasn't room to debate anyway; it was time for sword-work. He drew his blade as the two soldiers in the lead bellowed their war-cries and charged towards the cleft the fugitives were defending. Aram drew his sword, though he'd never held a real sword in all his life and had little idea what to do with it now.

Darya aimed and loosed and the first pursuer fell with an arrow in his throat.

Aram propped the quiver against her leg and backed away from her to give her the space to work. His eyes were drinking her in. She was magnificent in that instant, touched by the divine: Durga, slaying the demon armies in her fury. Careless of her ruined clothing, all her focus upon her next target, she was a thing of power, beauty and death, carved in stone. He almost fell to his knees in worship. Then the sound of the charge tore his attention away: the first man had reached the cleft.

Shastri rose in a blur and stabbed downwards, punching his blade through the man's breast, and he fell with a surprised gurgle, his face a mask of shock as he rolled down the slope.

A cloud of Jeet's warriors stormed past the dead man, shouting in fury.

Aram clenched his fists in despair, his head sinking. There were too many, surely, and he could do nothing to help . . . He dropped his head, and found himself staring down at the rock before him, terror and despair fogging his mind. Then metal and leather scraped the other side of the boulder, and he looked up—

—then darted backwards as a curved blade, gleaming silver in the moonlight, flashed and struck the rock where his head had been, sending a ribbon of sparks into the air as the steel chimed.

He yelped, stumbled, and lost his sword.

The man with the scimitar darted around the boulder, grinning fiendishly, and Aram quaked, groping for the lost sword and instead coming up with just a rock. He hurled it, and more by luck than judgement, he caught the man in the face. The soldier, knocked off his feet, then tripped backwards. He was trying to get up again when one of Darya's arrows appeared, quivering in his chest. The man gasped breathlessly, then he sagged and his body slid into the darkness.

Aram threw her a grateful look, but her eyes were already fixed on the next target. Her hands a blur, another man cried and toppled backwards with an arrow jutting horribly from his eye socket; a third clutched a shaft in his shoulder. But her fourth arrow missed and a huge warrior immediately filled the gap between the boulders, roaring in rage.

Shastri took a massive blow on his shield, but he retaliated immediately, ramming his sword up and through the man's guard, straight into his chest. He planted his foot in the man's belly and kicked. Curved blades intruded from either side of the narrow gap, but the captain was already moving, parrying one with his blade and the other with his shield, punching the shield into the soldier's face, and then sweeping his sword in a great arc, snapping the talwar that caught his blow. The man holding it was caught unaware, and unable to stop himself overbalancing, he took down the man behind him as well. Somewhere below, Aram could hear One-Eyed Jeet as he bellowed and cursed, driving his soldiers on.

Another man came around the boulder and ran at Aram with his curved talwar straight before him.

Never had Aram regretted his insignificant stature more. He felt so *useless* – and not just useless, but a burden – surely without him, Rani Darya and the senapati could have escaped their pursuers . . . But this was survival. He screamed out his fury as his hand finally found his sword-hilt, and for want of anything to do with it, he threw. It missed, but the man had to jerk sideways, and his right leg slipped and got wedged under one side of the boulder, kicking loose some small stones . . .

. . . and the boulder rolled back about a hand's-breadth, and crushed his ankle. The man shrieked in agony, then one of the rani's arrows shut him up; he sagged and went limp. Aram stared at him, and then at the boulder.

What if . . . ?

He placed both hands against the boulder he was cowering behind and shoved, using every bit of force he could muster. But it wouldn't move further, wedged as it was on the fallen soldier's leg, cradled by the rocks beneath. He cast about him, thinking, *Leverage! I need more leverage!*

A spear jabbed through the gap beside his left shoulder, but Shastri just managed to catch it on his shield. The senapati managed to push aside the viciously barbed head, then hacked at the shaft until it broke in two, but an instant later another had snaked out, and this one pierced his shoulder.

He grunted and staggered, and Queen Darya screamed something in her own tongue and fired an arrow at point-blank range into the face of the spearman.

Aram dived for the nearest piece of broken spear-shaft and found himself tugging against the weight of its wielder, who was trying to pick it up. He let go instantly, and the spearman, suddenly pulling against nothing, yowled in horror as he went backwards and fell down the slope.

Aram picked up the length of broken spear and looked up to see Shastri still fighting, still protecting them. Beside him, Rani Darya was out of arrows, but she'd drawn a sword and was stabbing at the flanks of anyone trying to get through the gap in the two boulders to engage the captain. Between them they were holding their own; but it couldn't last as more and more men were reaching them, and Jeet's voice was terrifyingly close.

Aram rammed the broken shaft into the point where the boulder had moved, where it met the rocky slope, ignoring the splinters that pierced his hands; he shouted through the sudden, unexpected pain, and heaved once, twice and then again.

'Get them!' Jeet shouted, only yards away now. 'Get around both sides of those rocks! *Bring them down!*'

Aram's terror lent him a strength he never knew he had. The shaft almost broke, but this time the boulder shuddered, sending stones rippling away down the slope, skittering among the feet of the advancing men. He looked up, saw the first of the new wave of attackers begin to appear around the boulder, stumbling over the body of the man with the crushed ankle. There was time for only one more pull on the spear-shaft . . .

Beside him, he saw Shastri stagger back from the cleft, his left arm limp, and the gap was filled almost immediately with another of Jeet's inexhaustible supply of warriors. With his eyes fixed on his captain, he started shouting something, though Aram couldn't hear what. *Not very respectful, I don't think.* The senapati parried weakly, while beyond them another man was rounding the far boulder, grinning savagely at the rani.

'Put the sword down, girl,' he taunted. 'It'll go easier on you.' He reached out, his expression filled with complacent lust.

Aram opened his mouth in horror as Darya looked as if she'd just lost the will to fight. She sagged into the man's open arms, almost gratefully . . .

Then with a vicious two-handed blow, she buried a hand's-breadth of steel in the man's throat and ripped the dagger sideways. Blood sprayed and the man gurgled, clawing at the wound, and fell backwards.

The soldier fighting Shastri made the mistake of letting that sight steal his attention, and before he could recover, Shastri had stepped in, smashing his hilt into the man's face, shattering his nose and rocking his head back with the force of his blow.

As the soldier collapsed backwards, Aram turned to the boulder, and *heaved* with all his might, and at last it rocked in place, then went over with a thunderous crash and careened down the hillside, rolling straight over the man who'd been coming at him. Aram heard the *crack* of bones and the hideous *squish* of crushed flesh as the boulder went careening down the slope, smashing over every man in its path.

Then the whole world shuddered, as if the gods themselves had pounded it with great hammers. There was a dull roar and the top of the slope fell after his boulder. Jeet's men howled in terror as they were swept away, their captain among them. Even in the darkness Aram could see the black cloud that arose as the ground disappeared.

He'd already moved backwards, but before he could grab them he saw the packs vanish – then, in a heart-stopping moment, Senapati Shastri teetered on the jagged edge. But the rani was there; she reached out and grabbed his sword-belt and threw her weight backwards, hauling Shastri down with her. The two of them crashed to the ground, a pace away from the new edge.

Below them, the men on the slope were still crying out, but now most sounded frightened or injured, wailing for aid as the slip bore the rest away.

Shastri clutched his shoulder, wincing as his hand came away slick with blood. As the adrenalin of the fight dissipated he felt nauseous with pain – but there was no time for weakness. He looked at the woman lying beside him. Breathing hard, her hands trembling, she was re-tying the cloak he'd taken from dead Biltan around her waist. But her gaze was level as she looked at him, somehow both vulnerable and remote. His rani. His queen.

'Thank you, Rani-ji,' he panted. 'You have great skill with the bow.'

Her eyes flickered and she looked at him warily. He wondered if she had seen something in his face that frightened her; it wouldn't have surprised him. Women were not used to seeing battle. *And I probably look a mess*. But they couldn't stay there and discuss the matter. He clambered to his feet and staggered to the edge of the slope. The near-full moon was falling away to the west, but the night was barely half done.

The rockfall started by the boulder the poet had thrown down the hillside – *How did a man that slight manage such a feat?* – had changed the whole slope. The boulder itself now lay shattered at the bottom, with earth, broken branches and shattered rocks piled up around it. For all that the slip it had triggered had been dramatic, it had not dealt with all their foes. There were a few bodies unmoving, but most were gathering themselves and clambering shakily to their feet. There would be a good few broken bones and cracked ribs, he hoped, but Jeet was down there, cursing his men, exhorting them to get up and get back to the job, and they were reacting. He counted quickly: ten . . . fifteen . . . seventeen . . . and more were coming; he could hear the horns summoning the rest of his men.

He took stock of their position: it was still possible to climb the slope, but without that huge boulder, it was less defensible now. Where before they'd been able to restrict Jeet's men to attacking two or three at a time, now they would be open to the whole squad, and there was no way they'd be able to repeat Aram's trick with the other boulder. Darya had found eight or nine arrows among the equipment of the fallen, but that wouldn't be near enough.

'There are too many, Rani,' he told her. 'And we cannot hold this place a second time. We must go now.'

Aram Dhoop groaned; his hands were bleeding and his eyes were glassy, but he rolled to a sitting position, breathing heavily, as the rani asked, 'Where will we go, Senapati?'

Shastri cast his mind back to previous expeditions to the Hill of Birds, trying to remember the lie of the land. Ravindra-Raj had talked of building a fortress up here – as had the Maharaja before him – but such a project was beyond the resource of Mandore. He couldn't recall anything useful from those visits in their current predicament.

'I don't know precisely where to as yet, Rani, but we must find a more defensible place quickly, or we will be overwhelmed.' He looked back into the shadowy broken top of the hill. 'We'll go south along this flank and try to ward off any attempt to take us with bow and sword. Then before dawn we must slip away.'

He offered a hand first to the queen and then to the poet, pulling them both to their feet. They were bloodied and filthy, and all were exhausted, but their eyes glittered with resolve, heartening him. They would need all their courage to seize what little chance there was. He liked the grim set of their jaws. There was more steel in them than he had expected – even the poet. He clapped the man on the shoulder and said, 'Well done, Aram Dhoop. Your quick thinking saved us.' He squeezed the man's skinny shoulders. 'Hanuman-ji himself could not have moved that boulder!'

Aram Dhoop ducked his head, looking embarrassed, especially when the queen also beamed at him. *He saved us*, Shastri acknowledged silently. *There's more to him than just songs and verse.* He remembered the heart-stone Padma had given him, still in his belt-pouch, and made a mental note to give it to the poet when there was time. But that wasn't now.

He turned and bowed to Darya. 'Do we have your permission to move, my queen?'

She drew herself to her full height, looking admirably composed, and agreed. 'Yes, Senapati, please, lead on.'

He'd seen commanders on campaign with less self-possession in a crisis. He was warming to her more than ever.

He took them along the western face of the hill, as fast as caution would allow. At the next gully they saw men moving; they'd run along the gully below to get ahead and were now ascending towards their new position. He let them get nearly halfway up, then sent a shaft among them that nailed one on the arm and scattered the rest of them, at least temporarily deterring further ascent.

But all too soon they heard shouting behind them: Jeet's men had gained the top, the place they'd previously defended. Shastri cursed, but he kept them moving and they found themselves in the middle of a maze of boulders, following a vague, meandering path leading downwards into some kind of dell deep in the middle of the hill. Looking back, they could all see tongues of fire strung out across the summit, a loose cordon of men with torches, each only a few paces apart. 'They are sweeping the hilltop, Senapati,' Darya commented, her voice commendably steady.

'They mean to herd us south.' Shastri looked about them. 'If we climb to the heights, we will be seen in silhouette. We must find a low place and let them slip past us in the darkness.'

'But where? Or do you have somewhere in mind?'

He did; a memory of a previous expedition had finally come to him. 'Last time I was here, I came across a small shrine to Hanuman, near the south end. I spoke to the hermit who dwelt there, and though he did not come out and say it, I got the firm impression that he actually lived in a cave behind the shrine – there might even be more than one, perhaps even with exits lower down, if the gods are with us.'

'Can you find this place?'

'Yes . . . and to my knowledge, Jeet knows nothing of it.'

'Perfect, then.' She looked up at him, searching his face. 'Or is it?'

'It could be perfect, or it could be a death trap. I don't know.'

She reached out and put her hand on his. 'I trust you, Senapati. I trust your judgement.'

Shastri was shocked to find how *right* that small moment of connection felt. 'Then we will try it, Rani-ji.'

He looked at the poet – and found himself staring into a face burning with jealousy.

Oh no, not that. Not now . . .

Aram hated the way the man moved, like a big cat, afraid of nothing. He hated his competence, and his frank, open face. He remembered Shastri's guarded, reserved manner at court, and how he had always feared him, believing him to be nothing more than just another butcher in the service of Ravindra-Raj. He hadn't seen the nobility, the courage and the burning loyalty, for it had been hidden, waiting to be brought to light: waiting for *her*.

She is my *queen – I pulled her from the fire! She is* mine!

But what could he say, when he was riven with such envy and shame? Their lives hung in the balance and they needed to depend on each other – it was dishonourable to have such base thoughts at such a time.

But why does she have to look at him with such an admiring gaze?

He prayed to Vishnu for fortitude and Shiva for inspiration, but mostly he prayed to Parvati, the good wife, for forgiveness.

It was still some time till dawn, though in the east there was a subtle light in the sky. After some more painstakingly careful, silent creeping, Shastri suddenly gripped Aram's arm and pulled him to a halt. 'Behold,' he whispered.

A large grey shape sitting upon a rock beside a dark cleft moved suddenly, emitting a soft screech that almost sounded like a greeting, and then it vanished down the cleft. A powerful animal smell rose from the hole: dung and urine and fur, strong and musky.

Aram glanced back, then grabbed Darya's arm in alarm.

Behind them was a chain of men, maybe a hundred paces to the north, walking slowly towards them. For an instant he thought they'd been seen, but then he realised that they were low enough down and deep enough in the shadows to be invisible, especially as the moon was now almost gone, and only the starlight lit their way – at least until the torches came much closer. He looked southwards: the maze of paths resolved itself in a climb towards a bare knoll. There was no way forward that would not expose them against the southern skies. The only place they could hide was at the bottom of this cleft, where the shrine lay. The senapati had placed them in Hanuman's hands. For good or ill, they would live or die here.

'Come,' Shastri whispered. 'We must link hands, to keep together in the dark.' He held out a hand to Darya, who took it, and try as he might, Aram couldn't watch them together, despite all the terror he felt. Then the rani reached out her other hand to Aram.

'Come, my good poet, let us brave the darkness together.'

Her hand was sweaty, and quivering with suppressed terror, and also the most valuable thing he'd ever grasped.

Thus linked, they inched their way step by step into the blackness of the shrine.

Using his free arm to feel their way along the wall, Shastri inched his way downwards, each step tentative for he had no idea what lay before them. Queen Darya's hand felt tiny in his, but terribly precious. Looking back, he could see a rough triangle of deep blue: the sky, glowing softly in the pre-dawn light. But down here in the darkness, unseen things skittered away, chattering angrily. Every moment he expected to hear sudden screeching, and huge teeth tearing at his throat, but though they were surrounded by the beasts, so far, the monkeys had kept away from them. When he looked up, he could make out several of them clinging to the sides of the cleft, above and behind, and it felt like they were following them down.

Then they heard voices shouting from above: 'Did you hear that?' someone yelled.

Then another bellowed, 'Look, another hole!'

Shastri pulled Darya against him and bending them both low, almost carried her forward, seeking a place where they might not be visible from above.

An orange torch filled the triangle of sky, and its light stabbed the darkness about them.

'Lo—'

The soldier's voice suddenly cut off and the torch tumbled into the cleft, starting a riot amongst the monkeys, who shrieked and screamed as they flinched away from the unwelcome light. Cracks and holes in the ceiling and walls were revealed, along with dozens of nests – and what looked like hundreds of glinting eyes, and everywhere, yellowed teeth bared in fury. Then a body toppled into the crack and thumped to the ground, his mail rattling against the stone.

Shastri recognised Roshan, one of Jeet's thugs – and his throat had been opened from ear to ear. The torch he'd been holding fell with him and landed in the sand where it lay flickering.

Darya and Aram gasped, and Shastri stared, then looked up again.

There was shouting above them, and the clatter of arrows rattling against the rock, then a dark shape holding a lit torch leapt from above and crashed against the wall before landing heavily beside the fallen Roshan: a familiar bulk, his face lit by his torch.

Shastri grabbed Darya's shoulder as she went to draw an arrow. 'No, Rani!' he warned, then peered at the newcomer, scarcely daring to hope. 'Til?'

'Captain.' Tilak's laconic voice rolled down the cleft. 'Sorry about this. I'd hoped we'd manage to pass this place by, but Roshan saw you, so I had to act.' He grunted with brief regret, then grinned. 'So, how're you faring?' he asked casually, as if this were nothing more than a friendly hunting expedition.

'Better for seeing you. Now get yourself out of sight before they start shooting again.'

Tilak grimaced and hurried towards him, sure-footed in the torchlight. When he reached Roshan's fallen torch, he swept it up. 'Shall I bring this?'

Shastri nodded. 'Give it to the poet, and I'll take yours. Can you cover the rear? I'll lead.' He waited until Til nodded agreement – this wasn't a place for orders and rank – then turned back to Aram and Darya. 'This is Tilak. Rani, you may trust him, as I do, with my life.'

Tilak grinned suddenly and bowed low. 'You two stay in the middle and light the way for us.'

'Let's go,' Shastri said. 'We may yet get out of this,' he added with a sudden surge of conviction. He lifted the torch Tilak had handed him and ducked through the doorway to the shrine, fearful of presenting a target to the men above. 'Quickly, get inside!'

Voices echoed from above as they hurried into the bowels of the hill, and loudest was Jeet's voice, swearing and cursing like a market-square harridan. Shastri prayed to every god in the pantheon that this cave was not a dead end. But it had the feel of one.

The actual shrine to Hanuman was at the bottom of a long slope. It was a crude place, little more than a small, flat-ceilinged chamber where someone had carved a rock into the likeness of a squatting monkey, garlanded it with marigolds and basted it with orange and red paste-dyes. Old blackened stubs of votive tapers were stabbed like the quills of a porcupine into a mound of sand before the monkey statue. The place stank of monkey; the tribe watched them from their untidy nests in the walls, hissing and chattering indignantly. There was no sign of any priest.

'It's been abandoned,' Shastri guessed, casting about him.

Aram lifted his torch, illuminating the darkness beyond the shrine. After a moment he said, 'Not abandoned.' He couldn't quite hide the quaver in his voice.

The torchlight revealed a slumped form in rotting robes. There was long white hair still attached to the skull, but many of the bones were lying scattered about, gnawed and broken.

Shastri wondered whether the old man had been dead before the monkeys had started on him. He shook his head. *Now is not the time.* Queen Darya was breathing heavily, and when he gripped her shoulder, he could feel her shaking. 'Come, Rani,' he said calmly. 'We must move.'

Aram laid a protective hand on her shoulder. 'She doesn't like being underground.'

Shastri swallowed. 'Is this the paralysing fear?' he asked her. He'd seen grown men, hardened fighters, frightened of heights, or spiders. Some people had that type of weakness.

Darya shook her head bravely. 'No, I am just not used to such things,' she said, as if defying her own nature.

Shastri sympathised, but there was no choice. 'I am sorry. We must still go on.'

Darya jerked her head in assent, her face distressed, but she fixed her eyes on Shastri and followed him as he led the way through the cleft they found at the back of the shrine. Aram followed them, holding the torch to light the shrine.

Inside was all that was left of the hermit's home: smashed pottery, some rotted leaf bowls, a little dried-out rice the monkeys obviously hadn't wanted. An old staff hung with ribbons leaned against the wall, and a torn blanket was piled in one corner: all that was left of a lifetime of devotion.

'Look!' Aram held the torch up to the far wall, illuminating a monkey – and when the creature spat and fled, a narrow crack, just barely wide enough for them to crawl into. Darya groaned.

Shastri turned to Aram. 'I'll need to go first, then the rani. She must use that torch, poet,' he told Aram, taking the light from Aram's reluctant hand. He thrust it into Darya's hands, then held his own torch out in front of him. To his relief, the narrow crevice that the monkey had vanished down widened considerably, just a few paces in.

Heartened, he looked back at Til's silent bulk, silhouetted against the glow of torchlight from above. He was kneeling, his bow nocked and drawn.

'Follow me closely, Rani-ji,' he told Darya, looking at her fevered eyes. He would have given much to take this ordeal from her, but somehow, she would have to bear it. 'It is only fear, Highness,' he said, hoping he sounding sympathetic and not uncaring. 'Fear cannot kill.'

She bowed her head wordlessly, but then Tilak's bow twanged, and someone cried out in pain. He had another arrow ready in a heartbeat. 'Get moving, sir. If they rush us, we're dead.'

Shastri didn't want to say anything; that might be tempting fate. They were soldiers, after all; this is what they did. He clapped Til on the shoulder and silently turned back to the narrow hole. Thrusting the torch before him, he crawled in, head-first, and was soon forcing his way down the crack, hoping they were not just heading towards something far worse.

Once Shastri had turned and twisted out of sight, Aram seized the queen's hand. 'Rani, we will keep you safe,' he promised her. 'We will give you our lives, I swear.' He hoped he sounded more certain to her than he did to himself.

'Hush, my poet,' she whispered. 'Hush.' He felt her inner battle against the weight of rock and darkness that pressed down upon her, for he shared it. He too hated this place, the oppressive closeness of the air, the stench of animals, the feeling of being trapped – but he was more terrified of what pursued them and that was the only thing that kept him from fleeing back to the surface, gasping for pure air.

'We must follow him, Rani,' he said, his voice hoarse with fear. But he could see she was even more afraid. 'I'll go first,' he offered, stiffening his resolve, but she pushed ahead of him, trembling.

'No, I'll go.'

Of course: whoever came third would be crawling in almost

total darkness. His own fear almost made him push past her, but with fatalistic resignation, he stepped aside. She was the important one; his turn would come soon enough. She met his eyes for an instant, a moment of understanding, before she pushed the torch in her hand into the gap where Shastri had gone, and followed it. In a few moments she'd crawled through and was gone.

Aram looked back at Tilak, hunched over his bow: just a silent shadow, not even his breath audible. The poet had not really been aware of this man before. In his enclosed, perfumed world the common soldiers were brutish, hulking creatures, stinking of sweat and, too often, the metallic tang of blood: uncouth, illiterate creatures, subhuman, even, and very far removed from the heroes of the epics he loved so much. But this man was different. He was like Shastri. In the little time he'd been with them he'd shown humour, poise and fibre. He and Shastri were brothers-in-arms, true princes from the old tales. The contrast between them and the studied cruelty of Ravindra or the bestial corruption of Chetan was palpable – so how had he missed these virtues? And why did they still twist his gut so? Was he so low on virtue and character himself that a mere soldier could reduce him to such envy and self-pity?

Do you really think you could ever be the equal of such a 'heroic warrior' in her eyes?

He felt a hollow swelling of despair inside his chest and an insidious feeling crept over him: that no matter how this ended, for him there would be only tears. Swallowing a choked moan, he took a gulp of the foetid air and crawled into the dimly lit hole, following the flickering light of Darya's torch before it vanished. Already it was only the faintest glow, several bends ahead of him. The cave looked entirely natural, and he couldn't tell how high the ceiling was, only that judging by the air-flow, it was some distance above. As if to make the point, somewhere above his head a monkey chattered, then fell silent.

As he braced himself to follow Darya, something hissed outside, sounding like a chorus of snakes – but he recognised this sound now: it was a volley of arrows. He heard the shafts shattering and crashing against the rock walls, and men shouting from above, urging each other on. Then a bow twanged from close behind him, and outside the cave, someone screeched.

'Come on, boys,' he heard Tilak taunting them. 'I got lots more shafts, enough for all of you.'

There was silence from above and then suddenly someone screamed, and Aram heard Tilak fire again, and then Til shouted something himself, and his voice sounded hollowed out by fear. Then came the sound of falling rocks, more terrified cries, and the thud of metal, leather and flesh on rock. Aram gasped as a lit torch – presumably one dropped from above – was thrown into the shrine, then Tilak squeezed himself into the tunnel, his armour a real encumbrance, but at last he was in and for a moment he just lay there panting, his legs still in the tunnel. In the light of the dropped torch, Aram could see his face was plastered with sweat – and terror.

'What happened?' he asked anxiously.

'I – they—' Tilak looked panicked, as if he'd seen something far worse than the killers who were chasing them. 'I don't—'

'Soldier!' Aram tried to imitate an officer snapping at a junior to reassert discipline, and to his enormous astonishment it worked: Tilak flinched as if slapped, but at once regained control of himself.

'They fell – they all fell! It wasn't me – they were already dead!' Tilak's normally dry voice had a distinct quaver. 'Move! We've got to move: something worse is coming! It's co—!' Then his voice was cut off mid-word. He gave a sudden heart-rending scream, his eyes bulging as he spewed blood, then he flew backwards as if a giant had grasped his legs and pulled. The darkness behind him swallowed him whole.

The tiny tunnel, scarcely more than a womb-shaped crack, widened and then dropped at a sharp angle down into the depths. Shastri could hear water, the slow dripping of droplets into pools far below, far from the light. Once a black snake confronted him; it hissed and sidled away down a hole. He had never really been underground before, not like this, and he wasn't enjoying it, but the queen was behind him and her face was a mask of barely restrained terror. For her sake, he made himself appear calm.

The tunnel had changed, widened enough that he could turn himself around and slide down on his backside, descending feet-first. He kept up a smooth litany of instructions for the rani – *mind that rough edge, beware that loose rock* – to keep her focused on the practical, the achievable. He couldn't hear Aram Dhoop behind her, though. He cursed silently to himself: the poet and Til were too far behind them; they'd be descending blind. He would have to slow the rani down so they could wait for them.

The poet had done well so far – not a fighting man, but he'd shown some resourcefulness despite that, and a true heart. The very fact that Aram Dhoop had found the courage to snatch the queen from the flames when he himself had done nothing to save his own sister shamed him; and goaded him on. Yes, the poet was loyal. As he was.

And he was in love with the rani.

As he was.

Shastri couldn't put his finger on it, that moment when the realisation had come over him – perhaps at the top of the slope, when she fought with such skill and poise, the equal of any warrior of his command. Or maybe during the stalking that followed. Perhaps it was even as recently as the last time he had glanced back and met her eyes.

My queen, I would die for you.

He dropped the last couple of feet into a small chamber, landing smoothly on a floor of compacted sand, and then lifted the torch high to light her way. Queen Darya slid nimbly down the slope and dropped onto the floor beside him.

She looked around. 'This looks like a man-made tunnel, Senapati.' She sounded curious despite her fear.

That had been his first impression too – but before he could reply, their attention was distracted by a dreadful shriek that echoed through the tunnel, and the sound of the sudden scrabbling of a man descending in blind panic.

'Steady, Aram!' he called as the poet appeared, holding a torch – part of Shastri's mind asked, 'A torch?' – as Aram battered against the walls and ceiling in his panicked flight, gashing his limbs on the rough stone of the caves. His eyes were wide and his mouth was working silently, as if he were too frightened to actually speak.

'Aram!' He jumped aside as the poet launched himself from above and tumbled heavily to the sand. Even then he didn't stop, but rushed to the far wall, clawing at it as if to tear a hole through.

The rani threw her arms about the poet, trying to restrain him. 'Aram? Aram! You're safe! You're safe—'

There was no sign of Tilak following, and Shastri looked back at the poet. Something was very badly wrong; he'd not been this panicked before, not even in the midst of battle. He went over and put a hand on his shoulder. 'Aram, we're here. We're with you.' He looked up, straining his ears for movement. 'Where's Tilak?'

The poet just stared up into the darkness, panting and whimpering. Shastri bent over him, fear making him angry. 'Aram Dhoop!' he cried, his hand clenching more forcibly, 'tell me – where's Til?' He grabbed the young man's arm. 'Poet! *What's happened?*'

Aram looked up at him and swallowed hard, then visibly steadied himself. 'I . . . I was readying to follow you – I had entered the tunnel – when I heard Tilak being attacked. I heard him shooting arrows, and then I heard bodies hitting the ground, lots of them. Tilak ran back to the tunnel and threw himself in, though at first he got stuck, because of the armour. He was – he was very frightened. And he said the men who were falling into the crevice were already dead . . .'

'Already dead?' Darya asked, her voice shaky. 'What do you mean? Surely he killed them? He had a full quiver—'

Hearing her voice had a calming effect on the poet. He took a deep breath, and when he spoke again, he was far more composed. 'No, it wasn't Tilak who killed them; he said the men dropping from above were *already dead*. And then . . .' He closed his eyes, shuddering, and had to force himself to go on. 'Then someone seized Tilak's legs and pulled him back out of the tunnel. He struggled and cried out for help, but he was yanked back so fast – he was gone before I could reach him. I'm so very sorry,' he said to Shastri, tears filling his eyes. 'I thought I heard him cry out, just for an instant, and softly, as if through a gag, and then . . .' He stopped, unwilling or unable to finish the sentence.

'Go on,' Shastri said gently. 'I think we need to know, however dreadful . . .'

Darya nodded, and Aram whispered, 'There were these awful sounds, like . . . like flesh being torn.' He looked up at Shastri with haunted eyes. 'I ran, sir. I ran—'

Shastri tried to picture the moment, and confronted with

that, he decided he would likely have run too. He looked up at the hole in the rock, straining his ears to catch any signs of pursuit, but all he could hear was the poet's panting.

Darya looked at him. 'What's going on? What happened to Tilak?'

'I don't know, Rani.' Shastri looked up again, trying to think. Were there other men up here? Bandits? A war party from another kingdom, who'd been drawn to the pursuit? That was the only answer that made sense. Either way, he doubted these newcomers would be any more merciful if they found them.

'We must move on,' he told Darya and Aram at last. 'There is no safety behind us, and we cannot stay here.'

They examined the tunnel they'd dropped into, looking for a way out. Neither direction offered clues, beyond the fact that one direction went upward, and the other down. He'd tried to keep his bearings since they'd entered the cave, and if he was right, the downwards tunnel was heading roughly southwest.

'I don't know,' he repeated. 'I don't understand anything, except that we must keep moving.' He pointed in the downwards direction. 'Perhaps this way leads out of the hill? The other way feels unsafe – it goes back towards the area we just left – perhaps it's another tunnel to the shrine.'

And to whatever killed Tilak, and all Jeet's men, he added silently.

Both Darya and Aram looked around, then they shook their heads and faced him. 'Downwards, then, Senapati,' Darya said, with some of her earlier decisiveness. It made him wonder what it would be like to serve such a queen.

Or to be her consort.

He turned and took Aram's arm. 'Come. There truly was nothing you could have done for Tilak, of that I'm sure. We must see our rani safe, you and I.'

Their eyes met, and he knew he'd struck the right tone because the young poet's face hardened with determination and the faint whiff of belief.

Well done, Aram Dhoop.

Then cold air slithered down the shaft from which they had come and someone whispered, 'Sister. Sister, come to us.'

Darya gasped and stared at Shastri, then peered upwards. There was no one visible, but they all knew that voice – they knew it too well.

It belonged to Halika.

Dinner Date

Jodhpur, Rajasthan, March 2010

'But, but . . . Dad, I have plans!' Vikram spread his arms wide.

'No doubt,' his father replied, 'but we are both invited, and therefore we will both attend.'

Vikram bit his lip. 'How long will it take?'

'Vikram!' Dinesh looked at his son in puzzlement. 'I thought you would enjoy spending time with your friend Amanjit. Anyway, I have accepted, and considering the lady is a widow, it is proper that family should be in attendance.' He pointed a finger upwards. His voice took on his 'no arguments' tone. 'Now go up and get ready for temple – and wear your best clothes. We will go straight to Mrs Bajaj's afterwards.'

Vikram hung his head. 'Yes, Dad.'

He trudged upstairs, not really sure what it was about going to lunch at Amanjit's mother's that was upsetting him so much – maybe it was the possibility that being in the same house as Amanjit and Ras might draw these ghosts to them? After what had happened last night, it didn't feel safe.

Then there was the idiotic – and increasingly disturbing – thought that this really might have some link to the *Ramayana*.

The similarities were mounting up, which made no sense to him, but not even he could ignore the emerging string of coincidences. It couldn't bode well. But there was a third thought too, the one Amanjit had hinted at last night: that if this was somehow linked to the *Ramayana*, then that made him Rama – and that was just too ridiculously stupid to be true. So perhaps that made the rest of it rubbish too . . .

At the temple, a small shrine tucked in behind a gaudy doorway three blocks to the north, Vikram and his father joined the throngs coming with Sunday-morning offerings. Vikram had packed a rucksack with the clothes he'd need in the afternoon, which was when he, Amanjit and Deepika were planning to go to the fortress. But neither he nor Amanjit had realised that their parents had made lunch plans. He wondered how easily and quickly they'd be able to get away.

The crowds at the temple this morning were busier than ever and he wasn't able to relax and clear his mind; there were too many faces in the crowd, and he was too caught up in the mystery they were chasing. The smells of the food stalls and the offerings, the bells constantly chiming as people entered, the loud conversations of those outside – it was too much and he just couldn't concentrate. He found himself comparing this to Canterbury Cathedral: he and his mates had gone there on a sixth-form school trip. He'd been to Anglican churches before, of course, but this was his first cathedral, and though it was huge, and had very cool gargoyles, it was dark and grey and austere compared to the colourful squalor that surrounded him now. He'd always liked the Hindu temples: the sense of being part of something so energetic and vibrant. As he gazed around him, enraptured by the bustling rainbow-hued worshippers, he almost felt like a tourist for a minute.

There were real tourists here, of course: Asians, and Europeans too, all with camera-phones and high-end Nikons and Canons clicking away madly. Some of the foreigners were fascinated by what they were seeing, but others appeared to be completely overwhelmed. A stony-faced Australian man – Vikram could tell his nationality by the flag on his rucksack – was snapping at a persistent beggar. An English girl in a too-short skirt was getting hassled by leering men. Once he glimpsed someone he thought might be that one-eyed thug – Jeetan? – but when he checked again, there was no one there. But that was enough to remind him of the danger they were in, and he began to feel jumpy and nervous all over again.

He went into the temple with some trepidation, worried he might trigger another strange episode like he had in the shrine in Mandore, but everything was completely normal as he filed in with the rest of the crowds and bowed to an ochre-daubed image of Rama with his bow, hung about with flowers. Sita sat at the god's side. *Protect us, Shield of God*, he whispered to the image. *If this mystery is somehow a concern of yours, then watch over us, please*. A priest applied a pooja mark on his forehead and Vikram turned away, feeling strangely heartened. And he hadn't turned blue . . . that had to be a good omen!

Then his heart sank a little as he noticed his father was praying for an extra-long time to Krishna and Radha, the God and Goddess of Love. *No, Dad, please! Surely you don't want a third wife!* But it felt mean-spirited to ask Krishna to ignore another man's prayers, especially his father's.

'You don't seriously want to court Amanjit's mum, do you?' he asked as they forced their way out through the crowds jamming the winding streets. They'd walked from home – they had been in Jodhpur long enough to know there was absolutely no point trying to drive anywhere in the old city on a Sunday.

'Don't you like her, son?' His father looked especially dapper today, with slicked-back hair and carefully trimmed moustache, and the unmistakeable scent of his most expensive aftershave. The orange pooja mark was vivid on his brow.

Vikram shook his head. 'No, it's not that – she seems nice.' *How on earth do I put this . . . ?* 'It's just . . . well, wasn't last time bad enough? Do you really want to go through it all again?'

Do you really want to put me *through it again?* he didn't quite dare to add.

'It's only bad if it doesn't work out.' He put a hand on Vikram's shoulder. 'Listen, son: you should never be afraid to love – and believe me, you are never too old for romance! Man does not live by bread alone!' He beamed happily and rubbed his hands together. 'You watch your old man and learn, son – and remember, romance is not what you see in the movies, thank Krishna, for I am neither handsome nor dashing, and I cannot sing a note, as you have never been backwards in telling me. And as for my dancing . . . But here's the thing—'

He stopped in the street and looked at Vikram, a serious look on his face. 'Love is about real people, and real people don't sing and dance to each other. They are discreet and positive, they listen before they talk; they are considerate but not obsequious, and they have more than ninety minutes plus intermission to get to know each other.'

He obviously meant every word, but he was also bouncy and excited, almost like a kid the night before Christmas, so Vikram groaned and gave up. There was no point saying anything else; his father was a hopeless romantic and a totally lost cause.

His father was as good as his word: over lunch, Vikram was treated to a two-hour master-class in old-style courtesy and manners. Dinesh had not only brought flowers and sweets for the table but also produced a bottle of red wine – *French!* – that he had purchased on a trip to Mumbai. And the charm offensive didn't end there. He produced a pretty scarf for Amanjit's mum, and then proceeded to listen attentively to her stories of trips to the city with her late husband and military balls on various army bases. Amazingly, his dad recognised many of the names she mentioned, even important military men. 'It is amazing who one meets when one has a reputation for quality cloth,' he said at one point, managing to stay just the right side of smug.

It was all pretty dull as far as Vikram was concerned, even if he was grudgingly impressed with his father's patter, but Amanjit's mum was clearly captivated. Across the table, Amanjit's brother Bishin looked out of his depth; he ignored everyone else and spent the whole time talking to Amanjit about cricket and the latest Bollywood gossip. Vikram caught Amanjit's eye every now and then; he was clearly just as anxious to get to the Mehrangarh.

Ras was asleep upstairs. The encounter with the ghost in the library had left her weak, which was troubling Vikram, but at least it stopped her coming to the fortress with them. She was in no fit shape to face danger, not in her condition. At least Amanjit had managed to warn Deepika they'd be late; he had moved their rendezvous back to 3 p.m. He looked at his father and Amanjit's mother, locked in conversation, and sighed. *Are we ever going to get away in time?*

In spite of all the reminiscences and funny stories, they were all conscious that it was the person who was missing who subtly dominated the conversation: Uncle Charanpreet, who, it appeared to Vikram, ruled the family with a rod of iron, at least metaphorically speaking. He was away in Bikaner, and although no one said so, it was pretty clear his visit to the neighbouring city was the only reason this lunch was able to take place. His absence might have been the catalyst, but his name was carefully never mentioned.

Even though he was desperate to get away, Vikram thought it was kind of sweet, watching the way Mrs Bajaj was blossoming as the lunch passed and the wine flowed, even though she scarcely touched her glass – her husband had liked a whisky, she admitted, but Uncle Charanpreet was a teetotaller and expected the same of everyone in the family. All the same, she sipped it once in a while, and Vikram wondered if the wine tasted like freedom to her.

'Dinesh, this is lovely,' she said warmly as she finished her glass.

He watched his father incline his head with pleasure. 'It is hard to find a quality bottle out here – too often they are not stored well and go off. But that one was a bottle in a thousand, I am thinking.'

'I have not had wine in so long. Not since my husband and I . . .' She paused, and then smiled. 'Would you like chai? Or even coffee?'

'That would be a pleasure. And then we can let these two young people get away for their oh-so-important research trip to the fortress.'

Amanjit's mother laughed. 'Yes indeed! Your Vikram is such a good influence on Amanjit – I've never known him to be in the least bit interested in a school project before now.'

Amanjit rolled his eyes, while Vikram basked in a little adult approval for once.

Suddenly the door crashed open and Uncle Charanpreet filled the doorway, his eyes bulging. He was in full-dress uniform, from crisply wrapped turban to highly polished shoes; in his hand was a military cane.

'What is the MEANING of this?' he roared.

As Uncle Charanpreet pushed his way into the room, Amanjit and Bishin rose and pasted themselves to the wall behind them.

They knew what came next. Charanpreet was a soldier, and he had never been slow to use the rod; they had become inured to his beatings. He even struck their mother sometimes, and he was heading straight for her now as she put a hand to her mouth. Her face had turned from blazing scarlet to deathly pale.

But Vikram and his father clearly knew none of this. The dapper cloth-buyer stepped between the towering Sikh soldier and his sister-in-law, his face calm. 'Mr Singh, calm yourself. There is nothing untoward happening here.'

Uncle Charanpreet stared down at him. 'How dare you come here behind my back?' he bellowed, his spittle flecking his beard and Mr Khandavani's face. 'How *dare* you?' He raised his cane.

Amanjit waited for Vikram's father to cower away, but instead he looked up at Uncle Charan, his face a mask of calm. 'Before you strike, sir, let me warn you that to commit violence against me or anyone here present will result in immediate legal proceedings.' His voice was measured and firm, with a steel Amanjit would never have suspected.

Charanpreet sneered. '"Legal proceedings?" I *spit* on your threats, you effeminate little powder-puff! *Real* men settle their differences man to man – and they do not shrink from disciplining those in their care.'

'"Real men" may have done so hundreds of years ago, Mr Singh, but where there is the rule of law, "real men" obey those laws.'

Uncle Charanpreet hawked and spat down his shirt, growling, '*That's* for your so-called "laws", you toadying sycophant! Let me tell you: there is not a policeman in Jodhpur who would touch *me*. You don't know who you are dealing with! This is a *military* town, a town of warriors! We are Rajputs, not fucking *lawyers*!'

But to Amanjit's amazement, the tailor didn't flinch. 'I do not refer to the police, though even the most military of Rajputs must obey laws, sir. I refer to my very dear friend Brigadier-General Ramesh Bikanaryan, whom I have personally apprised of your tyranny of this family.'

Amanjit, Bishin and their mother all stared at him, and then Uncle Charanpreet, whose visage had gone from crimson wrath to purple apoplexy, now began to display a sickly, confused sort of fear none of them had ever seen on his face before. 'General Bikanaryan—?' He swallowed, then he gave a hard laugh. 'You're bluffing! How would the likes of you know such a man?'

But it didn't look like Vikram's dad was bluffing, for a slow smile had spread across his own face. 'Why, sir, the general has *always* made time for me – after all, my family has been supplying tailoring services for his wife and daughters for many, many years.'

Uncle Charanpreet looked like he wanted to strangle the intruder – Amanjit could see his hands flexing in the way that usually presaged violence – but he didn't. As he and Bishin stared at him with disbelief, Amanjit felt no sense of triumph. *This is all very well, but as soon as they leave, this is going to get bad*, he thought nervously.

But Uncle Charanpreet was not finished. His face took on a sly aspect. 'Since when have honourable men slipped around behind the backs of family to woo vulnerable women? And gone *crawling* to authority figures? If that is a measure of the man you are, then it is a good thing for my sister-in-law that she will never see you again.'

'Any head of a family who refuses his charge the chance to remarry is negligent of his duties and abusing his role,' Dinesh Khandavani retorted calmly. 'And as to "sneaking behind your back", I did no such thing – I had no idea you were not going to be present here today. And as for my conversation with the general – I am well in my rights to enquire after the family of one whom I am considering courting.'

His words just goaded Uncle Charan even further, and he bellowed, 'You will *not* pursue her! Your courtship is forbidden, you hear me? *Forbidden!* Now *get out*!'

Mr Khandavani stood up even straighter. 'This is the house of Kiran Kaur Bajaj and I will depart at her request and not before.'

Amanjit was not the only one to turn and stare at his mother. She pushed her hand through her fringe, wiping away the sweat. She looked frightened and upset, reminding Amanjit just how fleeting and fragile a thing her earlier happiness had been. He couldn't remember the last time he'd seen her that relaxed.

Uncle gave an ugly laugh. 'Then she will demand you leave now, won't you, Kiran?' His voice was menacing, and suddenly strangely confident.

Amanjit watched his mother disintegrate. All poise left her and she swayed where she stood. Vikram, who was closest to her, stepped in to support her, looking worried that she might faint, but then he said, quietly but clearly, 'My father knows, Mrs Bajaj. He knows, and he is still here.' He met her eyes, projecting a calm and certainty that startled Amanjit, hinting at depths the young man had not previously shown.

His mother sucked in a breath as her eyes went wide and flicked around the room. 'He knows?' she whispered, looking shamefaced.

'He knows, and he still cares,' Vikram affirmed, then added confidently, 'He wants you to be free.'

Amanjit wasn't sure what Vikram was talking about, but his uncle gave a strangled cry, shoved Vikram's father aside and stormed towards his mother – but Vikram stepped in front of her as Uncle Charanpreet's huge fist came up, preparing to deliver a blow that would have smashed Vikram's jaw if it had landed.

Vikram was staring at Uncle, almost paralysed – but Amanjit wasn't. He seized his uncle's arm and held on desperately, even as the huge soldier roared and whirled on him, and for a moment they contested, muscle against muscle, and Amanjit realised to his surprise that he could almost match his uncle's strength. Then Bishin made up his mind: he caught Uncle's other arm. Together – just – they held him immobile.

Then with a flailing shrug, the big man finally shook them off, but only by giving ground. The two brothers closed ranks in front of their mother.

Uncle Charanpreet puffed himself up, glaring, and for an instant Amanjit was afraid he would attack them again, this time using his full strength – then suddenly he deflated, as if their defiance alone had taken away his aggression. He turned and stormed out. They heard him stomp down the stairs and smash the front door closed, leaving it rattling on its hinges. His absence seemed to echo all around them.

They all let out long breaths, and as Amanjit clapped Bishin on the shoulder their mother pushed past Vikram and hugged them both. She was crying. Amanjit held her tightly, trembling with relief. He couldn't quite understand what it was that had goaded his uncle so badly – he didn't really want to understand; he just wanted his mother happy and safe.

Vikram's father was mopping at the spittle on his shirt when the lounge door opened and Ras tottered in. 'What's happening?' she asked weakly. 'I heard shouting – was it Uncle Charanpreet?'

Her mother rushed to her and wrapped her arms about her. 'Nothing, nothing, baby. All is well. All is well,' she kept repeating, although Amanjit thought she was on the verge of bursting into tears again.

'Funny kind of nothing,' Ras sniffed, hugging her back. She still looked dazed and unsteady herself.

Amanjit turned to Vikram, feeling a sudden and profound

sense of kinship for his new friend. 'Hey, thanks, bhai,' he said in a low voice. 'I don't know what you meant, but then, I'm always a bit slow about that sort of thing.' He frowned. 'So what did you mean?'

Vikram bit his lip. 'I'll tell you later.'

'Well,' his mother broke in shakily, 'who wants tea?'

'Mrs Bajaj – Kiran – we will leave if you need time alone,' Vikram's dad told her in a gentle voice, but she shook her head emphatically.

'No, no, thank you. I would like you to stay, if you will?'

He hesitated no more than a polite second, then agreed with a beaming smile.

Vikram looked at his watch. It was nearly three, and the fort was across town. 'We've got to go if we're to make it to the Mehrangarh in time,' he announced. He turned to his father for permission; he looked at Amanjit's mother, and the two adults nodded slowly.

'Go and do what you must,' he said. 'I am quite sure we will be all right here.'

The auto-rickshaw crawled through the packed streets. Vikram, clinging to a roof-strut to steady himself, looked sideways at Amanjit and sighed. 'I'm sorry, but you're going to find out some time. What I said to your mother, "My father knows"—'

'Yeah, so, "knows what"?' Amanjit asked apprehensively.

Vikram took a moment to pluck up his courage. 'That your uncle was sleeping with your mother,' he blurted finally.

Amanjit went scarlet. 'But she *loathes* him!'

'Yeah, I got that. I don't for a moment think it was her choice, do you? He must have used his authority, bullied her into it . . .'

Amanjit shook his head and said emphatically, 'No! *No!* That can't be – I'd know! I'd *know*!'

'You didn't want to see . . . And he was discreet.'

'Then how the hell did you know?' Amanjit glared at Vikram. 'How *could* you know?'

'I didn't – I guessed. Right before I opened my mouth.'

Amanjit buried his face in his hands. 'But . . .'

Vikram went on remorselessly, 'I guessed, but because I wasn't *completely* sure, I said it in such a way that she could deny it or pretend she didn't understand my meaning. But she didn't, did she?'

'But . . . How did your dad know? You said he *knew*!'

Vikram shrugged. 'He didn't, but he caught on fast – I knew he would.'

Amanjit shook his head. 'You're unbelievable!' He looked away, his hand over his mouth as if he was about to be sick, blinking fast and hard. 'Did he force her? If he forced her—'

'I don't think so. Coercion, and some very unpleasant "persuasion", I think. Dad asked around about him and apparently he doesn't have a good reputation in the forces, but he keeps his nose clean.'

Amanjit put his head in his hands, moaning aloud. Vikram let him recover, before going on. 'I'm sorry – I really am. Will your family be all right?'

Amanjit thought, then nodded. 'Yeah, we'll be okay. I think . . . Bishin is going to call some of my mum's relatives, get some bodies around. Normally they wouldn't get involved, but once they know what's been happening they'll keep my uncle away.' He looked worriedly into space. 'At least for a while.'

'I'm sorry it had to come out,' Vikram said again.

Amanjit looked at him for a long time, then sighed. 'No, don't be. It's probably the best thing that could've happened.' He stared forward for a few minutes, then he turned back and added, 'I guess we'll be seeing a lot more of each other then . . . *bhai.*' He stuck out his hand.

Vikram felt a flush of embarrassed pleasure. No one had ever called him 'brother' before. 'Yeah, I guess. Bhai.' He took Amanjit's hand, beaming happily – then as the auto-rickshaw broke out of the jumble of houses and began to climb he caught sight of the fortress. 'That's assuming the ghosts don't get us, of course.'

Amanjit forced a laugh. 'I ain't afraid o' no ghost,' he rapped in a hoarse whisper. He seemed to have reached 'sing or cry time', a feeling Vikram knew well. With a forced attempt at merriment, the Sikh youth went on softly, 'Who ya gonna call?'

'Ghostbusters!' Vikram responded, slapping his thigh.

The auto-driver threw a bemused look back over his shoulder.

They sang all the way to the fortress, to push their fears away.

Ancient Shrine

Mandore, Rajasthan, AD *769*

Aram Dhoop shuffled behind Darya, who was leading the way. They were travelling slowly, even though they each had torches now. The tunnel had suffered several small collapses over the years, which made the going difficult. Shastri was guarding the rear; they moved in silent dread of hearing movement behind them.

Even this far underground, the air in the tunnel moved in strange currents. Now it was carrying the dank tang of stagnant water. For some reason Aram was finding the weight of the rock above easier to bear, maybe because this was obviously a man-made passage: outcroppings had been visibly chiselled away and the roof was much higher. There were some droppings on the sandy ground, but they saw none of the monkeys. From ahead came the steady dripping of water. As yet, there was no audible or visible signs of pursuit – but they could all sense the feeling of cold purpose that stalked them, half-heard imprecations and threats carried on the breezes harrying them from behind. That presence was definitely growing stronger, not weaker, no matter how far they went.

The tunnel descended sharply, curving first to the right and then back towards the left. It was hard to gauge distances or to picture where they might be relative to the world above, but they must certainly still be within the Bhaurcheeria. As the tension built and the feeling of being followed grew more and more tangible, Aram wanted to hold his torch in one hand and take the queen's hand in the other and to run headlong out of here – but instead, he just followed Darya as closely as he could as they made their careful way, step by step.

He was fighting a rising tide of panic that kept pushing up inside him like vomit when the rani's whisper brought him back to the present. 'Look – a doorway!'

'Wait,' Shastri ordered them both as he squeezed past to get to the front, holding the torch before him. Aram was more than happy to let him go first, even though this left him rearmost as they waited. He noted that the tunnel had changed in the last few dozen paces: though still hewn from the rock, the rough edges had been smoothed down. The ancient wooden doors of the doorway before them had long since rotted away, leaving nothing to bar the way. The solid lintel above the door was carved with ten symbols – they looked somewhat familiar to Aram, but meant nothing to the other two. The young poet stared at them, the memory nagging at him.

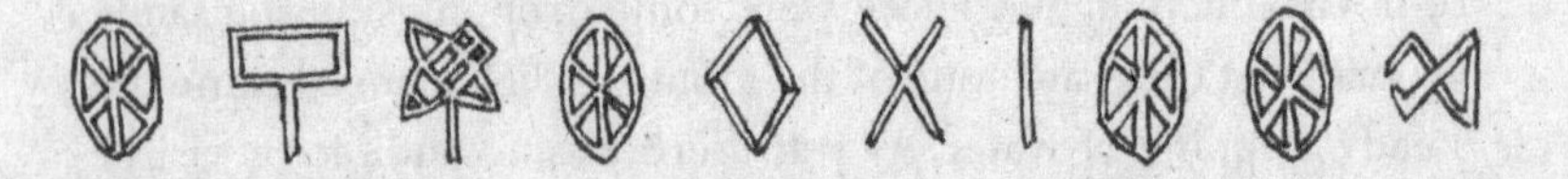

Shastri stepped through and lifted his torch high, illuminating a large chamber perhaps a hundred paces to the far side and almost as wide. The high roof, rough-hewn but still showing the hand of men, rose away into the darkness. There were raised platforms, and the channels between them were bearing slowly trickling water.

Once he was certain they were still alone, Shastri waved them through into the chamber, past huge statues on either side of the door they had entered; Aram couldn't decide if they were stylised dogs or lions – it was hard to tell, so crumbled were they by age. There were even larger statues facing the entrance, and these they did recognise: Shiva and his consort Parvati, though the style was strange, not at all like the idols in the temples of Mandore. Shiva had a snake coiled about his neck, but the god's head had broken off and was lying to one side. Parvati sat on Shiva's left, seated within the curved body and paws of what might be a tiger. Her left hand rested on the beast's head, but there was no sign of her right hand, which had been broken off at the wrist – maybe on purpose, perhaps just a result of the ravages of time. The statues, carved out of sandstone, glistened wetly.

When Aram looked closely, he saw another line of symbols, similar to those on the lintel over the doorway, adorning the plinths at the feet of the idols.

Queen Darya looked at him. 'Poet, you are a scholar, are you not? What is this place?'

Aram's mind had been worrying at where he'd seen something like them before. He walked forward, raising the torch he held to illuminate the symbols. After a few moments, it came to him.

'The style is old, Rani-sahiba, very old – I have seen fragments only, in a ruin northwest of here, which I visited a few years ago. The priests there said that they came from kingdoms overthrown thousands of years ago by a demon-people: the Asuras.'

Shastri shuddered and warded himself with the soldiers' gesture against ill-fortune and the evil eye.

'Asura? Demons? What rubbish!' muttered the rani, unmoved. Presumably she only believed in Mohameddan evil spirits! 'This was clearly some secret Hindu shrine. But we must find a way to leave, Senapati, before our pursuers find us.'

Aram was a little aggrieved to have his scholarship so brusquely dismissed, but he was in no mood to delay them further so he could debate it. 'Yes, let us go!'

'Yes, we must go on, find out if there is a way forward,' Shastri agreed. He swung his torch around, then gave a satisfied grunt. 'Look, that way—'

Aram went to his side and saw that the chamber opened out even further beyond the giant statues of Shiva and Parvati, into another large space so big their torches did not light the far wall. But as he moved, Shastri's torch guttered in a sudden chill breeze and almost went out. The senapati jerked his head about and stared back down the tunnel, then repeated urgently, 'Come – we must move!'

They hurried forward between the two idols – and then pulled up in frustration. Before them was a pool of black water, caked in dark algae. Their hearts sank.

After a moment Aram and Shastri started swinging the torches around, looking for a way across, but neither could see anything helpful, until Darya gripped Shastri's arm and exclaimed, 'Look!'

They all followed her pointing finger, but it took a moment for Aram to make out what she'd spotted.

'See there?' she whispered, gesturing at a low shape pulled up on the far bank, above the waterline. 'A boat, I'm sure of it.'

Aram stepped forward, eager to be doing something. 'I will retrieve it, my queen.' He dropped his pack and shield, handed her his torch and stepped into the water. He'd been anticipating a step below the surface, but there was none and he fell headlong into the lake. He floundered for a moment, then emerged, spluttering and gasping and covered in scum, trying not to feel hurt at Darya's peal of laughter – then Captain Shastri glanced back at the doorway and murmured, 'Hurry, poet! And be silent!'

Feeling inordinately foolish, Aram pushed off from the shore and paddled as his father had taught him, kicking like a frog and propelling himself forward swiftly with flat sweeps of his arms. His hand caught a stone edge and he groped his way along it until he found a treacherously slimy stone ledge beneath the surface of the water. He carefully pulled himself on hands and knees onto the step, then crawled forward up another shallow step, and then heaved himself onto dry stone, right beside the little boat. Even in the gloom he could just make out another doorway on the far side: the exit to the chamber.

For an instant he was tempted to just keep going, but almost immediately he chastised himself. *Unthinkable! Not without my rani.* He turned back, and glimpsed something grey, moving in the far doorway, like a cloud of ash blown by an unfelt wind. The whole chamber turned cold, their breath suddenly clouding, and he saw Shastri and Darya were facing the entrance way, their backs right against the water's edge. Shastri took five paces forward, placing himself in the gap between the statues, in the way of any danger.

'Poet,' Darya whispered, without turning her head, '*Aram*, please, *hurry*!'

Shastri caught their presence in the cold air that washed into the chamber, and the half-heard sounds became thirsty, lip-smacking whispers. He had always counted himself less superstitious than most men; he thought himself a realist, a rational man. But his mind could not disallow what his eyes showed him.

Clouds of ash swirled in from the tunnel and took shape: five darker pillars solidifying amidst a shroud of shifting white dust, sucking heat and moisture from the air. His exhalations were sucked into those clouds and a cold, deadly laugh echoed from within.

'Senapati Shastri,' purred Halika as she stepped from the shadows.

The three fugitives stared in horror at Ravindra's chief queen. The Rani of Mandore was impossibly alive – or something like life; for all her seductive tones, the ghost was a blackened, charred thing come crawling fresh from the sati pyre. She looked only part-formed, composed more of dirt and smoke than flesh and bone, but she moved with a sensuality in revolting contrast to her decayed, half-formed appearance. Her face was the most whole part of her, though the skin on her left cheek was missing and teeth gleamed from within. There was fresh blood on her lips and her eyes danced in the firelight. Her body beneath her sari of smoke writhed horribly, though it was growing more and more tangible by the moment.

'Senapati,' she whispered, 'won't you stay?'

He lifted his sword and whispered a prayer to Vishnu as behind her, the other queens took shape. They were barely visible, far less solidly fashioned than Halika, like ash streaks in the air, but they looked feral and bloody-mouthed, bestial reinterpretations of the women they'd been. Even though they were almost translucent, he could still recognise them: plump and foolish Meena was staring at him as if she were dying of thirst and he was water. Pretty, guileless Rakhi was licking her lips, reaching out as if begging, while Jyoti was beyond skeletal with half her wraith-form made up of bone. Aruna gurgled wetly, nostrils flared as if she could inhale him like the opium clouds she'd spent her life encased within. Each of them wore a blackened heart-pendant on her breast, pulsing darkly.

Shastri's heart leapt when he realised that his sister was not among them.

As they floated towards him, he found himself almost frozen in place – he couldn't move, couldn't react – until Queen Darya's voice cut through his paralysis.

'Senapati!' she hissed. 'Senapati Shastri: stand firm!'

I . . . must . . .

Halika snaked towards him, the other wives behind her, their mouths opening bloodily, those vivid scarlet holes the only colour amidst their grey forms.

'*Shastri!*' Darya screamed as Halika's mouth opened, revealing sharp fangs shining within: a tunnel that led all the way to Death's realm.

Suddenly orange fire blossomed about him and five mouths screamed. In a daze he saw the rani step before him, brandishing her torch, which ignited the smoky-silk of the ghost-queens' saris. They shrieked like demons, howling in fury and pain as they jerked away, beating impotently at the flames that roared through them.

The sight cleansed his mind and in one swift move he raised his sword and thrust it through Halika's breast. The blade sliced effortlessly through insubstantial flesh and motes of dust; she barely noticed his action, but seized his hand with hers. It was icy, and horribly strong, and in reflex he thrust the torch in his left hand at her – and she immediately ignited.

She too flickered backwards, shrieking, and he mirrored Queen Darya's movements, brandishing his torch as a weapon, sweeping it in great circles that forced the queens away. Behind them he heard frantic splashing and prayed it was the poet, returning with the boat – but he dared not take his eyes from the spectral queens to check. The fires that lit their forms were fading, but when they drew closer this time he thought them less substantial than before.

But though undeniably weakened and wary, the dead queens were still driven to attack. Halika circled at the back as she beat out the flames, out of his reach but goading her lesser sisters onwards. They pressed their assault, though none laid another hand on either of them, but it was to the rani they called, pleading with her to submit, threatening her with far worse.

'The raja is coming,' they snarled. 'He will make you join us. *You must burn!*'

'Never!' Darya hissed back.

Behind them, the boat scraped against the lip of the pool and Aram panted, 'I'm here—'

'Highness, go!' Shastri snapped as he lunged forward, thrusting the torch in a great sweep that pushed the queens back. He sensed the rani's leap and heard her land, and the splashing of the boat rocking on the water.

'Go!' he shouted at the poet, 'get moving – I'll catch you up!'

The queens pressed in on all sides but he was still twisting and turning, brandishing the torch to keep them at arm's length as he ran backwards to the water's edge. He planted his foot and threw himself across the space that had opened up as Aram pulled away. He landed in the little boat – but there was a great rending of ancient timbers disintegrating at the impact of his weight, and his left leg went straight through the bottom of the hull. He fell into the side of the boat, and he clung on, gasping at the impact and a sudden and unexpected pain.

The boat lurched and he felt a gash the length of his thigh open up, torn by the jagged edges of the rotten wood he'd punched through. He reeled at the hurt, but managed to gasp, 'Row! *Row!*' There was nothing he could do to help, for he was stuck and helpless, cradling his torch in shaking hands.

Behind them, the queens gathered at the water's edge, snarling like beasts, still pleading and hissing and menacing, scratching at the air above the water as if it were a tangible barrier. But they came no closer.

Shastri remembered folk tales his dada had told him, in which ghosts hated and avoided water. Or maybe they feared him and Queen Darya too much now to pursue them. Either way, he was grateful that they had stopped coming at them, for the gash in his thigh was agonising and he felt giddy with the pain, until the numbing effect of the icy water started to take effect. His leg was plugging most of the hole, though the bottom of the boat was still filling fast as they crossed the small lake, Aram rowing frantically, though with little skill.

The queen laid a hand on his arm and they both looked back, staring at the things the queens had become. Strains of hope were echoing inside his head, despite the horrifying image.

My sister was not among them – but why not? What has become of her?

Her heart-pendant throbbed against his hip.

It had been a real act of will for Aram Dhoop to return with the boat when freedom might have lain just a few paces further – but how could he not? *I've sung too many songs of heroes not to try to emulate them*, he decided as he helped the queen onto the landing. Together, they pulled the senapati from the imprisoning hole in the boat. There was blood on his leg and he could not hide his pain as he hobbled from the craft. While Aram held his torch to illuminate proceedings, Shastri hurriedly cut a wide strip from his leggings and wrapped it tightly about his wound.

'They don't like fire,' he panted. 'Remember that! Use it!'

Aram turned to the queen, who was looking back at Halika and the other queens, just a short distance away across the water. 'They are bhoots, Rani: unquiet spirits of the dead. The tales say that they fear water and steel, and the scent of turmeric. They seek to possess the living and thus return to life.'

He half-expected scepticism again, but Darya stood stock-still, gazing at her former sister-wives with wide eyes.

'I would have been one of them, if not for both of you.'

She may yet end up that way, Aram thought. *We have to run if we are to save her!*

'Sister, come back to us!' the five queens called, but she turned her head away and would not look at them again.

All they had now were swords and daggers, and the bow and quiver over Darya's shoulder – but they had kept their torches and now Shastri lifted his and lit the way forward, through the doorway in the far wall that Aram had spotted.

'Stay!' Halika called. 'Stay – the raja is coming. He is coming for you all. You cannot hide from his might.'

Aram hurried towards the doorway, and Shastri pushed Darya after him. The tunnel beyond swiftly swallowed the cries of the dead queens.

Frosted Glass

Jodhpur, Rajasthan, March 2010

Rasita Bajaj sat cross-legged on her bed with her elbows resting on the sill and her face pressed to the window. She had a blanket wrapped about her shoulders, but she couldn't stop shivering. Amanjit and Vikram had gone off on some errand she was sure had nothing to do with schoolwork and everything to do with what they'd been talking about at the library yesterday.

She felt that she should be angry to be left behind, but anger was difficult to sustain. Ever since that stricken-looking spirit, the ghost of Padma, had touched her and fled, she had been feeling ill, much worse than normal, as if something vital had been stolen from her, although of course that was crazy. She felt listless and being upright for long was making her dizzy. Part of her was furious, thinking that she might be missing out on something, but the rest of her was just relieved. Either way, she scarcely felt capable of standing up.

Once the boys were gone, she had tried to turn her room into a spiritual fortress. She had gone shopping that morning; her list drew on all she had ever read of ghosts and ghouls around the world; she'd considered every culture from Asia to Africa and even Europe and America, and now the room was festooned with garlic cloves and various cheap gemstones and perfumed with incense. Marigolds were scattered along the sill as well, and plaster statuettes of eight or nine deities filled every corner. She'd even found a crucifix – the shopkeeper had assured her it had been blessed in holy water – and she'd hung a rosary and a set of Muslim worry beads from the door handle. Since she wasn't sure what she was seeking protection from, she was trying to cover all the bases.

When she looked around at her efforts it was almost funny – but it also wasn't: the memory of the spectral Padma, with those frigid hands and sharp ivory teeth, made it far from amusing.

Right now though, Ras had something far bigger to worry about, much more tangible than any ghost, bhoot, vampire or rakshasa. From her window she could see Uncle Charanpreet, standing there and staring up at the house. Even from this distance she could see his whole frame was visibly shaking; she was pretty sure he was hyperventilating, the way he always did when he was in an uncontrollable rage.

It was frightening, everything being out in the open now. Her uncle's treatment of her mother – and everything it implied – was suddenly clear; all the comfortable little lies they'd told themselves so they'd be able to cope, they were all gone now. Ras shuddered, remembering the way Uncle Charanpreet had begun watching her, all those compliments, his admiring comments about how beautiful she was becoming. She felt physically sick just thinking about it. And what had become of Father's money in Uncle Charan's hands? She'd always wondered how they'd gone from pretty well-off to dirt-poor almost overnight . . .

What will happen to Mum, and to me? What will become of the family taxi company now? How will Bishin and Amanjit find a living?

Mum was downstairs with Bishin, who was helping her clean up. Mr Khandavani had gone, but not without a hundred flowery promises to host them all soon. She liked the trim little man, though he was as opposite to her father as she could imagine. But he'd made Mum smile and that hadn't happened for so long she'd thought she'd forgotten how. He might be nothing like the sort of man girls dreamed of, but she could see why her mother liked him. And he had courage, and honour too, to stand up to Uncle Charanpreet like that, and in such an awkward, fraught situation.

And his son had shown the same qualities. Ras smiled involuntarily at the thought of serious, studious Vikram, with his round glasses and earnest manner. He had looked so different, there in front of her uncle, facing him down with the sort of courage Bishin and Amanjit had never shown in the face of their uncle's wrath.

She peered out the window again. Uncle Charanpreet was walking away, but as she watched he turned and glanced back up at her window – she instantly pulled back from view – but when she looked next, he was gone.

Feeling dizzy again, Ras returned to her well-protected bed. The doctors had always been worried for her, all her life, but her family wasn't wealthy enough to pay for the sort of treatment she really needed. In the end, all they really said was, 'Enjoy life, and don't give up.' *Give up!* she always replied with an audible snort. *I am a Sikh and we do not give up!*

But there was no doubt the constant illness was wearing her down and no matter what she said in public, sometimes she did wonder what it might be like just to lie back and let the weakness take her . . .

As the minutes dragged by fatigue overwhelmed her again, although she had done little but sleep for the last eighteen hours. With a sigh she snuggled back down into bed. Closing her eyes, she curled into her blanket. Within minutes her breathing had become slow and regular.

Gradually, as the sun sank in the west, the temperature in the room dropped. Her breath began to frost and the condensation running down her window first turned sluggish, then froze.

From the doorway to her room came a soft sigh.

The Chasm and the Bridge

Mandore, Rajasthan, AD *769*

Aram's mind was trying very hard not to dwell on what they had seen as they wound downwards in a slow, spiralling descent through the rocks beneath the Hill of Birds. He was soaked to the skin and his wet clothing was chafing him, and leeching his body heat until he was shivering. The low sound of rushing water somewhere ahead hinted of more soakings to come; more worryingly, it also masked the sounds of any pursuit.

Try though he did to dispel them, the faces of the immolated queens haunted him. He kept looking at Darya, lit by the torch she carried, and trying not to picture her formed of ash and blood. The rani's face was pale too, and her eyes were haunted, constantly flicking behind them. Halika's threat – that Ravindra was coming for them – felt all too real.

Shastri guarded the rear now, his wounded leg making him limp, but he was still the strongest of them, and best equipped to guard their backs, for they were all more afraid of what was behind them than anything that might lie in wait. Their unspoken dread was that the tunnel would peter out into a dead end – and there was every sign that this might indeed be the case. The man-made smoothing of the tunnel hadn't lasted more than twenty or thirty paces from the lake and now the walls were becoming rougher, the floor less sandy, more bare rock, with every step of their descent. Even the roof was closing in, until Shastri, the tallest of them, was forced to hunch over as he shuffled along behind them.

Just when the tunnel had narrowed so drastically they were sure they were about to reach a dead end, they found themselves spilling out onto a platform of flat stone, twenty paces wide and almost as deep. Beyond the platform was emptiness.

As he stepped to the edge and peered down, all Aram could see was blackness; he couldn't begin to guess how deep the chasm was. Two stout timber uprights had been driven into the rock and thick ropes had been secured to it: ropes that ran horizontally out into the darkness: a rope bridge, stretching out across the chasm.

Darya and Shastri joined him, and together they thrust their torches over the chasm. The combined light gave them enough visibility to make out what lay before them, though what they found was not reassuring. Far below was the source of the watery sounds they had been hearing: a stream visible only as a shifting gleam and white froth. Every now and then, Aram thought he could make out a rippling effect, as if something were moving beneath the surface, but they were a very long way up and he wasn't convinced his eyes were not deceiving him. The far side was at the very edge of the light, but he thought there was a wall of stone beneath a high, jagged ceiling.

As Shastri examined the bridge, the other two cast anxious glances at the tunnel behind them. There was no other way forward than over this precarious span of rope. It was long, passing almost out of the range of their torchlight, but if they squinted they could make out the far side, eighty paces or more across the chasm. The glistening roof wasn't far above, and the stalactites that lined it were dripping constantly into the stream below.

'The first pool of water, in the chamber of statues, was completely still,' Darya commented. 'But the water below is moving. They are probably not connected.' She looked at Shastri. 'Is the bridge safe, Senapati?'

The soldier was prodding thoughtfully at the timber braces, but they weren't budging. He looked out at the bridge itself. It was a basic thing: the person crossing had to balance on the bottom rope while holding on to the two upper guide-ropes on either side. When he pulled hard on them they remained taut.

'It looks safe enough, Rani-ji,' he announced at last. He pressed a hand to his wounded thigh – blood was already starting to stain the bandage – and winced, then straightened. 'I will guard the rear.'

'Then I will go first,' said Aram quickly, before he could change his mind, 'to see that it is safe for you, Rani.'

'But I am lighter than you,' Darya protested.

'And I am expendable,' he told her. Perhaps it sounded like courage to her, but the reality was that watching and waiting would have destroyed his nerves. He just wanted to get it over with. He swallowed the rising lump in his throat, stamped out his torch and thrust it into his belt. 'I think I can see well enough for the crossing, and I need both hands free,' he said, eyeing the void below nervously. He'd been battered, soaked, and scared witless already. Surely this would be no worse!

'Then take this,' Shastri said, pulling a flint striker from a belt-pouch, 'so that you can relight it on the other side, to light the rani's way.' Aram took the crude device, and pocketed it, then sized up the bridge.

Just as he was about to go, Shastri grabbed Aram's shoulder, and said awkwardly, 'Aram Dhoop, your courage and honour do you credit . . . Here – she wanted you to have this.' He pulled something from another belt pouch and handed it to Aram, and as he did so, Queen Darya gasped softly and clutched at her own throat.

'What is it?' Aram asked curiously, reaching out to accept the gift: a heart-shaped pendant, opaque, but with strange dark veins. He looked up at the rani, who was holding a similar jewel in her own fingers. As his fingers wrapped around it he jerked suddenly, because he could have sworn that the pendant *pulsed* . . .

'It was my sister's,' Shastri told him. 'She wanted you to have it. She said it was her heart, and that it belonged to you.'

'Padma . . . ?' Aram felt greatly discomfited by this. Though he'd been aware that Padma had become inordinately fond of his singing, enough that he'd felt at risk to be in her presence too often, lest Ravindra take it ill, he had never suspected her feelings had run so deep. In truth, he'd had eyes for only one of the queens, and it had never been the senapati's pretty little sister.

'It means she loved you, poet!' Shastri snarled, reading his face all too well. 'The last thing she said to me – the last words we ever had – were of *you*, poet. She told me that she *loved* you.'

'Padma?' Aram repeated, and he stared at his feet, with no idea what to say to make this dreadful situation any better. It was too late to make his apologies to Padma, but at least she would never know he had not returned her affection. He started to speak, but instead he thrust the pendant into his waist-pouch, abruptly turned away and staggered to the rope-bridge, unsteady as a newborn colt.

'What *wasted* love,' Shastri whispered. 'She wasted her heart on you, who did not even notice her: a man who pulled another woman from the pyre instead.'

At least I saved one of them, Aram thought resentfully, but that thought was overtaken by the sudden realisation that Queen

Padma had felt deeply for him. *Padma* loved *me?* He couldn't remember exchanging more than a few words with her, though he'd sung for her many times, as he had for all the queens. That she had felt anything at all for him was inexplicable . . . or was it? *She was lonely, and the only men she saw were Ravindra, a few eunuchs . . . and me.* He swallowed again. *Have I been so blind?* he asked himself. But when he tried to envisage what might have happened had he tried to rescue city-born, gentle Padma instead of the athletic and brave Darya, he could not see how they'd have survived even half a day.

I did the only thing I could have . . .

The only thing now was to go on. He clambered onto the rope-bridge, his legs still weak, but the peril of the crossing swiftly focused his mind and gradually he regained control of his wobbling limbs. Within a few steps he was wrestling with the ropes: they might have felt taut where they were anchored, but the further he got from the tethering posts the more wildly the bridge swung. For a moment he wondered how old these ropes might be – surely the priests in the caves above must have been responsible for their upkeep, for there was no way ropes could last for centuries, not in such good condition as these. Then he determinedly turned his mind aside; it didn't pay to dwell on such things.

He looked back just once, and something inside him twisted painfully when he saw Shastri kneeling before the queen; she had her hand upon his shoulder. He drove the image fiercely from his mind, focused on his feet and willed them forward into the darkness, one step at a time.

It felt like the crossing took for ever, though in reality it wasn't long at all before he reached the far side. He stepped onto another platform, smaller than the one he had left. At first his heart sank, for he could see no further way forward – then his eyes alit on a hole, half the height of a man and almost camouflaged by the broken rubble piled against the uncut rock wall. From it issued a foetid smell that doused hopes that they were nearly free.

'I'm over!' he called, despite his fear that the next tunnel went nowhere. His voice echoed about the chamber. 'I think it's safe.'

'*Safe . . . safe . . . safe . . .*'

The word echoed eerily across the chasm, mocking their hopes.

Senapati Shastri and Rani Darya were watching Aram Dhoop's wavering passage across the void, when to her shock, Shastri fell to his knees at her feet. 'Forgive me, Rani-ji,' he whispered.

'For what, Senapati?' she exclaimed incredulously.

'I fear I chose wrong. If we had gone upwards at the point where we dropped into the man-made tunnel we might have been free of this place by now.'

'Who can know, Senapati Shastri? The choice is made, and we were all a part of that decision. No blame is yours alone.'

In my heart, I think we choose right, and either way, I would rather die here than be taken alive . . .

'Lady, more than that . . . I beg you to forgive me for every time I wronged you. For the times I held you down whilst Halika drugged you. For the times I manhandled you like a criminal at the raja's behest. For not acting in concert with Aram and organising a coherent rescue. I was a craven man. I do not deserve your respect.' His voice was filled with shame. 'I am the worst of men.'

She laid her hand on his shoulder. 'Senapati, the worst of men are those who pursue us. You are the best of men. I absolve you of everything for which you ask absolution. I would forgive you *anything*.'

He bowed his head. 'I'm not worthy, Rani-ji.'

'But I say you are,' she answered thickly. 'And I am your queen, am I not? So what I say must be so.'

'Yes, Lady. Yes, yes you are.' His face was stricken. 'But my sister . . .'

She bent and wrapped her arms about his shoulders and pulled his face to her. 'She forgives you too, Senapati.' He shook, and the thin cloak wrapped about her soon became sodden with his tears as he sobbed out his grief and pain. She cradled his head and stroked his hair. 'Take courage, Senapati: Padma is not among the ghosts who pursue us.'

She whispered her comforting words as if to a child, all the while wishing they could just fly away to somewhere safe, to be alone, to heal together. It felt strange to hold a man against her without feelings of utter repulsion; even as she had that thought, vile memories arose, of the only man she had ever known, her husband Ravindra, and all his cruelty. It took an effort, but she defied those memories, pushing them away. *Aram was always good to me, even before this, and now this man too has laid his life on the line for me. Not all men are evil.*

'I will look after you, Senapati Shastri. I will be yours, for always.'

Always . . . The word mocked her, when she truly could not see them lasting the night.

'I'm over, I think it's safe,' shouted Aram Dhoop, far across the bridge. His slight figure was just a silhouette in the darkness, but his voice echoed about them. Then his torch flared up on the far side, like a beacon to guide them home. Darya helped Shastri to his feet. He was clearly in distress, his gashed thigh obviously paining him, but his eyes were dry again.

'What is your given name, Senapati?' Darya asked.

'Madan, my queen. I am called Madan.' He bowed his head and she stood on tiptoe and kissed his forehead. Then she took his hands and pressed something into them, something she had pulled from about her own neck.

'If Padma's stone belongs to Aram, then this belongs to you, Madan Shastri,' she whispered, and she tied the pendant about his neck. The heart-stone pulsed against his breast and she felt a strange tingling in her own chest, as if both their hearts had skipped a beat, then resumed again, each in time with the other. His eyes were full and brimming, and her own stung.

I could kiss him now, she thought dreamily, tilting her head.

But their moment came to an abrupt halt as a foul stench suddenly emanated from the tunnel behind them, filling their lungs with the smells of smoke and roasted flesh. Something rattled, deep in the tunnel, making Darya flinch.

'Go, Rani-ji! *Go!*' Shastri snapped, pulling out his sword. '*Go!*'

She backed away, then extinguished her own torch and thrust it through her belt to free her hands for the crossing, as Aram had.

Shastri lifted the torch for her to illuminate her footing at the start and she sprang for the bridge, with no time to even retrieve the bow and quiver from against the wall, as he turned to face whatever new horror might be emerging from the tunnel.

Beneath the Fortress

Jodhpur, Rajasthan, March 2010

Amanjit and Vikram sat on an old wall beneath the fortress gates, staring out across the city as they waited for Deepika. Tourist buses filled the car park, disgorging tourists – Indians, Asians and Europeans – by the dozen. Drivers milled around paan vendors and chai-wallahs, joking, stretching their legs or squatting for impromptu card games. Vikram had texted Deepika; she was on her way.

From up here the city spread mostly south and east below the fortress, basking in the afternoon sun. It was a flat maze of pale blue-painted brick and concrete, punctuated by the occasional tall building. Gulab Sagar, an artificial lake filled with dirty green water, gleamed dully from among the buildings, and here and there little mounds of solid rock still endured among the urban sprawl, like fingers of the earth sticking up through the clutter. But it was the immense structure before them that constantly drew their eyes: a giant's fortress of gleaming sandstone, with sheer walls over a hundred feet high. Amanjit felt proud to belong here, to such a place. It lifted his spirits, and distracted his mind from the vicious swirl of recriminations over his uncle's behaviour.

'So, what do you think?' he asked Vikram. 'As big as the castles in England?'

'Oh, *way* bigger,' Vikram replied. 'Most of the mediaeval fortresses there were pretty small to begin with – and anyway, the kings weren't all that keen on their nobles having bigger palaces than the royal family, so a lot of them forbade really epic castles.' He grinned. 'So yeah, I'll give you this one: you *definitely* win "Castle Top Trumps" – I'll bet this is one of the greatest in the world.'

Amanjit was surprised at the pride he took in that statement, and especially that it had come from Vikram. 'We'll make a Rajasthani out of you yet! Do you know the history?' he asked.

Vikram went to reply, then noticed the look on Amanjit's face and jabbed an elbow in his ribs. 'What, you actually *know* something historical?'

'Just this one thing,' Amanjit laughed. 'I love this place: we used to come here all the time with Dad – as a soldier he could get us in cheap. I even know the year the building began: 1459.'

'I'm impressed! What else?'

'Well,' said Amanjit, happy to share one of his favourite stories, 'By 1459, the raja, Rao Jodha, had rebuilt Mandore – yes, *Mandore*, bhai! – but the fort there was too small for his needs so he decided to relocate the court to Jodhpur, where there was now a thriving town. But to build on the Bhaurcheeria – that's this hill here – he had to displace a hermit called Cheeria Nathji, who was known as the Lord of Birds. The hermit was pretty pissed off at being moved on, so he cursed Rao Jodha. "Jodha," he said, "may your citadel ever suffer a scarcity of water!" And so it was that the monsoon failed and the building went badly and everyone said that the curse would prevent the fortress from ever being built.

'So Rao Jodha consulted with his astrologers and priests, who told him that only the most powerful magic could break the curse and make the site propitious: a human sacrifice.'

Vikram looked up at that. 'What – really? What is it with you people?'

Amanjit waggled his head. 'I knew that'd get your attention! And the astrologers divined that it couldn't be any old sacrifice, either: whoever it was had to actually go *willingly* to his death – that was the only way to undo the hermit's curse. So there was this soldier named Rajiya Bambi Meghwal, and he offered himself as the sacrifice, to be buried alive in the walls so the building could be completed. In honour of his great heroism, Rao Jodha and his descendants have honoured Rajiya's family ever since.' At Vikram's sceptical look, he added, 'No, honest, I'm not having you on! They set aside a part of the palace for his family and they've lived there ever since, even now. Their bit of the estate is called the Raj Bagh – that means Rajiya's Garden.'

Vikram took that in, and then said slowly, 'I wonder if that relates to what we're doing?'

Amanjit pulled a face. 'I hope not, bhai. Ravindra and his ghosts are enough for me.' He studied Vikram and found himself smiling. *I can't think of anyone I'd rather have with me right now*, he realised. *Except Deepika, and she'll be here any minute.*

They noticed an auto-rickshaw puttering half-heartedly up the hill and into the car-park, and both jumped to their feet as Deepika stepped out and waved. Like them, she was dressed casually in jeans and a denim jacket, with the addition of a pale blue pashmina, fashionably casual. She looked ready for some serious exploring, and something in the way she dressed and walked reminded Amanjit of his mother. *She's got that effortlessly elegant thing going on, like Mum used to have when Father was still alive.*

She walked towards them, but though she tried to pretend she was her normal confident self, her steps were quicker than usual and her laugh a little nervous.

She's terrified, Amanjit realised. *But she's here . . .*

Vikram was staring up at the battlements silhouetted against the sky. 'This is insane, isn't it? How are we going to find something that was on this hill centuries before that fort was even built?'

Amanjit shrugged. 'I don't know.' He looked at Deepika. 'But we will.'

She smiled grimly and repeated, 'We will.'

They bought their tickets and Vikram added maps and headphones for the audio tour. He was obviously looking forward to the history lesson, but Amanjit wanted his senses undistracted. They joined the other tourists winding their way up into the fortress. There was a gate buttressed by stonework that was pockmarked with cannonballs, a sharp turn and a long climb to the next gate, where they passed a stone monument below the sheer walls that seemed to climb into the apex of the sky. Vikram, listening to the audio commentary, announced that this was where Rajiya had allowed himself to be buried alive in the walls to alleviate the curse. Amanjit touched the small memorial reverently, but Deepika shuddered.

'What a waste of a life, for superstition's sake,' she muttered.

'It was a noble self-sacrifice,' Amanjit retorted.

'Only if you believe it was necessary,' Deepika replied, her voice brittle.

At the top of that stone road their path turned sharply to the right and they passed beneath more fortified gates into the fortress proper. Deepika stopped with a sudden intake of breath. There were handprints moulded into the stonework of the wall on either side of the gates. They had been painted over in vivid orange. Marigolds and candles lay beneath them. She approached them unsteadily, holding out her hand.

'Deepika! Be careful!' Vikram called out.

She turned back, and Amanjit could see tears running down her cheeks. 'What did you see?' he muttered under his breath.

'Nothing,' she said hastily. 'I just thought . . .' She set her jaw, talking more to herself than him. 'It's okay, they've gone. They've gone. It's okay.' Her voice sounded bereft. A tourist photographed her, nudging his fat wife, staring at them until Amanjit glared back, and they moved on.

Vikram removed his headset. 'This is where the wives of an old maharaja of Jodhpur committed sati, here at Loha Pol Gate, in the 1800s.' He hung his head, and whispered something under his breath.

Amanjit was about to comment when Deepika, beside him, gave a sudden hiss and grabbed his hand. He followed her eyes, and where he could have sworn there had been no one just a second ago, there was now a girl standing a few feet away, looking right at them.

The girl looked scarcely fifteen, with a sparrow's build and twig-like arms and legs. She was dressed in rags and her face was filthy. When he looked closer, he saw that those rags were the burned remnants of rich clothing, heavy with gems and sequins, and her skin was smeared with ash. She held up a hand, and placed it on the smallest of the stone handprints on the gate wall.

Amanjit dragged his eyes from her as a cluster of tourists came past. They all looked at the place where the girl stood, but didn't appear to see her, because no one commented or stopped to photograph her. When they were gone, she remained, staring at them with big, sorrowful eyes. He held his breath as she turned and took a stair on the right, on the inner side of the roadway. It led away from the tourist trail, up towards a footpath which became a narrow alley running between the main bulk of the maharaja's palace and one of the lesser buildings of the huge complex. At the top of the stairs the girl looked back at them, then with slow dignity, raised a hand and beckoned.

They looked at each other. Vikram had gone pale. Deepika wiped her eyes. Her voice was a throaty rasp. 'We have to go with her. She wants us to follow.'

Deepika led the way up the stairs. The ash-streaked girl – *she's a ghost, she's a* ghost*!* – was already fifty feet ahead of them, waiting before a shadowy doorway. They were sweating, though they were all shivering beneath their perspiration too. As Deepika reached that doorway she found it open and the ghostly waif they were following was now a dimly seen presence at the far end of a shadowy passage. Deepika soundlessly held out a hand behind her and felt Amanjit's strong, reassuring grip close about hers. She needed that strength, to give her courage to go into the darkness ahead. Then she remembered Vikram and glanced at him guiltily. He looked back at her, and at her hand.

Sorry, Vikram . . . You can write as much poetry to me as you like, but I'm with Amanjit. She lifted her head, challenging him to deal with it. Amanjit and Vikram seemed to be getting on, but they were heading into something she couldn't foresee, where the deeds of these other people – Shastri and Aram Dhoop – would loom over them. The shadow of something unresolved in Vikram's eyes was troubling as he turned away.

She turned, focusing her own eyes forward again, seeking their eerie guide.

The ragged girl was now at the end of a short dirty corridor, barely visible against the blackened walls. She vanished around the corner as soon as they saw her.

'Come on,' Deepika hissed, and pulled Amanjit behind her.

She could tell he was fretting at letting her go first. *Let him fret – we Delhi girls don't need a man to lead the way!* When she reached the corner the girl was at the next, beckoning them on. Here in the gloom she was all monochrome, a black-and-white photograph, or a sketch drawn in ashes.

They followed her, on and on, deeper and deeper into the keep, maybe heading southwards, though Deepika couldn't really follow all the twists and turns. They never saw another person, and soon lost all functioning electrical lights too. Vikram handed Amanjit an electric torch and turned on another for himself. 'Sorry, I could only find two,' he told Deepika apologetically. She didn't care; she felt she could almost see in the dark down here anyway.

'I don't like this,' murmured Amanjit.

'What part in particular don't you like?' she asked quietly. There were endless possibilities for unease right now.

'The way the light of my torch shines through that beggar girl and hits the wall behind her.'

She didn't like that herself, now that he had mentioned it. 'I wish you hadn't pointed that out.'

Then they heard a sound from ahead: the dripping of water, echoing like piano music in a concert chamber. A few seconds later they were staring down from a small stone landing over black water.

'It's a baoli,' murmured Vikram. 'An underground water tank. Old buildings used to have them to store water for emergencies. I didn't know there was one here, but I could have guessed. All these old places had them.'

Deepika stared into the blackness and felt the chill rising from the water. Amanjit's hand found hers again, and it was the only warm thing in the world. She glanced left and right, unclear where their path now led. There was no way forward. Then she looked down at the water and sucked in her breath.

She cast no reflection.

Instead, she saw the ghostly child staring up at her. She waved up from the water, then slowly faded from view, leaving Deepika's own reflection behind.

'What do we do now?' Amanjit asked.

'I think we have to swim,' Deepika replied.

'Not swimming!' Vikram groaned. 'My most miserable holidays were spent at English beaches. No sand, no sun, and the water was cold enough to freeze the balls off a brass monkey, as they say over there.'

'I love the sea,' Deepika replied. 'You should go to Goa; the water is so warm you can stay in all day, and there are bars and cafés all along the sands.'

'This isn't exactly Goa,' Amanjit said, staring across the dark, oily pool. 'Are you sure that's what we have to do?'

'Can you see any other way forward?' she asked, testing the water with her finger. It was freezing cold. Of course the heat of the sun didn't permeate this deep beneath the rock. 'No? Didn't think so.' She looked around, found a bamboo stick and poked it beneath the surface. The bottom dropped out of reach three steps down. 'See, we'll need to swim.'

The two young men were both unhappy at that. 'Come on,' she said, then stopped as she realised. 'You don't know how, don't you?'

Amanjit and Vikram shook their heads in unison.

'What do they teach you here?' she complained.

'Lots of useful stuff,' replied Amanjit.

'Just not swimming,' Vikram added defensively. 'It's a desert, see.' He put his hands in his pockets sheepishly. 'I tried to learn in London, but I hated it. I can stay afloat, I guess.'

She snorted derisively, to mask her fear. 'I'm going to have to take off my jeans, because there's no way I'm wearing wet denim for the rest of the afternoon. So you two can turn round, teeka?'

'Okay,' Vikram said, preferring the English word for 'teeka'. He spun around, while Amanjit grinned, winked insouciantly and ostentatiously turned away.

Once she was certain of this modicum of privacy, she whisked off her trainers, jacket and jeans, wrapping her pashmina around her waist as a skirt and knotting it firmly to protect her modesty a little. Then she dipped her feet in, stood on the top step and slowly lowered herself into the frigid water. The cold was enough to leave her gasping.

'Can we turn around yet?' Amanjit asked, with a teasing lilt to his voice.

'Yes, yes,' she said impatiently. 'Sweet Mother, it's freezing!'

Feeling her core beginning to chill, she kicked off and pushed out, and then yelped as something tangled with her foot.

'Deepika!' Vikram called anxiously.

She thrashed about, put her feet down and realised she could stand, and that she wasn't in any danger. 'No, it's okay!' she told them. 'Look! This is what that ghost girl was trying to show me!' She paddled back to the ledge and pulled herself up, then reached down. She dragged at a piece of chain, hung with slime and crusted with rust. She climbed out, trying to pull it, but it defeated her. 'I got wet for nothing,' she grumbled.

'Here, let me help,' Amanjit said, leaning in. He gripped the chain and began to pull. At first nothing happened except for his muscles bulging, quite impressively, she noticed, then the chain began to move.

'Look!' gasped Vikram.

A wooden dinghy hoved out of the darkness, the other end of the chain attached to its stern. They all seized part of the chain and drew it in until the dinghy was lying alongside the platform. It didn't look old, maybe a few years at the most. More importantly, it floated.

'That's lucky!' said Vikram.

'Lucky? Ha! I notice I'm the only one who got wet,' Deepika retorted. She felt chilled to the bone, but curiously excited now. 'Does anyone else feel like they're dreaming? We've been guided by a ghost of a burned woman, who must have been a queen judging from her jewels, into the bowels of the castle,' she said, a little breathlessly. 'Who'd've dreamed?'

Amanjit sniffed the dank air and said, 'Try not to use the word "bowels" down here. It smells like a cistern as it is.' He winked. 'I do know how you feel, though. I keep pinching myself.'

While Deepika wrung out her pashmina and used it as a towel for her legs, then tugged her jeans back on, Vikram put the audio-tour equipment in a pile to be retrieved later, and Amanjit went to the wall and pulled two old-style torches from the walls.

'These still smell of some kind of oil, so we might be able to use them,' he told them. He showed them a lighter from his pocket, then put it back. 'Can you believe that they're still here? We'll bring them, just in case.'

He climbed cautiously into the dinghy and steadied it. 'I think it'll hold – and look, there's even some oars!' he announced with satisfaction as he fumbled around in the bottom of the boat.

Vikram caught Deepika's arm as she went to climb aboard. He leaned towards her, and spoke in a whisper, his voice almost inaudible. 'Amanjit was a bad guy in both of our dreams,' he reminded her. 'He was Shastri, the raja's captain. He killed people.'

'Amanjit isn't him. Just as you aren't the poet. We are who we are now. Past lives mean nothing.' But she didn't really believe that, she realised, even as she said it.

'I know . . . and I trust Amanjit Singh. It's Shastri I don't know about.'

Deepika swallowed, realising that this was what was gnawing away at her too. The scene that had played out on the movie screen flashed before her eyes. But she gritted her teeth. 'I trust Amanjit,' she said firmly, to ward off the doubts. 'As I trust you.'

But what about these other selves? Shastri and Aram Dhoop . . . do I trust them?

Their new bonds of friendship suddenly felt flimsy, here where older, darker secrets and actions might be so much more powerful.

Vikram wished he could make Deepika see: Amanjit was a menace to her, not through who he was now, but because of who he'd once been: Shastri, the raja's captain.

What if he turns on us? What do we do then?

If only he could get her alone, out of Amanjit's earshot. The deeper they went, the more his fears grew . . . instinctive suspicions clouding his thoughts. And then there was the way he felt for Deepika: he could almost feel the presence of Aram Dhoop in the way he wanted desperately to protect Deepika, and it was increasingly hard not to stare at the way her damp clothes clung to her body.

They paddled into the darkness, down a low tunnel, until the boat beached itself on a little rocky subterranean beach, where more ancient torches were bracketed. The rough natural rock of the ceiling was only a few feet above their heads, and water was dripping slowly into the pool, a subterranean music that never quite found a tune. The air was cool and dank down here, enough to make them shudder involuntarily. They shone their torches about them, sending a pair of rats scuttling away, and Vikram shivered as a snake detached itself from the shadows and entered a crack in the rock. But there was a door in the wall before them, and it was ajar. Through it wafted cold air.

There was no sign of their ghostly guide. Perhaps she'd played her part. Vikram glanced backwards, thought he saw her, back on the platform they'd left, one hand raised. Before he could react she'd gone, if she'd been there at all.

Amanjit leapt out and hauled the dinghy as close to the water's edge as he could, so that Deepika and Vikram could jump out without getting wet feet. He helped Deepika, then turned to Vikram and clasped his hand, staring down at the smaller youth. 'What were you saying to her?' he hissed.

'Nothing,' Vikram replied. Their eyes met, and the fragile trust they'd been building seemed to fray slightly. Amanjit hauled him up and out of the dinghy. Vikram could tell that the Sikh didn't believe him. But suddenly they were plunged into darkness. Both of their electric torches had winked out at once. They all gasped. Vikram hated the fear in his own voice.

Amanjit chuckled to hide his fright. 'Let's see if these old things work,' he said, lighting the oiled torches with his cigarette lighter. 'Could be a good thing I brought them, huh?'

The flames on the primitive torches flared and guttered fitfully, making the shadows dance. Any light was welcome, though. Vikram felt a nervous chill as he stared back across the water, into darkness. It was as if something dark was huddled where that ghost-girl had been, and a foul stench drifted across the surface of the water, propelled by an icy breeze . . .

'Come on,' he said tersely. He was suddenly afraid to stay still. He took a torch from Amanjit and held it aloft, pushed past the Sikh and led the way through the door. It led to stairs of stone, spiralling downwards into the depths of the hill. It felt to Vikram like all the weight of the Mehrangarh had settled on their shoulders.

One hundred yards down, the stairs opened into a long, narrow passage, roughly hewn but functional, too long for their torches to see to the end. They walked down it in a line. Vikram noticed that Deepika and Amanjit were holding hands again, and something inside him crumbled a little further. His brain began to gibber at him: It wasn't fair! Amanjit was an oaf! How could she be so blind to Amanjit's faults and his own virtues? He bit his lip angrily, trying to force such feelings away, but they hovered over him no matter how he tried.

Gradually though, the fear and wonder of being so far underground, in a place so mysterious, buried those emotions, or at least pushed them below the surface of his mind. They had other, more immediate concerns. At the far end of the passage there was a broken door, the wood so old it was silvery, and the stonework around was somehow, subtly, far older than the passageway they'd just traversed. There was a tangle of debris strewn around the floor of the small chamber behind it. On one side a rough-hewn path curved down from above. If they lifted their torches, they could see the entire chamber was walled from above by a massive rockfall, as if one side of the cleft had fallen against the other, sealing this space from above.

Deepika peered at the debris, then gave a small cry. Vikram pushed his torch up close and gasped too as an empty-eyed skull grinned at him from beneath a rusted helmet. There were more, dozens more, and armour and weapons – swords, spears, even a discarded bow and a quiver of arrows.

'Great guru! Look at all this – there must have been a hell of a fight here!' Amanjit picked up a rusty curved scimitar, and waved it about thoughtfully. 'What do you reckon these are worth?'

But Deepika wasn't interested in rusted weaponry; she'd been examining the walls of the chamber and now she lifted her torch up and peered closer, then cried, 'Look—!' She strode forward, towards outlines of stone in the right-hand wall. Amanjit and Vikram hurried after her, when something caught Vikram's eye and he stopped.

Lying among the debris was a bow, still intact, the string loose but unbroken. He seized it, and a quiver of arrows, with a dim recollection of sports days at his London school involving archery, at which he wasn't entirely useless. The leather quiver holding the arrows was rotting, and the bow was so decrepit it looked as if it would snap if he tried to draw it, but at least it was intact. Just holding it made him feel more complete, somehow, as if he might be able to do something if things went badly.

'I feel like Indiana Jones!' Amanjit exclaimed with forced levity, still brandishing the rusted blade.

Vikram felt like nothing of the sort. He felt like an intruder.

Deepika was holding her torch before her. 'This place must be a Hanuman temple,' she said, shining her torch on a cobwebbed idol coated in grime that stood in an alcove set into the wall. All about the floor were bones and little skulls filled with big, ferocious-looking teeth. 'And look, there used to be monkeys here, too.'

'A long time ago,' Amanjit commented. 'A hell of a long time ago. I wonder if they got sealed in here by the rockfall above?'

Vikram went to the back wall and found a crawl-space there. 'Look, there's a little tunnel – it looks like it's the only way we can go on. I guess we have to try it.' He felt another twinge of nerves and looked around. There was something he didn't like about the way the light was flickering around the doorway they had just left. 'Let's go now.'

But before they could move, a dark shape stepped through the doorway behind them, just a dozen feet away, with three others crowding in behind.

The newcomer's eye-patch identified him instantly, even

before his voice rolled into the chamber like a breaking wave. It was the one-eyed thug, Jeetan, who'd pursued them at Mandore. He held a fiery torch in one hand and metal glinted in the other: gun-metal.

Vikram felt his gut tighten at the sight as beside him Amanjit and Deepika stopped dead.

'Stop! Stop right there! Or we'll shoot!' Jeetan's teeth glittered. He looked and sounded immensely satisfied. 'Don't move, any of you.'

Amanjit stepped in front of Deepika, almost earning himself a bullet as the muzzle of Jeetan's gun swung towards him.

'Who are you? What do you want with us?' he demanded.

'Not me, boy,' Jeetan replied. 'I'm just doing what I'm paid to do. And as for who . . .' He shrugged disinterestedly. 'I've never even met the man.' His eyes narrowed, focusing on Deepika. 'It's the girl he wants. And the short kid.'

Vikram felt his heart skip at those words and he stepped closer to the other two, while the three men with Jeetan fanned out. They too were armed.

Jeetan grinned evilly. 'Sadly, he wants you two intact,' he said, addressing Vikram and Deepika regretfully. Then he leered at Amanjit. 'But you, Sikh, you are all mine.'

Burned Flesh

Mandore, Rajasthan, AD *769*

The thing that stepped from the tunnel was scorched and blackened. Every inch of its flesh was seared. What skin was left was cracked and weeping. There were a few bits of smouldering cloth still clinging to the frame, and the crown and metal breastplate had melted into the remaining flesh, like some creature constructed by an insane jadugara. There was no way it should have lived. Yet it did. It stalked like a panther into the chamber, a long curved blade in its grasp, glowing red and smoking as if it had just been removed from the forge.

'Shastri,' it snarled in a chillingly familiar voice.

'*Ravindra?*' Shastri couldn't believe the calm voice that responded was his own. How could it be Ravindra, and why wasn't he dead? But Ravindra it was, and that was all that mattered. Behind him, the ropes of the bridge lurched as Darya fled. He placed himself before the posts, jammed the torch into a metal ring set on the side of the bridge's left stanchion and steeled his heart. With his life he would buy her time to flee.

'You may come no further.'

The thing that had been his king chuckled darkly. 'Shastri,

Shastri. Jeet warned me of your treachery months ago. He begged leave to do away with you, but I thought you still had some honour left in your heart. Is this how you repay me?'

Shastri flexed his bleeding left leg, which felt hollow and unsteady. 'What have you done?' he asked, not wanting to know, but trying to buy time.

Ravindra spat sizzling spittle the colour of blood. 'What have I done?' He shuddered. 'What indeed? And why should I explain the least of it to you, Madan Shastri?' He halted though, and his ghastly face became reflective, almost as if he could not resist the opportunity to brag of his cleverness. 'The rakshasa speak to me in dreams, Shastri! Can you imagine that? They directed me to ancient texts. Seven queens, bound to me by the gemstones I gave them . . . seven *specific* women . . . they guided me to my queens, though I had to scour the north to find them all! They told me how to free my spirit – and the spirits of my ranis – so that I would be returned to my past glory! Do you know who I am? Who I really am?'

Shastri shook his head thinking, *The man I served is insane.*

'I am Ravana, Demon King of Lanka! Ravana, Lord of the Asuras!'

Shastri stared, speechless.

Ravindra went on, rapt in his own glory, 'And that damned poet ruined everything! Instead of rising in glory, with my glorious Rani Mandodari at my side, I am reduced to this!' He looked down at his burned body, and then stared fully at Shastri. 'For which you shall all pay dearly!' He glared at Shastri with hooded eyes. 'Enough! I will not be delayed!'

He leapt and swung, and Shastri barely reacted in time. Their swords smashed together and the chime of the steel rang through the chamber. Their blades slithered together, sending sparks like fireflies dancing into the air. With his back to the chasm, Shastri had to parry desperately as Ravindra, relying on brute strength, started hacking away at him in a relentless attack.

Then their blades locked, and Shastri shoved the hilt of his blade at Ravindra's face and pushed the king away, gaining some respite. The hideously maimed raja was moving with all the grace and power he'd had in life, though, and with no little skill. Shastri would have backed himself against anyone in Mandore, but his leg was throbbing, and Ravindra was as dangerous a foe as anyone he'd ever faced.

'Madan!' cried Darya, from on the rope-bridge.

'Go!' he shouted, striking back at the fearsome thing before him. 'Do not wait for me!' Then he had to focus all his attention on facing the serpentine movements of Ravindra's sword.

Ravindra lifted his talwar and swept it into a figure-of-eight, cleaving the air. 'I see you use the Roman-styled straight blade, Shastri. Poor for mounted fighting, but superior in a duel. A good choice, but it will not avail you.' Ravindra attacked again, a frenzy of blows executed with tigerish speed and ferocity. There was nowhere to retreat, and no place to manoeuvre.

Shastri stood his ground, parrying in desperate reaction to each stroke. Time and again the smouldering blade whisked past his face, but each block brought a snarl of frustration. Then in a flash of inspiration, he reached back and pulled the torch from the metal loop, then lashed out with it, driving the fiery tip at the king's face.

Ravindra staggered back, his eyes furious. 'You dare!' He swung wildly, but Shastri stepped into the blow, met it, and lashed out with his left foot. Though pain wracked him as the gash in his thigh spasmed, his boot took Ravindra in the chest and slammed him backwards. The king staggered, hit the wall behind him, and leapt sideways as Shastri followed up. A straight thrust that could have skewered Ravindra's heart was turned aside and the raja countered, slashing with blinding speed, driving Shastri back to the bridge, lunging ferociously, but this time it was Shastri's turn to parry and disengage. They pulled apart, each seeking a new opening. Shastri was gasping for air, but he noted with a sinking heart that the raja was not even panting.

'Give me the girl, and I'll let you live, Shastri,' Ravindra purred. 'I don't care about Mandore: you can have it for all I care. Chetan is dead. So is Jeet. If you went back and claimed it, no one would resist. You could establish a new dynasty, Senapati. Your blood could rule Mandore for ever.'

Shastri swallowed air thankfully, grateful for the respite. The offer meant nothing to him; only his queen mattered now. He desperately wanted to look back, to see how Darya fared, but he dared not take his eyes from the circling blade before him.

Flee, Darya, he willed her. *Run far and fast*.

'Madan, I'm across!' Her voice, frightened, full of concern for him, carried over the chasm.

He felt a small surge of relief.

'If you're going to cross, you'll have to kill me first,' Ravindra rasped. And with a bellow of rage, he sprang at him again.

Aram jammed his lit torch into a holder that had been screwed to one of the wooden bridge posts, then pulled Rani Darya the last few steps, wrapping his free arm about her to steady her as she stepped onto solid stone again. She was shaking with terror. The crossing, her horror of enclosed spaces and her fear for Shastri had combined such that she could barely stand.

'I've got you,' he whispered. 'I've got you.'

For long moments she stood there trembling, saying nothing, and Aram began to wonder whether her mind had been turned by the horrors she had faced. It was up to him to see her safe now.

Across the chasm, Shastri's torch waved about, and steel hammered on steel. They heard the soldier cry out, a stricken sound, then the clangour of metal on metal resumed, louder than ever.

Aram pulled her torch from her belt, placed it in her hand and lit it with the flint. Once she had recovered enough to grip the torch, he pulled her towards the crack at the back of the cavern, repeating, 'Rani, we must go on!'

She whimpered something in shock, trying to pull away from him, back towards the bridge. He had to drag her with him, then pushed her ahead of him as Shastri cried out again.

She wailed with grief.

Her distress angered him in ways he didn't care to examine. *I've got to see her safe – nothing else matters!* He shouted in her face, trying to shock her into movement. 'We must run, Rani! Run! Run! RUN!'

It worked, but too well. His shouting and Shastri's cry of pain panicked her. Her eyes went suddenly wild and she scrabbled back into the rotting, heavy darkness of the tunnel, brandishing the torch in her hand wildly. Aram chased her a few paces, crying, 'Run, Rani! Go! RUN!'

Reduced to animal fright, she fled, leaving him alone. He went to follow when a dark impulse took him.

Does it even matter which of them crosses the bridge?

Both will take her away from me . . .

He acted before he had had a chance to come to any sort of considered decision: as if his body had made the choice for his brain. He drew his dagger from his belt and went back to hack at the rope-bridge. His side of the chasm was lit only by his own torch, which was guttering low. He slashed wildly at the old ropes. *No matter who survives*, he told himself, *I do not want them on this side of the chasm*. But the ropes were still strong, though bound with rusted wire. *Too slow!* Every sound from across the chamber – every enraged roar, every hammering blow – frayed his nerves faster than he could slice the rope. He glanced over, and gasped. Shastri was on his knees and the huge figure of the king was raining blow after blow down on his wavering guard.

Then the captain's torch spun into the depths and all light was gone from the far side. Aram's own torch, beside him, was going out. He could barely see to cut the ropes, and then he heard them creak as they took the weight of someone at the far end. Terror swept the rational part of his mind away. He slashed one more time, then backed away as his torch went out. The only light now was the faintest glow from the tunnel Darya had entered.

Praying he had done enough, he turned to face that dim glow and stumbled towards it, pursuing the queen.

The first time Madan Shastri faltered, Ravindra's burning blade slashed open his arm. The fire cauterised as it cut, and the stink of seared flesh, already prevalent, became stronger. His cry echoed through the chamber, and at once he began to believe in his own mortality.

Ravindra purred, and licked his lips. 'Soon, Shastri,' he gloated. 'It's just a matter of time.'

Shastri lashed out, but Ravindra parried comfortably and closed in again. The king's sword flashed about him, and each parry Shastri managed was weaker than the last. The king did not even tire. No man could sustain more than a few minutes of such fighting, and Shastri, in peak condition, felt like his lungs were on fire and his limbs slowly turning leaden. Yet Ravindra continued to attack with inhuman power and endurance.

Shastri's injured leg gave out first. He stumbled, the knee buckling as he sought to lunge, and fell. He thrust blindly with torch and sword, gouging the king's breastplate, but though he won a respite, he couldn't make his limbs respond. He could not even lift his left leg.

Ravindra roared, towering above him, and smashed downwards, blow after blow battering at his guard, all finesse abandoned. All Shastri could do was hold his sword aloft as Ravindra's blows hammered it like a blacksmith at a forge. Abruptly Ravindra changed stroke and smashed a blow at the torch, splitting it in half. It fell to the ground between them and the raja kicked it into the void.

The only light was gone, and darkness closed in for the kill.

Aram caught up with Darya at the end of a long, narrow tunnel that hardly warranted such a name; it was more a large crawl space between vast boulders. The torch in her hand was barely flickering, and then he heard her wail again.

He redoubled his speed and scrabbled up behind her, seizing her from behind and pulling her into his arms. He'd dreaded confronting a snake, or worse, more soldiers coming from this direction, but what he saw was bad enough: a blockage of fallen earth.

He almost broke down and wept. 'No,' he whispered. 'No, oh gods, no!' He pleaded with the Fates as he scrambled up the mound of earth, pulling Darya with him, then shovelled at the stone and dirt with his bare hands. They both cringed as part of the roof gave way – not a large area, but it covered them for an instant.

He had to grab the rani to stop her from bolting back the way they had come. 'No, no, Rani. We will yet prevail!' He held her face to his, covered it with kisses. 'We will escape, I swear! I will dig us out – I will protect you! I love you! *I love you!*'

She stared at him with a blank face.

'I love you!' he told her, demanding a response, but she gave none.

With a wild sob he pulled out his dagger and swarmed further up the mound, to where it met the roof of the passage. He stabbed and pulled, loosened a handful of rubble. Again and again he stabbed and dragged, bringing down another spray of earth. He felt his nails break, and then the dagger snapped in half, but still he burrowed into the mound, digging in a blind frenzy and showering earth and rock and pebbles around him . . .

. . . until a sudden blast of chill, fresh air slapped his face.

'Rani-sahiba! My love,' he sobbed, 'I can smell clean air! There's a hole! We can get through! We're saved!'

He turned back, in time to see the rani and the torch vanish down the tunnel behind him, going back the way they'd come.

'My Rani!' he shouted at the darkness. 'Come back!'

His voice echoed.

Bullets and Rusted Blades

Jodhpur, Rajasthan, March 2010

Jeetan raised his gun, strode across the chamber towards Amanjit and placed the muzzle against his temple. 'Drop the sword, kid, or I'll splatter your brains on the wall.'

For a mad instant Amanjit found himself trying to measure reaction times, as if he could somehow do some insanely heroic move, something Salman or Aamir or one of the action-types might do in a thriller. But the cold reality of the circle of steel against his skin brought its own kind of sanity. He dropped the sword, which landed point-first and fell propped against the wall, a foot from his hand.

Jeetan frowned as his henchmen began to sidle forward, a trifle nervously. 'I don't know what you did back in Mandore, but if I think for even an instant that you're going to try it again, you're dead,' he said. He ground the gun painfully against Amanjit's temple. 'Don't move a muscle.' He looked at his men and indicated Vikram and Deepika. 'Seize them! Take them back to the boat.'

Amanjit watched helplessly as the other men laid their hands on Deepika and Vikram and hauled them away. One gave a leering look at Deepika's chest and sniggered under his breath in a way that made Amanjit's blood boil. But that gun muzzle stole his courage.

I'm a Sikh! I am a lion! I am a warrior, a son of warriors!

Why am I so scared?

In a few instants, they were alone, he and Jeetan. The man stank of whisky and sweat. 'You've led us a merry little dance, boy. But we've got you now.'

'Who is paying you?' Amanjit asked, playing for time as he tried to work out what he could do, though that metal circle against his skin terrified him.

'None of your business,' Jeetan said mildly. 'He really does just want the girl and the boy. You, I can have for myself, he said. I don't know why, but he seemed to think there was something between us. "An ancient debt," he called it. Whatever. It's not like I need an excuse to slaughter a strutting piece of dung like you.'

He chuckled and gouged the gun muzzle into Amanjit's temple again. 'Kneel, scum.'

'Never.' Amanjit tried to respond bravely, but it came out weak.

'As you wish, kid,' Jeetan snickered, and Amanjit tensed and shut his eyes tightly.

Jeetan pulled the trigger.

The weapon clicked impotently, and Jeetan stared. 'Wha—?'

Amanjit moved by instinct. He shoved the man in the chest, making him stagger, and snatched at the hilt of the sword propped against the wall.

Jeetan nearly overbalanced, then roared and fired again.

Click.

'Huh? What are you doing?' the man bellowed.

Amanjit didn't hesitate. With a fluid movement his body

appeared to know, the blade flashed into a sideways slash that chopped into the gunman's wrist, and through.

Jeetan howled as his hand, still gripping the gun, spun away in a slow arc and flopped to the dust. His wrist-stump fountained blood as he fell to his knees, his mouth goldfishing soundlessly.

Amanjit stared down at the man, panting. He felt no pity, only grim satisfaction. On the floor, the fallen hand went limp and the gun slipped to the sand. They both stared at it.

Guns like that don't misfire . . .

'My hand, my hand,' Jeetan whispered, his one eye gleaming wetly as he swayed.

Should I just kill him? Can I? Could I really kill a man, even this one? But I can't just let him be . . .

Jeetan himself solved the dilemma by fainting. He sprawled amidst the monkey bones.

He'll die if that wound isn't staunched . . .

. . . there's no time . . .

Amanjit heard questioning shouts from the other men, getting nearer: at least one of the gunmen was coming back to investigate Jeetan's absence. He strode to meet him, and nearly bowled him down as he exited the chamber.

The man's mouth was open, as if about to ask Jeetan what was happening, but when he saw Amanjit his eyes went wide. 'What the—?'

Amanjit slammed the pommel of his sword into the man's face. His nose splattered, his head cracked backwards, and he flopped bonelessly to the ground. The young Sikh never even broke stride, though he was marvelling inside at just how instinctive the blow had been.

When did I ever learn to fight with a sword?

He burst from the tunnel to find the last two men herding

Deepika and Vikram towards the dinghy. The man holding Deepika was laughing and pawing at her.

Amanjit saw red. He heard some kind of battle-cry trumpet from his mouth and he leapt.

Two guns clicked and their owners gaped, and tried to fire again.

He thrust the sword into the belly of the man holding Deepika, where it snapped, centuries of rust finally claiming it. The thug doubled over, collapsing with a scream. Amanjit whirled, and saw the last man fling his useless gun away and run for the water.

He went to chase him, but the man had already dived into the black waters and was thrashing away. Amanjit stopped at the edge of the water, put his hands on his knees and gasped for air.

Behind him, the man impaled by his broken blade whimpered weakly. Vikram looked down at him, at the blood, and then swayed and barely caught himself.

Deepika stared at Amanjit, her eyes round with shock. 'What happened?' she asked in a hollow voice.

Amanjit just tried to get his breath back; he was unable to talk and too scared to think.

Then a cold blast of air washed over the water and they heard the fleeing gunman cry out, a cry of absolute terror that was cut off in mid-voice.

They all stared into the darkness. Vikram held his guttering torch aloft and Deepika snatched up the other one before it went out. Three sets of eyes tried to pierce the gloom. Nothing moved. Something was there though, they could sense it. Something ancient and hungry, creeping closer, rippling through the water.

'We can't go back,' Vikram whispered, looking pallid, even in the dim light. 'Something's out there.'

'Then we must go forward,' Amanjit said, taking command. 'Come on! This way!'

He took them the only way available, back to the Hanuman temple chamber where Jeetan lay motionless in a pool of blood, his severed hand beside him. He looked dead.

Amanjit stared, nauseated, yet unable to feel regret. Vikram and Deepika looked at the dead man, then back at Amanjit.

'How—?' Vikram began, but Amanjit shook his head.

'No time.' He pointed the way forward: a tiny tunnel in the wall. 'Something's coming, I can feel it.'

Worse than that . . . I can hear them: wet footsteps on the stone . . . Cold voices . . . Somehow he felt that if he went back to that pool, he would see five ragged shapes rising from the water, coming for him . . .

'Come on,' he said more urgently. 'We've got to hurry!'

Rasita woke suddenly, shaking with cold, facing the wall, huddled over. The air was gelid, the whole world was deafeningly silent and she knew instantly that she wasn't alone.

There was an extra weight on the bed, sitting beside her legs; she could feel the chill radiating from it.

'Mum?' she whispered, in hope but not expectation.

Silk rustled, and a smell like old fireplaces washed over her, cutting through the scents of garlic and flowers and incense.

'No, child,' a woman answered, in a voice that was like an echo of sorrow and pain.

Ras turned and shifted to the top of the bed and with her back to the wall, pressed herself into the corner, trying to putting as much distance as she could between her and the other presence. Her heart was pounding painfully, hurting her chest. It was hard to breathe.

The figure in her half-lit room was hard to look at: she could only really be seen clearly from the corner of the eye. She was wrapped in a silk sari that was no colour and every colour, and hung with blackened silver and gold jewellery of a rich, ancient style. Her skin was very dark, as if she had been exposed for years beneath a pitiless sun. Her eyes were lost beneath the folds of her veil, but Rasita thought she was about her own age, just a soft young girl.

Padma.

Every marigold she'd placed on the sills had dried and withered away to orange dust; every candle and incense stick had guttered and gone out. The garlic was blackened and rotted, the statuettes had all cracked and fallen over. Padma fingered the Muslim worry beads and the string frayed. Beads of onyx and camel bone fell to the floor and went rattling and rolling away into the corners of the room, almost as if fleeing from her touch.

Ras fought for air. 'Who . . . who are you?' she asked in a quivering voice.

'Do you not guess?' the ghost-queen answered, and when Ras shook her head, unable to answer, she whispered, 'I am you.'

The Rope-Bridge

Mandore, Rajasthan, AD *769*

Aram felt his control dissolve as he fumbled in complete darkness, feeling his way back down the narrow, low tunnel towards the chamber of the bridge. The rani's torch was out of sight, and she wouldn't respond to his cries.

He heard her ahead, calling out, 'Shastri! *Madan!*'

She's gone back for him!

'No!' Aram groaned. 'Wait, wait,' he called after her. '*Wait!*' He couldn't see her yet, lost behind a bend. The undulating floor tripped him and he sprawled, but he got up and went on, regardless of the pain emanating from where he'd landed on his damaged hands. 'Wait! Please, wait! My love, wait!'

Suddenly, there she was, before him, waiting – somehow his cries had stopped her, and his heart leapt to think that his love for her had finally penetrated her mind. Her face was tear-streaked, almost hysterical, her expression torn as she looked back at him, then forward, to that dark chamber where Shastri was surely dead already.

And where Ravindra lurked . . .

Then a voice echoed weakly down the tunnel, 'Darya! Aram!'

Shastri? But he was losing . . .

He caught her up, seized her arm. 'Don't go back, please,' he begged. 'Please! It's a trick, a trick of the raja's. It's not him. Ravindra can't be slain – it's not Shastri, it's Ravindra!'

She threw him off contemptuously, her sudden strength, dredged from some hidden reservoir, startling. He found himself on the floor of the tunnel, his knees bloodied, as she shouted, 'We must help him—' She started backing away from him, edging towards the cavern and the bridge.

'Please,' he begged from the floor, on his knees. 'I love you. I *love* you.'

She turned away, straightening as the tunnel widened, and was gone, hurtling down the rough passage, calling Shastri's name. Darkness surrounded him again.

The poet was calling after her, but what he was saying, she had no desire to know. He didn't understand: Shastri needed her. They couldn't just leave him behind – they had to help him somehow.

She couldn't recall just when her feelings for the senapati had changed, but she knew they were real. Maybe it was an accumulation of things: the way he had continually placed himself between her and danger. His courage and daring; his confidence and capacity to act in the face of terror – how could she not respond to that? And she had finally recognised the expression in his eyes whenever he had looked at her at court: it was pain, the torment of wanting to help her and being walled about with enemies, unable to aid her. His secret was out now, his enemies named and faced. He was calling her – she would find him, and they would never be parted again.

'Madan—'

Behind her she heard the poet slithering and scrambling. She felt some brief pity, then forgot him. The man she loved needed her. Yes, Aram Dhoop had rescued her from death, but that was not an act that obliged her to give herself to him. She loved with her heart, not to honour her debts. She would always be grateful but she could never love him.

'Madan!'

'Darya!' His voice came, weak, but closer.

The distances had looked so far when slowly working her way into the unknown, but going back seemed to flow past in moments. She strained all her senses, following the sound of his voice.

'*Darya!*'

She burst from the tunnel into the chamber, her throat raw and her breath ragged. Her eyes sought him through the darkness: he was making his way laboriously across the rope-bridge, though his left leg was hanging uselessly, a dead weight. He was blind in the darkness until her faltering light lit the chamber. She saw the burned-out torch jammed into a loop on the bridge pillar, pulled it out and tossed it aside then jammed her own in it. It flared up as it hit a new seam of pitch, enough to light the chamber, all the way to the far side.

Madan saw her, and forced a grin. His armour was gouged and pitted, and blood glistened wetly on the metal and on his limbs. His eyes were black and his face streaked in scarlet. His hands were empty, but when she strained her eyes, peering through the gloom, she thought she could make out his sword-hilt, jutting from the chest of a fallen man, lying immobile on the far ledge.

He had triumphed. *My warrior!* Her heart almost burst with relief.

Madan inched forward, closer and closer to her, as Aram Dhoop stepped through the crevice behind her and gasped, 'Shastri?'

From the bridge, the soldier shouted, 'It is done. It is over.' He hissed in pain as he moved, the bridge swinging wildly under his weight. 'Stay there,' he grunted painfully to Darya. 'I'll come to you.'

'No, I'll help you,' she called.

His eyes gleamed as he came closer, shining with adoration. 'I love you,' he called.

His words rang in her mind, eternal and perfect. She replied instantly, 'I love you too. Come to me, Madan Shastri!'

After Shastri had lost the torch, Ravindra had stalked him in the darkness, gloating as he attacked, slyly slashing at him, opening cuts on arms and legs and in his side. But what the raja hadn't realised, as he played with his foe like a cat with a mouse, was that Shastri could still see him.

The king's whole body glowed faintly when seen in pure darkness, like the dying embers of a fire; barely discernible, but enough that Shastri could make out his form.

Shastri gritted his teeth and set about feigning total blindness, letting the raja worry away at him, ignoring the pain of the dozens of cuts that now bisected his flesh, harbouring his strength for one final blow. When Ravindra carelessly raised his blade, preparing to administer his final killing stroke, Shastri sprang off his right leg and drove his blade straight through the raja's heart, piercing him with such power that the sword went straight through his ribs and burst out his back.

As Ravindra staggered back, choking for breath, Shastri could make out the glare of total incomprehension on his face. He clutched at the sword-hilt and slumped against the wall beside the door, then onto the ground, and the weight of his body forced the tip of Shastri's blade into the floor and anchored him there.

The raja laboured for breath and attempted in vain to rally himself.

As his head dropped to one side, five chilling voices started wailing somewhere in the darkness.

Shastri looked at the body. Some part of him feared to remove his sword; it looked as if it was physically pinning the raja to the ground. *Is Ravindra dead? But hadn't he been dead already?* Perhaps his ruined body had taken all the punishment it could sustain – but maybe not; he didn't know the rules. In the end he opted to play it safe and heed his instinct: he left it there and backed away until he reached the posts of the bridge.

He clambered onto the lower of the ropes, gripped the two guide-ropes with hands sticky with blood and lurched along. Every movement was agony, tearing open all those vicious wounds a little more with every correction of balance, each forced step. Only Darya's fierce, beloved face sustained him.

One more step. Just one more. Then another.

Darya stepped right to the lip of the chasm, one hand on a pillar, the other extended towards him. She was very deliberately not looking down. How odd to think that his beautiful, courageous love feared heights and depths . . . And how magnificently she fought those fears!

A dark shape loomed behind her, on the ledge. The poet.

Relief washed through him. They were all alive – that was a miracle in itself.

And like a deva, his angel had come for him out of the darkness.

'Just a few more steps, my love,' she called. 'Just a few more.' She was so close . . .

Then the rope in his right hand gave way and Darya screamed. He tipped sideways, swaying furiously, and as his left hand clung to the other suspension rope, his right was ripped raw by the broken guide-rope as it whipped across his palm.

For a second he thought he was falling, but the bottom rope was holding. His eyes sought Darya desperately: she was staring out across the chasm at him, both arms wrapped about the right-hand pillar at her end. Her eyes were as wide as her mouth, but he could see she was poised to come for him. His gaze went to the frayed ropes and he bellowed a warning.

Aram loomed behind her and wrapped his arms about her shoulders, pulling her back.

'Aram, hold her,' Shastri called. 'Hold her tight—'

Then the suspension rope in his left hand snapped as well.

For an instant it was as if gravity had forgotten him, then he teetered, wobbled, tried to step forward, tried to leap for the bottom rope. It felt for a moment as if he could walk on the air. He bellowed out his fear, reaching for Aram and Darya.

Then he struck the bottom rope, fell through it as it snapped, and the darkness gobbled him up.

Remembered Lives

Jodhpur, Rajasthan, March 2010

Vikram was at the back as they ran into the tunnel, but it got smaller almost immediately, and they all had to drop to their knees and start crawling as it dipped and led them deeper beneath the earth. He held one torch and Amanjit had the other, so both had to crawl one-handed, which was turning out to be a nightmare way to travel. He kept imagining some awful thing would come slithering along the tunnel behind him, so he crawled mostly backwards so that he could put the flame of the torch between him and pursuit. It made things very awkward, and after they'd been descending several minutes, Vikram began to doubt that this could be the right way.

Suddenly Amanjit called out, 'Hey, I've found another tunnel – and it's bigger, too.'

Vikram exhaled with relief and waited impatiently as Deepika followed Amanjit, dropping down a short shaft into a wider and higher tunnel that looked distinctly man-made. He gave a sigh of relief as he landed beside them, relieved to be out of that narrow confine.

The air was colder down here and their breath was frosting as they wound deeper and deeper beneath the rock of the hill. He wondered if they'd make it as far as the level of the plain itself, but there was no way of knowing. Oddly, the path was becoming more slippery now, and despite their fear they had to slow down to negotiate the treacherous footing.

Finally they reached a doorway with a great carved lintel and ran out into a chamber that took their breath away.

The doorway was guarded by two huge statues of lions, and opened onto a large chamber dominated by more ancient statuary, half crumbled and unrecognisable. Vikram felt curiosity and excitement overtake fear and he pulled out the notebook he always carried and copied down some of the symbols, half-wishing they could stay so that he could search for more. He felt they might be important somehow. But the feeling of pursuit that had been hanging over them since the encounter with Jeetan – or 'One-Eyed Jeet' as the sadhu had called him – drove them onwards. They clambered over what might be a dried-up pool littered in filth, with the rotting ruins of a boat which crumbled where Amanjit laid a hand on it.

They climbed between the two largest statues and saw a doorway beyond.

'That way!' Amanjit said, his voice confident. All this danger was bringing out something in him; he was very much the man of action now.

Just like Shastri, rose the thought in Vikram's mind.

Amanjit strode towards the door he'd pointed out. Deepika looked at Vikram, mouthing, 'Come on,' as she followed Amanjit through the chamber and into the darkness of the next tunnel.

Vikram followed. Part of him was longing to stop and investigate further, but the fear of what was following them was too great: *something* was coming – something he felt he could almost name. The bow in his left hand and the torch in his right clattered on the rocks as he climbed up after them.

They're gaining on us. They're getting closer.

But five minutes saw them still moving, down another man-made tunnel that ran straight and level, and there was still no tangible sign of pursuit. Then Amanjit called out, 'Look, another door!' It was broken, and he led them through, then swore. 'Chod! It's a dead end!'

Vikram swallowed as he scuttled through behind Deepika. He cast a fearful look back down the tunnel, but nothing showed.

Beyond the door, he saw the reason for Amanjit's cursing. The tunnel had deposited them on a wide ledge.

There was no way forward.

Amanjit's torch lit the area, and they looked about them despairingly. The ledge they stood on was around thirty yards wide, and jutted out about twenty yards over a black chasm. Two wooden pillars were set on the edge, wrapped about with thick dirty ropes, which fell out of sight over the edge. The torchlight revealed the far side of the crevice, fifty yards distant at least: a smaller ledge, slightly above them, also spiked by two pillars. Rope also fell from those, but only for a few feet; they could all see where they ended, frayed and useless – the ropes had evidently given way or been cut. Amanjit walked to the edge and peered down, holding the torch out.

The light revealed sheer drops on either side, but it couldn't reach the bottom. Water was trickling somewhere below, far out of sight. There was no way to cross: they were trapped.

'Now what?' Amanjit groaned.

Deepika was panting for breath, sounding distressed.

Vikram joined them. 'Look,' he said, 'there are only three strands. It was just a rope-bridge – one central rope for walking on, and two higher guide-ropes to hold on to. The ropes snapped at the far side.'

'How deep is it? Can you hear anything?' Deepika demanded.

Their voices echoed eerily.

'Listen,' said Amanjit, 'there may be an underground river down there. Maybe we can slither down? 'I'm sure I could . . . if I used the ropes . . .'

'What's that?' Deepika said, pointing to a large lump of debris on the floor beside the wall, near the edge. It had something jutting out of it. She went to approach it, but Amanjit stopped her.

'Don't,' he warned. 'I'll check it out.'

Vikram blanked them both from his thoughts and tried to imagine a way forward. *This is just a puzzle*, he told himself, *like a computer game problem: something we have to solve*. As he walked to the edge he wondered how much time they had. Momentary vertigo upset his balance and he wobbled and reached out a hand to steady himself, grasping the nearest pillar.

A jolt ran through his body and mind like electricity and he gasped, his eyes shutting and then flying open, and he saw a different scene altogether . . .

. . . a small man with a serious face was standing at the far end of the bridge. The ropes were still connected to this side, one for balancing on, two to guide the hands. He knew, as much from instinct as from the ancient clothing style and jewellery, that he was seeing the past. And he knew the man . . .

It's Aram Dhoop . . . it's me, my previous life . . .

Vikram felt dizzy and sick, especially when the poet began hacking at the supports to the bridge. The ropes held, but he understood now that they had been fatally weakened. Dhoop was clearly trying to block some pursuer. Beyond the poet he saw down a tunnel entrance, and suddenly his vision swooped and darted forward, like a movie camera, showing him a fleeing woman dressed in rags, looking dazed and distressed as she stumbled on alone. Despite the poor clothes, he knew that she was a queen: Queen Darya. She had Deepika's eyes.

He blanked the vision out as a sense of bitter irony momentarily filled him.

Aram weakened the bridge – Aram, who is me. So I trapped us here, in my past life.

But then that emotion passed, to be replaced by something worse as the visions beat at him once more, bringing him back here, to this near side of the bridge, where two men were fighting in near-darkness. He could just make out a warrior who had to be Shastri, fighting a larger man whose body glowed like coals in a fire. That hideous figure's blade was a blinding flicker, but his body was a hulking and horribly burned ruin, and he knew beyond doubt that it was the same being who'd sent the vision of the sadhu at Mandore . . . and no doubt who'd set Jeetan upon them too. This was Ravindra himself!

Shastri fought Ravindra on this side of the crevice, and all the while Aram Dhoop was weakening the bridge . . . Intuition told him why: *Aram believed Ravindra would triumph* . . . His eyes went to the mounded shape that Amanjit was bending over.

Then he relived the rest of it.

Time passed in a split-second, and in that brief instant, he understood and remembered it all: like a hot-wired download from a computer to his skull, like a torrent of fire from a flame-thrower, like a bolt of lightning that made him shake and stagger, almost sending him over the edge of the crevice, Vikram *remembered*.

In an instant that seemed to stretch for millennia, he remembered not just this place, but *everything* that had followed.

Visions dazzled him – illogically linked fragments making no sense and yet incandescent scorched his mind. Images, faces, places and names; betrayals and failures, over and over again. Flashes of past lives like half-remembered dreams crashed into his consciousness: fighting red-jacketed British soldiers in the south, and battling Muslims in the north, kissing a white woman in one life, the hand of a plump, dusky-skinned maid in another; an insane girl nuzzling his feet as he dangled on a rope. Sitting at the feet of gurus and rajas and generals and governors. Swords and spears and muskets – and arrows, always arrows. Arrows, and chants that went with them, that made them something more. His lips mouthed the phrases as they flooded back into his mind. Then the visions changed again, and brought him something worse.

Images of past lives were supplanted by images of death: every death in every life his soul had ever lived. Over and over they hammered into him, each and every fatal moment – and always the same eyes blazing as they stood over him and thrust, or shot, or stabbed, or gave the executioner his orders: Ravindra's eyes.

He moaned in despair, feeling his vision blur with the tears of so many years. He could even remember going through this moment, this eternal instant of remembrance, in almost all of his past lives – but not in the life in which he was named Aram Dhoop. His first life.

But he wasn't Aram any longer . . . and he wasn't really Vikram any more either. He fell to his knees, not needing to see any more, not when he could recall what had happened here so long ago.

He let go of the pillar and his normal senses returned. Had years or seconds passed? He looked at the others, but they were still looking at the debris on the edge of the ledge and neither of them appeared to have moved, although Deepika glanced up at him and paused, as if noticing something in him that was odd.

His voice sounded ragged as he blurted the first thing that

came to him. 'Aram cut the ropes, from the far side. That's why the bridge is broken.' Vikram felt his heart shuddering erratically.

The other two straightened and turned to face him. Amanjit's face looked older in the torchlight, his demeanour commanding and capable, and Deepika had a regal air that took Vikram's breath away. But his brain was still swirling strangely, because he saw other faces overlaying theirs, as he had in the professor's office a few days ago.

I've known them both in the past, he realised. *But we've never resolved what Aram did here . . .*

Cold air wheezed out of the tunnel behind them and Deepika looked back, dread in her eyes. 'Aram cut the rope-bridge? Why? And how do you know?' She looked at Amanjit, but to Vikram's relief he was staring at the debris, which looked like an old man sleeping, with something sticking from his chest, like the sword in the stone in English legends of King Arthur.

Amanjit pulled it out and stared at it. 'It fits my hand,' he whispered in awe. 'As if it was made for me.'

'So it should,' Vikram replied. 'It's yours. Or rather, Shastri's.'

Amanjit looked at him, then back at the weapon. 'It's rusted all to hell.'

'Wait, let me see it!' Vikram said quickly, striding towards him. Amanjit handed over the old weapon while Deepika just stood staring down into the depths of the chasm.

Vikram took the sword and closed his eyes. He said something softly as old memories flooded in, and did something he'd done before, many times . . . in other lives. The sword thrummed in his grip, then the cloth and leather of the hilt reformed and the rust fell away, revealing clean steel, gleaming as if freshly forged.

He gave it back to Amanjit, who was staring at him.

'What did you do?' he breathed, looking at Vikram as if he had just sprouted horns.

'It was just dirty,' Vikram answered, meeting his eyes. 'Nothing out of the ordinary. It was very well made,' he added.

Amanjit continued to stare at him, but nodded as if he feared to know more. 'How weird is that?' He swished it experimentally. 'So, what do we do?'

Vikram could barely bring himself to think. He felt numb, overloaded, disconnected, and he was struggling to rein in his galloping mind. 'I saw something when I touched the pillar. Aram and Queen Darya were on the other side, and I – he, Aram – weakened the bridge. He did it while you – er, Shastri – was still on this side.'

Amanjit looked back at the stones from which he had pulled the sword and stiffened. 'That's an old body—? So is that – *was* that – me . . . ?'

'I don't know,' Vikram replied. 'You were fighting another man, so perhaps it's him.'

Dear gods, I hope so, because then perhaps Shastri escaped after all.

But other memories were rising through the dizziness inside his head.

No, Shastri never escaped . . .

Amanjit frowned. 'What are you saying, that Aram and Queen Darya left Shastri to die?'

Vikram started to nod, then shook his head and said unhappily, 'I think it was worse than that . . .'

Amanjit's face changed strangely and his voice took on a different cadence, sounding older, more mature – stronger. '*You bastard, Aram! You cut me off and left me to die!*' He raised the sword and pointed it at Vikram.

Deepika clutched at his arm, suddenly alarmed as Amanjit shook her off. 'Hey, past lives, guys!' she hissed. 'This one amends it all, right?' She stepped between them, looking from one to the other until the anger subsided. 'What we've all got to do is get out of this alive ourselves and make this life count. And we've got maybe five minutes.'

Vikram knew she was right, but he was fixed on the gleaming sword in Amanjit's right hand. Amanjit didn't take his eyes from Vikram for a long time, but at last he lowered the blade. 'Later,' he warned. 'Later, we'll talk about this.'

Vikram swallowed and turned away. It seemed odd to him that they were not remembering everything the way he was. But there was still a problem to solve. *How on earth can we get across?* But even as he set his mind to it, old skills were flooding into his mind, and not just any sorts of skills either . . .

Yes . . . that would work . . .

He stared across the gap, looked up and down, calculating, then removed the bow and arrows he'd picked up earlier and murmured the same spells that had restored the sword. The bow lost its grime and rot, becoming as clean and flexible as new. He strung it and nocked an arrow, feeling a long-lost emotion rise as he did. The bow was his weapon, the one skill he'd mastered down the centuries that Ravindra feared. 'I've got an idea how I can get us across, one at a time – Deepika needs to go first.'

'How?' Amanjit demanded, his voice still filled with mistrust. 'What are you doing?'

Old memories yielded the required spell. 'Watch, and I'll show you!' He looked at Deepika. 'Get ready. Make sure you've stashed everything you need, because your hands need to be free.'

Deepika looked at Amanjit uncertainly. 'Vikram, have you gone nuts?'

'Probably. But this works, I know it. I can get us across. Are you ready?'

Their torches flickered in a fresh draft of cold air that made them all shiver. Vikram saw Deepika make up her mind. 'Okay. But what do I do?'

'Be ready,' he told her, full of confidence. Memories were bouncing through his mind, memories of dark places and dangers – but he was no longer afraid . . . not for himself, anyway.

He stepped away from the edge, aimed past her shoulder at the far side between the two far pillars of the bridge and muttered a chant over the arrow. It took time, this one, but it was the only one that would do what he needed. The slow burst of energy made him reel . . . *as it always had before* . . .

The arrow left the bow . . . very, *very* slowly.

'Grab it!' he told Deepika.

She stared at the shaft as it glided slowly through the air, as if completely immune to physics and logic. 'How—? But— What—?'

'It's the Dhimayastra – the slow arrow.' He grinned. 'I invented it myself! Grab hold, both hands.'

'An *astra*? The arrow of the gods?'

'Not just of the gods,' he told her. 'Go on, quickly!'

She reached out as if in a trance and took the arrow as it moved past her at walking pace. Her face was disbelieving as she laid first one hand, and when that didn't change the flight of the arrow, the other on the shaft. It dragged her to the edge.

'This is impossible!' she gasped.

He nodded cheerily in agreement. 'Yes, it is – every law of science just went out the window. Don't let go, will you?' He blew on the arrow and it suddenly accelerated to about six feet per second.

Deepika gave a little shriek and her legs kicked as she was pulled out over the void, but the arrow didn't deviate from its flight an inch as it soared onward towards the other side, bearing her with it.

Amanjit stared at Vikram as if he was a circus freak. 'Who *are* you?'

'Vikram Khandavani. Aram Dhoop. A few others. Are you ready?'

'That was impossible,' Amanjit whispered. 'Even Rama himself couldn't make that shot.'

'I bet he could,' replied Vikram. 'Come on, your turn!'

But before they could act, something clattered in the tunnel behind them and an icy breath of air washed out of the cave-mouth. There were whispers, and muttered curses, and the two young men turned to face it, Amanjit with his sword held high, Vikram with another arrow ready.

On the far side, Deepika landed and let go of the arrow, which flew on inexorably until it struck the wall, where it bounced and clattered to the rocky floor, as if gravity had suddenly claimed it.

'I'm here!' she shouted. 'That was incredible!' But the boys heard more stones rattle in the tunnel, and neither dared to turn their back.

'Come on, come on,' Deepika called. 'Both of you – *both* of you!'

Vikram nocked an arrow to his bow and said urgently, 'Amanjit, you need to go first. I've seen how this ended last time. It's got to be you first this time.'

To make amends . . . In all the teachings of Hinduism, we can only move on to the next stage of spirituality when we have made amends for our failings . . .

But before Amanjit could respond, a soft, feminine sigh resonated from the cave-mouth and pale shapes slid into the half-light of the torches: the chief queen – Halika, Vikram recalled from his pool of new/old knowledge – with four other queens gliding behind her.

Vikram cursed. There was no time for another Dhimayastra.

Amanjit crouched, flexing his sword arm. 'I don't leave people behind,' he snarled.

Vikram wished Aram Dhoop could have said the same. 'It's your choice.'

'Damn right it is.'

The five queens grew more and more substantial and the torchlight flickered, illuminating the dust motes that clung to them. Only the cavernous holes of their eye sockets were not lit.

'Madan Shastri,' they called, reaching out in a chilling mockery of seduction. 'Aram Dhoop. Come to us . . .'

'Is the Raja hiding behind his women again?' Vikram taunted them. 'Some things never change.'

'Ahh. It has come back to you now, has it? All life is a circle, Aram Dhoop,' whispered Halika. 'In this one, as in all the others, you will die alone.'

'Not alone,' snarled Amanjit.

Halika smiled. 'There is a skeleton down that hole behind you,' she told the Sikh. 'It's Shastri's. We'll send yours down to join it when we've finished with you.'

The ghostly queens raised their claws, hissing hungrily as they closed in.

Ras stared into the empty eyes of Padma, dead queen of Mandore. The ghostly shape raised a hand with long nails like sharpened tusks, yellowed and curved.

'Please,' the girl whispered, 'I don't want to die.'

'Neither did I,' the spectral woman replied. Her hand splayed as she rose to her feet and reached for Ras' throat.

Ras shrank against the wall. Though almost paralysed by fear, she wriggled desperately to preserve herself for an extra second. Something cold pressed against her leg and she gripped it almost by reflex.

Her fingers traced the outline: her letter-opener, a silver one she'd been given.

'I'm sorry,' Padma told her, 'but I need you. You will make me complete.' Her hand closed about Ras' throat and seared her skin with cold. Rasita's lungs felt like they were collapsing as if punctured; suddenly she could scarcely breathe. Pale light shone in the queen's eyes and with a satisfied gulp she inhaled the frosted air that Ras choked out. The young woman's vision swam and she felt all of her volition and self-control weaken as her body ran dry of energy.

With what little strength that remained, Ras raised her hand and buried the blade of the letter-opener into the dead queen's heart.

The ghost shrieked, a noise that rattled and then shattered the windows. Both her hands flew to her breast and seared against the silver as if it were cold fire. She flew backwards across the bedroom, fraying as she went, until all that hit the far wall was a bag of bones wrapped in mouldy cloth and leathery shreds of skin.

As the body struck the wall it felt like something exploded in Ras' chest. She jerked once and tumbled in a faint to the floor.

An Honourable Way to Die

Mandore, Rajasthan, AD *769*

Aram clung despairingly to Darya, stopping the queen from hurling herself to Shastri's aid as the first rope gave way. Her cry tore the air, echoed by Shastri as he fought for balance. Aram held fast, sensing that her weight on the remaining ropes would snap them too. Then the second one gave way.

She thrashed in his grip, but he held on to her grimly as the third rope began to part. For a second, the scene etched itself on his retinas, to burn there ever after: Shastri hanging on desperately, his eyes on Darya, blood spraying from the rents in his armour. Darya twisting and clawing, turning her face back towards his, her arms splayed. Her eyes were so full of enmity, her face so contorted with hate that she could have been Halika. Then she turned back to Shastri as the last guide-rope gave way and cracked like a whip across the void.

Shastri roared as his hands flailed, reaching for the final rope. Then he was gone, falling away from them while Aram held Darya to him with all his strength. The darkness swallowed the senapati with an echoing wail, then a clattering smash met their ears as he hit the rock walls, then splashed into the waters.

Darya cried out his name, and her harsh, agonised voice echoed through the chamber.

Aram tried to drag her from the edge, but she saw the cut rope-ends and she *knew*. She whirled on him and slapped viciously, her face livid. 'You did it – *you* cut the ropes . . . it's your fault he's gone!'

He edged backwards, pleading for her to understand. 'I had to – Ravindra – I *had* to—'

She turned away and leaning out, peering downwards, called despairingly, 'Shastri! Madan—!'

But there was no reply.

She turned back and looked down at Aram with contempt and fury on her face, but he read her intention too late.

She turned and jumped.

Aram Dhoop stayed alone in the darkness. Hours passed and still he called her name, and sometimes Shastri's, but no response arose from the darkness below. The torch guttered and burned out and he cried alone, weeping and tearing at his face with his broken nails. She was gone. He had betrayed them both. He was nothing.

I am a weakling and a coward.

Finally, he dropped to his knees and prostrated himself. He rubbed away his tears, swallowed his bile and began to pray for the opportunity to redeem himself and those he had failed.

How long he remained there he could never afterwards say. Or why he was heard by the powers who hear such prayers. Perhaps he was delusional. Perhaps he was insane, but something was torn inside him and closed doors inside his skull blew open.

It seemed to him that there was a powerfully built man sitting cross-legged on a tiger's pelt, with tangled hair and a third eye in the middle of his forehead. There was another being, sitting on the coils of a many-headed serpent, with face stern and impassive, almost too brilliant to look upon. A tiger coughed behind him, ridden by a beautiful woman with terrifying eyes who watched him without compassion. They were each so massive that Aram could have walked inside their mouths without bending. He hung in the air before them like a small hummingbird, trembling under the stress of their dreadful gaze.

'She was meant to live,' She who rode the tiger hissed.

'But you let her fall, and her lover too,' He on the tiger-pelt accused.

'You betrayed your brother,' said He enthroned on the snake. 'You must make amends.'

'Please! Please!' he said eagerly, desperate to do exactly that.

'Your prayers are heard,' they chorused. 'You are heard. In every life you will remember your pledge and all that has gone before. At every turn of the wheel you will recall this moment, and so you will be driven to fulfil your oath.'

The man on the snake throne gestured, and flaming symbols blazed in the air. 'Now it is written. So shall it be. From now until your pledge is fulfilled.'

A gong reverberated, its vibrations tearing at his flesh and his soul, and it felt like he fell, for aeons, through darkness and then clouds and then earth, and into his own body with a cry that echoed throughout the lonely chamber far below the ground.

How long Aram lay there, he could not tell, but finally he woke. The torches had burned out, and he had neither food nor water. His body was battered and his heart aching as he crawled sluggishly along the passageway for an age, until he emerged into the daylight world.

The earth was still brown and the sky still blue, but it was empty, as empty as his heart.

He understood that in every future life he would be given the chance of redemption . . . but not in this life . . . in this life, he had nothing to hope for.

There was nothing left for him but to find an honourable way to die.

The Return of Ravana

Jodhpur, Rajasthan, March 2010

Vikram crouched between the ancient wooden posts of the bridge with an arrow nocked. Amanjit, at his side, had the renewed sword in his hand.

The five queens fanned out, two on either side of Halika, a dozen paces away. Vikram knew their names now – Aruna, Jyoti, Meena and Rakhi – and he remembered them too, how they had been before the pyre claimed them: sweet girls, pampered, frivolous, frightened of their lord, but indulged in every luxury. None of them deserved this endless torment – except for Halika, who was as deep in evil as Ravindra himself.

'Lord Rama, be with me,' he prayed.

He felt eyes on him, eyes from other times and places.

In the forests of ancient India, said the *Ramayana*, the Sage Vishwamitra had taught Rama and his brother Lakshmana how to enchant their weapons. The words and ways of those enchantments had been whispered into Vikram's brain in another life, when the world was younger and far stranger.

Now he took aim, and as he murmured Vishwamitra's words, his arrow blurred into five shafts; he loosed the string as

Ravindra's queens gathered themselves up, mouths open and teeth flashing, talons flexed – tigers set to pounce.

The five arrows flashed, each with a comet-tail of incandescent power, and as each struck the heart of a queen, that power coursed through them, jolting them with the impact, for this was an astra, a magically enhanced arrow, the favoured weapon of the Hindu gods.

The dead queens howled, unbearably loud, as if knives of white-hot steel had been driven into them, and their hands flew to their chests. All five fell convulsing to the dirt, burning from the insides, their skins turning from deep red to white-hot – and then each burst into flame. A sickening stench rose all about him, making him choke, but he had no choice but to watch further, even as each of the five beings collapsed into ash and then blew away down the tunnel in a dark stream of flecks.

'Holy Father!' gasped Amanjit, awestruck. 'How'd you do that?'

'Technically? That was an astra called a Mohini, and its special power was that it dispelled magic. I combined it with an Aindra-astra, for multiple arrows. I was thinking that those dead queens need magic to remain in existence.'

Amanjit stared at him, his jaw dropping. Then he said, disbelievingly, 'Did it work? Are they dead?'

'Probably not, because they weren't alive to start with. I suspect they're just temporarily inconvenienced.' He pulled another arrow from the quiver. 'I don't know how to tell you this, Amanjit, so I'll just say it outright: there were five queens. There should have been six.'

Amanjit stared at him. 'What do you mean?'

'There were seven queens in ancient Mandore, Ravindra's seven wives. Darya escaped; six queens burned. That' – he waved an expressive hand – 'was five. One was not here: Padma, the one who attacked your sister in the library.' He frowned. 'Though what the ghostly sadhu said suggests Ravindra doesn't actually control Padma . . .'

Amanjit had stopped listening to him. 'Ras . . .' His voice trembled.

Whatever he might have said next died on his lips, for a larger, darker shape was forming at the mouth of the tunnel: a shadow framed in the cave-mouth. Red eyes gleamed from the dimly rendered head.

Vikram took a shot, but the dark shape raised a hand and somehow his arrow veered aside and shattered explosively against the rock. The whole chamber shook, and splinters of rocks pinged across the cavern.

But the dark shape had merged with the deepest shadows and now a low, rasping voice filled the chamber. 'You have remembered your old skills just in time, little poet.'

The mere sound of that voice made Vikram shudder; it triggered memories that started replaying in his mind, but he forced himself to keep his eyes open, trying to pierce the darkness.

'Would you like a taste of what your wives got?' he called, hoping to provoke a misstep.

Ravindra's dark voice slithered from the shadows again. 'I need them not. They have served their purpose for now. All you have done is dispersed their essence for a time. Do not think that I am weakened by the loss of those irritating bitches. Alone I was born. Alone I shall triumph.'

'I'll send you to the loneliest part of hell if you step into the light.'

Ravindra chuckled evilly. 'Seven queens I have: seven lives for the seven gates of the underworld – so the rakshasa whispered into my mind as I sat on the throne of Mandore. My rising again should have been a triumph – but you stole Darya, and Chetan was fool enough to let Padma give away her heart-stone. It left me and my ranis stranded in the void, half in this world, half in the next; we have never passed on . . . For more than a thousand years I have endured, stealing the bodies of others to hunt my two stolen queens and their heart-stones. We have crossed paths before, many times, as I know you now recall.'

Vikram certainly did, and he also recalled the results: until now life after life had always ended in his own death.

Ravindra rumbled on, 'It has all been in vain, until now – but in this life we are *all* gathered – and I can almost *smell* those heart-stones: they are close, I know it! This is the key life, Aram Dhoop, in this life I shall complete the ritual. In this life, I shall finally gain true immortality, and become Ravana reborn.'

Vikram heard Amanjit gasp in astonishment, but for him it was just the confirmation of what he'd suspected. 'Ravana died,' he reminded the shadows.

Ravindra ignored him and his sulphurous voice rose anew. 'Yes, that is my goal: to be Ravana, Priest-King of Lanka, risen again and immortal, with all his wisdom and power – and thus shall I take revenge upon the sons of Ram – no, upon mankind itself!'

Ravana . . . reborn . . . The mere thought made Vikram tremble. 'You're mad. Ravana never existed,' he said firmly. 'What you're saying is impossible.'

Ravindra chuckled. 'After all you have seen and experienced, you still believe that such things are impossible?'

Amanjit stepped forward, his expression thunderstruck. 'I remember,' he said to Vikram, his voice shot through with wonder. 'I *remember*: I fought him. I fought and I won.' He brandished his reborn blade, which reflected the torchlight. 'Vikram, I fought him right here – and I *won*.'

'Aram Dhoop never believed you could win,' Vikram replied. 'That's why he weakened the bridge. And he wanted Darya for himself. He . . . *I* . . . failed you both.'

'You weren't to know, and it was a long time ago,' Amanjit replied. He looked Vikram in the eyes and said clearly, 'I forgive you, Aram.'

The instant he uttered those words, something bright flared inside Vikram's mind.

Beside him, Amanjit gasped. 'Did you feel that?'

Vikram had: it felt like fetters broken, like the first shaft of sunlight at dawn. But he couldn't think about that now; they still had a major problem to sort out. He kindled another arrow and tried to find Ravindra.

Perhaps I can . . . ?

He stared into the shadows, but couldn't see anything, although he could tell Ravindra was moving, flowing through the darkness like an unseen river.

From across the chasm, Deepika cried a warning, just as the pile of debris from which Amanjit had pulled Shastri's sword stirred and then rose. A blackened sword detached itself from the fossilised dust in the grip of an animated right arm. Ravindra swung it experimentally and sighed in pleasurable remembrance. 'Ah . . . it's good to have my own body once again . . .'

Vikram fired, and Ravindra's blade swatted the arrows away in a flash of flame. The dead raja laughed and shambled forward, his huge form grimed and hideous.

Amanjit whirled and lunged. Steel chimed, pure and untarnished against the raja's rusted, filth-encrusted blade. They hammered at each other while Vikram sought an angle for another shot.

Amanjit was moving incredibly, like a man born to the sword;

for all his foe's size and speed, he was faster. Then the black blade shattered in Ravindra's hand and with a cry, its wielder vanished.

Vikram spun around, desperately seeking the raja, then flung himself sideways and rolled as a massive claw swiped at his skull from behind. Amanjit whirled and thrust above him.

Ravindra was gone again. They turned, both of them, seeking their foe—

—as Deepika screamed from the other side of the crevice, her cry echoing back from the rocky walls until it filled the cavern.

Ravindra was looming behind her, his left arm about her throat. 'My queen,' he snarled, 'you belong to me.' He leered across the chasm and announced, 'I have finished playing with you two boys. I have what I came for.' He laughed. 'Farewell, fools!'

His face mocking Vikram, Ravindra was poised to leap and vanish.

Amanjit roared in anguish and Vikram took aim, despairing, as Deepika grasped the nearest bridge-post and clung on for dear life as the demon-lord lifted her into the air.

For an instant she held him still—

—and in that instant, Vikram's arrow took Ravindra in the throat. An Agneyastra: the fire arrow.

Ravindra howled and let her go as he spun and contorted in the air, then crashed to the ground. He ripped out the arrow, which crumbled to ash, but his neck had gone searing white. As Vikram prepared another shaft, smoke poured from the wound. Deepika rolled away, scrambling frantically to put distance between them, but Ravindra had leapt upwards and now clung to the roof like a spider. His throat wound gaped and black blood sizzled and smoked.

His voice, contorted by pain but still virulent, thundered, 'I am Ravana! I am immortal!'

'Only the gods are immortal,' Vikram said, and fired again.

Ravindra twisted fiendishly, and the second fire arrow took him in the shoulder instead of the heart, but the impact still slammed through him and with a roar, he fell into the crevice. He struck the wall, and was gone. They heard the raja hit the water below with a sizzling splash.

Vikram stared after him and cursed.

Amanjit peered down into the crevice, panting. On the far side, Deepika was on her feet again, her eyes wide with shock. They listened to the thrashing in the water below, then everything fell silent.

'Is he dead?' Amanjit asked. 'Did you kill him?'

Vikram shook his head. 'No – no, it didn't kill him. I'm sure of that.' *I used the wrong arrow . . .* But there had been so little time to re-absorb all those past life memories, too little time to become again what he once was. The sensation that this was a chance lost ate at him as he stared down into the void.

'Damn!' Amanjit cast about desperately. 'Can we get down there and finish him?'

Vikram considered the question, looking around him, and inside himself. Slowly he shook his head. 'No, we'd never find him down there. There are too many shadows, too many places to hide. He'd have the upper hand.'

'But we can't just let him get away.'

Vikram closed his eyes. There were so many things coming back to him now, prodding at his mind – so much he had known: past lives, skills, memories. He whispered a just-recalled spell and his mind showed him Ravindra, slithering through shadows beneath the water, kicking through narrow places where no mortal man could go, black blood flowing but the wounds sealing, though flames still licked at them, even underwater.

He said regretfully, 'He's already gone.'

Amanjit hung his head and cursed. 'Then we'll never be free of him.'

Vikram straightened himself and looked Amanjit in the eye. 'Yes, we will,' he said, trying to sound confident. 'In this life, we will be free of him.'

'You know this?' Amanjit asked.

Vikram almost nodded, but that would have been a lie. 'Maybe. I hope so. I really hope so.'

Because this is my seventeenth life, and he's killed me, either directly or indirectly, in all the previous sixteen . . .

After the fight with Ravindra, escaping the darkness was just a matter of logistics. Vikram and Amanjit used the slow arrow to get to the far side and took the same path out that Aram Dhoop had once trod alone, more than twelve hundred years before. They had to push their way out from behind a rockfall to regain the surface, but it wasn't too big and took them only twenty or thirty minutes. It looked like no one else had found this path in all those years.

And this time, there were three present, and the sun greeted them, kissing their skin, as a cooling wind caressed their hair. It was early evening, only a couple of hours since they'd descended beneath the fortress.

For Amanjit, it was like regaining sight after being blind, or walking again after a crippling injury. Deepika's hand in his was warm and firm, and she met his eyes steadily. He knew, he just *knew*, that this would be their time. He pulled her to him and closed his eyes. She felt like a part of him, restored to him, bound to him anew. He had never felt so complete.

Deepika clung to Amanjit and it felt like coming home. Something echoed inside her and she felt for a second that she could, if she just knew how, remember all the other times, just like Vikram. But no . . . she didn't want to. All she wanted, all she could ever desire, was *here* and *now*. That Ravindra had escaped frightened her, but they'd come through so much, and there was a wholeness and rightness in how she felt right this minute that she'd never experienced before. It was as if she'd been hunting through her room for a lost heirloom that meant a great deal and suddenly found it.

He and I were fated to be, but it has never happened before . . . until now.

It should have frightened her, but it didn't: it felt like the best thing that could ever be.

Vikram stared at the setting sun, his mind so far down memory's paths that every moment was a waking dream. He saw life upon life, each dropping new knowledge and memories into his mind. It had always been like this, in every past life except the first: he was always in his teens when he regained the memories of each preceding life – if he actually made it that far.

Amanjit had been in many of those lives, and so had Deepika – though not Ras, thankfully. In past lives of danger they had often fought together, and died together, but always in defeat. Even when they'd been reborn into quiet lives of seclusion, the darkness had found them. Ravindra – his nemesis, his personal demon – had appeared in so many guises.

It was too much to take in.

He looked at Deepika, longing to hold her, just as Amanjit was, but he no longer felt compelled to act on his desire for her. He'd let her go, and been rewarded with a new certainty: that there was someone else for him, someone out there he was yet to meet. Though that old yearning for this unattainable woman – Darya who was now Deepika – was still there, from the moment he and Amanjit made their peace in the caves below he'd moved beyond Aram Dhoop's tragic, unreciprocated desire.

But he also knew just how delicately balanced everything was now. He and Deepika had met in many other lives, and in none of them had she ever loved him as he did her. In none had he ever found the woman of his heart. For an instant, caught up in an aching loneliness, he lost his certainty. All of the past times he had failed her came flooding back and he turned away, breathing deeply. There was so little time to make everything right this time round. He had *maybe* solved the riddle of Shastri and Darya, but there was so much more to do.

A hand touched his shoulder. 'Vikram, stop worrying,' said Deepika. 'It might not all be over, but it's a beautiful day to be alive. We can solve tomorrow's problems tomorrow.' She put her arms around him and hugged him.

He drank in the sensation, aglow with curious satisfaction. He could have repeated the mistakes of Aram Dhoop, but he hadn't. He found this time he could let her go – she wasn't his and she never had been.

The weight of history suddenly choked his throat and froze his limbs, until Deepika squeezed him again. He forced a smile – and felt himself begin to heal.

'So, what shall we do now?' Amanjit asked him. There was no question any more of who led them.

'For now, we get on with life, I think,' Vikram said. 'But first, I have to recover a book.'

'What book? The *Ramayana*?' asked Deepika with a doubtful smile.

Vikram couldn't share the humour. 'No. A book of poetry.'

I last buried it near here . . . about thirty years ago, I reckon . . .

'But the *Ramayana* is involved, isn't it?' Deepika asked. 'I heard what that – that *thing* said: that he's Ravana, reborn.' She stared at Vikram, and at the bow he still carried. 'Does that mean you're Rama?'

'No, definitely not!'

'So is Deepika really Sita?' Amanjit asked, holding her possessively, his voice betraying the anxiety that somehow she might not be meant for him after all. 'Or Ras?'

'No,' Vikram said heavily, 'Deepika is Deepika, Ras is Ras, and I don't think she's really involved at all – at least, I hope not. And you are not Lakshmana, you are Amanjit Singh Bajaj. We're just people. Even after . . . well, what just happened. We're just people who are sometimes actors in a play that keeps repeating, over and over. Don't ask me how I know that, but I do.'

He looked at first one, then the other, and sighed. 'This isn't the end at all, you know. I'm sorry, but it's only the beginning.'

Throwing Down a Gauntlet

Jodhpur, Rajasthan, March 2010

'Hey, have you ever been inside a gurdwara?' Amanjit asked.

Deepika pulled a face. 'A Sikh temple? I'm a Hindu – it's not really encouraged.'

'There's one in Ratanada, near the railway station. I'll show you round.' He winked at her. 'We can get a free meal.'

'Really?'

'Sure, there are always kitchens at a gurdwara – it's just daal and rice and chapatti, but hey, no charge. Come on.'

She let him pull her along, not really minding. They'd been walking all morning, holding hands, not really heading anywhere, just going wherever the streets of Jodhpur took them, stopping for little cups of chai occasionally. They should have been in school, but after the last few days, they'd managed to wangle a sick-day off. They felt they needed to make sense of everything they'd learned and been through, and doing that together felt as natural as breathing.

'Where's Vikram?' Deepika wondered.

'He was going to visit Ras,' Amanjit told her. He'd done so himself that morning before meeting up with Deepika. His little sister had had another relapse while the three of them had been trapped beneath the Mehrangarh. Amanjit suspected that the unaccounted-for ghost of Padma had been the cause of her relapse, but she was safe, or so the doctors had assured them, though she wouldn't be going back to school for a while. So that was another thing to worry about, as if raving lunatics who thought they were the reincarnation of Ravana and used knife-wielding thugs and murderous gunmen to do their dirty work weren't enough.

And then there was all this past-life stuff.

'So Vikram can remember his past lives,' Deepika said quietly. 'Has he said anything more about it?'

'Not much,' Amanjit said worriedly. 'I got the impression it wasn't good.' He looked at her sideways. 'I haven't had any memories return . . . I just *know* that I was once Madan Shastri and you were Darya. But I have no memories of it.'

'I know, me neither.' She looked up as they turned a corner and saw lines of turbaned men and veiled women filing into a gate, and beyond it, a white and gold dome beyond a high wall. 'Is this the gurdwara?' She lifted her scarf to cover her head out of respect for the temple.

'Sure.' Amanjit let the strange subject of past lives and past loves lapse and led her inside, walking barefoot through shallow running water to clean their feet, then on to the temple itself. Amanjit showed her the darbar, the central hall, where the *Guru Granth Sahib*, the holy text, was continuously recited. There were no statues, which Deepika found strange – Hindu temples were crammed with colourful statuary and symbols. For his part, he liked the pristine feel of a gurdwara, where one could clear one's thoughts without all the distractions of colours and art and icons.

After they'd filed past the holy text and listened to the

chanting in silence, he took her out to the sarovar, the pool for sacred bathing. There were fish in the big rectangular tank, to keep the water fresh, which Deepika found amusing.

'Look at those catfish: they're huge! You bathe in there, they'll eat you up,' she giggled.

'If anyone gets eaten, it won't be me,' he laughed. 'Catfish curry, yum! Come on, let's go and get some food.'

He took her down to the langar, the free kitchens, which were full of the poor and the not-so-poor, many with drawn faces and broken teeth, wolfing down the food with their fingers. As he found Deepika a place and went for food and water, he thought she looked like a shining, beautiful bird amidst the crowd – a Delhi-bird, far from home. When he returned she looked up and caught his eye, and he had a feeling of absolute belonging: not to this place or even this town where he'd spent all his life, but of belonging with her.

'Fish curry?' she asked lightly.

'No! Just daal and chapatti, I told you.'

Eating around the lump in his throat was hard.

After they'd finished, they wandered down to the far end of the sarovar, well away from the crowds, and held hands as they watched the water reflecting the dome and the sky.

'Amanjit—'

'Deepika—'

They stopped, laughing awkwardly. 'You go first,' she told him.

He would have rather she had, in case she'd been about to tell him something that might have changed what he was going to say. But he swallowed, clung to the hope in his heart and spoke.

'What I did learn from yesterday is that you and I should have been together, many lives ago, and I feel – *really* strongly – that we should be together in this one. I know that there are a thousand reasons why this is foolish, but there is one good reason that outweighs everything else, and that is that even though in some ways we've just met, I already know that I love you.'

Her eyes grew big as he said that, and her lips pursed together, trembling. But she didn't pull away, or shake her head, so he kissed her, tentatively and quickly, just a fleeting taste of her mouth that set his blood pounding through him.

'I love you too,' she whispered, making his soul sing. 'But if we keep snogging in a temple, we'll get thrown out,' she warned him. 'This is a holy place, remember.'

He glanced furtively towards the darbar and saw one stern old man peering at them disapprovingly. Deciding she was probably right, he stepped away a little, dropping one of her hands. 'Okay, no more PDAs until we leave. But I wanted to ask you something.'

She looked at him levelly. 'Teeka,' she said. 'Ask away.'

'Well, I'm thinking that if Vikram is right, and there really is something out there trying to be reborn as the king of demons, then we're not going to be safe until that situation is resolved. And if we are involved, then anything we do that might run counter to his will would be a direct challenge to him – like throwing down a gauntlet. He'll most likely pick that gauntlet up and then the duel will be on.'

She nodded apprehensively, then glanced around, checking they were still alone. 'If you don't want—'

'No, let me finish. I was going to say: I am not afraid of him. I will not stop living for fear of provoking that madman. And if it means our time is short, then that makes what I ask all the more urgent. Deepika, I am just a Sikh boy from a struggling family – I am young and I have no great prospects, but I know already that there is no one else in this life or any life for me but you. So there is no point in waiting and looking when I have found you already.'

He swallowed, then said, 'Deepika Choudhary, will you marry me?'

She went to reply, as tears sprang in her eyes, then she choked out, 'Yes, of course I will.'

'You will? But your parents—'

'—will go mad.' She smiled helplessly. 'Well, they'll just have to get used to it, because for me there is also no one else but you. Apparently I've been waiting for you all my lives.'

She fell into him, and he into her.

They were thrown out shortly afterwards.

Vikram stared at the girl in the hospital bed behind the clear plastic curtaining. Rasita Kaur Bajaj was off life-support, but not entirely out of danger. Until they found the cause of her relapse, she was under full electronic monitoring. There were tubes and drips and wires everywhere, screens that bleeped and pinged.

He'd heard the doctors speaking: '*A weak heart . . . not expected to ever lead a normal life.*' It made him wonder if this fragile girl was a part of the puzzle of his previous sixteen lives after all, even though he was sure their paths had never crossed before.

Who are you, Rasita? Have we ever met, in our past lives? Are you involved in this drama, or is this just your misfortune in this life, to meet Amanjit, Deepika and me?

All the electronic gadgetry in the world couldn't answer that question.

To not know pained him, because he liked her sparky, positive nature, especially in the face of such a hard situation. To be confronted with mortality so young had to be heartrending, but she just got on with things. But his life was about to get bloody and dangerous: he knew that from the experience of all those other past lives, showing him the outcomes of all the other times he'd gone up against Ravindra-Raj.

They had made a good start in this life, but he'd seen that before too, and there was no guarantee it wasn't going to be as disastrous as any other life he'd led, from the Muslim invasions, to the Mutiny, to the World Wars, and everything between and since . . . He'd never won.

But I've never quite lost, either . . .

That was something to hope for.

But as for involving Rasita: that would be cruel and wrong.

'Get well,' he whispered. 'Have a happy life.'

He turned and walked away.

EPILOGUE
The Past

Mandore, Rajasthan, AD *769*

With Chetan-Raj dead and his captains dead or gone, the Mandore kingship faltered.

The town was handed to one of the emperor's relatives, but the new dynasty never took root and a decade later the palace was abandoned. Once it became apparent that no new royal favourite would return to occupy it, the townsfolk raided it for building materials, leaving only fragments. The pit where Ravindra's funeral pyre once burned was turned into a midden, its previous use soon forgotten.

Memories faded and vanished. Lives went on.

Legends grew all over Rajasthan of five ghostly women who preyed on the lost and alone, and a burning man whose eyes were death, but over time even they were largely forgotten, recalled only occasionally, usually when someone died in mysterious circumstances.

But Aram Dhoop's memories never faded. He wandered alone, an itinerant holy man begging food for blessings and spending whatever he could on writing materials. He wrote hundreds of verses, love poems of loss and futility that no one read during his lifetime. All were in praise and adoration of an unattainable woman. He also wrote obscure odes about the darkness beneath the Hill of Birds, and a strange retelling of the *Ramayana* that verged on heresy.

His most secret labour was a journal that he kept hidden beneath a distinctive rock in the desert. When he felt his final sickness begin to claim him he buried it with a distinctive pendant, an opaque crystal with dark veins running through it. He was eighty years old, and every day had been a torment of regret and remorse.

He smiled as he felt his soul depart his flesh.

The old priests read his poems and considered burning them, but in the end they just tucked them onto their shelves, alongside far better works, and forgot him.

Though little was known of Aram Dhoop, one-time court poet to Devaraja Pratihara, Raja of Mandore, occasionally someone would stumble across the poems and bring them out into the light. Eventually someone made a selection of verses, bound them together and distributed a few copies, to see if they might take, keeping them alive for the next generation. Over the centuries more of the poems were discovered, and a biography was added, and copies were printed and circulated.

It seemed a lot of trouble to go to for an unknown poet of little skill, but somehow there was always someone who would find a hidden copy and ensure the poems survived. It was almost as if they knew where to look.

EPILOGUE

The Present

Jodhpur, Rajasthan, March 2010

It was official: Amanjit Singh Bajaj and Deepika Choudhary were engaged and would marry once they had graduated and found jobs for themselves in Deepika's home city of Delhi. Amanjit's mother was surprised and not a little troubled that her second son was planning to go to Delhi, and apparently Deepika's mother was very put out that her daughter had got herself engaged at so young an age – and to a provincial Sikh boy at that! But those closest to the couple knew that Deepika and Amanjit were made for each other.

That was not the end of the matrimonial news that summer: Vikram's father had proposed to Amanjit's mother and been accepted. Dinesh Khandavani and Kiran Kaur Bajaj would marry as soon as they had found a new family home in Jodhpur, where they could all enjoy a fresh start. Uncle Charanpreet had been forced to relinquish his control over the family purse-strings and to her joy, the widow had found she was far richer than she had ever been told. Even so, a lot of the money and possessions mentioned in her dead husband's original will had disappeared and her brother-in-law Charanpreet was facing charges for embezzlement.

Vikram was happy for his father, and proud to call Bishin and especially Amanjit brother. Both their families had been enlarged and enriched, but more importantly, they were all happy – even if the new household did look uncomfortably like the royal family of Ayodhya in the *Ramayana*. But he wouldn't have long to get used to the new arrangements; he was off to university in Mumbai in August.

When they had returned from the Mehrangarh that evening, they'd found that Ras had been rushed to hospital. When she'd recovered enough to talk Vikram and Amanjit had asked her if she had been revisited by the ghost of Padma, but she swore she hadn't. Vikram was positive she was lying: her mother had found her on the floor in her bedroom, which had been strewn with stuff like mouldy flowers and rotting garlic. Of course he'd recognised it was all anti-ghost stuff, but Ras wouldn't talk about what had happened, just that she'd felt faint and collapsed. At least her health didn't appear to be any worse.

Vikram really hoped that Ras, who had never figured in his past lives, would be left alone now that Padma appeared to be gone, but he couldn't be certain. There were too many gaps in his knowledge and his new memories to be sure. He had no idea why the ghost had latched on to Rasita in the first place. Perhaps it was just because she was weak and sickly, but that was unlikely. Even her name still troubled him: he knew there were no coincidences any more.

At least none of them were having bad dreams now; the nightmares had all stopped and it looked like they could all enjoy a slice of normality. It was only a couple of months until he, Deepika and Amanjit graduated; their new adult lives were beckoning. But he was afraid it felt like the lull before a new storm, and the others sensed it too.

On his last day in Jodhpur before leaving for Mumbai, Vikram visited Mandore again. He found a marked flagstone, and pulled his old journal from beneath it, where his previous self had buried it thirty years ago. There were holes in his past-life memories, but he knew they would gradually fill, and the journal would help fill some of those gaps, he was sure. He sat on the steps where Ravana was said to have married his virtuous queen Mandodari, but no visions came this time.

Was this truly to be his final life, the one in which the tangled strands of Aram Dhoop, Madan Shastri and Darya ak'Alitan would be resolved? Was this the time for the battle with Ravindra to end, once and for all?

For better or for worse, he prayed it would be so.

The story of Vikram, Amanjit and Deepika and Ravindra the demon king of Mandore, continues in

THE ADVERSARIES

Glossary

achaa	Equivalent to 'I see' or 'I understand'.
Agneyastra	The fire arrow.
Aindraastra	An astra (magical arrow) that splits into many shafts.
astra	A magic arrow.
asura	A magical 'demon', which in Hindu mythology is more akin to a nature spirit than a being of evil, though many asura are apt to be evil in nature.
baba	Father.
bahut mast	The English equivalent is (approximately) 'cool'.
behan	Sister.
bhai/bhaiya	Brother, as used by a sibling. Bhai is used by males, bhaiya by females.
bhoot	A ghost.
chai-walla	Chai is tea. A wallah is (more or less) 'fellow' or 'boy' – hence chai-wallah is 'tea-boy' or tea-seller.
channa daal	Chickpea curry.
chod	A swear-word.

33 crore gods	A 'crore' is a number equivalent to 10 million. So 33 crore gods is 330 million gods.
darbar	The central hall of a Sikh gurdwara.
dhaba	A small family restaurant/road-house.
Dhimayastra	The slow arrow.
dupatta	A woman's long scarf worn traditionally with a *salwar kameez*, used to cover the face for modesty and protection from the sun.
gurdwara	A Sikh temple.
Guru Granth Sahib	The central text of Sikhism, revered as the teachings of the Ten Gurus. The huge volume of 1,430 pages is a source and guide of prayer and is pivotal in Sikh worship.
jadugara	A sorcerer.
-ji	Ji is an honorific, approximately meaning 'revered one' or 'sir'. It's used to show respect, but can also have a connotation of holiness.
kabaddi	A playground game similar to British Bulldog.
kheer	A rice-based pudding. In the *Ramayana*, the gods bestow a bowl of magical kheer upon King Dasaratha and his queens which enables them to have children.
kotte	Donkey.
kurta	A long knee-length overshirt.
langar	The common kitchen in a gurdwara where food is served for free to all-comers, regardless of their background.
Mohini	A magic-dispelling arrow, an 'astra'.
namaste	A greeting, spoken with hands pressed together, palms touching and fingers

pointing upwards, while bowing slightly. Used on arrival and departure.

Naraka — Hell.

pooja mark — Pooja means 'prayer'. A pooja mark (a tilak) is a spot of coloured paste daubed between the eyebrows, usually given by priests to worshippers at the temples. It is used in both Hinduism and Sikhism.

punkah-wallah — A servant who wields a large fan to keep people or rooms cool.

rakshasa — A demon with magical powers. Though they are not necessarily evil, most are. They are more powerful than the asuras.

Rani-sahiba — Rani means queen, the feminine of raja (king). Sahiba is the feminine form of sahib, another honorific meaning 'lord/lady'.

sadhu — An itinerant holy man who typically wanders the country accepting charity and living (usually) at temples.

salwar kameez — A traditional outfit worn by both men and women. The salwar is a pair of loose trousers, wide at the top and narrow at the ankle; the kameez is a long overshirt or tunic.

sarovar — The pool for sacred bathing in a gurdwara.

sati — Sati is the now-illegal practice of burning the widow on a man's funeral pyre. It was supposed to signify the ultimate form of womanly devotion and sacrifice, and derived from the legend of Sati, the wife of the god Shiva, who threw herself into a pyre and self-immolated when her father

	insulted Shiva. When sati was outlawed by the British Raj in 1829 they estimated upwards of 500 women were committing sati (not always voluntarily) in their territories every year. In 1988 the Indian government passed a law, not just further criminalising the practice, but forbidding the aiding, abetting or glorification of sati as well.
senapati	Captain.
talwar	An Indian curved sword, like a sabre.
tata	Grandfather.
teeka	A Hindu word, meaning 'Okay'.

A Brief Introduction to the *Ramayana*

The Story of the Ramayana

The Indian epic called the *Ramayana* is the core mythic background for the four books of *The Return of Ravana* series. Here is a very basic summary of the story.

In ancient India, Dasaratha (or Dashrath), king of the northern Indian kingdom of Ayodhya, is childless. He makes an offering to the gods and is rewarded with a bowl of magical kheer (a rice pudding). His three wives each eat a portion, and each becomes pregnant. They give birth to four sons: Rama, Bharata and the twins Lakshmana and Shatrughna.

The princes grow up under the tutelage of the sage Vishwamitra, learning all the skills of the warrior-prince. Rama, who is outstanding in everything, is the heir apparent. He kills demons that plague the land and is loved by all the people – as are all the brothers. When a neighbouring king announces a swayamvara (a bridal challenge) for the hand of Sita, the loveliest maiden in the land, Rama competes, and by breaking the supposedly undrawable bow of Shiva, wins Sita's hand in marriage and returns to Ayodhya with his bride.

However, Queen Kaikeyi, mother of the second prince,

Bharata, is goaded by her maid (who in some versions of the tale is really a rakshasa in disguise), who plays on her jealousies and insecurities. The maid convinces her that if Rama ascends the throne, he will ill-treat her son Bharata. To prevent this perceived threat, Kaikeyi calls upon the king to honour a boon made when she saved his life years before: she demands that Rama is banished for fourteen years, and her own son Bharata made heir. The king is honour-bound to grant her wish, and reluctantly he banishes Rama.

With his wife Sita and his devoted brother Lakshmana, Rama goes into exile in the forest. When his father Dasaratha dies of sorrow, Bharata becomes king, but in defiance of his conniving mother, he goes to Rama and begs for his return. Rama refuses, for this would compromise his father's honour, so Bharata takes his brother's sandals and places them on the throne in token that one day Rama will return and become king.

Kaikeyi and her maid are ostracised, and eventually the queen pines away and dies.

For twelve years Rama, Sita and Lakshmana lead an idyllic life, troubled only by the occasional demon (asura), which the two princes destroy. In one such encounter, they dismiss the advances of a female demon called Surpanakha, who has taken a fancy to the two brothers after spying on them. Rama spurns her seduction attempts, as does Lakshmana, who mocks her. When she attacks him, he wounds her, cutting off her nose and driving her away – but Surpanakha is in fact the sister of the demon king, Ravana, who is mighty in war and magic, and very proud. When she tells her brother of these men and their insults, and of the beautiful Sita, Ravana resolves to have revenge for his sister's injury. He sends a shapeshifter demon, his uncle Maricha, to lure away the princes – he takes the form of a deer and whilst he does succeed in luring Rama and Lakshmana away, he is hunted down and killed for his trouble. But while the princes are distracted, Ravana kidnaps Sita, killing Jatayu, the giant eagle which had sworn to protect her. He takes her to Lanka, his island kingdom, and sets about trying to seduce her, but Sita resists all his advances. Frustrated and obsessed, Ravana ignores all his wives, even his chief wife Mandodari, daughter of a celestial sage – and before Sita's arrival, accounted the world's most desirable woman.

Rama and Lakshmana go hunting for the missing Sita, following clues and encountering various perils, and fall in with Hanuman, the monkey god, son of the wind god. Hanuman flies off and locates Sita in Lanka; he talks to her, but is unable to rescue her from Ravana. The monkey god then takes the heroes to the monkey king Sugriva, who agrees to aid Rama; he assembles a monkey army and they invade Lanka. Normally the monkeys would have little chance against the asuras, but Rama and Lakshmana are master archers, using arrows with magical powers called 'astras', so the odds are evened and in the battles that follow, despite various setbacks and crises, the princes and their allies gain the upper hand, killing many of the rakshasa (demon-lords) who surround Ravana.

Finally Ravana has no choice but to come out and fight in person. In an epic duel, he is slain by Rama, and the demons flee or surrender and Sita is recovered.

However, knowing that his people will suspect Sita of infidelity during her captivity, Rama asks that she undergoes a test of fidelity. Though insulted to be doubted, Sita is determined to prove her loyalty to him. She invokes the fire god and asks that she be consumed should she have been unfaithful. She is surrounded by flames but is not burned and is therefore accepted as having been faithful. The couple are reunited and are free to return home triumphantly, reclaim the throne of Ayodhya and live happy lives.

Only at his eventual death does Rama learn that he is Vishnu, the Protector God, sent in human form to save the world from the demon king Ravana.

Holy Book, History or Myth – or all three?

There is considerable debate on how much of the *Ramayana* is history and how much is mythology. It is also a religious text, as the hero Rama is believed to be an incarnation of the god Vishnu, the protector of mankind in Hindu mythology.

Some Indians have described the text to me as a sacred holy book and therefore one hundred per cent fact; others have told me categorically that it is history, and yet others maintain it is only a fairy-tale for kids.

Most seemed to regard the *Ramayana* as similar to the *Iliad* or *Odyssey* and other such mythic epics: it contains divine characters whose actions can be studied to provide moral examples, but primarily it is heroic myth with a possible basis in real-life history.

Putting aside this issue (because everyone will have their own opinion and I'm sure no mere fantasy writer is going to change yours), the next question is: if some of it relates to real events, when did these take place? The *Ramayana* epic was composed around four hundred years before the birth of Christ (it's claimed Valmiki, the composer, taught poetry to Rama's sons). The question is when it is set.

There are many extravagant claims, but one possibility is that it looks back to the first great civilisation of the Indian subcontinent, now known as the Indus Valley Civilisation and dated to 3000–1200 BC. Believed to be the most advanced society in the world of its time, it flourished in and around the Indus River valleys, now the modern India–Pakistan borderlands. The people of the Indus Valley pre-dated Hinduism; they had sophisticated mathematics, science, trade and art. The civilisation failed when climatic and tectonic changes caused the rivers to dry up and the land to become arid, leaving the major cities without water. The people largely abandoned the region as it turned to desert and they migrated south and west across the Indian subcontinent, in what is known as the Vedic period. Many believe the *Ramayana* to be a fanciful reimagining of the fall of India's first great civilisation, written with a religious slant.

A second possibility is that the *Ramayana* looks back on the battles and rivalries of the North Indian kingdoms during the Vedic period (1500–500 BC), the period during which Hinduism was codified, although this option isn't entirely satisfactory as the historical tie-ins to known events are tenuous.

I don't pretend to know which is right, but I have taken a stance in the story – you'll find out which in Book Four.

While it is probably fair to say that the *Ramayana* is regarded more as a legend and quasi-historical tract than a purely religious document by educated Indians, the religious aspects cannot be ignored. Rama was seen as an exemplary king, a model for all rulers, and his role as Protector mirrors that of Vishnu in Indian cosmology. Gandhi invoked Rama during the creation of the Indian Republic. The incident of Sita proving her fidelity by walking through the fire is also often invoked, and is full of meaning. The tale remains as much a part of the fabric of Indian culture, society and religion as tales from the Old Testament do in Christian countries.

The origins and meaning of the *Ramayana* are hugely contentious, and I certainly don't claim any expertise: I've incorporated conventional truths if they suited the story and ignored others that didn't. *The Return of Ravana* is an adventure series written first and last to entertain, and if this sounds like a plea not to be hounded by historians and scholars – it is!

Hinduism at a Glance

Hinduism is the oldest living religious tradition in the world, and the third largest, after Christianity and Islam. However, almost all of its adherents live in one country, India, with the remainder primarily in South-East Asia. It has a plethora of holy texts which include the Vedas, Upanishads, Puranas, and the epics *Ramayana* and *Mahabharata*.

Until the nineteenth century Hinduism was not even seen as one religion; it still has huge regional diversity. Taking one set of rules and saying, *this is Hinduism*, is never entirely correct. To outsiders Hinduism has a great many gods, but this is not entirely true, for every god – and there are *millions* if you take into account the local deities and ancestor worship – is believed to be part of one supreme being.

Nevertheless, here is a broad outline:

The supreme being (called variously Ishvara, Om or Bhagavan, amongst others) created and maintains life. The goal of existence is to merge in eternal bliss with the supreme being. Attaining this state requires purifying oneself spiritually, for which a pathway of dharma (righteousness), artha (livelihood/wealth), kama (sensual pleasure) and moksha (release) is prescribed: a person should experience all the world has to offer and learn from it, before setting life aside in favour of the spiritual/divine. It is believed that people keep reincarnating, living many lives, until they attain moksha.

To guide mankind, the supreme being manifests in many different forms. As different people find moksha in different ways, so there are a great many gods and goddesses in Hinduism to help them.

Nowadays, the three primary male gods are known collectively as the Trimurti: Brahma (the creator), who made the universe, is usually seen as having done his work, and is therefore seldom actively worshipped – he is portrayed as resting until he is needed again. Hinduism teaches that the universe has been created and destroyed several times over.

Vishnu (the preserver) protects and champions mankind, especially against forces of evil, like asuras and rakshasas. Vishnu is a deity embodying the manly virtues; he is said to have become an avatar (a god embodied in flesh) in many forms, including the god-heroes Rama and Krishna, always to guide and protect mankind.

Shiva (destruction and rebirth) is unlike Vishnu, for he teaches the putting aside of worldly concerns and the seeking of moksha. He is said to have invented yoga to facilitate this. He is normally portrayed in furs and a loincloth, dancing or practising yoga. He is also, with his consort Parvati, the prime fertility deity.

Each of these gods has a female consort:

Saraswati, the consort of Brahma, is the goddess of music and learning and a favourite of school children.

Laxmi is the goddess of wealth, the consort of Vishnu. Her image is to be found in most business premises.

Parvati is Shiva's consort, the perfect example of the good wife and beautiful woman, the most sensuous and loving of the female deities. She is also the most dangerous – when roused she becomes the warlike Durga, who embodies the female warrior spirit, and when pushed to the limits she becomes Kali, a bloodthirsty force of destruction.

Other important deities include Hanuman, the monkey god, a spirit of fidelity, cleverness and courage, devoted to Vishnu; and

Ganesh, the elephant god, who is lucky and provides good fortune.

There are also beings akin to 'angels' and 'demons' – the devas and asuras respectively, although asuras are not always evil. Both cooperated with Brahma in the creation of the world, but devas are celestial and asuras are baser and more malicious. Rakshasas are also demons, but more powerful than asuras.

In the Hindu cosmology we live over and over again, seeking release from life, seeking the divine. The gods help with their wisdom and interventions as we make our way in the world, become wiser, and eventually attain moksha.

A Quick Note on Sikhism

One of the major characters in this series is a Sikh. Sikhism was founded in the fifteenth century in the Punjab in northern India. It teaches of a universal god without form, and that salvation comes from merging with that god. The 'Five Evils' (ego, lust, greed, attachment and anger) are seen as the main obstacles to oneness with God. There are a number of behavioural tenets (wearing turbans, bearing knives, etc.) by which traditional Sikhs may be recognised. The religion is guided by gurus (teachers) and worship is carried out at a gurdwara, where the holy texts are read; there is traditionally a bathing pool and a kitchen dispensing free food. Sikhism is the fifth largest organised religion in the world, though most followers live in the Punjab.

Acknowledgements

This series was initially inspired by seeing the handprints of the burned queens of Jodhpur, in the Mehrangarh (the wives of Maharaja Man Singh, who cast themselves onto his funeral pyre in 1843), and refined over red wine with Mike Bryan. The entire Mandore section of the story is fictional, but the setting is real – Mandore was the imperial capital until it was abandoned in favour of Avanti in the eighth century, as noted in the story, and fell into decline, until a revival in the 1200s, before the building of the Mehrangarh in 1459. The gardens and fortress remain, a lovely spot and a refuge of green in the harsh desert. It is also the site claimed to be the wedding place of Ravana to Mandodari, his favoured wife until he became besotted with Sita.

There are no caves under the Mehrangarh – at least, that I am aware of – but there was a very long tradition of hermitage on the hill where the fortress now stands. The fortress is stunning, like a castle made by giants stuck on top of Uluru/Ayers Rock. Look up photos online or, better yet, visit it!

I'd like to thank Jo Fletcher Books for re-issuing this series. It was originally released by Penguin in 2010 in India and New Zealand. I'd especially like to acknowledge Mike Bryan, Heather Adams,

Sudeshna Shome Ghosh and Tanuva Mujumdar for their parts in bringing the tale to life, and of course Kerry Greig, my wife, love and muse, for all her proofing and ideas, and for taking me to live in India in 2007 and opening so many new chapters in my life.

Thanks also to Jo Fletcher, Nicola Budd and all the team at JFB for their faith in the series, and especially Patrick Carpenter for the cool new cover.

David Hair
Auckland, New Zealand

About the Author

David Hair is a New Zealand fantasy writer, the author of three fantasy series. His first novel, *The Bone Tiki*, was winner of Best First Book at the 2010 *NZ Post* Children's Book Awards, New Zealand's most prestigious awards for children's fiction. *The Bone Tiki* and its sequels, the six-book Aotearoa Series, are set in New Zealand and are based on New Zealand's colonial and Maori history and folklore. The Moontide Quartet, an adult epic fantasy series, is set in the imaginary world of Urte.

This quartet, The Return of Ravana, is set in India. An earlier version of the first book, entitled *Pyre of Queens*, won the New Zealand Librarians' Association Award (LIANZA) for best YA Novel of 2012. This book, *The Pyre*, is a substantially revised edition of *Pyre of Queens*.

David has a degree in History and Classical Studies. He has lived primarily in Wellington, New Zealand, but also in Britain and India. Apart from writing, he is interested in folklore, history, travel and wine, and has a passion for football.

About the Author